Some Other Time

Andrea McKerlie

authorHOUSE®

AuthorHouse™
1663 Liberty Drive
Bloomington, IN 47403
www.authorhouse.com
Phone: 1-800-839-8640

First published by AuthorHouse 6/11/2009

ISBN: 978-1-4389-6429-4 (sc)

Printed in the United States of America
Bloomington, Indiana

This book is printed on acid-free paper.

For those who will remember the past,
acknowledge it, and let it go on its way…

To Shannon and Ethan.
Thank you for everything.

BOOK ONE
INNOCENCE OVERTURNED

ONE

THE BEGINNINGS OF THE END

Citrosine drifted in and out of consciousness, all the while feeling stifled, as if wrapped in a heavy blanket. She could pick at frayed strands, twist them in her fingers, but the blanket was made of millions of tiny threads. There was no way that she could pick her way out, if it would take this much work. She tried to relax, but her heart would not slow—she was overwhelmed by a sense of urgency and needed to wake. Something outside her was terribly wrong.

After what seemed like days of panicking, she was roughly brought to life again. Her eyes still closed, she had the sensation of being shaken by an invisible hand. She finally wrenched open her eyes and found herself lying in a field surrounded by dark brush and scrub. Comforting night sounds arose from every last crevice of the darkness. This had a calming effect on her disorientation, but she knew that she must discover what was wrong just the same. Citrosine stood, shakily, and discovered a biting pain in her left forearm.

She raised her arm and looked at her wrist. It looked as if she had gained a Faerie's Blessing, a vein of extra magic for her to wield. It was an honor to gain one of these, and allowed one to incorporate magic into his or her life in much more useful quantities.

But…Citrosine didn't remember being given a Blessing. *When would that have happened that I cannot remember it?* She rubbed at her eyes and looked at her silvery new vein more closely. *This is no Blessing,* she thought. Just as she was about to touch her arm, a bright light shone from the vein, temporarily blinding her. She felt a crack in her bone, and screamed in pain. The light abruptly extinguished itself, and the Elf saw that her skin was peeling away from her muscle and bone. A new kind of form under her old skin had grown, as if she had been possessed by some kind of demon.

This can't be happening! Wouldn't I know if I were being possessed or controlled? she reasoned, as she felt her skin peel from her face. She screamed, but no one came. Now she realized that she did not have her sword with her. She always carried it when she traveled at night, even though she was just a young Elf.

Skin continued to fall away; more bones melded and broke into different forms. Citrosine lashed out and shrieked in pain, but still no one came. The new skin rising out was leathery and hard, almost like the scales of a Dragon's skin. She felt a nauseating shift in her shoulder blades, and two huge, thin wings sprouted out, extending the full length of the clearing. Claws tipped the ends of her wings, and monstrous talons replaced her fingers. She knew that these could tear through bone—she had heard stories.

Now all of her Elven skin had fallen away, and she stood there in the forest as a demon. Her new skin was black and was writhing with magic that was bursting to get out. Her eyes burned and watered, and everything seemed foggy. She was filled with a desire to hunt, to kill, to run through the dark, cold night...

Would she resist? Or would she run through all the Big Lands hunting however she wished, against all rules of nature, and regardless of the Men? Being a demon now, she had no choice but to surrender to the latter. Her humane Elven instincts were quickly being replaced by sheer energy. Her wide, fanged mouth salivated as she pictured Elves, Nymphs, Men, other demons, and Changelings fleeing before her, only to be caught in her grasp and mangled. Of course, after she had a bit of fun with her new victims, she would eat them.

She began to run, the cool air filling her lungs, and her new heart racing with adrenaline. She extended her long, bat-like wings, letting them pump up and down in the air, cooling her face, before she took off high above what was necessary to catch helpful updrafts. Soon she could not make out any clear shapes in the night. *I can go to the edge of the land now! No more silly rules to limit my power...* And then she woke up.

"Tie, stop it!" Citrosine giggled as her young sister, Palgirtie, climbed onto her back and tickled her. Citrosine spun a few circles until Tie got dizzy and fell off. Their mother, Leenka, laughed, and scooped the staggering Tie up into her arms, setting Citrosine free to walk outside to find her father, Gya. Gya studied the magics of every being. *His* father had been a Nymph—the beings who possessed elemental powers, and whose magic could only be overpowered by the Faeries. Since Gya's father had been an Air Nymph, his powers ran though Gya, Citrosine, and Tie's blood.

Citrosine had always wanted to join her father and traverse the land, observing all the magics of the Enchanted Realm, but she still wasn't as experienced with her own power as she should be.

"Father?" she called when she got outside. She looked around through the surrounding trees, but didn't see Gya anywhere. She squinted, trying to find him. "Dada!" she cried, louder. *He might have gone to study some more,* she thought. He sometimes left without warning, but…he had been sitting outside in their front garden just a few moments ago.

Citrosine felt for her magic—though there was little to summon up. She focused on seeing her father, and sent out a string of her power to find him. She closed her eyes and visualized him: he should have been…right next to her! The Elf opened her eyes, startled. Was she mistaken? She looked to her right and half-expected to see Gya standing there.

"Citrosine!" a voice called through the trees ahead. She looked up to see her father appear from the forest. She smiled, and ran over to him.

"Father," she said lovingly, "where were you?"

"Watching you," he replied gleefully. "You almost found me, but thought I was closer." Citrosine laughed with him, bashful. "Did you need me for something?" he asked her, more seriously. "I thought that you might wish to speak to me alone, once your sister and mother had their way with you."

"Yes," she replied slowly. "I had another strange dream last night." They stopped walking. Gya looked at his daughter knowingly, and asked her to continue. Citrosine took a deep breath, and told him all about the demon transformation dream, where she had gotten a false Blessing and was then turned into a strange demon.

"I think that it could be a warning of some kind," she told him nervously, finishing her story. "It felt horrible; I woke up and could almost feel the pain. Am I all right?" Gya was rubbing his chin, where a tiny beard was growing. He nodded, and looked into her eyes. Citrosine looked back into his bright, wise gaze for a moment, until she felt awkward. She blinked, and looked up at the darkening sky.

"I have heard talk of a Faerie that is coming to give someone a Blessing," Gya said mysteriously, changing the subject smoothly. "No one is sure of who will receive it, but the Faerie comes only in a day or so and it could be you, I suppose. Maybe the dream was only a bit of disguised, worried foresight." he concluded. Citrosine's dark eyes widened.

"Me? Selected for a Blessing?"

"Perhaps," Gya smiled, "it could be you."

"But this dream...does it mean that I should refuse the Blessing? Aren't I ready to receive it?" She looked up into her father's oceanic eyes, playing on his fatherly affection. Why shouldn't she receive a Blessing? It wasn't as if her magic had been getting any stronger; a Blessing could help her mature her power.

"Personally, I think you are a little young," Gya murmured, much to Citrosine's dismay, but he continued, "However, I am still studying Blessings. They are somewhat of a new development, so there is much to learn about such factors as age, readiness, anxiety..."

Citrosine shivered. Her long, brown hair stirred around her shoulders as a slight wind danced in the trees. What if she *was* to be Blessed? Since she was so worried about the Blessing, would her body reject it? She had never thought of it this way, though she had anticipated the extra power since she had been old enough to understand it.

Gya smiled at her, assured her not to worry—"Dreams are just dreams,"—and let his optimism overtake Citrosine.

Citrosine and her mother were the more thoughtful in the family, both with dark eyes, slender builds, and moonlit skin. They would often sit outside and watch the sky together, stars filtering through the trees around their secluded, eastern cabin that was such a comforting home. Palgirtie and Gya, on the other hand, could keep up conversations for days on end, coming right back into the discussion upon waking. These two were lighter in most ways—sunny hair, blue eyes, and tanner skin.

Altogether, it made for a content, balanced family that typically could share secrets and hugs easily.

As Citrosine and her father walked back into their cottage, Leenka was setting the table for dinner. Tie was running around, trying to find a doll or some other lost toy in her usual way, which was inclusive of a lot of shouting and laughing at seemingly nothing. Citrosine picked Tie up and plopped her into a chair next to Leenka, then sat between her parents.

Gya began conversation by reviewing what had been spoken of in his last Council meeting, in the central Stone Elf Tribe city of Haerthor, where he visited every few days as his primary occupation. There had been talk of the mortal Men that had approached the Big Lands from across the sea; the Old World, the Elves called it. The Men had run out of space there, and were now looking for lodgings and settlements here. Rumors had spread of all the magic folk being run out of the land, as the Men kept taking land for their own uses. Citrosine's family—in fact, the whole Elven population—had relocated themselves at least once before so as not to be discovered.

"Mama," Tie asked quietly, "have you heard about the Men? Are they going to run us out of the Big Lands?"

What could be worse than the exploitation of the Enchanted World? That was what had caused the desertion and extinction in the Old World—all the Leprechauns, ancient Dragons… they were slain, or hunted out of the sheer fun of it…

Leenka looked over at Tie warmly. "No, *lissa*, we will not be run out. The Men will not harm us, so long as we keep our distances. Isn't that right, Gya?" Her smile faded as she saw Gya's expression. He was staring down at his plate, a heavy scowl knotting his brows. He looked up at his wife, but said nothing.

"We shall see," he finally mumbled. Tie had already forgotten the conversation, and was heartily gobbling down her food. Citrosine pondered her father's uneasiness. If the Men reached the Stone Elf tribe *this* far away from the ocean, they would surely have to find another home. The Sea Elves must have been safe, as they lived under the very waters that the Men sailed across. Citrosine thought of each tribe, and how they would get along.

The Elves of the Air would surely prosper happily, as well, unless the Men found a way to pollute the very clouds they lived upon. That could never happen. The Fall, Mountain, Cavern, and Shadow Elves should be all right, as well, but the tribes that lived in plain sight, like Citrosine's tribe—the Stone Elves—could be in danger. The Stone Tribe had learned to build homes and cities out of stone without harming nature, and lived in individual homes located within a respectable distance from a central, communal meeting place.

"Citrosine, *lissa?*" her mother's voice intruded. She snapped into focus.

"Hmm?" she asked, looking up.

"Your sister is going to bed. Would you help me pull some blankets down from the attic?" Leenka pointed to the small ladder at the back of the one-roomed cottage. Citrosine nodded distantly and followed her mother into the loft.

When they entered the large loft, Leenka felt around for the blankets. She kicked something in the dark, and Citrosine got her second chance that day to attempt a spell. She held her hands in front of her and whispered the Elvish word for light. A faint flicker from her palms lit the room in a yellowish glow. Leenka gasped.

"Citrosine, brilliantly done! Now, see if you can keep it steady while I try to find those blankets..." Citrosine smiled, and the light flickered a bit.

"That's all right," Leenka encouraged, "but you must apply yourself to the light!" Citrosine quickly cleared her mind and focused only on the light. It grew slightly brighter, and stayed constant until Leenka found her blankets. She handed them to Citrosine, who, extinguishing her light, threw them down the ladder.

"Wonderful, wonderful! I am so proud of you, my beautiful Citrosine!" Leenka sent a wave of pure joy through her daughter's heart as she gave her a squeeze. "My first light spell was not as miraculous as that!"

"Oh, please tell me about it, would you?" Citrosine loved the way her mother sounded like a child whenever she would tell stories. Whether she told about her childhood or a tale of nonsense, her eyes lit up with a radiance that erased her many years of spellcasting and defending her race.

Leenka smiled, becoming Citrosine's own age once again, full of innocence and purity. She brushed her fine chestnut hair away from her beautifully heart-shaped face and then mother and daughter moved to sit like best friends on the hearth.

"Well, you know that I am part of the bloodline of Ghersah, the Elf we all worship for her powers of purity and goodness. My father thought it best that I learn to practice magic of Ghersah's kind—you know, light, air, and love—just charms, really." Leenka beamed, unaware that she sounded childish, wrapped up in memory. Her dark eyes shone as she continued. "I began practicing much the same kinds of light spells as you just have achieved. My first successful cast was a pitiful, flickering, almost *brown* spark, just the size of the pebbles that stick between your toes! It lasted for a fleeting moment, and then my father and I sat there in the darkness of the night for another moment." Her womanly yet still slim form hunched towards Citrosine in suspense, imitating her father to take a moment of silence. "Finally, my father said, 'Well, I suppose you cannot be the next Ghersah. Come away, I must go find you an occupation, for you shan't make profit out of magic!'"

Leenka and her daughter laughed together, for they both knew that Leenka was the best mage in the area, able to create clouds that could uphold trees and ponds, able to completely conceal a forest, able to defeat a sky-sized demon.

Once Palgirtie's sleeping place had been laid, the young Elf was put to bed. She fell asleep quickly, having no bad thoughts to dwell on. Gya, Leenka, and Citrosine sat on the ground by the hearth, where a small fire was dying out. Careful not to wake their youngest family member, they spoke silently through their minds.

"Father, Mother," Citrosine began, *"I worry of the Men. Have they overthrown any other races? What of the Field Elves?"* she thought back.

Gya and Leenka shared a significant look, and Gya sighed. *"The Men took the land in the Old World, long ago, having explored northwards from the Painted World."*

"Painted World?" Citrosine interrupted. *"I seem to have forgotten my knowledge of history…"*

Gya smiled. History was one of his favorite topics. *"Well… life itself began in the Painted World, the grandest expanse of land there ever was. There were wet, jungle forests; vast, burning plains; every type of animal you could imagine, mortal or immortal. There were mortal beasts that could hunt even the most skilled Immortals at night, immortal races that had such powers that whole areas would still retain such powers when the spellcasters had left them. All races flourished together, Man and Elf, Dragon and Beast. That is, until the Men began to exploit the magics of the Immortals. They needed rain for their crops, so they would perform all sorts of rituals that they believed would cause rain, even if it meant sacrificing one of our own kind—they thought releasing our magics into the heavens would appease their deities."*

"Gyardaute, do you think that you should—" Leenka broke in with an anxious glance towards Citrosine.

"Mama, I do not fear." Leenka nodded, giving her daughter a faint smile, yet obviously not happy with Gya for this.

"I am proud of your heart," she whispered audibly. Gya continued.

"So…the Immortals would not stand for this killing, so they fled northwards, and adapted to a new climate. This was what we now call the Old World, where the sea ruled the air, where almost everywhere one could taste the salt, until we expanded even further north, where one had to fight to see the sun past the gray,

11

ever-swelling clouds. The lands were always a rich, full green, and the animals were, if more sparse, more friendly and manageable. The Old World was not so wild, but all of us together in such a smaller place gave it ethereal, mysterious qualities that would seep through the ever-misty highlands. You cannot imagine, lissa, *how beautifully haunting it would be to see the glow of Faerie light through such sparkling mist.*

"Finally, it seemed as if the Men had forgotten us, but they, too, moved north. Our cultures seemed to blend again, in a peaceful, harmonious way...until they saw what we did not care to see about nature—they saw that by clearing away trees and ripping apart hillsides they could build homes and farms that would suit their needs of profit, greed, and ignorance. The Immortals realized that these people were killing themselves and the things around them. As their race multiplied and each generation became more destructive, forgetting their ancestors' treaties and peace with us, the Immortals resolved to disappear from the Men's history. They would forever incorporate us into stories and folklore, and we would forever avoid their self-made misery.

"In any case, all the Enchanted peoples sailed here. When we arrived in the Big Lands, each race and tribe went their own way. This way of settling distanced us all from each other, making communication and organization more difficult, but it made us all feel safer from being discovered and hurt.

"Your mother and I set up a dwelling near the sea, and you and Tie were born. You probably remember how we moved further inland after the Men almost saw us. We had to burn all traces that we left behind, so they couldn't find us again." He paused to poke the fire with a long metal rod. The chill of the autumn night had begun to seep through the walls like a probing fog.

Citrosine called up her memory of the day that they ran from the sea. The four of them had been sitting outside, a fire burning through the warm night. Then Leenka had looked around, and told them all to be very still and silent. She walked out into the woods alone. The other three sat silently in terror, and waited still for almost an hour, when they heard a peculiar cry, one full of rage as well as concern. It was Leenka.

The next thing Citrosine remembered was fire—lots of fire. Citrosine and Leenka had carried food and blankets as Gya threw burning wood into their cottage, then grabbed Tie in his arms, and caught up with them. Leenka was whispering spells of shadow, lightness, and invisibility; urgent, black spells that Citrosine had never thought she'd have to hear. They ran for days, putting as much distance between themselves and the Men as they could.

Finally, Gya had chosen this small clearing to build a new home. They were tired and frightened, but they finally got the cottage built, and they had been happy enough since. The Men had not yet moved inwards, instead locating along the rivers and gulfs near the coast; easy-to-reach places.

Presently, Gya continued. *"Now, as I have been traveling,"* he began, *"I have seen signs of Men closer and closer to us and the main village of the Stone Elves. We could be in great danger, but it is not certain. We may choose to change tribes soon. If we did, your mother and I have chosen to become Sea Elves. It would be a lot safer than the forest here. As for the Field Elves, Citrosine, they have vanished. No one has seen their kind for ages. Perhaps they have gone so far west that they reached ocean, and sailed off. None of us in the community are sure of what has happened. The Shadow Elves, also, have disappeared, assumed to have died off— presumed extinct, for they have attended no meetings or councils for over a century."* Leenka gave her husband a sharp look. Her usually sparkling eyes were now a deep, simmering black, and Citrosine noticed a touch of pain coloring her features, a distressed angel.

Dead? She thought to herself. *I can understand the Field Tribe disappearing, but the Shadow Elves? They could not have died off! They are the best fit to survive all of this, what with their dark spells and manipulation of the elements. I wonder if they have gone to where the great Ghersah was rumored to have gone; across the sea to a paradise of magic, and a tree raised by our ancestors…to redeem us after death… Did Ghersah tell them of this? The Shadow tribe was so removed from everything, ostracized for using their magic evilly… And, change tribes? Are we allowed to do that? Why would Dada choose to do something this way? It would be more fun, though, I suppose; a whole city to explore, all under the sea…and less danger…*

"All right, Citrosine," Gya stated flatly. Citrosine expected him to tell her that it was time for bed, but he did not. *"Come outside with me, would you?"* She did as he asked, nervously. Leenka bid them both a warm goodnight—such a change in mood that Citrosine could not help but notice the cheery façade instead of her mother's typical love—hugging Citrosine like a best friend and sneaking her fingers around to tickle her, and kissing Gya fondly on the lips, a little more ardently than every other night.

Gya made a failed attempt to gently speak of another subject. His voice was strained and tired, and it was apparent that he was trying to get both his and Citrosine's minds off the subject of extinct Elf tribes.

"Citrosine, I think the time has come for me to tell you about your Nymph blood. My father—your grandfather—was a Nymph. Nymphs possess much more magic than normal Elves, even those who use a Blessing." Citrosine gasped, making her father chuckle.

"Well," he continued, casting a small charm that lit the space around them. "Your grandfather was a Sky Nymph. That means that he could cast spells that had to do with night, day, and the stars. Since we are descendents of his, we have been passed some of his power. Not to mention the power you will inherit from your mother, who was born and raised an Elf of the Air Tribe.

"The Nymph blood in you may eventually stir up, and you will either have uncontrollable magic powers or none at all. I suspect the latter, as I had great trouble summoning mine whenever I wanted to use it as I developed my skills. It was only for a while, but it may be different in you—you are of a generation different than I.

"The Sky powers might interfere with your Elven powers, is what I am trying to explain," Gya continued, seeing his daughter's confused face.

Citrosine was rather perplexed. "You mean that I might not have any magic until I come of age?" she asked slowly. Gya nodded.

"Or, in a very, very slight chance, your powers could overwhelm you, growing completely out of your control."

Citrosine looked at him in horror. Gya frowned, eyes melting into warm pools of sky.

"I'm sorry, *lissa*, I don't mean to scare you. I just want you to be aware, and I didn't want you to be afraid if this happened before I could explain it to you.

"Just…don't try to look up at the sky too much, especially if that next Faerie's Blessing is for you. My father was almost swallowed up by the moon when he first felt his powers…Since his powers were of the sky, it was dangerous—these powers are elemental and quite difficult to understand. And your mother's powers are of the air…These together would be very unpredictable." Gya said. Citrosine looked into her father's eyes. Was that a trace of fear that she saw?

"How did yours work?" she asked.

"Pardon me?"

"What happened when you got your Blessing? How exactly did your powers not work, if that makes any sense?"

Gya smiled. "After I got my Blessing, I couldn't feel any magic inside me, none at all. I couldn't do any spells for quite a few years, and I felt almost mortal. It was a darkness, a blindness…a weakness I felt for almost a century…"

They both heard a loud clearing throat from inside.

"Isn't it amazing how acute your mother's senses are?" Gya smiled, both he and his daughter giggling a little.

"Finish up, love," Leenka murmured. Gya's lips turned up gently, and the love and obedience he felt for his wife were apparent in his gleaming eyes. He spoke a little quicker, a little softer, to his daughter.

"Then, on a day that I was especially frustrated, I created a thundercloud without knowing it, matching my mood, and I knew that my magic had appeared again. You and Tie might feel this in the same way as I did, or else you will have *too* much power, which is doubtful—hasn't happened in all our family's years. So do not worry."

Citrosine imagined herself not being able to do magic at all for a century, and shivered. Sure, her power was very limited now, but if she didn't have *any*...it was what made Elves Elves!

"All right," Gya whispered into the silent night air, "time for bed, before I scare you so much you shall never sleep again." They made their way inside, Citrosine's head swimming with so many new worries. She told her father how confusing it all was, and he laughed. Gya lovingly stroked Citrosine's hair.

"It would seem as if so many things are to happen, wouldn't it?" he chuckled. Citrosine nodded distantly, thinking that it might not be something to laugh about.

That night, Citrosine slept fitfully. She kept thinking back to the day when they had left their old dwelling, and the fire had burned all traces of Elven life. She also mixed this with visions of her not being able to do any magic, even if trying to defend herself against an unruly demon...unable to shield its blows...

She awoke with her sheathed sword quivering in her hand, and Tie's face hovering over hers. "What?" She took a moment to adjust to the sensation of being awake, and tried to remember where she was. "Oh, good morning, Tie," Citrosine grumbled. "What'd you get my sword out for?"

Tie beamed, and said nothing.

"What is going on? *Tie?*" Citrosine began to panic. Her sister was always silent when she was planning something against her.

"Calm down, Citrosine," Tie giggled. "Dada and Mama and I have made a surprise for you. Remember? Your birthday!"

With a gentle smirk, Citrosine looked over to where her parents' blankets were laid. Neither of them was in the room. The Elf got up and began dressing, as her sister began her daily ritual of telling Citrosine what the weather was like, what she had had for breakfast, and everything that had happened in the last few hours since the sun had risen. It normally bothered Citrosine, but now she was just wondering what kind of surprise was in store for her.

"*Nekka lissa?*" Citrosine's mother asked from the loft. "My little love? Tie, has Citrosine awoken?"

"I have, Mother," Citrosine called up the ladder.

"Oh! Well, good morning to you," she replied, startled. "Happy birthday, *lissa,* my love. We have special plans today."

"So I have heard," Citrosine murmured as she strapped her sword to her waist. "Tie told me there was a surprise." She ran a comb through her dark hair, pulling it up and away from her face only for it to fall back again, obscuring her eyes. Her mother noticed this, and grinned. She reached up into the loft and retrieved an old gown, bringing it over to Citrosine.

"I wore this when I was your size," she explained. Her fingers went to work at unlacing the back. "In the Air Tribe, we were raised to always wear gowns or dresses," she explained as she disconnected one of the laces, "and we were always the best-dressed warriors!" She put the gown back where she'd found it, and held a thick, shiny black ribbon in her hands as she descended the ladder, gathering the other things she had been bringing down before.

"Your sister wasn't supposed to tell you about your birthday surprise yet," Leenka said, laughing like a tinkling bell, "But then, she has never been very trustworthy with secrets. Go ahead and get your armor and waistcoat. You might want to pack a bag, as well; three day's worth of clothes should work." Citrosine's mother climbed down the ladder with three bows, two swords and scabbards, and a leather satchel for Citrosine to pack. How she carried it all, Citrosine would never know.

Leenka shifted the weapons to the crook of her arm, still keeping them perfectly balanced, and gathered Citrosine's lovely waterfall of hair into a graceful twist, tying it in place with the ribbon.

"Where's Father?" Citrosine inquired distantly, wondering why she was supposed to be packing. Palgirtie ran around and crawled through her legs.

"Dada's outside somewhere," she panted.

Leenka handed her eldest daughter the leather satchel and a pair of swords from under her arm.

"Will I need these?" Citrosine ran her fingers over the leather with exhilaration and worry blossoming quickly through her body. Leenka whispered into Citrosine's mind, oblivious of Tie hanging off her legs.

Do not worry, love. Just the sound of Leenka's voice eased Citrosine's panic. It was a gift of the Air Elves; Leenka could always be counted upon to soothe the atmosphere. *They are for extreme cases only, and a birthday present. You should use these two swords, rather than just your one. These are spelled; use them together. Your sword is so dull, anyway, isn't it?* She removed the belted sword from Citrosine's waist, and secured the pair of spelled swords. *Don't forget your armor; you never know when you could need it,* she reminded. The young Elf nodded, and began to put on her coat of mail and waistcoat. *Too bad it's not as cold as it was last night,* she complained silently, feeling the weight and thickness of her weaponry. Wherever she was going, it would certainly be an uncomfortable journey there.

As soon as her packing was finished, Citrosine stumbled outside into the dewy morning, where her father had shown up and was standing with Leenka and Tie. The sun was low in the crimson sky, having just barely woken up to provide them with any light. The forest surrounding the cottage looked like an ominous circle of pointed teeth, just waiting to gobble up the four Elves. Leenka had a bow slung over her shoulder, and carried Citrosine's older sword, unsheathed, in her hand. Gya had no bow, but a thin sword that he could swing with one arm, as he carried Tie in his other. His sword hand was currently vacant, and Citrosine could just barely make out the pulse of magic in his palm. She wondered what could be so dangerous in the few miles of forest between their dwelling and the harmless main city of Haerthor—the community where the Stone Elves collected.

"Surprise, Citrosine! Happy birthday. *Lissa ji,*" Gya called, as Citrosine walked out to join them.

"I love you, as well, Father," she replied nervously. "Where are we going that we need such heavy armor and weaponry?"

"*It's a surprise!*" Tie jeered. Citrosine made a sour face at her. "Thanks; that explains a lot," she mumbled.

Leenka calmed them down, and began speaking in hushed tones that made them stay quiet.

"*Lissa,*" she began—to Citrosine, "we are going through the forest to get to Haerthor, first. As we travel, we must be very careful. This is the forest *Bixoel*—Blackness—and it was created by Jygul the Dark Goddess. This is the same forest from the legend of Ghersah. Do you remember?

"When Jygul was fighting Ghersah, she resorted to trickery, and created this forest, in hopes that Ghersah would be lost while walking through and go mad. It is maintained by spirits that Jygul bound to the place. There are strange demons that may try to ambush us; eyes that can see your heart, fingers that can take hold of you."

Leenka nodded. "Your father will lead us, with Tie, and I shall be at the rear. The rest of our plan is a surprise, though." Citrosine rolled her eyes. Leenka laughed softly. "We must be as silent as we can in here: no speaking even through the mind," she instructed, pointing towards the trees.

"Why is that?" Citrosine asked, heart squirming.

"So that Jygul will let us pass unnoticed, and only her spirits will pay us any mind, without troubling her to see us."

Tie fidgeted, afraid, in her father's arms, and he stilled her. They proceeded into the wood.

Citrosine had not taken three steps into the forest when she was struck with a sudden awareness of all the magic it contained. She staggered, as if she had been hit with a dizzying scent entering a room. Leenka took hold of her elbow and steadied her firmly. She put a finger to her lips, and motioned towards her swords. Citrosine drew them shakily. The ground was spinning beneath her, the dark shades of the leaves blurring in her head. Leenka squeezed her elbow, and the spinning abruptly stopped. The warmth of magic crept through her skin, and spread through her whole body, finally reaching her head, and making the overpowering feelings subside.

She still felt the presence of a huge mass of magic in the trees around her, but it wasn't quite as overwhelming now. Every once in a while, she would feel the snap of a twig under her feet, and they would all freeze in their tracks, listening for any other noises. Occasionally, Citrosine thought she saw a dark shape skitter through the trees next to them, but she didn't alert her mother or father, as they seemed to dismiss the shadows.

The trees lived very close together, almost entwined with each other, fingerlike branches clasping above their heads. Picking their way through the undergrowth, and keeping vigilant for vile thorns and plants that caused severe itching, the family crept through. Citrosine could attest to feeling eyes fastened to her every movement. She looked over her shoulders every moment, to be met with small scuffling noises, and shifts in the currents of magic she was aware of. Once she swore that she could feel an icy hand on her neck, and she quickly rubbed her hand over it, but the feeling disappeared just before her own hand made contact.

She and Tie had never been through this part of the woods; they had come from another way when they first arrived. Gya would occasionally look up through the leaves to find the sun, which had only changed its position twice—two hours had passed. He finally turned around to Leenka and Citrosine, holding up a finger. He made a small gesture, and Leenka walked a few steps ahead.

She returned shortly, and motioned for the others to follow. They went a few paces, and then they could make out the outline of a silver gate between the trees.

When they came up to the gate, Gya took the head once more. The doors stood ajar, with two guards on either side. One of the men, clad in red and gray armor, approached him. Gya saluted sharply, startling poor little Tie, who just about fainted. The guard returned the salute, and addressed the family warmly.

"*Why, hello, there. Aren't we a nice little group here? What brings you to Haerthor?*" He smiled a toothy grin that looked quite silly on such a tall lieutenant.

"*I am Gyardaute Nakiss, of the Magic Study. I am here to...*" the rest faded out, not meant to be heard by Citrosine. Tie giggled again, obviously hearing. The guard looked at Leenka and Citrosine and frowned in concentration.

"*I'll be needing to see your Marks of the Stone, please,*" he requested politely. "*Sorry to pass such scrutiny over your family, Gya. You know that we recognize you, but it is our duty.*" Each member of Citrosine's family, in turn, lifted their sleeve to reveal a brown tattoo of a large, unevenly drawn ring. This was the Mark of the Stone Elves, drawn when a child is first born into the tribe.

"Thank you so much," the guard said, smiling again. He sidestepped and let the family pass with no trouble. They entered the gate, following a path that led into the city square. Once more, Citrosine had to imagine what it would be like if they were Sea Elves. This before her would all be under the water.

Haerthor wasn't an impeccably furnished town. A few stone homes scattered among various wooden cottages, all around this square. There was a slightly larger home in the center of the square, however. It was still in the process of being built; a whole west wing was littered with scaffolding and loose bricks. This was apparently to be a castle of some sort. The stone and wood structures were what made the Stone Elves who they were. Their ancestors, long, long ago had discovered the secrets to creating homes out of what nature discarded, using nothing more than they needed, harming nothing.

"That is the meeting place of the Magic Study Council," Gya explained, waving a hand in the vicinity of the unfinished scaffolding of the largest building. "The west wing is to be a home to the new king. The Royal Family is currently staying in the city of the Sea; King Hendius couldn't trust the infant twins in the East Wing—too many breakable treasures for little fists—so our Council has taken control until the West is finished."

Citrosine suddenly got a hunch.

"Dada, I would like to know why we are here," she asked, chuckling. Gya slapped his forehead with the back of his hand.

"Yes, of course, *lissa.* Just…just wait one more moment, would you?" He smiled teasingly, and turned to Leenka. They shared a secret conversation, Leenka looking extremely nervous.

"Citrosine! Don't you want your present?" Tie almost shouted as their parents spoke. Tie looked at Citrosine with incredulous eyes, as if her older sister had just refused an invitation to become queen of all the Big Lands.

"Well…" the older girl teased. She reached over and tickled Tie, who let out giggles of mirth.

"Stop! Stop! I'll give it to you if you only stop!"

Citrosine withdrew her hands quickly, genuinely curious now. Tie reached into her pocket and retrieved a small pouch made of woven grass. She seemed to ponder whether to give it up at all, then broke as Citrosine gave her an exaggerated, pleading look. Tie smiled, laughing. Citrosine took the pouch from her. Gya and Leenka were now paying attention and smiling at them.

The small pouch was flat and made of dry, woven grass. It looked like an envelope.

"Well, open it, would you?" Tie grumbled, hiding her excitement. Citrosine nodded, and unfolded the grass pouch, pulling out the glittering treasure within. The small silver mirror shone and sparkled in her fingers, as if it was generating its own light.

"Mama and I made it," Tie declared. "Well…I thought of it, and Mama actually made it," she added sheepishly. The mirror was laced with tiny glass leaves and flowers that made it appear as if a small round mirror had simply been tossed into a small plant, both becoming inseparable and intertwined. Citrosine looked at her face in the mirror, and realized how much she was beginning to look like her mother. A warm blush filled her cheeks, for she had always known that her mother was gorgeous, and now even acknowledging any resemblance in her own face was magical.

"It is beautiful!" Citrosine gushed. "I—it—oh, thank you!" She hugged Tie, then squeezed her mother, feeling all her curves squeeze her back.

"Just as beautiful as my little lissa,*"* she replied emotionally. Citrosine felt more of her mother's magic pour into her own body, probably unconsciously, just a product of her powerful love. Gya smiled at the scene.

"We should return now. There is a storm moving swiftly from the…south, it seems. It approaches our meadow soon. This is unusual…the south…" Leenka said, now to everyone, reluctance and edginess beginning to take over her musical words. Citrosine looked up at the sky, and then back at her mother skeptically. The sky was a beautiful cerulean sheet that had not one cloud to stain it, but she made no argument, as Leenka was quite advanced in her magic skills, and even more endowed than her husband.

"All right then," Gya began slowly. "Citrosine, here is your surprise from me. You are to help me on one of my studies with the Magic Council," He had barely finished when Citrosine threw her arms around him.

"Se lissa, mesta Dada! Mesta lissa, Dada!" She laughed and thanked her father. She had not been so content since… well…ever. Gya laughed, almost falling backwards under her sudden weight. Palgirtie let out a surprised squeal, clinging to his neck.

"Yes, Citrosine; I love you as well, and you are most welcome. Now, we should be moving on. Your mother and sister must go back home now." Citrosine sobered a bit. Palgirtie skipped from her father's arms and ran to Leenka. Gya hugged his wife tightly, giving her an innocent-yet-lingering kiss that would stick in Citrosine's mind longer than some of her other memories, just by the way Leenka seemed to crush her lips to his more passionately then was normal. Then it was time for Citrosine's birthday to continue, and her mother and sister to depart.

Two

FAERIES AND DEMONS

Leenka and Tie were heading through the dark, stifling woods again. It had nearly been necessary for Leenka to spell Tie's mouth shut. The little Elf did not want to be so quiet again for that long, not when she was already whimpering at the dark shapes that loomed between the brush and wiry trees. In tears, she had finally held her tongue. Leenka was almost in tears herself. The woods around them had an oppressing effect when too much magic was woven into it. She quickened her pace. They needed to reach a safer place to hide before such an unnatural storm approached.

The trip through the woods was more of a nightmare than it had been before. Branches were extended across the path, reaching out to scratch any patch of skin they could reach. Thorny vines, the likes of which Leenka had never seen—and she had seen many vile things—were the size of trees, snaking over logs and underbrush. Leenka breathed incantations, attempting to protect her and her daughter further, and resorted to speaking to the spirits within this black forest, careful to make sure that Palgirtie was oblivious.

"How long is the path this day? Do you warn us against returning home? Or do you wish us to be caught here when the storm comes?" She looked around her warily, catching glimpses of dark faces between the trees, as if they were shadows.

"Why do you weave such malice into your creations today? I have passed here many times invisibly, but now you are angry with me. What have I done?"

Tie closed her eyes tightly after watching a humanlike shadow reach out long, rotten fingers in their direction and beckon. She opened her eyes moments later, and could not see it any longer, but felt something catch the back of her sleeve. Looking around in terror the little Elf smelled what she imagined to be the invisible beast's decomposing flesh… yet she saw nothing. Clinging to her mother's arm, she closed her eyes again.

Never had a storm come from the south in the Big Lands, never in Leenka's long lifetime, until now. Some evil was at work. She could feel more eyes in the wood than ever before. Things were watching her and her little daughter. Her magic felt significantly weak at that moment, and she, Leenka Guidyr Nakiss, most powerful Elven mage in the Stone Tribe, family to the bloodline of Ghersah the Light—patron deity of all Elves—was frightened enough to lose her wits.

"So, what kind of work will we do? What magic will we learn about? Am I going to learn to use mine better? What—" Citrosine was cut off by a wave of her bemused father's hand.

"Calm down, *lissa*. We must wait to know until we are assigned to our exact duties. I can tell you, however, that it will involve Blessings." Gya took his daughter's hand like a princess's escort might, and led her to the large half-built castle.

Gya easily passed through the guarded gates in front of the castle, pulling an extremely curious Citrosine behind him. The younger Elf peeked at the large iron gates and shivered. She wondered what kinds of things might have been locked out once, or may have needed to be in the future.

When the pair entered the main hall, they were immediately greeted by several important-looking people. They all spoke very fast in the Common Tongue; the same spoken by the Men and learned by all Immortals, and Citrosine didn't understand many of their words. She did get the hint that her father was a superior here, however.

They were escorted to a long chamber. The room sported a similarly long table, with dozens of chairs running along it on each side. The room was elegantly decorated, with various crests and tapestries adorning the walls. The two large fireplaces were empty—with no traces of any ashes, or burning of any kind. The room was quite warm, and a slight ringing pressure filled Citrosine's ears. Everyone was seated, seemingly in a certain order.

"Citrosine," Gya whispered gently, "We all have special seats—those of us that are in this committee." He gestured towards the table, and then pointed out a muscular man in a red and black robe. "You should ask that man where you are to sit. Tell him that you are the Scout's oldest daughter. He should help you. Go, go!" Gya retreated, and crossed the room to sit.

Citrosine wove through all of the tall Council members until she found the man that her father had pointed out. She tugged at his sleeve politely and smiled up at him. When he looked down, she saw that he had a large scar across his face and had no hair, but he smiled pleasantly. The scar twisted from one eyelid to the opposite corner of his mouth, and was thick and white. The damaged eye was bloodshot and looked off slightly to the right of Citrosine's ear, and she tried not to stare at it.

"Hello, sir," she greeted him nervously. "My name is Citrosine Nakiss, and I am here with my father, Gyardaute... er...the...Scout? He told me to ask you about a seat...?"

The man clapped his hands together.

"Yes," he said, in Citrosine's native dialect of Elvish, though choppily and in a low, coarse voice, "Gya's daughter. You are going to help him with his studies, aren't you? You may sit at the chair on the end of the table closest to the door. You see it, there? Yes, that one. Oh, and you may address me as Leader, please. I will sit in the seat next to you, the head of the table. Now, I shall be over there in a moment. Off with you!" He smiled and gently nudged Citrosine towards the end of the room.

What a peculiar man, treating me if I was the age of Tie. I suppose that he is likeable enough, though, Citrosine thought as she sat down. She looked down the table and spotted Gya about halfway down the line. She waved, and instantly regretted it, because the jerky motion only made her growing headache worse. The unnatural vibrations in the room had grown, to fill her head with an unpleasant pulsation.

As everyone sat down, the room grew quiet. Leader was the only one standing. He raised his hands above his head, and Citrosine suddenly knew what the vibrations in her head were; the sensations of magic.

Leader's palms glowed, and a breeze filled the room, extinguishing the candles all around the room. Citrosine recognized the spell, but it was much stronger magic than the versions that she had witnessed. The buzzing, ringing was obviously Citrosine's awareness of all the magic that was built up and collecting into this room. There were so many Elves of sorts, and their magic was all pent up in the room together.

The room was darkened from Leader's spell, but the candles relit themselves almost immediately. When they did, he smiled.

"Welcome back, everyone!" He addressed the whole of the Council. He then proceeded to give a long speech in the Common Tongue. Citrosine resolved then to improve her skills in that language when she and her father returned home. Citrosine tried to pick out words from the man's dialogue, but couldn't keep up with him. So, she sat back and daydreamed for a while.

"...And we welcome Citrosine!" Leader mentioned her name, and the young Elf snapped to attention. She hoped that she hadn't missed anything important. Everyone was looking her way, and she could only smile, and pray that she needed not to say anything. She managed a tiny wave, blushing, and Leader began to speak again, in the traditional Modern Elvish.

"Citrosine has been invited to join her father in this meeting. Citrosine, you and Gya will be visiting the Faeries in the next days. That is a wonderful post, eh, friends?" Everyone chuckled. Citrosine had heard about this position. The Scouts that were assigned to do this were always the most skilled with their magic, and had to keep their thoughts absolutely straight. Gya almost always was assigned to these positions, as one of the more powerful magic-wielders in the Tribe. Citrosine thought that only Leenka would be able to perform Council duties better than Gya, but for some reason Leenka had declined from a permanent position in the Council when she was asked a few years ago. She had been a protector, a warrior, before, but for some reason quit and now forever declined such a high position.

When Leader was done speaking to the Council everyone adjourned outside to a courtyard behind the palace. Citrosine and Gya stood in the center of a bustle of Council members eager to introduce themselves. Citrosine wondered how she would ever remember any of their names or ranks. Most of them were about Gya's age, except for three men that were older with long beards, and two young Elves that were just older than Citrosine. Those two she met last.

One of the young Elves was a loud boy, with less respect for magic than would ever be imagined. Citrosine tried to keep a good distance, as he was quite rude, and she didn't want to stand too close to his jabbering mouth that seemed to be full of raspberry wine all night. His name was Mychael, an outlandish, almost Man-like name. He was a worker on the Council, meaning that he performed such tasks that other members required, like carrying heavy loads or doing jobs that no one more skilled had time for.

The other boy was quiet and more mature. He had beautiful cacao-toned skin and seemed to look off into dreams throughout the night, though that was only because he was blind, eyes obscured behind cloudy glaze. Citrosine had little chance to talk to him until food was brought out, and he remained on a bench a good distance away. Citrosine walked over cautiously and sat next to him, for lack of interesting conversations with her elders, the men too stuffy and the women too matronly and obsessed with seeing a young Elf girl for Citrosine's taste.

"Hello," the boy said distantly, a question in his voice, as if inquiring if he was actually being approached. He inclined his head towards her. "What's your name?"

"I am Citrosine—Gyardaute's daughter,"

"Ah, yes. I am Tyre. It is nice to meet you, Citrosine."

"And you, as well," Citrosine said politely. They sat in silence for a moment.

"Do you have a Faerie's Blessing?" Tyre asked bluntly. "Well, you don't have to answer if you don't wish. I'm sorry—I am known for being a little forward…" he trailed off, embarrassed. Citrosine laughed softly at how quickly he spoke.

"No, I do not have a Blessing," she answered easily. "I might get one soon, but I do not have much magic yet."

"Yes you do," Tyre argued.

"What do you mean?" Citrosine was startled.

"I feel a lot of magic pulsing around you. That was the reason for my asking. It's as if you have a full aura of magic, and it is very strong. I can sense things like that well. It gets somewhat irritating sometimes," Tyre finished mysteriously.

They sat in silence for a few more minutes. Citrosine watched the smiling moon climb higher in the night sky, as she felt a smile climb higher on her face, just from this odd boy's presence.

"Citrosine," Tyre began faintly, "Would it be all right if I felt the shape of your face, just so I have an idea how to picture you? It's easier to talk if you know what someone's appearance might be like. My apologies, it seems too rude and overeager, but I assure you my intentions are pure. Curiosity, really… Again, my bluntness astounds me. I've only known you for three minutes…so rude." He finished as if speaking of an irksome cousin, rather than of himself.

"It's quite fine," Citrosine assured him, amused. She led his slender hands to her cheeks.

Tyre ran his fingers smoothly over her skin. He focused on the area around her eyes. To Citrosine, it felt very nice, like a silk glove. For having such long hands, his were extremely soft and gentle…

Tyre, on the other hand, was having trouble keeping his hands from shaking. This girl had so much magic emanating from her skin, mainly in her hands and face. If he could feel—or see—her eyes, he knew that he would feel the highest concentration of it there. He felt the pressure that he always felt with magic, but Citrosine alone gave off more than a whole roomful of mages.

"Tyre," Citrosine asked gently, and the boy raised his eyebrows slightly, still running his hand over her cheekbones.

"Tyre, were you born blind?" Citrosine looked into the boy's clouded, entranced eyes. A long moment of silence followed. The rest of the men in the council were beginning to disperse, some leaving to return home and others returning inside, to begin on some of their studies. Gya was having a lengthy conversation with Leader, and he glanced periodically at Citrosine, perhaps wondering why his daughter's face was being caressed by a fellow Council member.

Tyre finally answered Citrosine. He seemed to be having trouble finding the right words, so he left great pauses between words. Citrosine didn't think it was in uneasiness, just in difficulty explaining.

"I...was not born...this way. When I was...very little, I received a Blessing...My father recognized that I was very skilled, and I was chosen to be in this council." He paused, and then continued—stronger, now that he didn't have to risk sounding like a braggart.

"I was designated a Scout, as your father remains—powerful man, he. I ventured to a demon hideaway, and was ambushed...It's not wonderful conversation for Elves so young, really...hot tongs to the eyes completely scorched out all the nerves, all the bits that pick up lights, shapes, color...That was quite an experience...I am still on the Council because I can sense magic, and can perform it decently without sight." Tyre placed his hands in his lap. Citrosine looked down at her feet.

"I am sorry to have mentioned it," she said softly. She hadn't needed to bring up such a personal subject. What had she been thinking? Blushing, she turned away.

"It doesn't matter," Tyre reassured her quietly, not insincerely, but perhaps hurt? Perhaps his hesitance *was* because of his feelings, rather than his words. "I am comforted to know that someone else likes to have the same boldness as I...to learn a person's soul before you have to go through the process of meeting them. It really makes things easier. You have a lovely face, by the way—thank you for allowing my rapacious fingers to touch it."

"So, *lissa,* did you have a satisfying visit today?" Gya asked his daughter as the pair walked out of the courtyard together. Citrosine nodded, and looked up at her father. She didn't have the energy to go into great length explaining her conversation with Tyre, and her father didn't seem to wish to know what had gone on.

They walked through several dim, not-yet-complete corridors, and up narrow, twisting stairs. Gya finally stopped at a small door, barely high enough for him to stand within the frame.

"This is where we will stay," he said, yawning. He opened the door and held it open as Citrosine passed through. "I always stay here when I come. We're only going to stay one night, however. We will be outside for the remainder of our study."

"How long will that be?" Citrosine asked, a sinking feeling forming in her spirit. "And where are we exactly to go?"

Gya laughed. "No need to worry," he said, ruffling her hair as Citrosine tied her mother's black ribbon around a wrist, "It should not be long. We are going to study some of the different types of Blessings—from the Faeries themselves!"

The warning intuition evaporated faster than ice on a summer afternoon. Citrosine almost sighed—loudly—with relief, but stifled it. She couldn't have her father thinking her too afraid to set out on her first quest through the lands she'd not yet seen.

"How many types of Blessings are there?" She had heard plenty about Faerie Blessings, but had only been aware of one simple, white-boost-of-magic, intended-for-no-evil Blessing.

"That is what we are to find out," Gya replied mysteriously, "is it not?" With that, Gya closed the tiny door, leaving only the thin burning candles strewn about the room to provide their necessary light.

A troubled sleep overtook Citrosine, and she was haunted again and again by disturbing dreams of demons and Blessings gone wrong. She woke frequently, often finding herself with a hand on one of her twin swords, unsheathed and dangerous. She would quickly sheath it, and push it under her coverlets, but one of the two would spring to her hand again regardless.

When Gya awoke, he looked over at his daughter, who had been allowed the single bed. Her eyes were closed gently, and she seemed at ease, until he saw the sweat lining her brow. Citrosine was not prone to nightmares, but apparently, that had changed. Thankfully, she was sleeping peacefully by this point of the dawn.

Gya dressed quickly, and pulled two loaded knapsacks from a large cupboard in the rear of the room, one for each of them. They contained food, maps, journals, precautionary bandages, and the like.

He piled a heap of papers on the low table in the center of the room, and decided to let Citrosine sleep a bit longer. They had a few days and there was no need to rush. He set to work on some notes that he was behind on, and listened to the deep, even breaths of his daughter's sleep.

"Do not receive Jay's Blessing..." These last words of Citrosine's latest dream rang in her subconscious mind. A strange sending had warned her against a certain type of Blessing, as if she would receive one soon. They were magic *intensifiers*, and had she any magic to speak of yet? Not as far as she could tell. The sending had been cut off in mid-sentence by some other supernatural force—not a demon this time, amazingly.

The young Elf woke with a start. She sat up quickly, black dots swimming through her vision, head spinning, but ignored this.

"Father," she cried out nervously, calling Gya's attention. *"Lissa ji, ne rathka volst..."* She continued on quickly: *I love you; could you answer a quandary of mine? I have been seeing strange fantasies. You know how I have never experienced such nightmares, but they have begun to haunt me. I think these dreams have prophesied my near future, and they scare me!* She told her father of the dream that she had just encountered, and broke down crying. Citrosine had *never* in her life had nightmares until these last few nights.

She lost her breath quickly, and gasped, silent tears storming her cheeks and filling her mouth with salt. Gya knew that she was not insincere. He had been exactly right, seeing her sweating earlier. He cradled her in his arms, rocking the both of them back and forth in a slow, calming rhythm.

"Shh…" he whispered, "It will be all right, my love, *se lissa.* Calm down; it's over now." The young Elf finally slowed her breath, and shuddered one final time. They would solve this mystery while they studied the Faeries.

The two set out a while later, slinging packs over mail and their identical red surcoats, emblazoned with the Council's symbol of two swirling lines together, reminiscent of a musical literature marking.

They stopped in the courtyard, the same one they had lounged in on the previous day. The fresh, crisp air kissed their cheeks and stirred their hair, making them stop to savor it; the first cool breeze of the arid, sticky season that was coming to a close. Citrosine closed her eyes and let the wind blow her troubled dream memories away into the dawning sky.

"Citrosine," a warm-yet-hesitant voice called out from the southern edge of the courtyard. It was Tyre. He sat on a bench, holding a long walking stick dormant in his lap.

"He is your friend from last night, is he not?" Gya asked rhetorically. "Go to him. We have time to spare this morn. I will go to the Council Hall and return in a few moments. I must retrieve some instruction for our assignment." He trotted off towards the huge double doors, leaving Citrosine no choice but to walk to Tyre. She crossed the uneven stones, wondering all the while how the blind Tyre had sensed her.

"Hello, sir. And what might you want on this fine morning?" Citrosine sat next to him and joined in his light laughter.

"I knew it was you," he said, seeming to marvel at his prediction.

"Yes; I wondered how you did."

Tyre said nothing, but rubbed his hands along his cane.

"How did you recognize me, Tyre?"

He smiled smugly. Citrosine pressed and badgered him for a few more moments, and then he finally gave in.

"There were two signs. The first; I heard two pairs of feet walking over there," he gestured out to the center of the courtyard, "—so I knew *someone* was coming. The second was your aura. It would give your position away regardless of your total silence."

Citrosine suddenly wished she hadn't asked. Tyre was smiling broadly in a secret thought of his own, so she said nothing.

"What I called you for," he began again, more seriously, "—was to ask you a question before you left." Tyre wrung his hands around his cane. Citrosine touched his shoulder. This inspired a little more confidence in him, and he continued.

"Have you had any kind of dreams lately that include some kind of...sending? You know, somewhat of a magical spirit sent to you for a certain purpose..."

Citrosine nodded, and then remembered his blindness. She blushed, and murmured, "Yes...just last night. It tried to tell me something about a Blessing... '*Do not receive Jay's Blessing,*'...something like that, and then it was cut off. Why do you ask?"

Tyre looked troubled. He shut his useless eyes. "I had a dream last night, as well. Only mine didn't say 'Jay's Blessing', but it was cut off. It said the Blessing of J...something that starts with the letter 'J'. Maybe in your dream, it didn't say 'Jay's', but perhaps the letter 'J', abbreviated? Is that a possibility?"

"Of course," Citrosine mused. Tyre was quiet, calculating for a moment.

"I only wished to tell you this, since the prophecy spoke your name. It wasn't as clear as your dream, but I suspected trouble—you are studying Blessings, aren't you?"

"Yes,"

"Well," Tyre finished, "be careful. Tell your father, as well. I shall see you after you return…" The last statement sounded more like a question or request to Citrosine, but Tyre then proceeded to stand up and walk away, his cane tapping against loose stones in the courtyard. Citrosine shivered.

"Tyre," she called, before he was out of earshot. The boy turned around. Citrosine bit her lip; she hadn't really a reason to call his name, but it had slipped out. She said nothing, and after a beat, her acquaintance left silently. She watched him walk smoothly, using his walking stick to tap loose stones and corners as if he could see them perfectly, just highlighting them instead of discovering them. He turned a corner and was gone.

Gya approached Citrosine a few moments later. He patted her hands gently. She stood and, without another word, they left Haerthor.

"Father, which way do we go?" The solemn silence was broken as the pair reached the gate marking the city's exit. Three paths merged into one, ending where they stood. Citrosine looked down each one carefully as her father studied his map.

To the west was the path they had taken through *Bixoel*. The sky looked peculiarly discolored above that forest, though it may have been just her imagination. She remembered the oppression that the forest had put on them, and shivered. She saw a few flashes in the sky, and was—almost—certain that the storm was not just her mind playing tricks.

The east road looked quite difficult, but seemed pleasant enough. A few cottages lined the rocky path, and when these ceased, the path veered upwards, encircling the mountains. Few went that way these days, for over those mountains laid the settlements of Men. Elves had abandoned loving elements over those mountains, including the Eastern Ocean, which Citrosine had never seen. Their old home had lain there, now scorched and only a memory.

The path that stood straight ahead was wild and overgrown, hardly a path. No one that had gone down that path had been of the Stone Elf tribe. It was rumored that the path ran due south the whole way, and reached another ocean. The Elves had come to believe that all of the Big Lands were surrounded by oceans, making it an island of great scale. The south path did lead to other tribes—the fabled Shadow Elves, at least where they used to be—and other kinds of villages. No Stone Elf had *ever* been that way.

Gya folded his map and stuffed it into his pack. He sighed. They must be taking the southern path, the most dangerous one of all. A heavy weight settled in her stomach.

"We go east," Gya said, much to his daughter's relief. But then she remembered the Men.

"How far east?" she asked quietly.

"That is where the map stops helping us. That part of the page was damaged by one of my less competent scribes. I do not know how long it shall take us, but we will find the Faerie Dwelling." With that, he turned to his right and began to walk. Citrosine followed suit, picking her way carefully through the fist-sized rocks.

"Mother, *what is going on?*" Palgirtie cried as another peal of thunder rattled the house. Leenka was gathering blankets and armor from the attic. She climbed down the ladder quickly.

"Tie, *lissa*, you must not ask questions now. Put on this armor, quickly," she handed her youngest daughter a small armor plate, which she strapped on hurriedly. Leenka outfitted herself in another plate, similarly glittering with magic protection spells. She gathered the blankets and grabbed for Tie's hand. They ran outside into the merciless rain. *I hope that they have only come for me, and not my family,* Leenka pleaded to herself. *I have made enemies, dealing with such magic, I admit to my mistakes...they should not want the others...*She led Tie around to the back of the house.

A large boulder stood in the center of the clearing behind the house. Leenka squinted, and it rolled aside sluggishly, inch by inch. She lifted a small iron ring on a recessed trapdoor that had been revealed underneath, and threw the blankets into the small space below. She nudged Tie down the pit firmly, and followed suit. The trapdoor shut, and the boulder was rolled across the door again. They sat panting in the darkness for a moment, hearing nothing but rain dripping from the trapdoor and their own bodies. Leenka suddenly sat up, listening motionlessly and holding a finger to Tie's lips. A thump on the door made them both start.

Citrosine and Gya had long since passed the last of the cottages along the eastern path, but now they stood at the base of the mountains. Gya allowed Citrosine to ascend first, and she did so very slowly, loosing many rocks as she scurried through the dirt. Gya looked behind himself, and then followed.

The mountains were not very high, nor was the path among them a great distance, but the path was instead quite steep. With few minor falls and scrapes, the pair arrived at the summit. They were weary, but not enough to make them rest. However, they did stop, for the view was amazing.

Citrosine was shocked to see what she did over the mountains. The valley was filled with cottages and farms! So close to the Elves? She reasoned that it was not as quick a walk for the mortals as it had been for she and her father, but... wasn't this supposed to be dangerous?

Milling about the mortal's dwellings were hundreds of the race of Men. Children chased each other among many trees of the same, needly type that Citrosine recognized from near their secluded home, and there were a great many horses and strange, fatter animals that she did not recognize, perpetually chewing on who knew what, between large square jaws. The older male Men were hurrying around, talking to each other loudly and rushing to talk to others. The females wore white bonnets and long skirts that brushed the ground.

They seemed to be doing chores within their farms. Some would sit next to one of the fat, black-and-white animals and do something Citrosine would rather not imagine, and then retreat, carrying the full buckets of white milk back to their homes. Others tried to get at the children and bring them inside.

Citrosine looked at her father.

"Have you come this way before? I mean, after we fled through this path from the old dwelling of ours?" Gya shifted uneasily at that question.

"Yes, I have, but these residents were not here then. Now, we have to get around here and up to that crag on the other side, and get through to the forest. From then on, I do not know what to expect."

Citrosine peered again at the village. There were no ways to pass by unseen, so they would presumably have to walk right through the center square. Gya was apparently thinking the same thing.

"I need to cast a glamour over us; we might be able to get there easier." Even as he said this, Citrosine felt the buzzing pressure of magic becoming present. Gya waved his hands over the two of them, and they changed. Tiny invisible shards of magic assembled over the Elves' skins, and the glamour was cast.

Gya now wore the form of a Man, complete with a flawless illusion of a dangerous, pointed metal tube that all of the real Men seemed to be carrying around with them. It looked quite out of place on Gya, with his soft eyes and fair hair. His ears had also changed; they were smaller, and seemed awfully unnatural to Citrosine. She looked down and realized that she had changed as well. She wore one of the long dresses that the women were wearing, and her hair that had been pulled back so gracefully was now piled under a bonnet. Her swords and pack now took the shape of a basket of food and a walking cane. She reached up to feel her ears and found that they, too, were rounded at the top. She groaned, imagining the trouble it would be to pick her way into the valley while wearing a long skirt. Recalling Leenka's story of fighting in gowns as an Air Elf, she smiled and followed her father.

"Your name will be Cassy, and mine Jacob," Gya was explaining as they began to climb down swiftly. "We are a father and daughter that are just passing through, as we are, but we must not say why; we do not know the names of places here, and must ask them how to get to the center of the wood. You shall take the guise of having a twisted leg, so pretend to favor it, and I will take care of all the dialogue. They do not understand Elvish, of course. Man's race considers women as a minority, so they will not mind if you do not speak. Do you understand?" Citrosine nodded obediently, and they moved to the village.

As they entered the center square, a mob of men and women greeted them.

"Hello, good day," they said. Citrosine didn't understand their meaning, for they spoke in the Common Tongue, which sounded like baby-talk. Gya acknowledged them, and began to speak.

"Hello, friends, and good day to you. I am called Jacob, and this is my daughter Cassy. We are only passing through here momentarily. Pardon her; she has a twisted leg…" He stopped, wondering how much their vocabulary let them understand. They accepted this, and led them to the tavern immediately. Citrosine almost forgot to limp, but she remembered just as they began walking, and hung back, almost being left behind. She shuffled along, rotating her left foot and ankle completely inwards, putting half as much weight on it as the other, and thus tottering along precariously. She felt silly, and the mortal children stared at her openly, but she pretended to ignore them.

One scruffy man approached the pair once in the tavern.

"Where was it that ye came from?" he asked, in a strange accent.

"Just a small settlement over the mountains," Gya replied politely, wondering if he should imitate this man's vowel sounds. *Too late now.*

"Aye? This was the furthest west we were able to go, but it suits us fine—better for the plantation we're planning on," the man said. Gya shifted in his seat, and gave Citrosine a reassuring look. "Yes," the man continued, "so welcome to the village. My name is Samuel, the innkeeper. What is it that you two are lookin' fer?"

"We were just in passing. It was said by the town soothsayer that a certain fairy-herb would ease the pain of Cassy's crippled leg." Gya almost winced as he said the word, as "crippled" was an unacceptable term, even when translated into his own tongue. "Say, Samuel," he continued, "how would we get to the center of yonder forest to the northeast?" Gya looked again at his daughter, who was looking around, somewhat apprehensively.

She was already fed up with these people. Many men were shuffling around and making fights in this place. It smelled strongly of ale and sweat, and there were no other women here. The one thing that peeved her the most, though, was that she couldn't understand a word that was being said. She looked around. The whole building was made of wood and mud packed together. She was not impressed. The only magic here was the glamour that her father had cast over them. Thankfully, no one else was attuned enough to it to notice.

Gya talked to Samuel for a moment longer, then he said something that made him go away, and he led her out of the tavern.

"What did you say back there?" Citrosine whispered, in Elvish—the only language she knew. Gya shushed her, as they were within earshot to a few of the women. The Elves practically ran to the crag on the opposite end of the village after skirting a meandering path among cottages. Citrosine—Cassy—shuffled along even more unsteadily, greatly exaggerating her limp. Gya led her around a few bends, and they were in the center of a forest.

"I told the men that we were being followed and needed to hurry to get an herb for your leg. He thought I was trying to avoid some band of creatures that he called, er, En-juns? and left us alone."

Gya said this as he waved his hands about and returned them to their former appearances.

They began walking through the forest, around rocks, over huge roots, and under leaning trees. Many animals they had never seen crept along next to them; Citrosine was amused by the small gray ones that hopped from tree to tree, with their bushy tails springing behind them. These seemed to be afraid of the presence of magic. Perhaps that was why she had never seen them before. Eventually, they could hear someone close by. Gya stopped, and Citrosine dropped to her knees and crept along a thicket, where the voice got louder. It was a beautiful, tinkling voice, and there was a magical quality to it.

Gya slunk next to her, and listened as well.

"Faerie," he said, mainly to himself. Citrosine nodded. No surprises there. They inched forward. The voice stopped, but a very high-pitched drone of magic reached their ears, and a figure approached them. It was indeed a Faerie, and it tiptoed towards them gleefully.

"Hello, Elven friends!" The Faerie greeted enthusiastically. *"What brings you to the realm of Men?"*

"Just some business," Gya replied, *"...for the Stone Elf Magic Study. It is a funny thing, because we are actually supposed to be studying the different types of Faerie's Blessings. The information is only to be shared inside the Council so as to keep us informed of the powers of our tribes; it will not leave our records."* Gya whispered quietly in Citrosine's thoughts that she was to keep her eyes at the Faeries' feet throughout this adventure. *"As hospitable as they seem, if you gaze into their faces without steeling yourself, they will suck you away to their otherworld: Tír na nÓg. It is in a different plane, and they would keep you for a thousand years as their slave...so please, lissa, be careful!"*

The Faerie looked thoughtful. She shrugged. *"Well, follow me!"* She darted away, and the Elves had to jog to keep up with her. She zigzagged through the trees, and then came to an abrupt stop in a clearing. The grass here was tinted blue and sparkling, so anyone would know that it wasn't a normal place. A ring of toadstools lined the outskirts of a quaint Faerie community, where the homes were made of vines and flowers enchanted to grow together. It was any young girl's dream come true: so much beauty and magic.

"Wait here!" commanded the Faerie. She unfolded her thin wings and flew briskly away. A white-auraed Faerie replaced her after a few seconds. This Faerie was slightly fairer, and sported black wings. She also wore a dainty crown and a flowing white dress, signifying her as the leader of these particular Faeries.

"Welcome to Faerie Village," she said in a deep, musical tambour in their minds, *"not that we wanted it to be called this. A group of Men's children called it this, what with the ring*

of toadstools, and otherwise, we live here in secrecy. What was it that you two wished of us?"

Gya cleared his throat. "We are here on behalf of the Magic Study Council of the Stone Elves. We request information for private use on your Blessings. It is not to be shared outside of the Council, save for my daughter Citrosine here. I swear it on my life." He bowed his head slightly.

"An Elf's promise is never broken, else he shall suffer as the Blue Lord," the Faerie reminded him. The Blue Lord was the Great Ghersah's greatest oppressor, and he was condemned to a tortured death that was worse than any other after Ghersah had seated herself at the peak of the Tree of Redemption. Gya nodded to the Faerie solemnly, raising his right hand.

"Oh, how glorious this is!" The Faerie tittered. "You will have to learn from witnessing the Blessings performed. Your luck is that we are busy in assigning Blessings today. We have the average of two of each Blessing to compose today, actually, so you shall have a good chance to learn. You must keep out of sight of each recipient, and cannot ask questions until later, for the Elves and beings who receive these Blessings will feel intimidated otherwise, and the magic will not flow freely. Do you understand? According to each of my kind at this moment, you are no longer here." Citrosine and Gya nodded. The Faerie smiled even wider. She then waved the Elves over to a large tree. Without being asked, they climbed up high into the branches, hidden from all.

Soon after the Faerie had resumed her duties in the city, a Sea Elf approached. She was clad in silver surcoat and leggings, and wore a small ring around her little finger. She was greeted by a bright green-winged Faerie, who led her close to Citrosine and her father's hiding place.

"You, Jyline Ress, Sea Elf, have been recognized and accepted to receive a Faerie's Blessing, the Blessing of Cayre. It is a Blessing that will strengthen only your light-bringing magics. You will be able to do more than you had ever been before in the ways of light-bringing and controlling." The Faerie continued her introduction to light-bringing for quite a time, occasionally asking Jyline questions.

Then, the Faerie touched Jyline's right wrist, and a bright flash of light illuminated the entire clearing. The Elf flinched. She bowed her head slightly, to look upon her arm. A white beam had begun to issue from it, and she let out a tiny cry...

Several more types of Blessings were given over the next few hours, and Citrosine gathered that all were, in the least of terms, painful. The types that she had witnessed were Cayre, Blessing of Light-Bringing; Hillsa, Blessing of Strength; Orla, Blessing of Water-Handedness (Citrosine didn't know what this was); Kyte, Blessing of Fire-Handedness (the opposite of whatever Orla did, Citrosine reasoned); and Fraam, Blessing of The Earth. She was trying to listen for a name that began with *J*, when a purple-winged male Faerie mentioned the Blessing of Jygul. She snapped into closer attention. *Jygul? There is a Blessing dealing with the darkest mage that has existed in Elven history?* Citrosine panicked. *Why on earth would I ever need protection from receiving* that? *I wouldn't want it!*

"You, Jaque Hurin, Cavern Elf, have requested and been accepted for the Blessing of Jygul. It will allow you to practice dark magic. You have been deemed worthy of this, but it shall be rather thorny to acquire. This Blessing will also strengthen the rest of your magic skills. Are you prepared for this honor?" The Faerie paused, clasping his hands behind his back.

"Yes I am," Jaqe replied, but his face told another story. The Faerie leaned closer to him, his dark and iris-less eyes staring into Jaqe's. He cast a quick spell, creating a goblet from naught but the moist air.

"You must spill three drops of your own blood into this goblet. One that will acquaint the dark magic with your old magic supply, one to sacrifice to Jygul, the Dark Goddess, and one to redeem yourself to Ghersah, the Great Goddess." He then acquired a dagger in the same way as the cup. "Use this. It is clean enough for you to use."

Clean enough, Citrosine thought, *but how clean is that? Washed, or wiped off in the grass?*

Jaqe's face was white, but passive. He gathered dagger and goblet from the Faerie's grasp. He lifted the dagger to his neck. He did not wince when it bit into his skin, and quickly withdrew it once he'd drawn blood.

Jaqe angled the blade towards the golden goblet. Citrosine had a crisp view of this, thanks to Elves' impeccable vision.

She clearly saw the tiny stream of blood roll down the blade. The drops seemed to fall very slowly from it. She counted, *One...Jaqe, two...Jygul, three...Ghersah!* Jaqe's hand shook greatly as he carefully dripped his blood into the cup. It was disconcerting to watch.

The Faerie nodded. "Wonderful!" he proclaimed. "Now, I must recite the mantra that will bring the darkness to your power. It will be extremely painful, and I am sorry for this, but you will be brought great power. The magic store will be in your non-dominant palm and both of your eyes. Now, the mantra." The Faerie took a deep breath, exhaled, and then took another. He then began Jygul's Mantra. It was chanted in Old Elvish, so Citrosine could not understand the words. There were a few she could pick out—*power, love, hate, darkness*—but only the magic in the archaic words gave her any sense of what was going on. By the force that stirred her mind from the mantra, she gathered essentially that *we don't like Jygul very much.*

The small Faerie ended in a loud, proclamatory voice. It was an odd sort of poem...not really having any kind of rhythm to it...chaotic, almost.

The Faerie lifted his hands to Jaqe's shoulders. He looked him straight in the eyes and said, "Prepare for the worst nausea that you should ever endure. Give me your left palm." His soft, musical voice had suddenly turned cold and sharp. Jaqe realized this, and raised his hand hesitantly.

The Faerie put both hands on the Elf's palm, and braced himself. A great darkness spread through all of the clearing, and the forest, and even the village beyond. Nothing was visible, except to the Faerie. He pressed down on Jaqe's palm. A small thread of light issued from it. It rose up past the trees. Jaqe observed, mesmerized. It swirled around, like smoke, and expanded and inflated into a large ball that spun around lazily, as if a soap bubble caught in wind. It shimmered, and then zipped down into Jaqe's hand in an arrowlike stream.

Jaqe screamed. The darkness around him was fading away into the sun's light, but seemed to be retreating into his blood. He couldn't see anything, couldn't feel the wind, or anything outside of his pain, and he fell onto the soft grass at his feet—which he also couldn't feel.

The Faerie remained with his hands in the Elf's palm. Jaqe closed his eyes tightly, bracing against the pain. He shuddered, and the agony appeared to recede.

The Faerie gathered himself up and prodded Jaqe with a nudge in the waist. He opened his eyes groggily, and he looked into the Faerie's eyes for a third time. He felt as if there was nothing else past the figure, that it was the only thing there was. He clenched his teeth, and looked away.

He braced himself. Everything else vanished, and he felt the darkness that was now inside of him stir. It fluttered around his body, and he knew that the Blessing had been fully cast.

Citrosine had let tears run when she saw Jaqe on the ground, writhing in absolute distress. She could somehow feel the magic inside her own blood moving around, in sympathy. It was an odd sensation, as if her blood grew restless and had changed form to occupy itself—turned into flitting dragonflies. She turned away from Gya, and raised her hand close to her face. She summoned the magic inside it, and a small black spark shot out from it, leaping away into the sky. She did this again, and knew that her magic was more powerful than it had been just moments ago.

As Jaqe stood up again, he looked at a small shadow under the trees. He convened the darkness from the Blessing into his eyes, and the shadow grew darker. He experimented with making it lighter, smaller, larger, and once gave it a three-dimensional body, before leaving it to its original form again.

He bowed to the Faerie, and immediately took off into the trees, though the pain that had been bestowed in him appeared still quite prominent, judging by the look in his eyes.

The white, queen-Faerie flew into the tree where Gya and Citrosine were still hidden.

"You may desist," she said flatly. The pair leapt from the tree, and landed where the Faerie was already waiting.

"That is the last Blessing we conduct today. I hope that you have learned all that you needed to, and will keep to your oath of privacy. Farewell on your next journey, may you be returning home, or pursuing another wish." She bowed her head and flitted over to her village, disappearing through an archway.

Gya and his daughter stood there a moment longer, and Citrosine tugged at her father's sleeve. He looked at her, and saw that she wore a look of wonder.

"Father," she said quietly, "I…my magic has just appeared to me. I do not…do not understand how…" Gya cut her off with a hoist of his hand.

"Show me," he said. Citrosine nodded, and showed him the spark that she had discovered in the tree. He was awed.

"Amazing," he muttered. "Are you sure you do not know why this happened?" he asked, with the slightest hint of urgency in his manner. This Citrosine did not notice. She explained that her magic had stirred right after Jaqe had acquired his Blessing, and how she had experimented with the spark. Gya rubbed his temples thoughtfully.

"It is probably the Nymph blood in you…" he mused. "I will bring this matter before Leader when we return. For now, try to develop some spells as we walk. Here, let me show you a smattering of what I know…"

Gya passed a bit of his knowledge of magic to his daughter, and they traveled invisibly through the village again, resuming the trail back to Haerthor.

Three

BLANKETS OF DARKNESS

When the two Elves reached Haerthor the next afternoon, they walked immediately to the Council's wing of the castle. There was a session that was to be held in only a few moments, so they took the seats they had used before.

Citrosine was greatly enthusiastic after this journey with her father. On the one hand, her magic was beginning to grow much more powerful, and on the other, the journey didn't take nearly as long as she had been dreading. One could say that she was the nervous type when it came to trying new things, but she was trying to amend that.

A sudden noise made the two of them start, but they sat down again quickly. It was only the bells chiming in the tower of the courtyard. The chimes rang out thirteen times. After the last echo of the last chime, the door at the end of the room swung open silently, and another group of Council members filed into their seats.

Leader walked briskly, getting a chance to shake hands with Gya before he had to sit. Apparently they were good friends, which Citrosine had not realized. He winked at Citrosine as he sat down.

"Friends," he called out in Elvish, his sharp voice silencing every whisper and murmur, "I trust that the past few days have been good to you, and that everyone's quests have been fulfilled as much as is possible. I see that there are vacant seats today, and let us all wish those Elves well on their journeys..." From then on, he rambled along in the Common Tongue, and Citrosine tried to look attentive. Was it really that important that he speak in Man's language? Couldn't all the Elves present understand him if he spoke in Elvish? Maybe he was practicing, or perhaps just speaking this way for spite.

She looked around the room; at the tapestries, various members around the table, and most of all, for Tyre. He had the right to know what had happened to Citrosine's magic. She subtly spotted him, and cursed inwardly as she remembered that he was blind, and could not make eye contact. For it would be rude to speak even in thought while he listened to Leader.

As Leader talked, his tone became more and more urgent, and Citrosine immediately focused again. She looked up at his face, and saw that it was wearing a stern expression. He continued like this for a moment, and then his face softened.

"Now," he began comprehensibly, "are there any questions or needs?" Gya stood up, along with Tyre and two other men. Leader called on one of the latter first, one with a long, wiry black beard.

Long Beard asked, "When will we hold our next counsel?" Leader rubbed his temple.

"In half a fortnight, at the thirteenth hour," he replied. Long Beard sat down, and the next man was called on. He did not have a beard, but a pair of transparent glass circles facing his eyes, held together by some wire; a device that Citrosine did not recognize.

"Are we to continue our research during that time, or do we share it tonight at the dinner in the courtyard?" he asked in a nasally voice that made Citrosine's scalp prickle. No Elf should have a voice so ugly, she mourned. Leader nodded, almost as if he had heard Citrosine's thoughts. She stifled a giggle.

"An imperative detail I had forgotten," he said. "Your information will be held until the meeting in half a fortnight, and we shall compile it then, since many have not yet returned. Scribes and the library facility will be available for use tonight and in the remaining time period until the next meeting, lest you forget your discoveries." He turned to Citrosine's father. "Gya?" he inquired quietly.

Gya bowed slightly. "If I may, I would like to hold private audience with you and my daughter after this meeting adjourns..." He shot Citrosine a subtle wink.

Leader said nothing, nodding slightly. Gya took his seat.

Tyre was the only member that remained standing, but he couldn't know this. Leader called his name, and the boy bowed at the waist before speaking.

"Leader, sir, I would like to ask if you know when our sovereignty's leaders shall return to the castle. I have heard some rumors that it is no longer safe here on land, because of encroaching Men from the north, and perhaps it would be better if our royalty remained in the sea...or relocated very soon?" Tyre bowed again and stood at attention.

Leader's brow furrowed. He turned his eyes to a man Citrosine presumed to be Tyre's father, who had taken a seat on his son's right side. The man was shaking his head and shrugging. Leader rolled his eyes.

"Tyresias Kendah," he began slowly, his voice quivering between disbelief and anger, "I do not know where you have learned this, or who may have encouraged you into believing it, but there is nothing that should worry you at this point in time. I grow weary of your advice for the future in the last few months, Kendah, and if it reaches my ears too many times more, you and your father shall be punished," he stopped, and then began in a more unbiased tone.

"The King and his family will return to Haerthor as soon as the central portion of the castle is finished. The other wing will be constructed soon afterwards. *Thank* you, Tyre."

"Yes, sir," Tyre proceeded, "but what of the mortal settlements so near to us? Will we only continue to build with the chance of their coming our way, into our lands? What of—"

"Tyre, that is talk for a meeting between tribes and races, and not for the Stone Tribe to decide. You may *sit*." Leader contained himself by just a tight, forced smile.

The Council dispersed, and everyone went to their rooms to prepare for the dinner, except for one pair. They met with Leader in the gathering room just outside the Council meeting room. Leader smiled as Gya and Citrosine approached.

"Please," he said, gesturing toward three chairs that had been swung round next to a small fireplace, "sit." They did so, and Gya expressed his thanks in meeting them privately. Leader made a dismissive gesture.

"Anything for you, my friend. Now, what did you wish to ask me about, Gya?" Gya smiled, directing his eyes to Citrosine. *"Do you wish to explain?"* he asked her. She nodded halfheartedly.

"Er…" she began nervously, "While we were doing our research on the Faerie Blessings, we saw one that made my magic…er…rise up, kind of. So I was wondering if maybe I could get a Blessing now…to…strengthen my…powers? Or at least kind of…solidify them."

Citrosine's face had gone beet red, but she got through her narrative. Leader asked Gya a few questions about his father being a Nymph.

Finally, he seemed to have reached a finale, and turned to Citrosine. "Darling," he said slowly, "I believe that you should try to get a good, strong Blessing. If it affected your magic just from watching one of these performed, then you may come into great power if you physically get one. I have a template you can send the Faeries if you wish to receive this Blessing, but…" he trailed off. Citrosine was not focused. She was thinking to herself.

I would 'come into great power', though it would be dark power, for the generic Blessing strengthens that power which is already present…they would try to assume that it was light powers, as Leader already has assumed. Would this hurt? Light and dark conflicting? I must be growing dark powers—did I not feel it rise in the course of the Blessing of Jygul? This would be the appropriate Blessing to receive, though I would be betraying the dream-prophet, as well as my father. He hates dark magic! Do I wish to expand my magic? Of course! But…why would a prophet come to Tyre and I, warning me away from it? Citrosine, have any of your other dreams—with the demons—come true? Not for anyone in the family! Don't spend so much time thinking on this, just get the Blessing and get on with your life! The last trail of her thoughts became a high, shrieking voice, encouraging her to just get the Blessing of Jygul and be done with it. She succumbed to it.

Looking up at Leader, she said, "Sir, I would like to ask permission of the Faeries to receive the Blessing of Jygul." Gya looked at her sharply. Seeing the determined expression on his daughter's face, he softened ever so faintly. He just didn't wish harm on her, as they had seen Jaqe go through. Black magic was unacceptable. He had lectured his daughters about the evil and corruption that that ghastly magic always seemed to cause…

Leader nodded solemnly, and stood. "I will recommend you to them, and shall notify you through a messenger when I hear a reply. I will, of course, speak to your father before both of you return home…just for reference's sake, and to determine whether this is a good idea or not. For now, you are both dismissed. It is almost time for dinner."

When Gya and Citrosine arrived at Gya's small chamber, they saw Tyre sitting against the door, eyes closed.

"Hello?" he asked, his apprehensiveness showing through his voice. "Gya?" Gya and Citrosine stifled a laugh. He sounded just like a child.

"Yes, Tyre, I am Gya. Pray, what are you doing in front of the door to my room?" Gya smiled, and took Tyre's hand. He helped him stand without knocking into anything. Tyre smiled meekly. He was silent for a moment. "Is Citrosine the other person with you?" Tyre seemed to already know Citrosine was there, but made a point of asking the question so as not to seem rude.

"Yes," Gya replied, something hard hiding in his voice.

"I…well…I was waiting here to ask if I…could…speak with her for a moment?"

"Yes, you may, Tyre." Gya winked at Citrosine, and retreated through the door to his room. Citrosine was deeply saddened to see the sorrow weaved into her father's brow. He must still be thinking of the Blessing…

Tyre reached out for Citrosine's hand. She gave it to him. "What did you want to say?" She asked, so quietly that she barely heard herself. Tyre clenched and unclenched his free hand.

"Did you find out about that Blessing? The 'J' one?" He was nervous, and thought his words cautiously.

"Yes, it's the Blessing of Jygul."

"Jygul? What does it do? Dark powers?"

Citrosine thought about her recent discussion with Leader, and tried to find the right words to tell Tyre that she was going to get this forbidden Blessing. Tyre recognized her hesitation.

"Citrosine,"

"Yes, er, that Blessing strengthens dark magic."

"Dark as if Jygul is giving this power?"

"Yes…and…well…"

"What *is* it?"

"I – Leader – it's…"

"Citrosine!"

"I am getting the Blessing of Jygul!" She hadn't meant to be so frank, but it just came out. Tyre's mouth hung open in disbelief.

"After all of this, you are still getting it?" he asked her incredulously, but kept his tone steady and measured, despite the volume it had gathered.

"Yes, well, I think so…my father is not pleased." Tyre visibly sobered at this.

"Wow…you are very courageous, Citrosine. You…I respect you for that, I always have, since you came…"

"Really?"

Tyre cocked his head to the side, as if he had heard a sound. "We should have been getting ready for dinner. I will talk to you in the courtyard?"

"Obviously. I will find you, Tyre, and we can talk." Tyre nodded, pleased. Citrosine sighed quietly, overwhelmed. She'd not wanted Tyre to react like her father had. Tyre must have heard her frustration, for he reached for her hand, gave it a reassuring, almost tender squeeze, and began on his way. Citrosine smiled, watching Tyre take up his cane and feel his way down the hall. Gya opened the door just after Tyre disappeared around a corner.

"Are you all right, *lissa*? I heard raised voices, and then silence." He looked into her eyes, searching for any hurt. She showed none, and they walked down to the dinner hall.

Palgirtie woke suddenly. She could see nothing, hear nothing. Where was she? She rubbed her eyes. Had she gone blind? Where was her mother? And then she remembered;

they had hidden in the little cellar. A storm was coming, and there was something trying to get in…She could remember no more than that, but she could feel the slight buzzing pressure of magic. Had she been put into a spell-induced sleep? Her head hurt, and she could remember nothing.

"Mama?" she whispered. Her voice was instantly consumed by the earth around her. She sat up on her knees, and felt the ground around her. *"Mama!"* Was she here? Tie couldn't feel anything on the ground, other than the coarse dirt and rocks. The blankets that had been covering her were gone.

She sat dejectedly, tears rolling down her cheeks.

"MAMA!"

She sniffled loudly, and then stood. If she raised her arms, her fingertips just brushed the top of the cellar. Maybe she could find the door, and have some light to look around? She felt only dust and muck for a long time, and walked for many moments. She began tapping on the surface above her, just to be sure that she would know where the planks were.

Thunk, thunk, thunk…rap! What was that? The wood! She could feel the wooden door above her head. She could just touch it with the tips of her fingers, and realized that she would not be able to push the door open. She lunged upwards at it, but accomplished nothing. She sobbed, and covered her head in her shawl.

"Mommy…Dada…Citrosine," she wept, their names giving her a bit of comfort; torches in the blackness. But then, they, too, were extinguished by the dirt, roots, and sorrow and Tie wept herself back into exhausted slumber.

When Citrosine and Gya returned to the courtyard for dinner, it was raining. A protective roof had been conjured by someone's magical prowess. It absorbed the water from above, and glowed enough to let them see what they ate. Tyre had sat down, and was the only one to do so as of yet. He sat in the furthest seat from Leader's appointed chair. As Gya and his daughter approached, the rest of the Council was heading to the table and taking empty places. Citrosine took her place aside Tyre, as she had promised, and Gya sat next to the nasally-voiced man wearing the glass-and-wire contraption before his eyes—at the other end of the table. Tyre placed his hands on the table and whispered something audibly in Old Elvish, which Citrosine perceived as gibberish. She looked at him questioningly, but said nothing.

"Friends, and members of the Council," Leader said in his grandiose voice, "let us eat in friendship, and enjoy each others' companionship! Whenever you wish, you may take your leave and be on your way home. I am sure that your families wait for you." And with that, everyone began to converse pleasantly.

Tyre reached for Citrosine's hands, which had remained in her lap the whole time. She allowed him to grasp them, but she moved them atop the table first so that no misunderstandings in common Elvish courtesy would occur. She kept an eye on her father, for she was not sure of his feelings towards Tyre.

Tyre whispered something through thought, once again in the archaic Old Elvish that only scholars and advanced mages learned. Citrosine knew few words in Old Elvish, only the few that could be put to good use in spells because of the power they held in themselves. She spoke fluently in the adapted Elvish that had come with the migration of Elves to the Big Lands. Old Elvish was for the Old World, across the cold Eastern Ocean.

"Tyre, I can't understand you."

"Never learned Old Elvish? Shame, that," he said, far more distantly than normal. Usually he would have been wordier and more joking.

"You're scaring me. What is the matter?"

"Citrosine," he said to her privately, *"I must meet with you after this dinner. I feel that something has...gone wrong."*

"Why must you wait?" Citrosine said uneasily. *"Tell me this way. No one will listen to us."* Tyre withdrew his hands

and wrung them. He bit his lip, and moved some food to his mouth, trying to appear jovial to those mages who would see his discomfort.

"*At your home…a storm of some kind…a demon raid. This was in another prophecy, and it was definitely centered on your home. I saw you, and your little sister, as I assumed. Taking away an older woman, your mother…? Demons; attacking,*" he stopped abruptly. Citrosine had lost thought, anyway.

Mama! No, she is too strong to be captured! Never could she be taken away that easily. But…could it have been the Men? No. They are not sturdy enough; she would have destroyed them. I must go home. I need to tell Father! No…after the dinner, do not attract attention.

"*Tyre?*" Citrosine asked him hesitantly. He nodded absently. "*Why are you having dreams about me, and my family? How do you know that they are correct? You do not know me well at all, so…*" she stopped. Some races shared myths in their histories, in which those with no sight could foretell the future, have almost involuntary hindsight, foresight, hypnosis…

And then Tyre did something that she half-expected.

"*Yes, Citrosine, I do have that kind of magic, as you imagine. It came with my removal from sight. But do not worry; I do not use it in bad ways. I have connections with certain people sometimes. It is quite complicated, so do not worry. By the way, you should make sure that you do not stick out from the rest of the crowd.*" Tyre flexed his hands, and rubbed them along his cane, all the while humming a familiar tune to himself, though the knots in his brow betrayed him.

Citrosine mouthed a few bites, only pretending to enjoy the dinner. What she really wanted right then was to be home, in the arms of her mother, listening to a nonsensical story.

Gya and Citrosine both left the dinner feeling uneasy. Gya had been completely left out of the conversations around him, and had been wishing to be home with his beloved mate the whole time. When his daughter reported Tyre's predictions, an unpleasant void began widening in the pit of his stomach. If any one of his girls was harmed...and that unnatural storm...

Citrosine went over and over through her dreams, trying to find any clue that she had anticipated this, but found none other than her own transformation into a beast.

The journey home through the dark wood went a lot slower than they seemed to be walking. They quickened the pace, jogging like mad, but still did not reach the clearing where their home should be. This passage through the wood held no foul plants or ghostly spirits, but it happened to be too long for the space it actually took up. Citrosine could practically see the clearing at the end of the path, but no matter how long or fast they ran, they could not reach it any faster.

"Perhaps we took a wrong turn?" Citrosine suggested hopefully, after an hour of straight running. Neither of them believed this theory. Gya took the map from his bag. The forest was indicated with two heavy dark lines. He studied the scale at the bottom of the paper for a moment, and looked back at the drawing.

"Only two miles...running past hours...makes no sense," he whispered in thought. Citrosine looked over his shoulder at the map, and couldn't figure any of the symbols out. For one, they were written in Old Elvish, plus, they were quite worn.

"Leenka could tell us," Gya whispered, *"for she knows about such abstract magics..."* His voice died out flatly, as if Jygul's spirits had eaten his words upon their arriving in Citrosine's mind, though they had not even been spoken aloud.

Citrosine looked out at the woods ahead of them. There was now no sign of the trees ending. A black lattice of branches cast eerie shadows across her father's face, making him look more ghost than Elf as he tried to calculate the remaining time before they reached home. The trail ahead grew narrower, and the very air seemed more ominous in the twilight, shadows becoming hiding places for any number of ravenous things. Noises began to fill the narrow space, and breaths of cold air fluttered between narrow trees.

Presently Gya put the map away, and Citrosine tried to read his expression. He looked worried, but also a bit excited. He took her hand in his with a firm grip, and walked slowly along the path. She could feel magic issuing from her father.

"Think not of the trees, but of the end of the path," he said icily, making Citrosine jump. His voice echoed through the still trees. Though it might have been her imagination, Citrosine saw the forest around them grow lighter, as if they had traveled back in time by an hour. The shadows faded slightly, and the ominous feeling of the creatures within lessened.

Palgirtie stirred in her sleep once more. She shifted her position on the wet, musty ground, and a crinkling noise startled her. She rubbed her eyes as she sat up. A scrap of paper lay wadded on the ground beside her. She was suddenly very alert and awake. A bit of light filtered through the door above her at this hour—whatever it was—and that was why she had seen the paper. Perhaps there was a note written on it? Some clue as to why she was hiding in a musty, underground cellar all alone? She grabbed the paper and positioned herself underneath the tiny beam of light. She could almost make out her surroundings—the faint outline where the ground and walls converged, the rocks that sat piled up in the corners of the area.

She unfolded the scrap of paper and wedged it into the sliver of light. Palgirtie had to stare at the words for a long time before she accepted them.

Remember never to forget, it said, in a hastily-scrawled Elvish phrase. The ink was a thin, magicked solution barely adhering to the paper that had come from who-knows-where.

"That's *all*?" Had she read it correctly? Was it from a book or something?

Tie flipped the page around, looking at every empty space upon it; perhaps there was something hidden there. She spent the better part of an hour looking this way at the sheet before her, and, finding nothing else, she tucked it into her belt. It could be a message from her mother.

The little Elf slumped down on the ground again. She was well past crying now. The only sound that came from her was the sound of nervous breaths, quickly entering and exiting her lungs. She began humming, to fill the silence. She recalled a lullaby that Leenka always sang when neither could fall asleep. The first part of the song went by easily, but Tie now had a hard time remembering the rest, as she would normally be asleep by then. A single tear rolled down her cheek. She watched as it fell onto a small pebble at her feet.

She thought a moment.

She could get out of here! The girl almost tripped herself as she scrambled up, and started searching for rocks.

She hefted one in her arms, discovering that they were strong enough to hold her weight, but light enough to carry. She dropped it directly underneath the trapdoor. Then Tie selected another from the pile and did the same with it. After a few more stones were stacked, she could reach the underside of the door. She had to rebuild the mound a few times, so that it would stop shifting under her weight, but it was done. She lifted her arms above her head and—

Hopefully the boulder had moved.

Tie froze.

...The trapdoor shut, and the boulder was rolled across the door again. They sat panting in the darkness when a thump on the door made them both start...

"No," Tie whimpered. *It must have moved if Mama is...not here. I can't remember what happened after...*

The Elf girl shook out her arms. She placed her palms on the rough, weathered door. She took a deep breath, and shoved with all her might. A creak emitted from the opposite side of the door, but it did not budge. She breathed more quickly, panicking. Her breaths became loud and labored, and she was on the verge of hyperventilating.

She readied herself again, but before she had the chance to push, the door was jerked open. Tie ended up jumping into the air, and then falling back into the hole, slamming her legs against the rocks.

She ignored the pain completely, still in shock from all that had happened. She looked up at the opening above her. Two figures looked in on her, talking loudly. She could barely understand them, and wondered if they spoke a different language. Perhaps they were kidnapping her, bringing her to wherever her mother was? What kind of hellish place could that be? She couldn't remember where her mother had gone… her head hurt so much…

One of the figures scooped her up in its strong arms, and lifted her out of the pit. She was handed to the other shape, which was smaller. It carried her awkwardly, her weight falling out of one side of its arms, and they made their way across the small field. When they reached the other side, Tie fainted.

The young Elf regained consciousness when a slight amount of frigid water sprinkled her face. She jumped and opened her eyes. Everything was blurry for a moment, but she saw and heard the two dark figures, and their garbled language trying to tell her something. Her eyes focused, and she saw that the figures were her father and Citrosine, and the words they spoke were hushed and muttered. She stared at her father's mouth as he spoke. He winked. It seemed that they were chanting some ancient healing rite that she did not understand. When they were silent again, Tie tried to sit up. She got only a few inches off the blankets that she had been resting atop of, and a huge wave of nausea washed through her body. Black dots swam before her eyes as she tried to discourage the bile from rising in her esophagus.

"Tie, are you all right?" Citrosine asked as she rubbed her sister's forehead. Tie nodded slightly. Gya sighed heavily. "What happened to you, *se lissa*? Where is your mother?" His eyes were overfull with worry. Tie screwed up her face, trying to recall what had occurred before she'd fallen asleep. Gya mistook this as a gesture of pain, and he let a blue wave of his magic pass into her, dulling any pain. Tie had not really accepted the fact that she was, indeed, in pain yet.

"That is all right, baby sister," Citrosine cooed, "You do not have to tell us right now." She smiled sympathetically. Somewhere in the back of her mind, Tyre's voice whispered *I told you so* and Citrosine couldn't help thinking that her mother was dead. Her vision clouded, and she turned her back on her kin, not wanting them to see her eyes wetten.

Gya handed Tie a water skin, which she accepted and drank from heartily. The extra droplets rolled along down her chin, cooling her labored, stiff body. She sighed.

"Dada," she said quietly, and he leaned in to listen to her. "Where were you and Citrosine? What happened while you were gone?" She tried to imagine her father running through the scary forest, sensing that something was wrong at home.

Gya and Citrosine took turns confiding in Tie the story of their journey; the Council meetings, the Blessing study, Tyre's premonition, and the rest. Citrosine withheld her bit about the Blessing of Jygul, and Tyre's other meetings with her. By the time they had finished, Tie's stomach had settled, but rage had taken its place.

Tie frowned. *So you didn't think anything wrong with an ungodly storm until some stranger warned you to "go home and check" on us? Fine. Now Mama is gone and...gone...Gone!* It was as if she had hit her head again—a gap of her memory had returned! Demons, Mama's bargaining with them, transforming...but Gya and Citrosine would not care...it was their fault. If they had returned in time, Dada could have stopped it...

Her countenance remained solemn as she fought back a stronghold of emotion. "I...I suppose you want to hear about the storm, then, eh? I can remember most of it now..." Gya and Citrosine shared a quick glance.

"Yes, Tie, if you wish to tell us," Gya said slowly. Tie's face showed no emotion, yet neither her father nor her sister wished to intrude upon her troubled mind.

"As Mother and I were walking back through the forest from...er...Haerthor...it was even scarier than before. There were so many voices and shadows, and it looked like a storm was upon us. But the storm was coming from the wrong way..." she pointed towards the south side of the house.

"South, *lissa?*" Gya's eyes darkened as he remembered Leenka's concerns.

"Yes, south. But we got out of the forest all right. Mother took me in the house and covered both of us in armor, and then she hurried me outside to the back cellar. There was thunder everywhere, it was very dark. Then, after what seemed like only seconds, the trapdoor was thrown open, and a huge demon—I think—came inside. Mother made me go sit under some blankets and be still, so it wouldn't see me.

"I heard them speaking in some rough tongue...maybe it was Old Elvish, or the language of the Men, but it didn't sound like anything...They were talking loudly and in an argument. I heard Mama's name a few times, and yours, Dada. I pulled up a corner of the blanket so I could see, and then..." She took a deep, shuddering breath. Citrosine saw that Tie looked much older than she had a few days ago.

"I saw...I saw..." she was whispering, "Mother was swallowed up into light, and then...*transformed!* Wampyre... she wasn't Mama any more," Tie collapsed into her father's chest and cried, failing to stay defiant and angry. "Fangs, blood, screaming...Mama...Mama..."

Gya made dinner without a sound that night. He said nothing to his distraught daughters, and they said nothing to him. Tie sat blankly in front of the hearth, her lips whispering something incomprehensible. She sneaked looks at a piece of paper tucked into her fist several times, but Citrosine couldn't make out what it was.

"Citrosine," Tie whispered.

"Eh?"

"What does '*jreah*' mean in Old Elvish?"

"Er…I think it's something like, 'remember', or 'don't lose the memory'; that kind of phrase."

"And '*grins*?'"

"Spell it,"

"G-R-I-N-S,"

"*Grins* is a warning. It means something like, 'don't go', or 'never do' something. Why?"

"I wanted to…er…make sure that I learned it right." Tie went back to staring at the fire. She crumpled up the paper in her hand, the one that said *Grins jreah nya—Remember never to forget*—and threw it into the ashes. It caught fire immediately.

Citrosine, other things on her mind, climbed up the ladder to the loft room, and made sure that a blanket covered the opening. She snapped her fingers together and thought, *light*. This reminded her briefly of her mother, and she tried to ignore the oncoming flood of memory.

A spark jumped from her hand, and formed a large luminescent ball that hovered close to the ceiling, as if dangling from a string.

Impossible. Citrosine now confirmed that her powers had, in fact, grown since watching Jaqe's Blessing. However, replacing the ball of gold light that she and Leenka had marveled over, her new sphere of light gave out a dark purple glow, and was tinged all around with a black aura.

She *was* growing dark magic, but was this a blessing or a curse?

After dinner, once Tie was asleep, Gya brought Citrosine outside to talk. They walked in large circles around the yard, talking softly through their minds, so that there was no chance of Tie overhearing.

"Dada, do you really think that Palgirtie was telling the truth about Mama?" Citrosine wanted under no circumstances to believe that her mother was now a foul demon.

"I think that it is possible, but not likely. Could you sense the sleeping spell your sister had around her? She may have dreamed any noises she heard into some fantastic story. As to what actually happened...well, your mother made many enemies back when she was a warrior, before she had come to terms with the other races. There used to be a lot of tension. However..." he paused, bracing himself, *"if an enemy had caught up to her, and she... was defeated, then we would have found her.*

"Your sister could very well be truthful. Leenka may have been captured, or even...sired...and might have fled...in order to protect us...? Also, there has never been a storm of magic from the south before; that is where the Field and Shadow Elves used to be, before they diminished so quickly. Tie could be right, and something could be amiss." Gya paused to rub at his eyes. Citrosine saw a flash of weariness that made her go numb. The pain in her father's face made him seem impossibly old, so different from the good-natured, happy man that he usually was. He continued gravely.

*"I believe that something is beginning to go terribly wrong in these lands. Leader and the Council begin to speak increasingly urgently of how many Men are coming and invading our homes without even realizing that they are destroying us. It was briefly proposed to find a new place for everyone—*everyone*—to live. All the Nymphs, all the Elves, all the Dragons, Sorcerers, Faeries; everyone."*

"Do you think that it will happen?" Citrosine's eyes opened wide.

"I cannot say, as of yet. What your friend Tyre suggested once was how the 'missing tribes', he called them, those poor extinct groups; they could be interfering with our affairs while we are pondering the idea of migration…perhaps they are in hiding, and using our confusion of Man's invasion to their own advantage. I don't believe him. The other tribes were more trustworthy than that. The boy doesn't give them enough credit…they would not be so selfish and leave the well-being of our way of life so unprotected. Were they actually still in hiding, protecting themselves somewhere, they would at least send us counsel."

"Do you have bad feelings for Tyre?" Citrosine couldn't help asking. They were such good friends already, and if Gya hated him, how could they keep seeing each other?

"No…" Gya thought, "but he is awfully outward with his thoughts, hunches…it gets wearisome. Sometimes." he added after seeing Citrosine frown.

"I think he is very intelligent. If he weren't so blunt, he wouldn't be my friend," Citrosine argued. She also kept to herself: *and I wouldn't know myself as well, had he kept all his 'hunches' to himself. Nor would we have come home so quickly to Tie…*

They walked together in silence a bit longer, but Citrosine noticed that Gya's eyes were moist. She delicately, subtly passed a tendril of magic into his mind, just to see what he was thinking about. She expected to see memories of Leenka, since she was missing, and could possibly be dead.

What shocked her was seeing the memories of *herself,* Citrosine, attempting to use magic, discovering it near the Faerie dwelling, and asking for a Blessing of Jygul.

She quickly withdrew her magic.

"Lissa, do you really wish for a Blessing of Jygul?" Gya's voice was strained. Citrosine feigned surprise.

"Dada, it's just that…"

"*That's the reason that your magic came up…through that Blessing, correct? I understand how you could wish to nourish this power, but Citrosine—it is black magic! Did you not see how much pain that Elf, Jaqe, was in? It isn't worth it, just to be able to practice the powers of Jygul, the Dark Lord! You know how I feel about dark magic! I do not want you to do this. You could lose control—*"

"*Father, I just want to—*"

"*I must forbid it! I know what Leader has arranged, but I have come to my senses—I didn't want to belittle you in his presence, but my love, I do not wish this upon you…Leader is too trustworthy of magic. I've warned him that he will eventually succumb to its powers—*"

"Dada!" Citrosine shouted aloud, and felt a cold, imagined blade twist through her stomach.

She suddenly felt as if something had gone horribly, irreversibly wrong.

The air itself seemed to have stopped circulating. Birds' songs were silenced. Gya stopped walking and stared at her. Citrosine's very heart turned cold, and seemed to slow.

"*Lis—*" Gya's voice was cut short in the middle of his pet name for his girls, almost as if…

Citrosine ran. She ran into the house, to see if what her instincts told her was true. She looked at the small fire in the hearth. It was still alive and burning, but every flame was stuck dead still. The smoky curls above it were frozen still, as well. Tie was asleep, and Citrosine knew she must be alive, but she did not move, did not breathe, did not stir. If she wasn't paused in time, she might be dead.

Tears formed in Citrosine's eyes, and she ran, tripping over her own feet, back outside to Gya. He, too, was frozen still.

Had she truly lost control so easily? Her magic had welled up in her frustration, and had overpowered her…She had hypnotized the world. It was dead and unmoving this very moment.

Citrosine sat on the ground and concentrated as hard as she could on motion, sound; any kind of sign that she had not just killed everything around her. She tried to summon her magic in such a way that the world could move again. Tears squeezing from her eyes, her head and insides shaking as if she would vomit, her veins stirred the air around her...

Slowly, Gya was set into motion again. The night-birds hesitantly began their calls again, and smoke began to rise out of the chimney. Citrosine and Gya slowly resumed their walk around the yard once more.

"Oh, lissa," Gya began slowly. Citrosine winced. She knew that Gya would immediately start scolding her for using dark power, even against her own will.

"Lissa, remind me of what I was saying...I seem to have forgotten..."

Citrosine gasped. Had he lost all memory of what had just happened? Surely, if the world stopped, and everyone was frozen solid, they would remember it as the worst thing that had ever happened in their lives!

She gulped. *"Er...you spoke of Tyresias?"*

"Eh? Yes, yes. Excuse me. I must have digressed..."

Citrosine's mind spun. *I just erased a portion of Dada's memory!* She tried her best to follow her father's one-sided conversation, while marveling at her own wrongdoing.

How did I do that? What did I say...I was thinking hard about him just leaving me alone about Jygul's Blessing... I shouted an angry word, and it happened!

Citrosine searched her father's memories as he spoke, prying for any hint of these last events, but she found nothing.

"Looking for something, lissa?"

"No, father...nothing."

"So why are you in my mind, then? Forget something I just said? Or weren't you listening?"

"I am sorry, father."

"Don't be—it's a gift to be able to see into minds, an Elven gift."

He remembers nothing—not Leader's permission, not my stirring at Jaqe's Blessing, as if he was never there with me when they happened? Will my powers always do this when I show great emotion? I must not do this ever again...

And Citrosine began learning how to keep her emotions in check.

Days later, a messenger from Haerthor came, with a letter for Citrosine. The messenger himself was a Dwarf, but he seemed very tense about coming through the dark forest to get to this dwelling.

> *Dear Citrosine,*
>
> *I know that you were quite anticipating getting a Blessing of Jygul, and now your chance has come. The Faerie that was meant to come to Haerthor to make a round of Blessings has decided to visit you. He will arrive at your dwelling at midnight tomorrow, if you still wish to go through with your proposition. Be sure to have had a hearty meal, and do not be afraid! If your powers have supported you thus far, they should continue for a long while.*
>
> *Say hello to your father on my behalf.*
> *My Regards,*
> *Leader*

Citrosine's heart fluttered as she read this letter, and she quickly threw it into the fire upon reading the last line, as a precaution against Tie or Gya getting hold of it.

The messenger Dwarf shifted impatiently, asking for his payment. Citrosine would have thought this unnecessary as it was the responsibility of the sender rather than the receiver, but the coy Dwarf begged all the same, since times were hard at home, and little Kett's cough was just beginning to worsen, what with the coming season and all. Citrosine shooed the man off with a hurried air, depositing one tiny coin of little value in his palm, and the Dwarf harrumphed and slowly walked his tired mule back towards the forest.

*Tomorrow at midnight...*Citrosine wondered if she would be able to get this Blessing in enough secrecy that her family would never suspect...but Jaqe...She thought back, once again, to the Blessing of Jygul that she had already witnessed. Jaqe's cries of pain had echoed all throughout the woods, as the black magic had stormed its way through his poor body...

Must I stop time again? I cannot let Father suspect... Her heart skipped a beat, and an uneasy, itching tingle spread through her own body.

"Dada," Citrosine crept up to her father later that day while he was sitting outside studying notes, and Tie was in the midst of a nap. "Dada, I was thinking about what you said the other day...about Mama's and your father's powers that I am to inherit..."

"What of them?"

"Well, I was just wondering..." Citrosine tried to construct an innocent enough question, "Are sky powers like dark magic at all?"

"Oh, *lissa*, you're worrying yourself so much about that boy's Blessing, aren't you? That must have shaken you all about, eh?" Citrosine nodded, deeply disconcerted that her father could still remember nothing of her stirring magic.

Gya put his papers down behind him. "My father, a Nymph, could do all kinds of things with his powers. Your mother can as well." She noted his use of the word *can*. "She has done the most amazing things, not because of her former tribe, but because of her bloodline to Ghersah. Anyway, my father could control winds, clouds, and sometimes, if his magic

73

was concentrated enough, or if there were enough of his kind cooperating, they could affect time, and the lengths of day and night,"

Citrosine's head grew dizzy.

"However, that kind of thing was outlawed, for it didn't seem right to disturb the natural ways of things. Soon, all that practiced the dark powers learned to do the same things, only they used their control over time for dark and evil purposes."

"All of them? Were—are—the powers of the Shadow Elves *all* used for evil?"

"Well, those that had the black magic but had learned to control it and harness it for good formed the Cavern Elf Tribe…"

"Thank you, Dada. I was just confused," she interrupted. Citrosine's face only showed the slightest flicker of curiosity, so Gya nodded, and returned to his studying.

Am I growing dark magic, or that of the air? Am I making a colossal mistake in receiving Jygul's Blessing? Should I instead receive…what…the…the Cayre Blessing—that of light and goodness? One that can nourish my inherent magics? Well, the Faerie comes tomorrow, so what am I to do?

Citrosine went for a walk in the woods that evening around her home, on the pretense of having an aching head. Her vision was blurred by the occasional flurry of tears, but few escaped her eyes. What *was* she to do? Remembering how the sparks and orbs she'd created were a dark, shadowy kind of tint, she realized that she had already shown signs of having dark powers, so she was obviously not inheriting the Nymph blood…yet. Conversely, she also remembered how firmly the one dream she'd had had insisted that she not get this Blessing.

Tyre, what should I do? What advice would her blind friend offer? "Get the Blessing and learn how to control yourself," or, "Try and develop your powers without risking being thrown out of your family, being possessed by powers you cannot control, or being killed painfully by Leader or another being of higher standards and control," perhaps? Maybe, "Talk to your father"?

What is going on with me? Who am I becoming?

Citrosine tried her hardest to seem happy and normal to her father and sister when she returned inside. They were oblivious to how harassed she was within her mind.

That night, she could not get to sleep.

She silently slid out of the house, and walked through the forest again. The night air was fresh and cool, and the sounds of all sorts of night creatures surrounded the troubled Elf. She reached a small clearing that she could not identify in the black night, and sat down to rest. She shivered as the windy night reached through her nightclothes.

She closed her eyes tightly, and tried not to let any more tears slip down her cheeks. *Calm…calm…get the Blessing and be calm…let yourself be calm and not be overtaken by feelings… calm…*Her eyes flew open in surprise as she felt her tears lift right off her skin! Wow…were her powers really growing this fast?

Oh, no…she listened, and the tears ceased their upward journey, falling down to the ground.

Silence. Not a bird, not a wolf. No sound. No wind. Had she stopped time again? But she had not let *any* magic out! Or so she thought. So time had been altered both when she was frustrated and when she tried to erase her feelings? *I can only hope that I can reach a middle ground…*

Citrosine hesitantly stood, and tried to determine where she was. There was nothing she recognized. She tried to send out a strand of magic to see if she could sense her home, but she was too tired, and too far away from home by now. Haphazardly choosing a direction, she began walking. The forest was thinning out here, and Citrosine became aware of a dull headache beginning. She kept walking, and the only sound to follow her was the crackling of the occasional leaf under her feet.

Her head hurt worse with each step, and the silence became more and more unbearable. She began stepping on twigs, on leaves, dead grass; just to make a sound, to know that maybe, maybe something else was not stuck in time…but no luck. She picked up a handful of small rocks and began tossing them as she walked, throwing them forcefully at tree trunks, letting them fall in dead leaves, anything.

Citrosine's head was consumed by a splitting pain now, and she'd walked for longer than she'd taken to reach the meadow in this direction. What was that faint light ahead of her?

As she tromped on towards the light, her head was throbbing. The trees thinned and she longed for a moving figure. She suddenly realized that she'd reached a camp. There were many tents scattered around a large fire, and a circle of figures were huddled around it.

Then she stopped dead.

What were this many Men doing this close to…well… wherever she was? What were they *doing* here? She'd been walking for less than a half hour.

There were almost no trees here, but a towering mass of felled tree trunks was piled up just beyond the furthest tents from the fire. This was obviously the reason for the headache. So many homes to so many creatures…taken away for this… She sensed the presence of a family of Changelings…but it was distant, as if they'd left this spot a few days ago. How could she know that? Were super-senses a part of her heightened powers?

She turned around a half turn and ran as fast as she could in the darkness. She ran for long minutes, stumbling finally into *Bixoel*, Jygul's evil forest. The trees were immobilized, and there were no movements in the forest, as time was stopped, but in its place Citrosine felt emptiness… She had to struggle a while to find the path, but then began sprinting as fast as her bare toes could propel her. Her skin was bruised with the lashes of many trees and branches that she had half-purposely run through, just for the sounds, and she reached the gates of Haerthor, the sleeping guards paused in mid-snore. Citrosine had run exactly the opposite way that she needed to, though not aware of this before she had reached this extreme point. She turned around, shuddering and panting, too weak to move with any haste. She'd run a full two miles in just minutes.

The forest was the worst part of the whole trip home—the spirits of the ever-changing hell sucking every sound out of Citrosine's steps, out of her very mind, she could not hear her thoughts, as if she was dead and running through the forest while the silence ate her inside out. It was as if the forest had known exactly Citrosine's greatest fear at that moment. As hard as she forced her breaths in and out of her lungs, she heard nothing. She stopped in the center of the path and could not hear the whimpering sounds from her throat. Her mouth opened, and she felt the vibrations and release that a scream would allow, but heard nothing. She trudged on, feeling tears but not hearing her sniffles or sobs.

At home, she walked into the room where she was supposed to be sleeping, ushered time on at the right tempo with difficulty to the extent of feeling as if she'd been turned inside out, and roughly woke Gya.

"Dada, Dada!" It was nice to hear the sound of Gya's tired muttering as he tried to listen to his terrified daughter.

"Eh, *lissa?* Are you feeling well? What is the matter?"

"Dada, I woke from a bad dream and then I went for a walk, but I got a little lost, and then I almost walked right into a camp…but they…there were no trees…a fire…there were…Men! It was a camp full of Men! They killed half the forest and are so close to our dwellings!" Citrosine gasped for breath, as she'd been running for over two hours, and was still in shock.

"How close, love?" Gya was wide awake and utterly attentive.

"No more than a half hour's walk from Bixoel!"

"You're sure?"

The look on her face was enough.

Gya was overwhelmed by her news just as much as she. He rushed to his study, lit a few candles, and scratched the opening of a letter. Citrosine followed him and read over his shoulder.

"Lissa, I want you to explain what you saw in as much detail as you can remember. This is a letter to Leader. I will deliver it to him myself in the morning." He handed his daughter the coal rod he'd been writing with, and she wrote furiously.

FOUR

JUST FORGET, FOR A MOMENT...

Gya had gone. Palgirtie and Citrosine were sitting in the backyard, and Tie was trying to persuade Citrosine to show her some "advanced" magic spells and charms. Citrosine finally gave in, but not before overtaking her sister in five-minutes of tickling, giggling, and squealing.

Citrosine removed the black ribbon from her hair and held it between her thumb and third finger. She closed her eyes and feigned struggle and toil, and the ribbon turned white. Then it was red, blue, silver, purple, crimson. Tie laughed, and removed one of her own stockings.

"Change mine! Change mine!" Citrosine smiled, and the two of them laughed as the stocking went red, green, gold, striped, dotted, and embossed in a floral pattern. Soon, their mouths and throats grew tired of laughing, and the girls lay in the grass staring up at the clouds.

Citrosine's hands were trembling as she counted the hours to the time she got her Blessing. *'Blessing' indeed,* Citrosine sulked. *Were that it was called a Faerie's Curse, I might be more at ease...then I would know what I have gotten myself into...*

Tie, on the other hand, was trying to think of ways to coax some kind of dark magic from her sister's hands, just to see if it was possible for an Elf to practice such enchantment...had Leenka practiced it before? Could that be the reason that the demons came for her?

"That cloud looks like a wolf," Tie said dreamily, "or maybe a Dragon. Eh, Citrosine? What do you think it looks like?"

"Which?" Citrosine shook her head, to focus on the present, not the future.

"That one, right...there," Tie pointed.

"It looks like...a man with a walking cane," Citrosine tried to participate.

"No, it doesn't!" And so the morning progressed.

"What do you think Dada's doing right now?"

"Probably talking with Leader,"

"Are you sure?"

"I don't know!"

"Well, why'd you say it, then?"

"You asked me what I thought!"

Tie shivered. She asked Citrosine to start a fire so it would be warmer inside. Tie sat wrapped in blankets, as Citrosine attempted to make a small meal, failed, tried again, and ended up throwing four bowls of wet, sloppy dough into the yard.

Just then, the door opened.

"Dada!" Tie forgot her coldness and hugged her father. Citrosine, relieved, came away from her cooking, and did the same.

"What did you find out?" She asked him silently, privately.

"Let me sit down, lissa. I have news to share with the two of you." His thoughts were unfocused, and Citrosine had to strain to catch all of his words, which were frailly floating through his mind, jumbled in other thoughts. Obviously, this was to be unfavorable news.

He sat where Tie had huddled, and warmed his hands. Citrosine watched him stare into the flames, his mind distant and sad.

Five

Midnight

"I talked with Leader today," Gya began later, after the glowing fire in the hearth had finally warmed the dark cottage, "and he was very distraught to hear confirmations that there are Men coming through these forests.

"He said that he'd heard a bit about this particular colonization from another Elf, as well as I, and that there were plans of our race moving to an island across the sea. It isn't inhabited by anything at all yet, not even trees or flowers. It's very large and not recognized by Man yet."

"Would we have to plant our own trees?" Citrosine was scared already.

"Yes, *lissa.*"

Tie panicked. "You mean we would have to...start our world over?"

"We will, somewhat, *lissa.* Every Enchanted being will have to begin a new life on this island. An Elf boat has been constructed already that is large enough to carry all the Elves in the Big Lands across, even those tribes that cannot get along as of yet.

"As for tribes, I have…news. I suppose that we will need to switch tribes. It would help us stay safe in the new lands, at least until we are entirely positive that we can be safe on land. We shall move from the lands of the Stone Tribe to that of the Sea." Citrosine nodded her head slowly, accepting the inevitable fact much more easily than her poor sister.

"The Sea Tribe? Dada, this isn't fair! What if Mama comes back, she won't know where to find us!" Tie cried.

"Lissa, I don't believe that Leenka is coming back. You said it yourself; she was transformed into…something else. If this is truly what you saw happen, she would not recognize us if she did find us. For all it matters to us, your mother is dead." Gya looked as if he had rehearsed this scene, as if he had said these exact words to himself over and over ever since he and Citrosine had returned from Haerthor. His eyes were a lifeless gray, like a sea after a storm, waiting silently for a sun that will never come to burn away the clouds.

"But, Dada!" Tie exploded into tears.

"No, Palgirtie. There shall be no argument!"

Citrosine watched quietly, and affirmed that Tie had changed—had shrouded herself in mystery—since Leenka had disappeared.

"But we won't even see any plants, the sky, the sun!" Tie was crying openly.

"Ssh," Gya rocked Tie on his lap, and tried to quiet her. Tie shed only a few more tears, and then sat smoldering.

"Father, when," Citrosine cleared her throat, "…when will we leave?"

Gya looked at her sadly, and his eyes wandered somewhere universally distant, as if he was looking at the dark side of the luminescent orb of the moon.

"I was told to be ready…in a fortnight."

His words sounded like a funereal bell.

Citrosine and Gya tried to calm Tie over and over that afternoon, but she would not be placated. Gya reasoned with her, but she just argued the same few points over and over in frustration. When Gya looked as if he needed to go mourn for his lost mate, Citrosine tried to take over the Tie job. Gya had not yet had a chance to grieve, and it was dangerous for him to keep it inside for too long. They had loved each other very much, and again Citrosine recalled their last kiss and the veiled passion and worry she'd seen.

After a few hours, Tie went to sulk outside. She ran to the boulder that still covered the door to the cellar, and stared at it dejectedly.

Letting out a cry of fury, Tie attempted all the spells she could think of, from what she had seen others do to what she only imagined could be done.

Nothing happened. She paced, letting all her powers come out. Then, upon walking in slower circles around the stone, she was startled to see the damage this stone had suffered before she had tried to attack it.

There were deep scratches all over one side, and punctures in groups of four. Claws? Some parts of the boulder were scattered with black-purple powder. She sniffed the powder, and her head took a dizzy turn. She sneezed. This was some kind of poison! Tie backed away from it quickly, and continued her path. There was a loud ringing apparent to her within a ten-pace radius of the stone, and she realized that it must be charmed.

Leenka must have tried her hardest to protect this trapdoor, but then whatever kind of demon had pushed the stone away had still done so quite easily, perhaps allowing physical strength to overpower Leenka's magic. Apparently, there had been more than one demon, by the quantity of the scratches around the stone. The earth kicked up around the base of the stone had the same patterns as the scratch marks. What kind of demons were these? Black, poisonous powder, fangs and claws that could bite through stone, and very strong muscles.

Tie crept back into the house, while Citrosine and Gya were talking in hushed tones on the front porch, and she tiptoed into Gya's study. Among his notes on magic powers, she knew, were illustrations and descriptions on all magic beings yet discovered. She leafed through until she came upon the notes on demons, and started reading.

"Dada, what do we need to bring to this island? I don't understand; how can no plants or creatures have discovered this place yet?" Citrosine tried to imagine what kind of place this must be.

"Leader said that he thought this dilemma might have come up once before. The theory goes that the founders of our realm once communed, raising land up from the darkest depths of the sea to create a new country. It was to be used if the well-being of the Enchanted World was ever threatened— kind of a refuge if we could not survive in the Old World, or the Big Lands…only this island would be secret; charmed.

"Their premonitions came true; a group of mortals ran the founders from their own lands, and chased them to the new island they had created. It turns out, however, that the land was too fallow then for them to use…they died out, and left few behind to continue on their way of life, sending them here, to the Big Lands.

"These Men invading us now must be ancestors of those who invaded the founders, back to finish what they began, hunting for land, food, or wealth, perhaps.

"The island is mostly a patch of fallow dirt and sand, presently, but some has developed into fertile enough soil to support life. Among the inhabitants of the vessel we shall travel upon to reach our new abode includes a collected supply of trees, weeds, wildflowers, crops, and just about all we can perceive. All of the population of this island will have to cooperate to build life anew. Leader has called another Council meeting in just a few days hence, and we will try to arrange another after that, in which at least two leaders from as many tribes and races as possible will attempt to map where we will all dwell on the island." Gya heaved a sigh, running a hand through his greasy hair, not yet washed from his quick trip to Haerthor.

"Eh? So, the Council will decide where we will be able to live?"

"Precisely. We will split new territories, and hopefully live in harmony for a few centuries." Gya was weary, and Citrosine kept all remaining questions to herself.

"You need rest."

"Aye, I do indeed. But my two daughters have not had a sufficient meal all day, so first I shall decipher Leenka's famous recipe for glazed *paliz*." The two smiled grimly.

Tie flipped page after page over as fast as she could decipher Gya's script. She heard Gya and Citrosine stand and stretch, preparing to come inside, and she flicked pages even more desperately. Wait…what was this demon?

Gya's script was hard to read. *Coulf Demon. Eight large claws, very sharp and penetrating. Two pairs of long fangs that inject poison. Covered with purple-black fur that secretes a powdery poison.* **One touch** *to any portion of the Coulf's body will be punished with a sharp dose of this poison: the* **longest an Elf has ever survived** *after being poisoned, in an* **extreme case** *and* **only trace exposure to the poison***, remains as* **one full day***. Coulf demons possess unknown amounts of magic, and are known for being strongly linked to the Shadow tribe, as they are impressionable.*

Was this what she was looking for? Of course! The powdery substance, strong, sharp claws and fangs…Coulf Demons had taken Leenka.

Tie pocketed the page, and stacked all the other sheaves of paper in as neat a stack as she could manage, then skulked back in front of the fire, just as Gya opened the front door. *Whew...*

"Time for bed, girls..." Gya had his eyes closed and sat on the front step, his cheeks wet. He opened his eyes tentatively, and looked up at the stars. All he could see was her face, outlined and dotted with flecks of celestial mass. The thick ribbon of stars trailing away from the moon now spelled out *Leenka Nakiss.* The constellation of the Great Archer was now Leenka, bow poised to protect their beautiful children. The moon was her face, almost the round face of a girl, but elongated, with womanly beauty, poise, wisdom, in the wrinkles that had begun to creep up alongside her eyes.

Tie had said she was transformed, not killed...but Tie always had an overactive imagination: why would any enemy put out an order to *transform* someone, as opposed to just putting one to death?

How about to torture her family?

So why wasn't the Wampyre Leenka here stalking them now? Had she realized this possibility? Would she be able to control herself enough to leave her family alone? If she knew that she was becoming a bloodsucking slave, perhaps she knew why...maybe she had realized what was going on, learned of her attackers' secrets. She was one of the most powerful Elves in history; there were legends about her. Had she been sired by a Wampyre legion, she would be able to control herself enough to protect the ones she loved. Whether that meant exile, a diversion or defeat of her enemies, or...preventing herself from being useable.

If she was the intelligent, strong-willed, compassionate Leenka that he knew she was, and if Tie was right, Gya realized that he would never see his wife again.

"Dada?"

Gya started, but turned the motion into the action of standing to tuck his daughters into their blankets. He followed Tie inside, wiping his eyes and nose on his handkerchief discreetly.

"Palgirtie, Citrosine, sleep well tonight. We must wake early tomorrow to prepare for our journey. Dream of all the things we've accomplished here in the Big Lands. Think of all the memories that you will detail to your own daughters."

"Sleep well, Dada,"

"Good night!"

Gya slipped into bed himself after the fire was extinguished, the shutters firmly closed, and the door barred. He attempted to block Leenka from his thoughts, but it was she who crept into his dreams, who finally kissed him and led him into sleep.

Citrosine listened to the dim echo of the bells in Haerthor. It was two hours until midnight. She took deep, slow breaths, to feign sleep, and listened to her father's nighttime routine. He rustled around in the darkness, extinguishing the fire in the hearth, pulling the lock over the door. This routine had taken longer in the last few nights than it did when Leenka had been there to assist him. It had also been lonelier, more of an ending to the day, without their quieted murmurs, their goodnight whispers to their daughters and one another.

After the house had been silenced, Gya flung himself into his blankets and breathed heavily for some time. Citrosine slipped one miniscule strand of magic awareness into his mind, and was overwhelmed with visions of Leenka and her father, the day they met, when they were betrothed, and images of Tie and Citrosine as infants.

Gya's heart was crushed with the loss. Citrosine wondered how he could stand to live without her.

She retracted her strand of power, and tried to resist the wave of sadness breaking over her. She succeeded, yet she still felt as if it was her fault. It was, after all, her birthday surprise that caused Gya to spend those days away from home, when he could have been shielding Leenka.

Half an hour until midnight.

Citrosine had stopped thinking about her mother and was slowly losing the ability to evade rest. She thought of Tyre's face as she'd told him about getting Jygul's Blessing. She saw Jaqe's features, contorted in pain, as the same Blessing was bestowed upon him. She heard the silence of time at a standstill, with only her breathing, her footsteps to listen to.

She watched as Gya's memory was erased. She watched the letter informing her of the midnight Blessing swallowed up in flames. She watched herself receive the wrong Blessing, and change her form into a huge, stalking demon. She watched the trees fall on a family of Changelings, and the trunks piled up into a cabin of sorts, where a family of Men grew and expanded, finally taking over all of the Big Lands...

Don-dong, don-dong, don-dong, don-dong, don-dong, don-dong...

Twenty-four strokes.

It was time.

Citrosine's eyes jerked open, and she flew up in terror.

Citrosine crept outside as quietly as she could, unsure of Gya's degree of slumber. She stepped outside into the fresh air, the slight wind brushing her nightclothes against her cold, nervous body. Should she have dressed herself? What would her Faerie think? It didn't matter, she assured herself.

As she reached the damp grass, she noticed a ray of light coming down from the moon, right into the center of the yard. Presently, a figure formed in that spot. A Faerie, come to endow her.

She wasn't ready for this.

The Faerie beckoned, and Citrosine walked over little by little. The Faerie was a male, tall, with shining blue wings flecked with silver. His face was sharp with lengthy, angular features, most prominent of which were the eyes. His deep-set, wide, violet eyes beckoned Citrosine to Tír Na nÓg, and she tried to steel herself.

"Citrosine Nakiss." His voice was calm, deep, and soothing. Citrosine nodded hesitantly, and the Faerie smiled. He had an extremely charming smile.

"Do not be afraid," he said, *"It will only make the time worse."* Citrosine nodded again, and she knew that there would be no turning back now. *"You, Citrosine Nakiss, Stone Elf, have requested and been accepted for the Blessing of Jygul. It will allow you to practice dark magic. You have been deemed worthy of this, but it shall be quite hard to acquire. This Blessing will also strengthen the rest of your magic skills. Are you prepared for this honor?"*

"I am ready," Citrosine said. She knew in her heart that this was true, so why couldn't she make her pulse slow to normal? Why wouldn't her hands stop trembling?

"Good," the Faerie replied. He magicked a golden goblet from his fingertips. *"Three drops of blood must be spilt into this cup. One represents your spirit, one for Ghersah, and one for Jygul. Here,"* he magicked a dagger in the same fashion, *"is the dagger which you must use. Cut from your neck."* Citrosine gulped and took cup and dagger from his hands. She found it disturbingly easy to form just a shallow cut in her skin, and then she angled the dagger to the slightest incline above the cup, so that she could count drops. *Who knew that it could be so easy to draw blood,* she thought morbidly, *at a time like this?*

"One...my spirit...two...Ghersah, the all-powerful Great Goddess...three...Jygul...the Deceiver..." She sighed in relief as that was done.

"Phenomenal. And the mantra is next. I shall recite this, and the dark power will come into your blood. The store shall be found in your...non-dominant palm...your...?"

"Right,"

"Your right palm, then, and in each of your eyes. I suggest bracing yourself for the pain, and I am sorry for how much will come to you. Now, the mantra," he repeated. He proceeded to recite the same chant as Jaqe's Faerie had. Citrosine's fingers trembled as if leaves, stirred and shaken by a breeze.

The Faerie put his hands firmly on Citrosine's forearms, looked her squarely in the eyes, and said, *"Brace yourself!"* Citrosine tensed all her muscles, and watched as the Faerie moved his hands to her right palm. A wave of darkness pervaded throughout the dusky night. The moon and stars were darkened, flickering like fireflies attempting to call out to their neighbors.

A tiny thread of light rose from her palm, and rose up past the tree line. Then it detached itself from her hand, and the thread wound into a ball, then changed from light to a dark purple, glowing form. It floated up there in the air for a moment, then elongated again and shot down back into its original place.

Citrosine almost collapsed in pain. She shut her eyes and bit her tongue. She would not undo herself by alerting her family. Her blood ran hot, slowly pulsating all throughout her body, and then turned cold. She could taste it pooling underneath her tongue.

Her blood was freezing! She felt it actually harden, as if it would not be able to flow through her veins anymore, but then the sensation was over. She couldn't feel the cool air any longer, and her head felt as if it had been cloven in two by a huge broadsword. She could not move, and then she felt a slight flutter in her heart, where the black magic had now appeared.

Her eyes opened, as did her mouth; she thought she was going to scream. But then she found herself staring right into the eyes of the Faerie. She saw herself in them, scared, weak, but then caught herself, and cast the charm of Unfairness, one which was created with the intention of giving Faeries an ugly appearance, so as to make them unattractive and repulsive. The Faerie frowned, and then reached his hand out to help Citrosine off the ground; apparently, she had collapsed. She took his grasp, and stood gingerly.

The world was spinning crazily, and Citrosine's head was throbbing. A cold sweat formed a thin, slimy sheet over her skin. She fell once again to her knees, gagging and coughing with a sudden nausea.

"You did much better than most," the Faerie stated, *"I would have expected you to have screamed at least a little."* He looked disappointed.

"I tried not to wake my family," Citrosine pointed a thumb back over her shoulder at the house, standing up with more confidence now.

"Well. I should probably warn you not to spend too much time around them, as they will notice that you are different." The Faerie shuffled his feet uneasily. *"It happens."*

"What? What is different about me?" Citrosine gulped, and looked down at her arms and legs. She saw that her aura of immortality had shifted to a dark purple glow. Her skin seemed almost translucent, though it had already been pale before. Her head still throbbed, but the pain had reduced itself to her temples and the space behind her eyes. She felt odd prickling tingles in each limb, every time her heart beat.

She saw that she had a black vein in the skin on her right arm, like a normal Blessing, only…black, and more jagged and slash-like.

"What is different about my eyes?" She asked faintly, recalling how the magic was to be stored in her vision, as well as her arm. The Faerie smiled grimly.

"They used to be brown, now they...somewhat resemble mine."

Citrosine tried not to think about how quickly her father would notice that she'd received this Blessing, seeing as he *studied* Blessings! She wished that she had the mirror from her mother with her, but now she just stood worrying and shivering in her silken nightclothes that hugged her body with the chilling wind.

"Will they change back to normal?"

The Faerie nodded. *"In a few days the color will recede, as will the vein of magic and the pain in your body. I would recommend feigning sickness."* That said, the space around him illuminated, and he vanished.

"Thanks for that," Citrosine breathed, her heart slowing for the first time in days.

Later that night—well, later that morning—Citrosine slipped into bed, groaning, as all her body felt as if it had just been sliced to pieces. Tie and Gya were fast asleep, deep in dreams. Citrosine fell into the sedative of sleep as her eyes closed.

"Citrosine, time to get up!" Tie shook her sister's shoulder hopefully after Gya had begun cooking the morning meal. "Citrosine!" She rolled her eyes. *Why will she never wake?*

"Dada, I can't get her to get up!" Tie shouted. It must have been a miracle that Citrosine could sleep while her sister's high voice pierced the still morning.

"Let me try," Gya suggested. He carried the plate of breakfast *paliz* that he'd just prepared over to Citrosine's sleeping area. He wafted the scent towards her, and she stirred immediately, lonely stomach driving her muscles. As she roused herself, he carried the *paliz* back to the table. Tie was running all about the house, so Gya barely heard Citrosine call for him.

"*Lissa,* are you all right? You look so pale," he put his hand on her shoulder, and wondered if she was feverish. He stroked her cheek, perplexed by how cool her skin was.

"Dada, I feel sick," she mumbled, eyes closed, and he nodded.

"Let me get you some herbs, and then you can sleep." Gya always kept a supply of medicinal herbs in the house to soothe headaches, sour stomachs, and other pains. Citrosine wished he'd just magically cure her sometimes, but she indulged Gya's love for the herbs. As the man strode to the kitchen, Citrosine removed from her pillowcase the silver hand mirror from her mother. She studied her eyes carefully. The brown irises had changed to a dark abyss-like indigo, nearly indistinguishable from the pupils. They did, indeed, resemble the Faerie's. She turned her eyes to the side, and saw that they still looked brown from that angle.

Gya returned with a sweet-smelling liquid into which he had mixed some herbs.

"Drink this slowly—it will be hot," he prompted, and Citrosine did so, keeping her eyes carefully averted from him. Gya saw that her skin looked very pale.

"Here, *lissa,* let me move your blankets into my study, so that you won't hear Tie and I moving things around so much. We're to be gathering our belongings together all day." Citrosine nodded, slowly, as her head still felt shattered, and followed Gya into his study, hiding the inside of her arm. Every muscle in her body was tight and drained, and she felt as if she'd become a spirit, wandering along with no purpose... Gya laid the blankets back down, kissed Citrosine on the forehead, only to find that it was wintry, and left her alone.

"Palgirtie," he said softly, as she ran up to hug him, "we must be quiet today, as Citrosine is not feeling well." Tie nodded.

"Can we have *paliz* now?"

Gya laughed. "Yes. Go have some *paliz,* and I'll be there in a moment."

After breakfast, Tie's mood darkened, as they were going to begin packing things up for the long journey to the new island. She wished that Citrosine had put up more of a fight to stay, rather than leaving it all up to Tie, because now Gya thought that Tie was just being a cranky child. Nonetheless, they began packing in the attic loft.

They sifted through boxes and boxes of old blankets and small toys that Citrosine and Tie never looked at anymore, and began a large pile of things to pack up. In two hours' time, that pile consisted of pillows, books, empty journals, storybooks, a few toy animals of Tie's, and a box of Leenka's jewelry. Later, they added armor, an old surcoat or two, and a few bows and swords.

"All right," Gya panted, wiping his forehead on his tunic, "that should be enough for a while." Tie nodded, and climbed down from the loft. She ran outside, where it was cooler. Gya followed her, and they ran for a while, until Tie fell in the grass, exhausted. She noticed something beside her. It was the ribbon that Citrosine had changed colors yesterday. It was no longer black, but the last color that it had been shaded with; a deep crimson, almost like blood. Tie picked it up and tied it around her wrist. She would bring this to her sister when she was feeling better.

Meanwhile, Citrosine, forced to spend the whole day locked up "sleeping", was experimenting. Any time she heard a sound from beyond the study door, she would pause suddenly, and listen for the door to move. After a few moments' silence, she would go back to whatever spell she'd just discovered.

One charm that surprised her in the worst way possible was one that was obviously to be used for battle. She was pacing around the room, and a loud noise from the ceiling above startled her. She twisted around and found herself in a fighting stance, but, where her nightclothes had been, she found a black surcoat with gray ripples stitched across it, and her hands gripped the two enchanted swords that Leenka had given her. Where they had come from, Citrosine did not know, but she quickly learned the reverse to that charm. Unfortunately, she had to practice it a little more slowly, because the first time, she made her underclothes vanish, along with tunic and weapons, leaving her standing completely unclothed and embarrassed in the middle of her father's study.

She also learned a few more entertaining spells, charms that didn't turn her stomach with the sickening thought: *this is dark magic.* One allowed her to create miniature creatures that could run around through the air at eye level and vanish into a small tuft of smoke. She tried this one with a werewolf image, and also a Dragon. They were quite accurate replications, but not nearly as threatening as the life-sized creatures would have been. However, after attempting a spiky shark-like beast, she learned that they could, indeed, inflict pain.

Gya only came in to check on her twice, and these two visits occurred within a period of Citrosine's genuine sleep. She had grown tired after being robbed of sleep the night before, and relished the silence one is granted when the world thinks one is fragile and infirm.

Gya opened the door silently, and crept over to where his sore, aching daughter lay, and kissed her gently on the cheek. He sat beside her for long moments, watching her sleep.

"You look just like your mother," he breathed, "save for Leenka was never this pale." He stroked her hair for another moment, and then left her side quietly.

Leenka used to live with her people among the clouds, in enchanted dwellings that floated above seas and mountains far below, and were never rained upon, for the rainclouds formed a distance below their cities. Leenka was a radiant young Elf who lived under her father's wing; her father was one of the eight founders and rulers of the city. This tribe was fabled to have been sent to live in the clouds by Ghersah the goddess on her way out of the world.

Ghersah had been a normal Elf who was unusually nurturing and compassionate. She worked with each tribe, each race; all the different Enchanted World leaders had taught her all that they knew, because they could see the sincerity in her heart, as well as the potential she had for great power. Eventually, Ghersah had become the singlemost powerful being that there was, and could do no evil.

Then war came. The migration of the immortals from the Painted World had begun, and tribes and races lost peace. The Shadow Elves and many of the Sorcerers and immortal beings turned away from their loyalties to everyone else, Jygul the Dark Elf becoming a major leader of the deceitful movement. Ghersah and Jygul fought for a solid century, so it was told.

Finally, Ghersah defeated Jygul's malice, but not without losing her own life. Moments after Jygul fell, Ghersah collapsed in pain. She was on the verge of death when Jygul's second found her in his lands. This man, the Blue Lord, he was called, kept Ghersah just barely alive enough so that he could wake her up to torture her in his chambers designed for just this purpose.

The great governing deity of the immortals and everything must have seen this and communicated it to all of its subjects, for everyone was again unified, and came to punish the Blue Lord. He was sentenced to be imprisoned inside the earth and keep it spinning forever.

Ghersah was taken up by the deity that binds the universe, as she would become the protector of the Enchanted World forever. She would be placed at the top of the fabled Tree of Redemption that served as the immortals' afterlife.

On her way up, she took eight Elves by the hands and carried them up into the clouds with her. The deity of the world had instructed her to carry on her power in new life, to instill hope, power, and love into all Elves through the generations. So Ghersah gave each man a daughter. Once a daughter of Ghersah's was born and of age, she would be sent down among the other tribes and coached to spread life. In this way the power of Ghersah diffused through the Elves.

Leenka, one of the daughters, had come to the Stone Tribe after she came of age, and immediately joined the Council as a protector. So endowed was she with her magics—as they were inherited straight from Ghersah, as the stories told—she became the most powerful Elf in the Council, and attracted Gya, who also had gained a high ranking. The pair fell in love rapidly, both beautiful and pleasant. They met for the first time in a clearing, both weary from Council expeditions and wanting time to reflect on the world. Here they planned their future together, here they left to live by the sea, here they returned to build a new home...

Palgirtie was, as Citrosine had guessed, growing to be wise beyond her years. She had been scarred by what she had seen the Coulf demons do to her mother, and she knew that neither Gya nor Citrosine would ever believe that what she had said was true.

Tie was slowly trying to form a plan. The first step of what she had come up with so far involved trying to decide if Leenka would ever come back home, in whatever form she had been transformed into. Tie would have to spend as much time as she could outside, looking for any signs that her mother might have left for her. But...would she ever be an Elf again? Would Leenka still try to kill her very own daughter? Would she recognize her own daughter? If Leenka was not a Wampyre any longer, what form *had* she taken?

Gya and Tie ate dinner in near silence, as almost all of the Nakiss' life was lived henceforth, since recent events had occurred. About halfway through the meal, Citrosine stumbled out of the study.

"*Lissa,* are you feeling any better?" Gya looked at his daughter earnestly, in hopes that maybe she didn't feel the need to be locked up an extra day. "We need your help with some packing."

"Dada, I'm feeling much better. May I sit with you while you dine?"

"Of course." Gya chuckled. "I'm elated that you feel a bit better. Care to eat?"

"Thank you, Dada, but I don't quite feel *that* much better."

Tie broke in with a round of giggling as Citrosine magicked a miniature butterfly that flew in loops and swirls around Tie's chair. She hugged her little sister and went to sit down, but Tie held her arm.

"You left your ribbon outside yesterday," she said, holding up the now blood-red ribbon. Citrosine smiled faintly. *Yesterday…*It seemed like a distant memory. Tie tied the ribbon tightly in a bow around her sister's wrist, and Citrosine sat down.

"*Dada?*" Citrosine reached into her father's mind quietly.
"*Eh, Citrosine?*"
"*When are we going back to Haerthor?*"
"*The day after the next…and Palgirtie must come with us.*"
"*Will all the races attend, or is that later?*"
"*The day before the journey, one or two representatives of every Elven Tribe, every Nymph colony, one of each colony of all the Nine Races, will meet in the Council Hall, and discuss the plans for our future. This will not include you, Tie, or I.*"

"*Citrosine, do you remember from your studies what the Nine Races are?*" Gya had taught his daughter as much as he could about Enchanted World history when Citrosine was younger.

"*Er…Elves, Nymphs, Dwarves, Faeries…Enchanted Creatures, Demons, Mortal Creatures, Men, Sorcerers…but the*

Race of Sorcery is very aloof, if still existent. They are more of almost a division or category and not really a race…"

"*Perfect.*"

Tie could hear what they were saying, but closed herself out, as she was working on her plans for trying to find out about the demons. She was having trouble thinking of anything that involved ever finding her mother again, but she easily scared herself with the daunting thoughts that she could come up with. One idea was to desert her sister and father, and pretend to turn evil, in hopes that she could come to terms with the demon ranks, and then be accepted as a powerful disciple of their kind, eventually discovering which demon used to be her mother…by searching their memories.

A few times, she had to actually poke herself with her fork to stop these chains of thoughts, and she poked herself *hard.* One such stab to her hand caused Gya to look over at her sharply, but his eyes turned fatherly as he saw a tiny dot of blood running over Tie's thumb.

"*Lissa,* are you all right?" He hustled to his study to gather a scrap of cloth. "I don't know what is getting into you, must be that age where little girls grow up…" he muttered under his breath as he hustled through the cottage.

Tie looked down at her hand, and noticed the wound for the first time. *Ghersah, help me…did I really do that without noticing?*

Citrosine looked at her sister with hurt in her eyes. She noticed the surprise that now filled Tie's countenance and wondered…

Six

EGAN AND PHERKUE

The remnants of the Nakiss family crept through the dark forest slowly, not making a sound but for the occasional muted rustle or chink of armor and swords. Gya carried a large sack that sported clothes, food, and papers needed for an overnight stay in Haerthor, along with his long sword, and, in his other hand, Tie's tight grip. Citrosine trailed behind, keeping an eye out for whatever might try and surprise them from behind. She recalled her last, timeless journey that spat her into the midst of this forest, and shuddered.

Fortunately, the spirits were not up to any mischief, as they happened to be readying themselves and all their kind for the journey to the new island. The forest didn't try any tricks of lengthening itself, either, for it was weary from so many travelers passing to Haerthor; representatives of all the Elven tribes streaming through it all day, shaking in anxiety. All that happened on this particular journey through was that heartbeats and footsteps were echoed severely, making it sound as if there were legions of things in the trees when it was really only the three travelers. Every breath reverberated a thousand times, making all three start and draw a louder breath together, which in turn would echo…It was the opposite of Citrosine's last journey, when there had been no sound whatsoever. Now she could hear her companions' very heartbeats, Gya's strong and hollow, Tie's light and fluttering.

Citrosine was edgy all day. She knew that there would be a lot of tension in the Council Hall today, due to all the dissonant tribes that would be present. She was also trying to imagine when she would see Tyre and demonstrate her new power to him.

The iron gate that had guarded the city was grown over with ivy and moss, as if the forest itself knew of the impending danger of the Men, and was trying to swallow any evidence of the Enchanted creatures' inhabitance. The guards nodded at the three of them curtly, allowing them past without a word.

When they arrived in Haerthor, Tie and Citrosine were warned not to disrupt any discussion they witnessed. Gya looked to each of them sternly.

"You two should not speak to anyone that does not wish to be spoken to. When in Leader's presence, I expect that you listen and pay him respect." His daughters nodded obediently.

Many Elves were milling about the courtyards, making acquaintances and waiting for Leader to begin the meeting. Many small straight-backed chairs had been arranged in concentric semicircles centered upon the edge of the courtyard.

The whole area was quite crowded as Elves of varying emotional states attempted to reach their seats. The Shadow and Air Tribe members were the easiest to distinguish, and, though Citrosine had never seen them, it was clear enough to her what tribes they were from. The many members of the Air Tribe wore flowing lace robes and surcoats emblazoned with wispy curls and cloud patterns. Their Marks were upon their arms, in the patterns of whorls and spirals racing down their arms and ending at their knuckles. They generally had olive skin and piercing gray eyes, most complemented by fair, silky hair.

The Elves in the Shadow Tribe had only a few representatives present, and Citrosine was afraid to look at them too long. Distinguished by the black, writhing wreaths that haloed around their brows, they contrasted the Air Elves with their blood-red eyes, white skin, and the black, weathered robes and cloaks they wore. She was amazed to be seeing them, as Gya had told her that they'd vanished into a secret hiding place a century ago.

The Sea Elves wore shimmering silvery-green garb with a silver ring on the little finger as each one's Mark, and all had tan skin and cropped, bleached hair. Citrosine caught Tie giving those few dirty looks, and nudged her in the ribs.

A few Mountain, Wood, and Fall Elves were scattered about, resembling the Stone Tribe closely, but for dress and skin tone. Citrosine realized that the Fall Elves all had the same dark skin as Tyre and his father, Marks not visible. The Cavern Elves looked like a hybrid of the Shadow and Wood Elves; they had the same sickeningly pale skin, with blue eyes and simple dress, each carrying an intricately designed bow. They were also quite interesting to look at, with the tattooed crescents on their cheeks and foreheads.

Citrosine spied Tyre sitting alone on a ledge near a flowerbox, in a sparsely populated corner of the courtyard. She received permission from Gya to sit with him, and she barely managed to keep herself from running. Tyre was the one person she knew she could trust with her secrets.

Before she could call out to him, he cocked his head to one side.

"Citrosine? Ah, how are you?" His eyes smiled, even as his face was unusually calm. Citrosine laughed.

"How do you know my gait?" she wondered aloud.

"You always sound like you're in haste, and that aura of yours…almost as if it grows every time we meet."

"Well it has, this time,"

His smile suddenly vanished. *"Did you get Jygul's Blessing?"* he asked suddenly.

"Yes, I did; just days ago."

Tyre smiled again. *"I could never be so brave. Did it hurt?"*

"Only as much as being burned to death,"

Tyre made a sound of concern and stretched out his arms to her, beckoning. Citrosine sat on the flowerbox next to him and placed her hands in his. *"You shouldn't make yourself hurt so much…isn't good for the mind."*

"Tyre," Citrosine giggled, "you are both comforting and silly sometimes."

"May I feel the vein, or is it tender?" Tyre's fingertips were already working their way up Citrosine's wrists.

"It isn't terribly tender," she replied faintly. She saw Tie giving her a questioning look from across the courtyard.

"My, isn't he overly intimate?"

Citrosine whispered to her quickly, *"He is blind, so he uses his hands as eyes. Forgive his bending of etiquette."* Tie nodded and continued in conversation with her father.

"She barely accepts your excuse…she'll ask you about me later, in a frenzied gossip, no doubt, wanting every detail of this meeting." Tyre's lips curved upward slightly, and his hand traced the Blessing on Citrosine's lower arm. He said, "I can feel the new magic here," and his smile lessened as the dark magic emitted a slightly louder pressure than Citrosine's triply-strong magic already did. His hands moved down to her wrists, and he started slightly when they brushed over the ribbon. Citrosine smirked, and then quickly changed the color of the ribbon, back to the original black that it had been. She pulled on the bow, and took up the ribbon to tie back her hair.

"Tyre," Citrosine said, just as Leader was emerging from inside the Council Hall.

"Mm?" He raised his eyebrows.

"What tribe do you belong to, if I may ask?"

"My father is part of the Fall Tribe, but I was born into Stone, and spend more time here in Haerthor than among my family. It is…it becomes very difficult to travel…when one cannot see the way," he stammered, still trying to understand why Citrosine had so much of an aura, though he was beginning to realize that this was futile. Perhaps she was just born with magic, like her mother.

"I see," Citrosine said shyly, "but I'm sorry to make you uncomfortable."

"I am not uncomfortable with anything you ask me." His voice was too quiet, too soft. Something was not in order.

"The sweat on your hands tells me that that isn't true," Citrosine laughed quietly. When Tyre didn't laugh along with her, she scrutinized his face. His eyes were troubled, and she knew he had a secret.

"You know that I hide from you," he whispered, stifling expression.

"*Tyre, you frighten me!*" Citrosine clutched her friend's arm.

"*Citrosine…I need to see you again—later, after the meeting. There are a few things I think I am responsible for telling you when we aren't so crowded.*" His hands grasped her shoulders, and Citrosine nodded. She noted that Tyre held her tightly, not hurting her, but with more emotion than he usually touched her. She shivered in nervous animation.

Then the meeting began.

Citrosine remained with Tyre, though Gya and Tie sat nearby. They were still in the corner of the courtyard, and had a sidewise view of Leader and many of the other Elves. Leader began with a greeting, first in Elvish, then in the Common Tongue.

"Friends, kinsmen, family, it is with a heavy heart that I welcome you here; a wonderful chance to meet, under a grave circumstance. I, the Leader of the Stone Elf Tribe, have been asked to speak on behalf of the Royal Family and King Hendius.

"It appears as if at least a handful of representatives are present from each tribe, though, as a formality, I shall call out names of those expected." Leader smiled warmly, and the representatives shifted in their seats, ready to begin at last.

"Will any representatives from the Wood Tribe stand, please?" Leader looked into the crowd as a mass of pleasant-looking Elves in the front few rows stood. Their Marks were tattooed on their necks; taking the form of a tree with a moon and a sun peeping out from behind on opposite sides. Leader nodded, and they sat.

"Lake Elves please stand," he called next. A smaller group—it looked to be only about ten—seated along the edge of the crowd rose. Again, Leader nodded, and they sat. The Lake Elves were heavily armed, as their magics usually failed the further they were from the Maiden who governed their establishment around the lake Kalta. Dark shapes on their foreheads characterized them. Citrosine wondered how they would fare in the new settlement without the lake, and if their Maiden would venture across the sea to protect them.

"Elves of the Mountain Tribe,"

These smaller-structured Elves stood. Marked by swirling shapes outlining their eyes, barely visible but intriguingly present, this group lived at the tops of mountains, so their bodies and magic dealt mostly with temperature spells. They had lower body temperatures than others.

"Sea Elves," Leader called hesitantly. Sea Elves usually came in small numbers, since it was such a long way to Haerthor from the bottom of the sea. A small group rose, smiling widely, silver cloaks shimmering.

"Fall Elves,"

A few scattered Elves stood, along with Tyre's father, across the courtyard. Leader nodded thoughtfully, and they all sat. There was a pause.

"Elves of the Air," he said more quietly.

Five Elves stood swiftly. It almost seemed as if the air grew more fragrant with their motions, and it was easier to breathe. These Elves had magic that affected light, darkness, weather, and they were said in legend to live atop the clouds.

"Cavern Tribe, are you here?"

Twenty Elves stood now. Citrosine felt a strange vibration in her chest, near the place where her dark magic store had first begun to stir, as if there was something kicking at her heart. *The Cavern Tribe practices dark magic...* She tried to reason why she was feeling this stirring again now. When the Cavern Elves sat, the sensation faded.

"Er...there are quite a few tribes in our race, aren't there?" Leader joked as he tried to remember the next tribe to call. "Stone Elves, please stand!"

Apparently, half the remaining onlookers were of the Stone Tribe, for nearly fifty Elves stood, along with Tyre, Gya, Citrosine, and Tie. Citrosine noticed Tyre leaning heavily against his walking stick next to her, his knuckles tight and trembling. Leader chuckled as they sat again.

"Are there any of the Field Tribe present?" His scarred face scoured the crowds. No one stood, and there was a penetrating silence. "That is a true loss," he murmured loud enough for everyone to hear. "May we hope that this meeting was simply too inconvenient for any remaining of this group." Each Elf present lowered his head, giving a moment of quiet for those disappeared. The clouds above shifted smoothly past the sun, and the wind rustled various tribe members' cloaks.

"Who have I overlooked…ah, yes; Elves of the Shadow Tribe, would you please stand?" Leader began more lightly, and many of the other Elves twisted around in their seats eagerly, to see if this mysterious tribe had also disappeared. However, the atmosphere was silenced again almost immediately when several Elves stood, and the air grew one hundred shades darker.

The eldest of the present Shadow Elves was very tall and severe. He had black hair, with eyebrows and facial hair the same color. His face was pointed, like a rat's, and had two sunken eye sockets, one of which housed an empty cavity, while the other had an eyeball that was blood-red. He glared around at the gawping Elves immediately surrounding him, and many of those Elves shrank back from his one-eyed scowl.

The Elf at his hip looked to be just a bit older than Citrosine. He was tall and thin, and also had blood-red eyes, although, yes, there were two, and they seemed to sparkle more merrily. He shimmered with a black aura, always outlined with a shadow, and appeared to be sending a charm over every female near him, as they all gazed at his flawless face in wonder, smiling and batting their eyes relentlessly, an embarrassment to their sex.

Citrosine found even herself staring, her heart an ecstatic sparrow flying in circles and fluttering, and quickly looked back to Leader, who presently nodded for the Shadow Elves to sit. Citrosine thought how similar to all those swooning women she must look, and cursed silently.

"As you all are aware," Leader began, "we have gathered here to discuss the plans for our migration to a new island off the southwestern coast of the Big Lands. Our ancestors created this island, in case this sort of occurrence—the invasion of Men upon the Enchanted lands—came about. They named this island *Ilthen,* meaning New Life. The idea of us journeying off can only be imagined if we illustrate how any tensions between our tribes can be forgotten. The Elves must all accept that we will be forced to build dwellings closer together than we have in these lands. Some of our tribes may end up living in new kinds of places—I cannot guarantee that there will be mountains or lakes to live within, much less waterfalls or caverns. We will all be forced to adjust our magics to lock together with whatever we can find; whatever we can create.

"Our races must be at peace; for this new land can know not the ancient grudges we carry with us, lest it be tainted with our own blackness and reject us to the mercy of the Men who will doubtless extort our magics and our very way of life.

"Present dwellings must be destroyed, retracted, erased from all visible history. Men are smart, and they continue to adapt to and analyze their new surroundings as they move deeper and deeper into our homelands. It will be imperative that we take everything with us; everything that cannot be spared for a new life. Ilthen will support us, so long as we can give it a jumping-off point.

"I have reached the end of the common public concern, and if anyone has any other discussion topics, this would be an excellent time to address them with the entire Elven community represented." Leader was pacing slowly back and forth, trying to gauge the opinions of everyone he could see.

The one-eyed Shadow Elf stood swiftly, just as a cloud ran across the sun. He raised his hand, and Leader nodded in his direction.

"Is there truly to be harmony on this island?" The man had a loud, coarse voice. Citrosine snorted at the strange question for a being of darkness to ask. The man continued.

"Leader, if I may," he curled his back into a snakelike bow, his one eye locked on Leader. "Are we to believe that the old prejudices shall be abandoned? For my tribe has been besmirched since before any of us present were alive, and only because of the stereotypes of darkness; of course we all must be evil and kill and devour everything we see—our 'dark' power *consumes* us, our 'black' magic kills everything we touch. This is asinine. Will we ultimately begin to fight the same wars in our new life as we have been forced to in the old? If this is so, then I may as well just tear out my remaining eye right here, rather than start another war! The last time my tribe was exposed to others, our ways of life were seen as *unfit* for peace, when we truly hurt no one—just because our powers scare others," his face glowed with rage, and his eye flashed recklessly, "doesn't mean that we will kill all life around us! For my tribe, darkness is a way of life, and not something that can be helped. We are an ecosystem, in balance with creatures commonly and ignominiously associated with both evil and good—" He was rambling with no more point to make, and Leader silenced him with a quick raise of his palm.

The younger Elf who accompanied this angry one surveyed the other Elves with curiosity. He didn't look irate, like his acquaintance, but purely curious of Leader's reaction to this argument. The females near him seemed unaffected by the one-eyed man's rage, still gawping at the boy, who shifted modestly in his seat to avoid their eyes.

Leader narrowed his eyes. "Egan of the Shadow Elves, I appreciate your concern, but you must let your anger go, as we all shall attempt. This is a meeting only to inform, not to scold or argue, so you will agree with me when I ask you to pause in your accusations.

"You may rest assured, Egan, and everyone, that we *will not* be forced to go through the same epic ordeals our ancestors faced. All tribes will be treated equally by rulers, and I assume that the tribes will all respect that. I wish only peace for all races, and hopefully the elders and higher-ups of each race will aid me in reaching that end." He nodded slowly.

Egan was still silently fuming. The younger Elf took Egan's hand and carefully helped him sit. After this was done, he himself stood to raise his hand. Leader nodded to him with a sick look in his eyes, as there appeared to be no other questions.

"Leader, our superior, sir," the boy began. There was an audible sigh from every female Elf present, upon hearing the boy's velvety, hypnotic voice. He looked about distractedly with his bright red eyes, shook his head, and went back to his question.

"Sir, about our new territories, I understand that there is to be an organized meeting, though I wonder if I could bring to your visualization a rather important matter in our tribe before the councils and whatnot are under way...?" His voice was detached, as if he was preoccupied by a noise somewhere behind him. Leader's brow furrowed, and he waved his hand for the boy to continue.

"The Dark Elves wish to express concerns of our tribe having an equal share of land as that of Stone, Wood, Sea, and other tribal lands. We have been living in various outskirts and shadows of leftover scrap territory ever since we became our own tribe, and I as a member of the Shadow Council have been asked to address this unease. More territory would allow us to congregate, so that our tribe does not die out, as our meager representative numbers illustrate that we nearly have, in fact, become extinct.

"If sufficient provision is not met, and we must go on living as we are, I am afraid to admit that all of our tribe will perish unless we intermarry within our own families, which is a suicide wish for our magic, not to mention sinful and disgusting. I am speaking, my fellow Elves," he turned around in a slow circle to meet the crowd's eyes, "of incest. If there aren't any ways to mingle the powers of our bloodlines, we shall become less and less powerful, diluting our magic, becoming eventually mortal, and...well, it would literally kill us over time—only a century, as our elders have predicted. We would become extinct as quickly as the Field Elves...and that loss is such a shame." He paused.

"I wonder if, Leader, sir, you wish that upon us?" He cast a wry, sour grin to Leader, who pulled at his ear in irritation and thought. The younger Elf continued.

"We have already been forced to—er—*mate*—within our own families for a decade or so, to keep our numbers up, so the youngest generations possess almost no magic anymore. It is as if we are wild animals, growing endangered every moment… we are almost mating for survival, no matter whom we must produce with…" He paused, again for effect. Citrosine noticed that his voice had not grown angry, only taken on certain inflections to speak his thoughts. He remained calm, with a retained smoothness and soft articulation of consonants that Citrosine felt would be able to beautifully say her name, to tell her its longings and fears…she slapped her hand.

"To better illustrate this situation, I will admit," a slight blush came over the Dark Elf's cheekbones, but he faltered not, "I will admit that, of this man sitting to my left, I am a nephew, step-son, step-brother, *and* step-cousin. Humiliating, yes, though true. It is unnatural for the younger of our race to be forced to become fathers and mothers…but it has almost become necessary…so necessary that marriages are no longer required before we—er—this is difficult for the other tribes to fully appreciate…We are a dying breed, and will vanish otherwise…but we simply fight for population!

"Leader, our tribe must be trusted once and for all, and given proper access to land. It was only our far distant ancestors causing havoc with their violent dark powers. We must be recognized, unless…Sir, surely you don't wish us dead?" The boy's voice turned smug, and he looked at Leader skeptically as he sat down with his uncle. Leader tried to keep a calm, levelheaded expression, but there was an evident streak of annoyance in his words.

"I understand the urgency in your tribe's situation, Pherkue, and of course we all realize the unnatural behaviors your circumstances require…" Leader drudged up more words.

"I will bring this issue up at the next meeting, where it will be better recognized and more relevant. I will keep your plea in mind and attempt to come up with a plan to share with the leaders of the other races. All of our tribes shall have more than enough land to thrive upon, and until this next meeting, I recommend to your kind to refrain from making any enemies.

"Now, are there any other questions? No? Everyone else is relatively happy? Then I open the doors to the Dining Hall, where anyone is welcome to join the Stone Tribe Council in a well-prepared meal. I believe there will be enough seats for everyone. Of course we also have plenty of rooms to make use of for staying the night so that those of you who have long journeys may begin when it is again light." With a sweep of robes, Leader turned and strode to the door that was thrust open at his approach. All the Elves stood and stretched, and the procession inside began.

Gya, Tie, and Citrosine stood; ready to at least move around a little after sitting still for so long. Tyre remained seated, but he caught the back of Citrosine's tunic in his fingers, preventing her from moving.

"Will you stay?" he implored with a lack of any humor or happiness.

"As long as you need," she replied respectfully, surprised by the urgency in his thoughts. She turned to Gya. "May I be excused to speak with Tyre for a while?" she murmured.

Gya gave his assent with a wink and boosted Tie up on his shoulders. They made their way through the crowd quickly, soon inside the Dining Hall.

"Thank you," Tyre said faintly.

"Of course," Citrosine replied, although she was uneasy. Tyre, who was of such good humor and energy, was not himself, and did not speak.

113

"Now," she went on, "you have concerned me with your reservation tonight. What did you need to tell me? What is on your mind that so perturbs your wonderfully light heart? You are my closest friend, and I will hear you with open mind."

Tyre did not answer for many minutes. When he finally spoke, it was so hard to hear him that Citrosine had to ask him to speak louder.

"I had a dream about you—several, actually," he repeated himself uncertainly. Citrosine's eyes locked on his. He said nothing more, motionless.

"…Go on…Come, you are always much more forward than this. What troubles you?" she prompted, trying to be encouraging.

"Well, it was very…I…There is no way to tell you, and so you must see, as hard as it might be for the both of us." He held his hands out, allowing the walking cane to fall clattering off of his lap. Citrosine timidly placed her hands in Tyre's, and he held them tightly. His mouth opened and closed a few times as he tried to come up with the right words that were bumbling around in his mind.

"I don't want you to get hurt, Citrosine," he finally said, voice wavering, "and I need to show you what I experienced in my dream. Don't be scared, I just want to prepare you… because I feel such love for you." There was false hope in his voice.

"Tyre," she whispered, trying to comfort him. But he wouldn't have it.

"Watch." His fingers trembled as those of a soldier's would, did he know that he was about to sacrifice his own life for some greater good—the greater good that escapes a being's understanding when he is at the face of death, as life is all he knows and all he now wishes for, the most precious belonging to his frightened, bleeding body.

Citrosine closed her eyes as a rush of thoughts, memories, and words came streaming through her mind.

There are bodies of fallen Elves strewn everywhere around a crowded field, where fires are just burning out, and, apparently, the victors of this war remain to be determined. Suddenly, a huge demon springs from a nearby ribbon of trees and lashes out at a more mature, battle-hardened Citrosine. Citrosine strikes it from behind while another soldier tries to attack the beast. The demon feels her spell and charges her. Citrosine shoots a pleading glance toward her fellow warriors, but is now forced to run. She sprints for the trees, trying to shake the demon off her trail, but the demon is unnaturally coordinated, with an Elf's reflexes, swiftly avoiding trees and vines rushing by.

There is a dark blur, and then the demon has pinned Citrosine down in a clearing. She is poisoned badly, and it would seem like death is upon her. The demon snarls and leans down to attack again. Another blur and Citrosine is stumbling across a forlorn beach. The sand around her is stained with blood, and the Elf screams, eyes rolling back and limbs convulsing.

She reaches out to a distant blurry shape in her clouded, hallucinatory vision, and then collapses. A wave from the green, frothy ocean abuses her limp and wilted body, and she is still.

Citrosine opened her eyes to see Tyre's shoulders shaking in silent hysteria. She was in shock. The image in the dream... she couldn't be that much older than she was now...

"I don't want you to get hurt," Tyre repeated, body quivering as he squeezed and squeezed the Elf girl's poor fingers. Citrosine slid closer to him, and wrapped her arms around him tightly. As her shock slowly gave in to terror, she remembered the promise to herself not to show too much emotion, or else her dark power would overcome her...she struggled to maintain control, but tears forced their way out of her eyes, and she felt a now-familiar sensation as time stopped once more...

Tyre's head jerked up, alert and listening. There was no sound, and it felt as though his ears were stuffed with cotton. Citrosine cried out in defeat, and tried to explain.

"Jygul's Blessing...if I show this much emotion so strongly... the magic leaks out and asserts itself! It's happened several times now..." She couldn't think of anything else to say, as the image of her poisoned body shuddering to a sudden stop as the ocean rolled over it again and again flooded her mind in overwhelming clarity.

"Why did you see this vision, Tyre?" she pleaded. *"Please, is this truly going to happen! Why..."* she stopped, as her energy was suddenly drained, her mind unable to fathom the vision of itself dying.

"Citrosine?" Tyre felt her faint. He struggled to keep hold of her so that she would not crash to the flagstone courtyard. "Citrosine! Stay with me, stay awake!" He tried to make her listen to his voice, to stay conscious. For one, he powerfully regarded her health and welfare, but he also needed her to make sure time wasn't stopped in one place forever.

"Tyre..." she whispered, letting him know that she was conscious again. Tyre breathed a sigh of relief, and put his hands under Citrosine's arms. He lifted her onto his lap, and pulled her arm around his neck, just to make sure she didn't collapse onto the stones below, should she faint again. She clung to him tightly, awakening.

"Citrosine...I had this vision because one small decision has been made in one person's mind. Things may still change...but as for now, you might *be put into this situation. You're stronger than that; I know you can last longer...just hold onto hope..."* He bit his lip, and waited to hear an answer. Citrosine was, at least, still breathing.

She opened her eyes slowly, accepting what Tyre had just said, and trying to grasp the idea. Her head hurt, as well as her eyes, neck, and limbs; but they didn't feel attached to her body, and she was now dizzy as if she would faint...again.

"Citrosine, come; Citrosine, *you must say something...*I'm blind, I cannot see if you are all right..." Tyre was frenzied. His clouded eyes were wide with fear and concern.

"I...I'm fine," Citrosine managed. Tyre breathed a heavy sigh of relief that Citrosine could feel, her head resting on his chest. His heart throbbed against her cheek, echoing the terrified beats that hers performed.

"Tyre, thank you for sharing this, warning me; it's just very...very perturbing," she whispered, her voice throaty and scared.

I'm worried for your safety," Tyre managed after a moment.

"We only met a short time ago," Citrosine chuckled darkly, "and you're already seeing premonitions of my death."

"Well..."

"'Well' *what?*" Citrosine snapped.

"That brings me to another thing I had to tell you..."

"I hope it involves happier news, Tyre. I still have to face my father as if my deepest concern is whether or not to *bring my fine clothes* on the journey to Ilthen." Her voice was getting hard and icy. Words were becoming difficult to control, forcing their way menacingly from her lips.

"I understand." Tyre was subdued and quiet again.

"So what *else* did you want to say?"

His mouth opened and closed.

"Pardon my temper, but I just learned of my death that is seemingly imminent, and it becomes a bit difficult to control one's words when one is forced to think of an upcoming loss of life."

"I understand," Tyre repeated, with such a complete identification of her feelings, despite the layers of disdain she'd given her words. She bit her tongue back in appreciation to this.

"Citrosine Nakiss, I haven't been able to think about anything else since we last met. I can only focus on *you*," he admitted, flushed. Citrosine recoiled.

"Me? You think about me?"

"Er, yes…I was just…I don't know…" His words foundered, and Citrosine was flushed now. Tyre located Citrosine's cheek, and traced her jaw, her cheekbones, her lips. She shivered, and leaned into his warm grasp.

"Have you ever heard of soulmates? The deity—"

"Shh!" Citrosine interrupted. "You can't speak of the—"

"The deity? I know that is what we are all told, but I don't believe that such a powerful force of justice and harmony could be so offended just by me speaking of it in praise." He managed half a smirk. "In any case, I believe that the deity struck me the first time I met you. From that moment on, since we became friends—or acquaintances…I am unsure of how you see our relationship—I have not been able to go for half an hour of my days without thinking of you. I feel so attracted to you, your voice, your gait, your laugh…"

"Is it the visions?"

"Not at all; that's a different matter. Well, there was one vision…a few nights ago…it's not my place to share… very improper etiquette to speak of such…" he paused, skin flushing.

"What else have you seen?" Citrosine whispered in horror, her heart resuming its frenzied dance.

Tyre's eyes sparkled like clear, calm oceans, and relief washed through Citrosine's thoughts. She waited more patiently for Tyre to speak.

"I saw a vision of…us, Citrosine…I mean *us,* truly! Together—we had a family, a home, a beautiful little child…I shouldn't be telling you of this, it is a rude fantasy that is better left to myself—there is that bluntness that strikes me around you—but…I *liked* seeing us there. You were with me, smiling at—"

"Does that mean that I am not going to die? You should have told me this first!" Citrosine spoke quietly, restraining the way her heart wanted to leap out of her chest and circle the universe.

"No…Citrosine…it came before. This was before…That… *other* vision was just last night." his voice broke before the end of his words.

The Elf girl did not know what to say, because her heart had just plummeted down to lay buried in the earth, black and icy and unmoving.

"What I wanted to tell you, however, is that that vision— it could still happen, we could be together, if you wanted to—Citrosine, you can't be afraid! My visions are only those things that the deity wishes me to see, to help me prepare. I can guarantee nothing, life or death. But I feel like I know you well enough to promise…you *will* last longer than this.

"Somewhere I can feel it, behind my fear and my selfishness; understand that I *desire* you to live…Citrosine, I believe that I love you," he breathed into her ear.

Citrosine looked up at him, and his eyes were brimming with tears again. She touched him to wipe them away, and his eyes flicked downwards, happening to lock directly on hers, which had never happened before, due to his blindness. Some force had chosen to allow his eyes to focus on hers, even if he still could not see her. Perhaps the deity was working for them, after all? Perhaps they could still be together, for a while? And now Tyre was leaning closer, closer, closer…

Citrosine met him halfway.

A rush of emotion sprang up from deep in Citrosine's heart, deep down somewhere that she didn't know existed. She felt her cheeks warm pleasantly, and hugged Tyre tighter, kissing him with all the emotion and passion she knew.

Here was Tyre, who was so infatuated by her and concerned about her welfare that he had premonitions about her; he loved her so much that this quickly he was already so intensely attached to her. What could she do but feel the same way? Her eyes closed slowly, and she thanked Ghersah that time was still stopped; she hesitated, and heard no sound—yes, it was still stopped; or she would already be under the inquiring gazes of Gya and Tie, for kissing in public simply was not done in Elven culture. It was almost like strolling unclothed through a Council meeting; it was simply unacceptable to display affection so boldly. Kissing was ultimately forbidden in public this way, although, if no one else could move through time at the same moment, would it really be considered public?

It felt as if that moment lasted ambiguously forever and not anywhere close to nearly long enough. Tyre's eyes remained closed, and Citrosine watched him curiously, trying her hardest not to see the pain that hid in the corners of his eyes, behind his love for her.

Suddenly realizing that she had failed to register a rather important detail, Citrosine caught her breath belatedly. Tyre directed his face towards hers in curiosity.

"You saw…we had a child?" Her words could barely escape her throat, which was filled with a lump.

Tyre nodded solemnly. All levity and happiness was gone from his face. Even though he'd been so pleased with the thought of their togetherness when he'd confessed his vision, the…*other* vision seemed to drain his energy.

"But that is not possible anymore. We cannot have a child after I…" Citrosine felt as if her insides had been frozen. She wanted to vomit. It would have been so wonderful to marry Tyre, to love him and see him all the time, to know that his child—their child—was growing inside of her…

Tyre still said nothing, but he held her waist tighter, his beautiful smooth face becoming dead and gray. He looked as if he wanted to tear himself into pieces for having such a prophecy. Citrosine knew from this that he loved her greatly, if he was so petrified to lose her someday soon.

Then Citrosine had a thought.

"Tyre…can you…would you show me? Us?" She stroked his face gently with her fingertips. "What we…could have had?" Tyre stiffened. His expression became even more pained.

"No." His voice was ice. "I cannot. I must not." Behind his hardness, Citrosine heard pain and weakness.

"Why?" she prodded, more carefully.

"Because…" he fought for control over his words, but lost it. "Because it kills me to hear you say that it cannot be. It tortures my very soul to see two contradicting futures in my thoughts and know that there is even a *possibility*," he choked on the word, for he was trying to make her death seem more unlikely and unpredictable than they both knew it was, "of a world where there is only me, and no Citrosine to be with me." He began trembling. "I cannot…I can't bear it!" He gripped Citrosine tightly, as if she would fly away from him that very second. Her skin turned white where he held her, but she did not register any pain.

"Tyre…" she paused to gauge her words, because she could not stand to see him hurt like this, "I need to see it. If I could see it—as you have shown me this other…vision…then it will be more real to me. Would you only show me, I could have something to believe in, something to—" she gulped with some difficulty, "to keep my heart beating for." Tyre flinched. "Right now, all I have is a very real image of my own death. If I had a vision of my life, and *our* life, then maybe I could overpower the terrible with the perfect. Let me at least have that…?" She faltered when she realized how much her words were hurting Tyre further. He was silently sobbing, which made Citrosine want to cry, too. She gave up her argument totally and wrapped her arms around Tyre's shoulders tightly.

And then she saw the house.

It was small, just a cottage, really, a few miles into a wood and flanked by trees that cradled the address and its little gardens between their loving trunks. Tyre stood outside, breathing deeply the scent of the forest, of a smoky chimney, of happiness. He was older, more filled out and grown. Citrosine could not help staring at him, at how perfectly content he seemed. Everything about him suggested that his life was perfection just then—his comfortable tunic that draped away from his body to show a V of brown chest, his shining expression, with no worries tucked into the creases any longer, and also the fact that his walking stick was nowhere in sight, suggesting ultimate comfortability. Citrosine watched as he turned towards the front door. It opened, and an older Citrosine who looked just like her mother walked out peacefully, carefree, and happy to see her companion. She flung herself into his arms, and they embraced tenderly. Citrosine could see that each of the couple had a small band on one finger: wedding rings.

Then the front door opened again, and a small face peeped outside. A pair of large, brown eyes twinkled as they spotted Citrosine and Tyre, and the girl bounced outside towards them. She was the most beautiful child that Citrosine had ever seen, with fluttering black curls, luminous tan skin, and the widest, brightest smile that could possibly fit on her immaculate face. Citrosine felt a surge of compassion towards her, and knew that the girl was *hers*. She recognized her own eyes, lips, and heart-shaped face, and Tyre's slender build, skin tone, and beautifully shining smile. They had made her together, taking their love for each other and multiplying it into this perfect being, this little girl.

And then it faded. Citrosine instinctively was filled with fury because someone had taken her daughter from her, but she softened, and remembered that it had only been a vision…a dream…and now it was gone…never to—

"Don't think that way," Tyre hissed. Citrosine looked at him in shock, forgetting for an instant that he had powers far surpassing her own. He continued, pained and almost—indignant? "This future is not *gone*. Not yet. You *are* alive, you can fight to *stay* alive, and *you will* survive. Do not overreact, or then there will be no hope at all. Do you understand?" He took Citrosine by her shoulders, eyes blazing, the deity seeming again to make them burn directly into her own.

"I understand," Citrosine breathed. She was not afraid of Tyre, but amazed by how strongly he felt for her, and for this future. She ever so gently reached into his mind, wondering what exactly he felt. As soon as she had done so, she recoiled; confused by the first thought she had come by.

Tyre cocked his head, softening, letting his emotions get control of themselves again. "What is it?" He had only somewhat felt the intrusion, then.

"I have only one question." Citrosine began to smile, slowly, and with more care than she had ever taken to smile before.

Tyre nodded. He breathed more deeply, slowing down his adrenaline, his heart, his pain.

"You named her already." The Elf girl smiled radiantly, withholding nothing.

"That isn't a question." A trace of a smile, just creeping up from the corners of his lips, illuminated Tyre's face. "And I want to hear you ask me. You can't just make me find your thoughts again; that isn't fair."

"What is her name?"

"It is in Old Elvish; it was given to me for her in my vision."

"That doesn't answer my question." Both smirked.

"Her name is *Dariya*. It means…"

"Hope." They said the word together, as if it were a miracle.

Citrosine glowed. "So, when you say there will be no hope when I overreact and blur this future, is that 'hope' or 'Hope'?" Tyre laughed lightly with her, answering, "Both," sincerely. His laugh filled her with rainbows and warmth; it came from deep in his lungs, resounding in quiet chords that she could feel vibrating through his chest. He kissed her gently on her cheek.

"I hope for Dariya; I hope that there is hope for Hope to live!" She giggled, forgetting her melancholy.

"There is hope," Tyre murmured into her thoughts as he kissed her hand.

She beamed, feeling a stirring of emotions that she had not known before. She *wanted* this child—their daughter—Dariya—to exist. Not now, when there was so much tension and fear in the world—and she was only a child herself, of course—but someday…when she *lived*. She must survive, if not for her sake or Tyre's, then for the sake of Dariya.

She took Tyre's face in her hands, realizing how cold her fingers were becoming in the darkening air. He waited for her to collect her words. When she did not say anything for a few moments, Tyre shifted towards her carefully. Citrosine felt him in her mind now, an almost imperceptible presence that felt as if it were her own mind. So she just thought about what she wanted him to know, going through her memory of this vision and all of her feelings that went with it.

Tyre, I will keep myself alive. I will not let the other vision come true. For you…us…Dariya. I want that second memory to be real. Memories of Dariya's face floated through her mind, and the image of Citrosine and Tyre together with their little girl.

"You can fight. I know that you can stay alive. You want it this badly, and you are stong enough." This time his words sounded much more genuine, less tortured. As if he actually believed himself.

Citrosine wanted to tell him more, but could not think; this whole encounter was starting to make her body weary, her mind drained. She focused on explaining the emotions she felt, knowing that with Tyre's strong powers he would be able to grasp her meaning.

Love, want, need…Frustration-anger-hate…wants…togetherness, connected, love, need…fear-rage-terror…

Tyre nodded. *Hush…calm…It is all right…There is nothing to worry about anymore, now that you are prepared…shh…*

all you have to do is be aware, be calm…fight when the time is right…shh…calm…peace…rest…

Some of the words and feelings Tyre let loose in her mind were empty, just for comfort's sake, she knew, but they still made her feel better. It was the way her mother had been able to pass on her own powers, her own emotions as she sang a lullaby or cooed in comfort after a nightmare. But Tyre felt as a part of her mind, giving her its own instructions, as if her own brain was calming Citrosine by itself.

"Thank you," she welcomed the comfort to her scrambled emotions.

"You are always welcome…just let your mind rest." He leaned towards her again, stroking her face. He pressed his lips to hers, and they kissed more gently, sweetly—Citrosine felt, however, that this kiss was full of more love than their first. She closed her eyes and hugged him tighter.

"Make time move again," Tyre whispered. Citrosine hesitated, as if she had not heard correctly. Of all the things to say after the most powerful kiss in her life: *Make time move again?*

"Eh?"

Tyre sighed softly. He gave Citrosine a loving squeeze. This sent a thrill of feeling through her body—fingers, toes, heart!

"We have been suspended in time for over an hour; this great use of magic will alert other mages, even if they have been frozen this whole time." Citrosine remembered her father telling her about the evil Shadow Elves that stopped time frequently, in order to better plan attacks and malevolent deeds. "They will feel a slight skip, and start asking questions."

"First;" Citrosine hummed, unable to control her heartbeats, as much as she tried to measure her breaths, "I love you, too! I don't believe I had told you outright yet." She kissed him again, not so lingering this time, yet full of love. Tyre let a smile overtake his eyes, and squeezed Citrosine against his chest. Citrosine looked up at his face, breathing in his scent. She stared into his eyes and saw that there was still something behind them—was it worry? Pain? Pretending that she hadn't seen it, she snatched up his hand.

"Tyre, I will not die on that hell of a beach. As much as your subconscious mind wishes it upon me...I will hold on for as long as I can. I want to fulfill that other vision. We can be together as long as you'd like." She kissed his neck gently, working her way up his jaw until their lips could share one more soft, sweet kiss. She was relieved that time was stopped.

"I would like to spend my life with you," he replied, more reflectively. Citrosine studied that twinge of worry she saw for a moment longer, and then was overcome with intoxicating love and had no choice but to stop seeing anything sad through her rosy-tinted vision.

"And I would like that," she agreed, hearing her voice catch while her moist eyes looked at him with all the love she had ever known, before the moment had to end.

Citrosine shuddered, thinking of the Shadow Elves and their manipulations of time, and summoned her magic. The sound of a nearby night-bird pierced her thoughts, and it was obvious that time had begun motion once more.

"You ought to go find your family," Tyre suggested. Citrosine groaned loudly, making Tyre chuckle, then shook her head quickly.

"No. In elapsed time, we have only been here for...a quarter hour? They won't mind. I think it'd be better for me to wait here for them, anyway; I wouldn't know where to look inside, or who they might be standing behind." She sent out a tendril of magic, and was amazed by the concentration of magic present in the Dining Hall.

"Would you like to strike up a conversation with that Dark Elf, Pherkue?" Tyre asked quickly, a note of irritation coloring his thoughts.

"Eh?" Citrosine didn't recall the name, her giddiness still controlling her.

"The Dark Elf that charmed all the women and girls earlier."

"No; he might cast some kind of entrancement over me," she giggled, an irrepressible action at this point.

"Then I suggest you pretend to be asleep. I can hear his intention to speak to us, and his footsteps are approaching." Tyre cradled Citrosine in his arms as she snuck one fleeting look over her shoulder, and, sure enough, there was Pherkue. She closed her eyes and leaned on Tyre's shoulder, inhaling his fragrance and becoming bound to it. It was something between crushed, smoky, autumn leaves and sweet apples, and had to be the most beautiful scent Citrosine knew.

"Hello, there," Tyre called out. The approaching footsteps slowed.

"Hello," Pherkue replied uncertainly. "Are you a Fall Elf?"

"A blind descendent of one—I am of the Stone Tribe Council, sir." Tyre said coolly.

"Ah... Well, excuse my unusually sociable manners for my kind, but I am of the villainous Shadow Tribe," the Dark Elf returned.

"An unfair stereotype, sir," Tyre replied politely.

Pherkue's footsteps stopped as he reached the pair. Citrosine sensed his eyes on her, and her heart skipped a beat. There was definitely some kind of unwarranted charm infused in this boy's presence. She shifted in her pseudo-sleep and wrapped her arms more prominently around Tyre's body, as if he were her stuffed toy.

"That girl," Pherkue said softly, "is she yours?"

Tyre chuckled. "After a fashion, yes. She fell asleep, and I'm guarding her," he said jokingly. Citrosine felt Tyre's fingertips stroke her arm lovingly, and she felt a wave of resentment for Pherkue's charm, trying to take her love away from this; this new feeling that was genuine and miraculous. How was it fair that such a false feeling should even try to compete with the genuine connection she felt to Tyre?

Pherkue laughed. His laugh…it was like the smooth trickle of water over sea glass… *No,* Citrosine scolded, *no, don't pay attention to him. You are sitting in the lap of the perfect. Do not give in to the lie…It is evil.*

"I understand," he chuckled. "I presume that you knew her before you took it upon yourself to let her sleep upon you?"

"Yes, you are correct," Tyre said, laughing lightly. "We are close, very close indeed." Tyre stroked Citrosine's hair delicately, and she reacted with a sleepy smile.

"Ah, I wish that I could have a relationship that was so genuine," Pherkue remarked. "My tribe is unfortunate in love, I must admit…but forgive me, this is unfit speak for a conversation between two strangers!"

"Forgiven easily, friend." Citrosine admired Tyre's unaffected tone. "I heard your plea to Leader earlier, and am sorry for your state of affairs."

Pherkue took a moment to answer. "Thank you, sir." Perhaps he blushed? Citrosine fought to stay still. "You say you are of the Council here?" Pherkue continued. "You seem very young—you must be either extremely gifted in powers or friends."

"Thank you, sir…I am very honored to be our youngest member, and the elder men were quite kind to allow me in." Tyre's modesty was seemingly genuine, although Citrosine knew of the rift between he and Leader.

Pherkue got to his point. "As kind as this meeting has been, I must reveal the initial reason of my approach. I wonder if you've seen—I apologize—if you know the whereabouts of my uncle—Egan, another of my tribe?"

"I'm sorry, no." A tiny note in Tyre's voice seemed grateful for Pherkue's apology on his small misuse of the word "see".

Citrosine wondered how many times she had made the same mistake...

"Ah. Well...I don't suppose, also, that you realized a little...shift in the flow of time?"

"No, sir," Tyre managed to say smoothly.

"It may have been just one of my own tribe—in fact; Egan may have stopped time in order to gather more of your fantastic raspberry wine, eh?"

Tyre laughed. This sound made Citrosine's insides dance warmly, more so than the flutter that Pherkue's charms caused.

"You don't happen to know which way a supply of wine might be, do you?"

"For your uncle or yourself?"

Pherkue chuckled again, a velvety-smooth sound that would have been pleasing if Citrosine did not know its source.

"The building behind the main hall houses such beverages...it is to your left."

"Thank you, sir—my, you have a remarkable sense of your surroundings for a blind man."

"My thanks, sir."

"Well, I must be on my way. What did you say your name was?"

"I didn't—but it is Tyresias. It was nice to have met you... Pherkue, is it?"

"Yes—wonderful making your acquaintance, as well." The footsteps proceeded back on their way, in the same direction that they had been going. Citrosine opened one eye, and saw Pherkue's back retreat, turn a corner and vanish.

"That was interesting," she mused, trying not to snarl and send curses flying after the Shadow Elf.

"Did he charm you?"

"I don't think he did it intentionally, but yes," she admitted. Tyre scowled.

"Those Dark Elves," he muttered, and Citrosine cocked her head.

"What?"

"I've heard that, at certain ages, the males take on that ability whether they wish it or not. I believe it is a charm cast by the fathers...They can't help who they entrance, be it girl, woman, or witch."

"Be that as it may, I must say that I know who is the most captivating being of all; one much more enchanting than he," Citrosine whispered directly into Tyre's ear. She saw the raised bumps that appeared on his skin and suppressed a giggle.

"I am most sure that you do not," Tyre whispered back, eyes closed and absolutely serious, "for the only creature who could be the *most* captivating is this beautiful one I have fallen so hopelessly for—and I know that Pherkue has seen it, as well." Citrosine almost regretted wanting to laugh at Tyre's reaction to her whisper, because now she echoed that reaction tenfold—her skin prickled all over, from arms to legs...and all in between.

"Surely you aren't jealous of Pherkue, sir?" Citrosine prodded. Her voice spoke lightly, as if in jest, but her eyes asked this question in utmost solemnity.

"As long as you keep kissing me as you were, then I would encourage him to find someone like you, for his own sake," he winked, squeezing her waist again.

Citrosine laughed out loud.

"Is that Gya I hear?"

Citrosine looked behind her. Sure enough, Gya and Tie were just coming out of the Dining Hall. Gya stopped to pick Tie up onto his shoulders again, and Citrosine took the moment to turn and kiss Tyre's cheek, enjoyably catching him off-guard.

"I'm going to go with them now," she said reluctantly. Tyre nodded thoughtfully to himself.

"I will see you some other time, then," Tyre agreed, equally as grudgingly. He stroked her cheek one last time, just before she jumped up and bounced off to her family. Gya called out a hello to Tyre, and he waved weakly in reply in Gya's direction, his fingers still warm of Citrosine's skin, as if some godly electricity had run though his body.

The three Nakisses made their way off to Gya's room to stay until the next morning. It had grown too dark to risk venturing through the forest again. Citrosine smirked when Gya mentioned this hazard. *Yes, who knows, we might have to walk through the dark—heaven forbid!*

"So, Citra," Tie opened as they were dressing for bed, using a childhood nickname, "who was that boy you sat with—or rather, upon—for the entire night? You must like him very much to be so forward with him in public. I'm surprised that Dada didn't even notice!"

Citrosine blushed behind her changing screen. "His name is Tyre, and he is on the Council with Dada. I met him when we last came. We are...very much in love." That seemed like such an understatement! How could she begin to explain the depth of what she felt for Tyre? It was as Tyre said, as if they were soul mates, created and placed in this world just to be perfect together.

"He is blind," Citrosine added, "but incredibly talented in his magic, so he may as well not be. There was even a moment when he managed to meet my eyes!" She stepped out into the room and shook out her hair.

"He is handsome," Tie remarked as she folded down her blankets, "and seems quite nice. Would you marry him?" she asked, looking up excitedly.

"I would do it today," Citrosine sparkled, "with no reservations!" She and her sister giggled, and Citrosine sent her a memory of Tyre's luminous face, and they went to sleep in amber happiness.

Tyre sat long after everyone had dispersed from the courtyard, and the night grew steadily colder. Still he did not move, replaying visions of his best and only friend, his love, his only, being killed by an unstoppable force and finally collapsing on a beach in a distant land…

He was spelled by her—how could he ever bear to lose her? It was hard enough to let the stunning girl leave him to be with her family, letting her angelic heart leave him alone here. Her name floated through his mind…Citrosine Nakiss…he could even feel her kisses coming from the end of her name!

There was so much that had happened in the last few weeks. From the first moment that he had encountered Citrosine, he had been irrevocably and unequivocally in love. Whenever he thought of her, his body was energized, his thoughts went fluttering around his mind. She was the only one, he felt, that he could ever feel this way about. He would give the world to her, if she would only stay with him. The morning after he'd seen Dariya, that morning had been so golden! He'd awoken to a known, inevitable *fact*, proven by a vision, that he *would* marry Citrosine Nakiss, who had made him feel that morning as if he were to split into bits of starlight. Could there be anything in the world that could be more perfect?

So what of the future? The imminent? The inevitable? He had distracted Citrosine from it with hope, but the darkest vision he'd ever seen had negated all the pleasure that could be possible. He would have no more reason to live if she died that way, alone, poisoned, leaving him no way to protect her, and with no way to protect that little angel: Dariya. What if she never got to exist? He already felt so attached to the very idea of her tiny hands, eyes, and smile. Even though it would be centuries until he and Citrosine would be able to have a child, physically…he knew that Citrosine didn't have that long. She would die in approximately fifty years. He knew this absolutely. His visions were never wrong, none had ever been wrong, save now for Dariya's future.

Of course he could not tell her this. Not only would it destroy the rest of the time that she did have, but he physically *could not say it*. It had been all he could manage to show her the vision itself; he could not put words along with it, the other bits of knowledge he'd acquired along with it. She would be chased, hunted, by something familiar and terrifying, which would turn on her at this last moment. She would die alone in a foreign place where she had never been allowed to go; she would see a false image of Tyre himself, conjured by her dying mind. In her last moments, Dream-Tyre would turn his back on her, walking away, making her feel rejected; as if Tyre had been okay with her dying all along. This was the part that pained him the most. Citrosine would die thinking that he was leaving her alone, that he did not love her enough to be with her in her last moment.

Though he knew it had to happen, he did not want her last memory of him to be like this. She would be misled, and die in misery.

Tyresias felt as if he was back in the past two centuries, back in the demons' lair in the south when he had been tortured for venturing in too closely on research business for the Council, when they had burned the nerves in his eyes away. Such was the physical pain he felt when he faced the thought of Citrosine's death, he compared it to this other pain, this dark, unprecedented agony he had suffered for years and years, finally resulting in blindness. If he lost Citrosine, it would be the same—he would never be whole again. He would feel torturous anguish for the rest of his life, resulting in a broken man unable to go on…for he simply could not live while she was not alive. He knew it, had known it when he had learned of Dariya. Without Citrosine, there was no purpose for his life.

This must not happen, he thought. *I must not let her die this way.* But there was nothing he could think of that could stop it. *What can I do? There must be a way to avoid such a fate!*

He remained on the cold stone, and he heard the flapping of wings pass nearby: a bat, returning home after a hunt, most likely. A strong wind blew, stirring the fallen leaves around him. He did not hear leaves skittering across the flagstone grounds; he heard a life being pulled and pushed away through time and forever, carried impossibly far until life was not bearable for those who had loved it.

And then, all too soon, the next horrifying vision came.

The absolute worst thing that could possibly happen was to happen.

Tomorrow night.

SEVEN

A LAST VENTURE

"I've just received a letter from Leader. It states that we must be ready to leave from Haerthor in two days." Gya's voice trembled, and Tie and Citrosine listened in sadness. They had safely returned home from the city, in an uneventful journey through the previously foreboding, now empty and harmless, forest.

Gya continued. "We will be provided with two Changeling-horses, and it will only be a day's journey to the coast. Make sure you have all that you would miss. I shall go prepare dinner, girls." He trudged away slowly, grief obvious.

"Citrosine, will you show me some pretty enchantments?" Tie tugged her sister's belt and looked up with her round, brown eyes, trying to look more innocent than she felt.

"Of course," Citrosine replied, and they strolled outside. Citrosine knelt in the grass, and tried to think of what she should show her sister. Then, she was struck with a brilliant idea.

First she created a luminous garden of blue and purple flowers. Tie ran through them gleefully. Next came a canopy of ivy and flowering trees. Petals and shimmering powder rained down gracefully. They fell in Tie's hair, making her look like a tiny Faerie. Citrosine thought for a moment, and then added in a small waterfall and some Nymphs. Finally, she struggled to create a unicorn that Tie could sit upon and ride swiftly around with. Tie was overjoyed, and looked at her sister in amazement. Citrosine smiled modestly, and then stepped back to take a better look at her work.

At first, she was shocked to see how real it all looked, and then her heart deflated when she saw Gya gawking at the scene from the window. She cursed silently; Gya hadn't known how strong her magic had become! Citrosine caught Gya looking at her questioningly, and she beamed. He smiled at her proudly, and she shrugged, as if to say, *I'm just as amazed as you!*

Internally, though, she was so relieved! It was so suspiciously convenient how all of the memories her father had of the Jygul's Blessing had simply disappeared. Citrosine still had a hard time believing it, expecting Gya to throw her out of the house any day now. Even though she had been inside his mind herself, she was not convinced.

Her father could have suspected so much more than the fact that her magic had simply come out of hiding, and all he did was lean back inside, grinning.

She collapsed on her back into the cool grass, and watched Tie laugh and smile until the scene finally faded away, and the yard was restored to its original appearance.

Tie fell back in the long, wet grass, and sighed. She folded her arms behind her head and watched the darkening sky. She had to relish these next few weeks with her father and sister, until the circumstances arose for her now nearly-complete plan to be set into action. *The plan…* She closed her eyes tightly. *No. The time to back out has now passed.* Her eyes flew open suddenly. Was this really what she needed to do? The first part of Leenka's mystery had been solved, but…was it really an evil solution that was shrouded within the second? She closed her eyes again, and gathered together all of the small reserve of magic she could, trying to remember back in time to what she might have forgotten…

Her eyes flew open. It was clear now. She remembered every word. And every word needed to remain a secret, until the time was right.

Her plan would take action as soon as possible, just as soon as she reached Ilthen. *Sea Tribe,* she laughed darkly. *Poor Dada.*

"Palgirtie?" Citrosine called. Tie sat up on one shoulder, and said, "Mm?"

"Do you want to see a *very interesting* magic trick?" Citrosine's voice was lilting and mysterious. She sidled up to Tie with all the grace of a landing falcon, and pulled her up off the grass by her fingertips. Tie forgot about her secret plan momentarily, and smiled devilishly. *Curse my sister's smile,* she giggled, knowing that Citrosine would have a very good trick planned if she was this excited.

"Of course," she answered slyly. Citrosine beamed, and then remembered her secret, mischievous-looking smile, looking like a conspirator of some dirty trick. Holding Tie's hand, she led her around the house, and they sat atop the boulder that guarded the cellar. Tie's face turned sour as she saw the scratches all around them embedded in the rock, but she looked at Citrosine's face and had to smile. *It isn't time yet,* Tie reminded herself. *I must make myself content…*

"Close your eyes," Citrosine said, crossing her legs and holding both of her sister's hands. Tie did as she was told, but took a quick peek from under her lashes. Citrosine's eyes were closed, as well.

"Concentrate...*focus your magic*..." Citrosine smiled faintly. Tie wouldn't need any magic at all—Citrosine's own would make up more than enough for the both of them. "Feel your spirit lightening..." She paused, as the magic was already working now. "Now," she ended in a dramatic whisper, "open your eyes."

Tie opened her eyes, and shrieked. They were still sitting cross-legged, holding hands, though the boulder, and the rest of the world, was far below them. They were hovering in midair. Tie squealed with delight, unable to make out the shape of individual grass blades.

She let go of her sister's hands carefully, and still she hovered. She stretched out her legs and arms, so she was spread-eagled in the middle of the air. Waving her limbs, she found she could move around, as if swimming. Citrosine laughed. Tie's movements were slow and haphazard, so she decided to help her along.

Tie started traveling in a large circle, not of her own accord, but Citrosine's. She giggled and laughed while looking down at the trees and animals below. It was beautiful.

Citrosine followed the same path, but more slowly. She saw the same clearing, she imagined, that she had fled to that night she was so depressed. Now sunlight filtered down into it through thin-leaved trees, and pooled onto the petals of blue, gold, and black flowers, and even a small pond that, thankfully, Citrosine had avoided falling into on that hellish evening.

Presently, a young Changeling was practicing its shape-shifting while studying its reflection in the pond. It went from a Man to a small Dragon, from a rabbit to an ant, and then from an extremely attractive Elf girl to a large black figure of whose nature Citrosine could only guess at. It appeared to be a Wampyre, but it could easily have been a demon of some sort. Whatever the beast was, it sent shivers through Citrosine's dark blood.

When Tie and Citrosine finished their revolution around their dwelling and the accompanying land, they slowly dropped back onto the grass. The sun was just setting, and they watched it from atop the aged, scratched boulder.

"Citrosine," Tie said softly, her voice quivering, "Thank you for that. It was...gorgeous." She looked up at her sister with her brown eyes wide in admiration.

"Oh, you are most welcome," Citrosine replied. She was suddenly struck by how much Tie resembled Leenka. Tie heard this thought inside her sister's mind, and her eyes overflowed. Citrosine hugged her, thinking that the tears were just from how splendid the spells had been. She had to admit, they were the most magnificent she had ever imagined magic could be. The two spells had actually quite tired her. They were the largest that she had performed yet. The Elf took a deep breath.

"We ought to return inside," she said thoughtfully. "Father might have been looking for us—ay! Palgirtie," she added quickly, "unless he asks, can this be a little bit of a secret between us, as sisters?" She looked at Tie with sincerity. Gya had seen some of her stronger powers, but Citrosine felt that this was not the time to show off.

"Yes, sister—unless he asks." Tie nodded obediently, and bounded off.

During dinner that night, Gya kept making remarks about Citrosine's spells that afternoon.

"I didn't know that you were so powerful already," he said in one instance. "Did you inherit that Nymph blood, after all?"

"No, Dada; well, I don't know. I might have," Citrosine replied, with a modest smile adhered to her face.

"I wouldn't have been able to do that at your age, *lissa*," he kept on. Citrosine nodded, and focused her attention on her plate, where she proceeded to poke the meat upon it with her fork.

Tie looked back and forth between them, and suspected that something was off. Citrosine never took her eyes off her plate for more than a fleeting moment, and usually ate what was to be expected of a growing young woman. But recently, she had appeared to be daydreaming, and had hardly touched anything on her plate. Now, she said almost nothing, and Tie wondered if she was hiding something. She was surprised that Gya sensed nothing wrong; but, then, he would never suspect his daughters of any wrongdoings. What could be on her sister's mind? That boy she was with earlier? Moving to a new home? Gya pestering her about her budding magic powers? *That would really bother me,* Tie reasoned.

"So, Citrosine," she broke in to break up the monotony, "tell us about Tyre!"

Citrosine looked up across the table piercingly, color rising in her cheeks.

"Yes," echoed her father earnestly. "How is it between you two?"

Most eloquently and with the most information she could muster, Citrosine answered, "Er." What did they want to know? She couldn't easily just tell them about the prophecies. Gya would lose his wits if she told him that she knew she was going to die, much to the same degree that he would if she spoke of having a child.

"We are wonderful…" she elaborated vaguely. "Erm… and we were thinking of staying together for a while…" She glanced meekly up through her lashes. As expected, Gya was caught off-guard.

"In what way? Staying together?"

"We'd like to continue our relationship…we are in love, Dada." Citrosine blushed.

"Have you spoken of marrying?" His fork was hovering a hair's breadth from his mouth.

How should she answer? They had not *spoken* of marriage, but they *knew* they would be married. At least if... She didn't follow the thought.

"Somewhat. We would like to consider it someday."

Gya nodded, stroking his beard and abandoning the fork. "Is it in *your* mind to marry Tyresias?" He did not see how Citrosine's heart exploded into sparkles in reply.

"Yes." She blushed harder. "I love him very much...I do not understand how it could happen in just a few meetings as it has, but...I know it plainly." She considered for a moment. "I love him more definitely than I have ever known anything." Gya looked into his daughter's eyes. Citrosine imagined that he saw the sparkles erupting and shimmering up into the shine of her dampening eyes. After a moment, Gya broke from a slight trance.

"Then that is enough. When you speak of this to him someday, you have my promise behind your own. I will let you marry him, should you as a couple agree to it." His words were soft, plush. Gya reached over and took Citrosine's hand tenderly.

"Thank you, Father." She could have sung! But still, with all the wonderful emotion she felt, the overshadowing of Tyre's prophecy hung like a thunderhead perturbing her euphoria... and it was all she could do to whisper and hold back tears.

Palgirtie sat and watched the proceedings.

As dinner was finished, Citrosine started a new conversation.

"Since tomorrow is our last day here, why don't we do something special?" There was an innocent question in her eyes, and Tie's suspicions were abated for the time being.

"That's a very nice idea, Citrosine," Gya agreed. "Do you have any ideas of what we should do?" He was too busy stacking up the plates in a box to see her bite her lip.

"We could…go for a stroll…?" She calculated a thoughtful pause. "What if we spent the night outside tonight, and then… we could walk to…er… Actually, I can't think of a place to go, but…" she stopped. "…never mind."

"No, *lissa,* that's all right. Maybe we will discover a new place, in our last travel of this homeland." Gya brushed his daughter's hair away from her face. "All in favor of Citrosine's proposal, say 'aye'?" he added in a businesslike tambour.

"Aye," Tie said enthusiastically.

"Aye," Gya seconded, chuckling.

"Opposed? None! Splendid," Gya concluded, "we shall pack up some provisions and have a last night of journey. Let us pack some bedding, girls. It's getting dark." He smiled rakishly, as if to say, *But we do not care about light; we're in the rough life now.*

The nighttime outdoor trek was quite uneventful, except for the fact that Citrosine gently guided them in the direction of the small clearing. She was almost certain that Gya had never seen it before, as it was so beautiful that he would have mentioned it, or told them stories about it. They walked leisurely without fear, aided by two luminescent orbs Gya and Citrosine carried.

When they reached the clearing, Citrosine purposely extinguished her light.

"Oops," Gya remarked, "maybe we should stop here. Getting tired, Citrosine, *lissa?*" Citrosine shook her head, looking like Tie, but Gya smirked. "Let's camp out here, what do you say?"

"Great," Tie said, as she tried to distinguish where exactly they were. With no luck in the darkening night, she sat down and unloaded the small bag she'd been carrying. She pulled out a pillow and blanket, and sat on them protectively.

Gya and Citrosine followed suit, and by then, they were all reasonably tired enough to sleep. Again, after a time of feigning sleep, Citrosine reached into her father's mind. She fought images of the recent past, and reached an overwhelming sense of fear.

Images of Leenka, Leader, Haerthor, the Dark Elves, a host of Men, and a field consumed by fire flew through his mind. He was afraid of what was to come, and of the past. Citrosine quickly recoiled. The future couldn't bring anything pleasurable if her own father was more afraid than she.

In hopes of finding something more cheerful to think of, she delved into Tie's mind. Well, she attempted to do so.

She was quickly met by a solid barrier. She pressed on it tentatively, but it showed no resistance. *What could Tie bear inside that is so secret?* She pushed on the barrier with as much force as would not wake her, but it held strong. *Hmm.* Well, Citrosine wasn't about to spend the whole night trying to figure that out.

"Citrosine!"

About halfway through the night, Citrosine sat up, wide awake. She had just experienced a feeling of sheer and utter loss, after a dream with images of menacing shadows racing through darkness. She'd heard her name, called out hysterically, in longing and despair. This was the most saddening, ghastly sound that she'd ever heard, multiplied by the power of words and dreams.

Her stomach was cold, and she was shaking all over. She felt as if everyone in the world had suddenly just disappeared, taken away from her by an invisible, massive hand. She felt as if she was standing, alone, in the center of a large, gray infinity, where nothing would ever make any sound, or change at all, and she was the only figure on it.

However, now, time was still in motion.

Citrosine stood, and walked around in a large circle, around the fringe of the clearing. She made sure that she knew where the pond was, as she didn't want to try and fall asleep wet.

She hummed to herself, thought of happy memories, and even conjured magicked images of Leenka, Gya, Tie, and Tyre. They walked around with her, but said nothing. Still she could not shake the feeling that she was utterly alone. Her stomach quivered as if she would vomit. Three times she knelt in nausea and pain, willing herself not to vomit and awaken her family. Something had gone amiss. Something in the very recent past had been lost forever. But *what was it?*

An idea began twisting through her head. Maybe she could try out her all-seeing vision skills, and try to look into time and see what had happened; figure out what exactly she had lost.

Every Elf, according to legend, had the power to travel the length of time and see things yet to come. Supposedly, it was something they were born able to do—to a point—much like their ability to communicate through thought. This was powerful magic, however, and difficult to bring about. It could also be dangerous: countless stories told of greedy creatures that looked to see the future, and then feared what was to come for the rest of their lives, thus dying miserable and lonely.

She sat next to the lightly lapping water at the bank of the pond. She closed her eyes, crossed her legs, and tried to empty her mind. She must let go of the sound of the water, of the insects, of the night-creatures, of her father and sister's gentle breathing, of her own racing heart, and of the frightened thoughts skittering through her mind.

Emptiness…selflessness…anonymity…

Yes! It was working! Citrosine caught herself rejoicing at her powers and thus lost the empty sensation. She refocused, returning to the selfless state that she had just achieved. She reached into herself…

She was racing along a stream of black, frothy matter. She couldn't tell what it was; she only knew that she was not in her body anymore, as it was a faint outline of mist below her. There was a pull in her mind, and she felt a sensation of being sucked into the dark matter. She couldn't dwell here too long, she knew, else her mind could be separated from her body, lost in a separate time forever.

She saw the dark, bubbling stuff melding and twisting into itself, yet she still flew along beside it, following its every move. Suddenly, the ribbon of whatever it was doubled back into its previous path, and she was aware of herself diving directly into it. Then, it was no longer a liquid-like stream, but a cloud.

She twisted and spun around within the cloud, all visibility ceasing momentarily. She was not afraid. Only her spirit was here, dancing through the stuff of time, and not her physical body, her worries, or her conscience.

Another pull brought her downwards from the cloud as she focused on finding the cause of her feelings of loss.

She was in the center of a large sandy area, where hundreds of Elves were all gathered. Every tribe was represented, and almost everyone held at least one overstuffed sack—clothes, papers, armor. She flitted over the beach, as it was apparent to her close-to-omniscient mind that there was more to see than this.

Now she was hovering over a large dock of some sort, where an enormous boat was waiting. This boat was already heaving with bags and sacks of varying sizes. Out of some leaked seeds; others revealed food or clothes. Many crates were neatly tucked under one another, and within these were sheaves upon sheaves of paper.

The deck of the boat was teeming with all the Elves from the field. She rushed with a breeze to the very rear of the boat, and she saw a young girl leaning over the rail. The girl turned, and revealed herself to be Citrosine from another time. She appeared to be the same age, but obviously she was in a slightly different instance. Citrosine reasoned that this was somewhere in the near future, for she could not remember this image in her recent past. She must have followed the bubbling black river in the wrong direction. The older Citrosine was crying, and she looked right up to from where the present spirit of her own past was watching. She clutched an opened letter, and her cheek was red with hot, dancing finger marks across it.

The vision grew blurry, and Citrosine's spirit receded further and further away. The image of her sorrowful face remained crystal clear, until the vision was completely out of reach.

Now she was receding through the black time river again. There was nothing else, just this flowing, writhing stream. However, now the spirit was rushing the opposite direction as the stream; she was moving backwards again, back to the present.

With a jolt, she leapt back into her body.

Citrosine kept her eyes closed as a shudder ran through every part of her body, as her spirit reacquainted with it. First there was a tingling in her feet, a tremor through her legs, up to her waist, a shiver up her chest and spine; her fingers trembled, her arms shook, her shoulders hunched, her neck was whispered upon as if by a small breeze, and then even her hair stirred. She opened her eyes suddenly.

It was nearly dawn. She could have sworn that it was hardly twilight when she had first begun her time-excursion. She figured that she had just lost at least six hours. What a way to spend the night!

Although…strangely, she felt completely rested now. She stood swiftly, feeling no fatigue whatsoever—no longer nauseous, no longer aching in restlessness. Even though she'd learned nothing of the loss, her body had healed. She turned away from the woods, and toward where she and her family had set up their sleeping arrangements.

She was startled to see Gya sitting up, fully dressed, and watching her. He breathed a visible sigh of relief. Citrosine walked quickly over to him, and sat beside him hesitantly.

"*Se lissa*, I was worried about you, Citrosine," he said as he squeezed her tightly. She looked up at him.

"*Why, sir?*" He looked down at her surprised.

"*You are calling me sir?*"

"*Am I in trouble?*" Citrosine smiled sheepishly in the creeping light.

"*Well, I knew that you had never tried to see time, and I didn't know if you knew how to get back safely. I was worried... if I had bothered or wakened your physical body, you would not have been able to return to it, for it would not be exactly as you left it. Remember this, if you ever try to see through time again: guard your body.*" Gya kissed her forehead tenderly. "*I thank Ghersah that you did. You are not in trouble, lissa;*" he squeezed her again, "*but I marvel at your strength...I have never been able to keep up a quarter of a day flying through time. Fly through time for too long and you will not have the strength to return!*"

"*Sorry to worry you.*"

"*Forgiven.*" He smiled at her, showing only a hint of sadness.

"*How long have you been waiting for me?*"

Gya shifted, and replied in false calmness, "*Two hours.*"

"*I'm sorry that I kept you waiting for so long. I didn't even realize all the time that I'd lost. It felt like only minutes,*" she said sincerely, as the images that she'd seen flitting through her father's mind in his dreams came back to memory. She had just created another worry for him.

"*That is perfectly fine, lissa. By the way...*" he paused.

"*Dada?*"

"*Rathka lya messi me noa?*" This Citrosine knew from Old Elvish—it was one of the few kinds of phrases that she could interpret. *How did you get so powerful all of a sudden?* This phrase was common in almost all of the legends involving the

Dark Elves, Jygul, and such—did that mean that Citrosine would become a villain?

"*I think…*" she hesitated carefully, "*I think that it was the Nymph blood you warned me to be aware of. It has budded up very quickly, no?*"

"It has indeed, it has." He got a puzzled look on his face. "*But nothing bad has come of it?*"

"*Of course not,*" she lied smoothly. She hated not being able to tell him what she had really been through, but she knew that gaining Jygul's Blessing was the one thing that would make her father angry enough to expel her from his family.

"*Wonderful, Citrosine; I'm prouder than you know. You have become full of such beautiful, light magic, just like your mother, daughter of an Air Elf…bloodline of the great Ghersah…*"

"*Thank you.*" Her stomach lurched. *If you only knew…*

They shared another embrace, and sat beside the pond, where the sunrise began reflecting. The sun rose gently, sending lazy beams first over the horizon and then the tree line. The sleepy orb climbed higher and higher, like a butterfly whose wings are not quite dried out yet, and so cannot fly. It crept across the leaf it was perched on, and with every step it illuminated a new vein or dewdrop. The dewdrops themselves winked back at the sky, which was being dreamily painted a light orange, green, and finally a blazing, cloudless blue, as if the day was dressing up in its best garb to see all the creatures out of the Big Lands that the communities dwelling within had lovingly inhabited for eons.

Tie stirred, and woke slowly.

"What have I missed?" she asked blearily.

"Nothing all too important," Gya said with a wink.

Gya started a small, controlled flame over which he laid a pan filled with pheasant eggs he brought on their journey from home. As they cooked, and Citrosine told her little sister about her experience of seeing a future time, Gya took a better look around at where they had stopped. He took in the golden flowers, the glistening pond, the lush, mossy trees, and the evidence of a group of Changelings. He swallowed forcefully.

"Come, girls; the eggs are ready!" Gya called his daughters over to the fire, where they sat gratefully, and accepted the plates of steaming yellow eggs.

"Thank you, Dada," they replied in inadvertent unison.

"You are both very welcome," he chuckled. The eggs had turned out perfectly, even though Gya's mind had been elsewhere.

"Isn't this place so beautiful?" Tie asked no one in particular.

"It most certainly is," Gya said distantly. Citrosine looked intently at her father's face. He was looking around nostalgically. It was almost as if…

"Dada, have you ever been here before?" she asked gingerly. Gya looked at her quickly.

"Is it that apparent?" he replied privately, bashful.

"It is glaringly obvious, begging your pardon."

"Yes, I have," he said, aloud again.

"When?"

Gya sighed. "Oh, it was a long time ago…"

"Tell us, Dada, tell us!" Tie trilled curiously.

He scratched the back of his neck. "Well, girls," he said, "your mother and I used to come here all the time. In fact, this spot is exactly where I asked her to marry me."

"Oh, tell us about it?" Citrosine asked enthusiastically.

"We called it the Bailey of Lost Beauty, because it reminded us of an overgrown courtyard, a bailey, perfectly flat, you see, and the first few times we tried to find it again, we got completely lost." He smiled reminiscently, his head nodding as his eyes wandered across the clearing.

"Wow," Tie breathed. "It's the most beautiful place to ever see in this sunlight."

"It is indeed," Gya agreed. "We were married here later. These trees around us were flowering that season, and your mother looked angelic, with the petals falling around her..."

Tie, unsuspecting of her father's loneliness, asked in excitement, "How did you propose marriage to her?"

Gya flinched. He took a few breaths, and swallowed. "Well, we had met properly for the first time here, and it became our secret place. We'd spend hours upon hours here, since it was so removed from everything, and we could forget the rest of the world. We had many talks here, and many wonderful times...

"On the day I asked for her hand, we were sitting right over there by the pond, dipping our toes in the water, and I took a few moments to watch her instead of the clearing around us. These golden flowers were blooming all around her, and there were golden leaves in her hair. It all made her glow, so luminous and beautiful. She looked so young then, knew nothing of war or darkness...I just looked at her for a while, and I felt as if she was the only thing in the world that would ever make me happy, and I knew that I wanted to be with her forever."

"So what did you do? Did you give her a ring? What did you say?" Tie chirped.

"I didn't have anything to give her, because my mother and I made little money, and I didn't want to magic something out of thin air—she could probably do a better job of that than I, anyway.

"So, I turned to her, and took her hands," Gya took Tie's hands, demonstrating, "and I said, 'Leenka, you are the most beautiful thing on this earth that I have ever seen, and if you leave my side tonight I think I shall die.' Leenka smiled at me, and I could see all the love she had for me in that one charming smile. I said, 'Leenka, will you be my wife?'"

Tie burbled with anticipation. "Yes...*and?*"

"She smiled, not saying anything, then moved toward me as if to kiss me, but she stopped."

"Why?" Citrosine chimed in, understanding exactly how frustrating that teasing kiss would be.

"She said, 'As much as I would love to, it's a great commitment, and I don't know...' I could see by the way she was smiling that she was just trying to keep herself from leaping at me in agreement. Not very good at hiding her emotions, Leenka."

"So what did you say?" Tie asked, a little concerned, despite the fact that she knew how the story ended.

"I made a deal with her. I said, 'Fine, Leenka. You leave me no choice, so I must win you. I shall secretly place a flower in one of my hands,' and I picked a little gold flower," he demonstrated by plucking one of the flowers by his knee, "'and if you choose the hand that has the flower inside, then you have no choice but to marry me. If you choose the hand without the flower, you may go home and never think of me again, but I will surely die.'" He closed both hands, hiding which had the flower inside, and held them both out towards his daughters.

His daughters gasped, and waited. Gya let the suspense build.

"Which did she choose?" Tie exclaimed in irritation.

"She chose the flower."

"Yes!" the girls shouted in victory. They all laughed giddily.

After a moment, Tie asked, "If she had not chosen the flower, would you really have killed yourself?"

Gya turned serious. "Never. I had reasoned this out before. If the love of my life really loved me back, she would have chosen the flower—she could have used her magic, if she took my words to heart, to determine which hand to choose. If she did not make this effort, then she didn't love me enough to stay with forever, then there would be little reason for me to love her enough to stay with her forever, true?"

"Yes," Tie agreed, relieved.

"Anyway," Gya added, "that doesn't matter, because both hands had a flower inside." He opened his hands, and, sure enough, a tiny, sparkling gold flower sat in each palm.

"You cheated!" Citrosine laughed in surprise. "You fiend!"

"I had to be sure," Gya tried to explain, but he was laughing too hard.

They laughed for a long moment. Finally they calmed enough to reflect upon their lost Leenka.

They sat in silence for a while longer, enjoying what was to be their last cooked meal in the Big Lands.

Once at home again, the three Nakisses gathered the bags that had been packed for this last journey away from their dwelling in the woods. They had been instructed to leave no trace of themselves, so as soon as all their necessities were congregated, Gya asked Citrosine to help him move the boulder in the yard away from the cellar hatch. She obliged, and then the cellar was lit aflame. Gya then slung the boulder over the hole in an attempt to collapse the cellar area, subsequently smothering the remains of the fire.

They all knew what was to come next.

Gya's eyes were tearing as he set fire to the home they had all helped to build. His mind's eye saw trails of memory— each with his daughters and wife pictured—slinking away up into the sky, trails of smoke, never to be seen again and evaporating into the clouds of this place they had inhabited for so many years. The tranquil family members bowed their heads in respect to all that they had just lost. After the moment of silence had passed, they set out for Haerthor.

They would never forget this place.

(Note: The area around where the boulder fell through the hollow ground left a circular hole in which the beginning of Tie's

later evil surfaced; she had cast every small charm and spell she knew of around that cellar, trying to discover what had happened to Leenka. Thoughts of hatred were cast into that spot as she dredged up any memories she could find of what had taken place that unnaturally stormy night. She had paced around and around the boulder, leaving a trail of magic behind in every step. When the boulder collapsed through the cellar, the ground eventually came back normally, with grass as found throughout the rest of the area.

The circular path she walked, however, so corrupted by Tie's intended evil magic, only ever sports wiry dark grass, and anything ever placed inside it, including sticks, rocks, seeds, et cetera, is absorbed into the trail of magic left behind and swallowed into the ground in a matter of minutes. This area has become known as the Devil's Tramping Ground, near Siler City, North Carolina.)

Eight

Formless

Through *Bixoel* Forest, Citrosine thought that perhaps the spirits of the forest itself sensed changes coming, as it allowed for filters of sunlight to arc down from the intertwining branches, sending lacing patterns along the unusually consistent ground. Birds chirped, insects hummed, and the normal sense of hostility had evaporated. Citrosine watched the motes of dust and organic particles swirl around and around in a dance of farewell in the slanted shafts of golden light.

It took less than a quarter of an hour to get through the forest, and it was refreshing, more so than a walk through a natural wood. Perhaps Jygul the Dark Goddess had relinquished her hold on the spirits of the forest. Perhaps, Citrosine reasoned, Jygul, wherever she was now, had realized that it was time to let go of the evil of her creation in this land, realized that Ilthen's time was dawning—it was to be a time of new life, new beginnings, time to get rid of evil grudges… perhaps this time of departure was recognized even by the beings that looked down on the world?

When the three reached the area where the gate to Haerthor had been, they were not in the least taken aback to see charred scars along the ground where the evidence had been removed.

What they were surprised to see, however, was the absence of Haerthor altogether. Had they not just seen it in full glory days before? Now, all that remained before them was a massive stone courtyard, and many, many Elves and horses scattered throughout. Leader rushed up to greet them as soon as they stepped onto the stone court, his scar whitened in contrast to his perspiring face.

He shook Gya's hand furiously, and gave the younger two a wink. He leaned dangerously close to Gya's ear, and whispered hurriedly. Gya nodded several times, and then Leader pointed across the courtyard.

"Come, my daughters," was all Gya said, along with a gesture. They made their way across the crowded place, until they stood before two tall, muscular horses. Well, they appeared to be horses. It was obvious by their ominous size that they were Changelings shaped as horses.

"Dada," Tie began, noticing this, "Why are all these Changelings going to take us to the beach?" She looked up nervously at the two before them.

Gya chuckled, and kneeled down before her.

"Changelings, when in the form of a horse, are ten times stronger and swifter than a normal, pure, non-magical horse. They will take us to the beach faster, and, well, the Changelings are coming to the new island as well, so why shouldn't they come with us?" Tie blushed, and Gya touched her nose with his thumb.

Citrosine looked more closely at the Changelings. Their shoulders were almost level with her head, and they looked as if they would be able to carry five Elves at a time. One was in the form of a proud black horse that paced impatiently, as if ready to run since birth. The other was a bit smaller, with large pools of white hair spotting its brown coat. Its face was almost completely white, and the beast looked content just to graze all day.

Suddenly, Citrosine felt a hand touch her shoulder ever so tenderly. She looked at it, and recognized in alarm that she did not recognize it. She whirled, and her stomach did a flurry of flips and flutters. Pherkue, the Shadow Elf, was standing before her.

"They're beautiful creatures, Changelings, aren't they?" he asked pleasantly. Citrosine nodded, already becoming very afraid; she could already feel the uncontrollable attraction toward the Elf. She tried to tell herself that it was only a charm, she mustn't let it become a real attraction, but it was difficult to resist.

"Excuse me, I'm not sure that we have met properly. My name is Pherkue; I became acquainted with your Tyresias at the Stone Council's meeting...I believe you were the one sleeping in his grasp?" He smiled charmingly, making Citrosine blush.

"Yes, sir. I am Citrosine...Tyre spoke to me of your meeting. He said that you were...quite courteous." She avoided Pherkue's eyes, for the crimson irises were alluring her.

Pherkue laughed softly. "I am pleased to make your acquaintance," he said, dipping in a casual bow.

"Of course," Citrosine answered.

"Citrosine...your name is familiar...Are you related to a Stone Tribe Council member, by any chance?"

"Yes. My father—Gyardaute Nakiss, and my mother was Leenka—"

"Leenka Nakiss?" Pherkue asked quickly.

"Er...yes...she...er, disappeared recently..." Citrosine blanched.

"Oh," Pherkue cast his eyes downward stiffly. "I am sorry to, er...but I have heard such wonderful stories about her! Your family must be proud to raise her memory."

"Yes, of course we are."

Pherkue began to speak, but then seemed to remember something and stop himself.

"Is, um, is there a reason you came to speak to me, sir?" She took half a step backwards, because she was beginning to notice the honeyed smell of his breath.

"Yes, of course, my apologies," he shook his head as if to clear his thoughts, or perhaps priorities. "I can't seem to be able to find that boy, Tyre, of yours, anywhere. I was wondering; could you tell me where he might be? I need to ask him about something we discussed last we met. Perhaps...?" He trailed off, leaving Citrosine fumbling to recover her voice. His skin was so white, so smooth; she just wanted to reach out and...

"No, I'm terribly sorry," she heard herself say politely, "I haven't seen him myself. Could you use a second opinion on whatever dilemma it is of yours? May I help at all?" She opened her eyes wide, innocently. She knew that Tyre and Pherkue had had no such deep conversation as Pherkue wished to imply; after all, she had been right there, listening! She raised a thick barrier around this thought as soon as it crossed her mind.

Pherkue smiled an alluring, apologetic smile. Was he making fun of her?

"I'm sorry, no. Thank you. But, if you should happen to come across him, will you please tell him that I was calling?"

"Of course," Citrosine replied smoothly, her attraction growing steadier. She willed herself not to show him any emotion other than polite courtesy.

"Thank you." He bowed slightly, keeping his eyes firmly on hers, maintaining his little smile. Then, as he was about to depart, he seemed to reconsider, took a step toward her, and reached for her hand. With a flourish, he knelt, kissed it, and was gone.

Citrosine stood there, not quite sure of what to do. Her heart was racing excitedly, her palms sweating and head reeling. The place where he had kissed her was warm and tingling. As

Pherkue receded further and further away her heart slowed back to normal and she began to think clearly again.

*That was…quite unnerving…*she thought. *I mustn't let that happen again. What would it have been that he would want to tell Tyre, anyway? They spoke only of the Council last they met, and they seem to have never met after that…what if…oh, no…* Citrosine put her hands over her mouth, and reminded herself to show no emotion. *What if he only wanted to get me alone here? What if he was lying about looking for Tyre…Does he have some plan for me? Or has something happened to Tyre?* She shook her head vigorously, her cheeks blushing nonetheless. *Fondness is a strong emotion to try masking,* she realized then. She turned back to the oblivious Changeling-horses, whom Gya was still loading up with bags.

"Interesting fellow, that one," he remarked quietly. A smirk twisted across his face, while his attention was still focused on the tying of the bags. Citrosine blanched.

"You think so?" she asked, as emotionless as possible.

"He was definitely trying to get your attention."

"My attention? Why ever would he want to do that?"

Gya's smirk inched upwards, growing larger.

"*Da*da,"

He sighed. "*Se lissa—my love*—do you not know how beautiful you are? Even to the Shadow Elves? He was just being a little flirtatious. Anyone could tell that he was relieved you were not with Tyre." He looked off into the distance, and sighed again. Citrosine made no reply, gagging at the thought of a Shadow Elf being flirtatious, if that was really what Pherkue had been doing.

"I'd rather let Tyre take care of the flirtatious bit…" she muttered.

Her father apparently heard her, and stopped what he was doing. Citrosine blushed. "I…he…" she waffled.

"He is a wonderful boy," Gya helped her, "and I approve of the two of you seeing one another as you are." He smiled. "Honestly, I do."

"Thank you, Dada." Citrosine hugged her father quickly. "We have been talking more and more upon our Haerthor visits, and we have…fallen in love rather quickly."

"He is charming," Gya conceded.

"Exceedingly so…especially compared to Pherkue," Citrosine giggled.

Leader, at the center of the square, used a charm to amplify his voice, and cleared his throat loudly to gather the attention of all the Elves about.

"Everyone journeying to the coast may leave as soon as I am complete in delivering the following instructions. We must all board the boat for our journey *no later* than dawn. Now we shall depart, Elves aided in swift transportation by the Changelings, whom we thank greatly. If all goes well, we shall arrive at the far beach by twilight—Changelings have been instructed as to the precise location of our next meeting. Anyone who comes across any misfortunes on their way is recommended to send *some kind of signal* telling me that you need help, or will be arriving late. Otherwise, the vessel launches at sunup.

"Changelings are reminded that any misbehavior will be noted in our records and your leaders may have you punished. You will be severely punished for any harmful use of your abilities towards the Elves until everyone is accounted for *on the ship.* The same goes for Elves; this is our last day in these lands, so why not save our energy for the times ahead, for they will be hard. I wish everyone a safe and swift journey; pace yourselves, and do not overtire. May Ghersah's eye be alert in watching for your well-being. *Sahme; kre mae voga rathka si!* Farewell, and may the magic in these, our homelands, see you off gracefully!"

159

Leader's eyes shone with the excitement that welled within nearly everyone's spirits at that moment. One lone Elf girl wondered if they would all be punished for leaving their former lives behind, and had a hard time pretending to smile with everyone else. She knew that she was leaving too many things behind…and for that they would all soon be punished. *Remember never to forget…*

Gya boosted Citrosine up onto the back of the brown Changeling-horse, and then lifted Tie onto the other. He himself climbed up behind his youngest, to make sure that she was all right riding such a tall mount. The Changelings began running as soon as the three were situated. Citrosine could feel no bounces or jolts as they ran. Their hoof beats turned into the beating of her heart, a background rhythm that turned into a pleasant stream bouncing through the blurring trees and undergrowth.

The forests around the travelers became long blurs of gray, green, brown, and black. It was impossible to distinguish anything from anything else, save for other travelers riding near. The Changelings ran with insurmountable speed and grace, diverting through trees, over felled logs, under strung vines, and out of the way of any Men that might have been around. Citrosine felt the wind streaming back through her hair, and she secured her black ribbon to her belt before it was lost. The wind *did* aggravate her eyes, however, so she closed them tightly, and imagined that she was straddling the back of a giant, snakelike Dragon, high above the mountains, and through thick white clouds.

She stretched her arms high above her head, fingers stinging because they were so wide apart. She opened her eyes, tentatively, looking sideways at her fingers. They seemed to pierce the air itself, leaving behind dark gashes in the rushing winds.

After a little while longer, the initial excitement wore off and Citrosine grew restless. It was difficult to look around for amusement, as the scenery consisted only of blurs. She wondered how the Changelings could stand this all the time.

"I understand," said a dark, low voice inside Citrosine's head, *"It becomes tedious, does it not?"* The voice was layered thickly with the accent of the archaic forms of Elvish.

Citrosine started, and then realized that it was the Changeling under her speaking.

"Well, it is quite exciting," she replied cautiously, *"but I don't see how you can go through this all the time. It's so hard to see anything!"*

"Indeed," the beast agreed, *"although...that is the very reason that allows my brethren and I to evolve anew so rapidly. I may change forms at any time I wish, and change back into this of a horse sort of beast, gaining a new euphoria, because it becomes new again; not like thine own form, which thy kind is so conformed to."*

"I think I understand..." Citrosine mused. She smiled; she'd never imagined talking to a Changeling this way, but at least it passed the time. The Changeling's words were marvelous to the Elf, as she seldom heard anyone use the old terms of language any more. It wasn't Old Elvish, but a hybrid of that and the newer terminology.

"Dost thou?" The low voice was somewhat threatening, although what it said was promising enough. *"I am called Dem, if it suits thy interests. And thou...?"*

"Citrosine Nakiss,"

"Daughter of Council Member Gyardaute," Dem stated admiringly. *"Thou hast much magic for such a young thing. Pray, why?"*

"Er..." Citrosine wondered whether she could trust Dem, or if she should keep this tidbit to herself.

"Well...? My secrets shalt not slip, if thou dost worry. What soul wouldst I reveal thy life to?" Dem's head shook impatiently, and the horse's mouth gave a whinny.

"I'm sorry, I just can't let my father or sister overhear, or I'd be damned to expulsion...I just recently received a very powerful Faerie's Blessing, and it reacted with the Nymph blood passed down from my grandfather, as well as my mother's Air Elf powers, so my magic is somewhat...er...immense..."

"Intriguing," Dem considered.

There was a few moments' silence, as they passed through a colossal field. The sun was just past the apex of the sky; it was almost two hours past midday. When the field had been ridden through, they entered a thick forest. The blurs of trees ahead of them were illuminated individually by the sun, and they were easier to pick out than they had been nearer to dawn.

"What is your favorite form to take?" Citrosine wondered to Dem.

"Ah, I regret not taking as many as I can as of yet..." Dem said wistfully, and then continued. *"At this moment, I love the Wampyre, the butterfly, and the Dragon most, I speculate, although there are so many remarkable feelings..."*

"Feelings?"

"Every creature has its own way of thinking, of seeing, of hearing, of being. We pick up on these when we change forms. Suppose I attempted a conversation while in the form of...a squirrel: imagine. My voice would be higher, more fluttery, I would shift my attentions faster than prudent, definitely not speaking in coherent sentences. They are shallower and vainer creatures than one would guess."

Citrosine giggled. *"Well...is there a form that is...I don't know...natural for you? One that is your true self?"* She wondered if Dem would understand.

"Ah...She asks if I was born to a certain element; is this that kind of question?"

"Yes, I think so." Dem's language was more than a little bit confusing to Citrosine.

Dem was silent, thinking. *"There is no single core form that I can sincerely call my own, and that is the most sorrowful bit of being a Changeling. I was born as a sort of slump, dost thou permit."*

"What is a 'slump'?"

"I was a puddle of substance; changing colors, forms, every moment; just a writhing pool of unidentifiable matter. Envisage a puddle of muck being stepped in and changing accumulation and position every instance. It only took a moment or two to learn to change forms. The first one I chose to take was a falcon, so I could get a feel for where I was."

"What do you spend most of your time as?" Citrosine prompted.

"Ah, I blush, I blush!"

"'My secrets shalt not slip, if thou dost worry,'" Citrosine said, smiling as she echoed Dem's words. The tang of Old Elvish energized her.

"Ay; the senses of memory!" Dem laughed; a deep, musical noise. *"Thou shalt please not laugh; I have created my own. It is a kind of permutation of the slump that I have only once been, a Wampyre, and a mortal Man."*

"Really? That doesn't sound humiliating at all; interesting, actually."

"Yes? I seem to have come upon a partiality for the way Men think. I cannot know why...Of course, I've formed countless Elves in my time, but I inexplicably like Men better. Their thoughts are more vulnerable, easier to communicate, and even more emotional than just about any beast I've yet to suit...The Wampyre, then, lets me feel so much coolness, control. As if I had the entire universe between the tips of my fangs...And lastly the humble slump, with all its chaos, brings me a balance of excitement, for I never am the same thing twice when the slump is involved. It all seems

forwardly mad, through my eyes." Dem let a sigh pierce its thoughts. A few beats passed.

"This sounds out of the ordinary for me to ask, but I wonder…"

"Yes? What does her mind cogitate?" Dem asked curiously.

"Do you prefer male or female?" Citrosine snickered to herself.

"Hah! That is the most blunt anyone has dared to be with myself! Yes, yes…There are many differences in the sexes' feelings, thoughts, mannerisms…" Dem paused. *"To be frank, male is my regular, for the lack of inhibitions and consideration, pardoning my sharpness."*

Citrosine laughed aloud.

There was another silence. This was a long pause, and Citrosine dozed off against Dem's neck. Dem continued running, running, keeping up with its own companions, and the rest of the Elves. The Changelings never stumbled once, keeping their paces quick and graceful. Dem was glad that its kind could add these supernatural kinds of qualities to the mortal beings they became, for otherwise it would take the travelers hundreds of days to reach the boat at the opposite beach.

Dem wondered if all the Elves and Changelings from every part of the Big Lands were really coming. It—referring in such a manner, for Dem was male or female when it wished—had heard that there was only a small gathering at the meeting the king of the Elves had arranged. Either the rest of the Elves did not believe that they needed to leave, and so would most likely be left forever, or had already gotten lost or died out. *How frightening to consider whether they would be any better coming to Ilthen…*

When Citrosine awoke again, sunset was drawing nigh, and Dem was running through a red desert. She was startled to see a long blur in the ground, where there was a long gash, as if the very earth was yawning up at them.

"Dem," Citrosine asked in surprise, *"What is that canyon off to the north?"*

"Ah, to be sure, it is wonderful to hear thy voice awake. That thither…that is what the Field Elves of this area once named 'Jygul's Grin'. There is a river at the floor. Would you like to go and have a look?"

"Would you mind?"

"Not in the least. It was *dawn when our seafaring vessel was to be setting off, was it not?"*

"That's what Leader told us."

"Fine, that's just fine. We are significantly ahead of many of my counterparts, so a slight detour should put us back in pace." Dem veered off towards the long black blur, and, ever so gradually, slowed to a trot. Citrosine's head grew dizzy as everything around her came back into focus. The barren land shone red and purple as the sun plunged itself into a lethal dive toward the quickly approaching horizon. The Elf wondered how long it would be before they reached the ocean. Dem, reading her thoughts as it continued to slow, replied shortly.

"We only have another slight auxiliary to reach. It should only be a further hour or so, at most. Please accept my apologies for intruding again," it worried.

"That's all right," Citrosine breathed, thinking briefly of Tyre, as she looked down into the gorge. Just a short way down was a gaping river, twisting and sloshing angrily around the jagged turns that the canyon made. *"How deep is it?"* She asked, eyes fastened to the dark water.

"I am not inclusively sure," Dem said mischievously, *"however, shouldst thou permit, I could discover this easily…"*

Citrosine blanched. "How much of our time would that require?" she asked aloud. The dry air seemed to swallow her words with a dry cough. Dem said nothing, but its mind was alight with the idea of shifting forms.

"Please?" it asked softly, hiding the excitement that coursed through its every vein.

"Make sure you do it quickly so that we don't get left behind," Citrosine sighed, wondering what she was getting herself into. Dem shook out its mane gleefully. *"But get me down off your back first, please!"* the Elf added quickly, seeing how high off the ground she was.

"Of course, milady," Dem replied, chivalry coating its tone.

Dem's legs began shortening, and the horse it had been now began shimmering and melding into something different. Ripples ran through its skin and bones, and Citrosine watched in amazement as Dem puddled into a shimmering mass of... well...something. She assumed that this was the slump Dem had mentioned. The saddlebags that had been securely tied around its body fell softly to the dusty ground.

Now the slump began shimmering and changing again, and before Citrosine knew what was happening, she was in the cradling arms of...Pherkue! She looked up at his face, and saw the same dark grin that Pherkue had last flashed at her, as he kissed her on the hand.

But something was different...she didn't feel the charm of attraction, drawing her eyes to his, filling her heart with his presence. She took a deep breath, and sighed in relief.

Dem looked down at her quizzically.

"I reason thou hast an elucidation here for such a sigh, Citrosine?" came Pherkue's velvety, disarming voice. Citrosine sighed again, and then thought of a way to evade explanation.

"Why did you choose to take Pherkue's form?" she asked, putting her arm around Dem's neck as it walked towards the river. This was an uncomfortable action, as she hated the life out of Pherkue, but she nonetheless enjoyed being carried this way, because this was *not* the real Pherkue. She could feel the smooth skin cradling her; the skin that covered tight muscles, the skin that had a faint, alluring scent…Citrosine bit her tongue and wished that Tyre was here with her instead—the *real* Tyre.

"Thou was't sharing a chat before we began journeying with this Elf, correct? Dost thou recall? Each appeared to enjoy the other's company, thus I reflected it might be more comforting for to see *his* body than my favorite form; the dark assimilation I told you about. That would more closely resemble the boy's relation; that ghastly monopic man…" Dem nodded reflectively, and gingerly placed Citrosine on her feet beside the edge of the canyon. They both looked down at the water, marveling at how dark it was, and how far away it seemed.

"Well…" Citrosine began, and then stopped.

Dem looked at her curiously. "*Is* his presence soothing? It certainly seemed—"

"It was…I mean, it isn't …er, it's a bit difficult—" Citrosine stuttered.

Dem looked at her with Pherkue's deep red eyes.

"He has a charm over himself that causes all females who look upon him to…lust for him, I think, would be a sufficient explanation." She blushed. "I hate him powerfully for this, because he tries—whether consciously or not—to draw me from the Elf I truly love, whom I now somewhat miss…"

"I see…but I noted that this particular Elf *quite* enjoyed being within thy presence," Dem remarked, "although, I repent; it is far from my place…" It looked back down at the water.

"You ought to start moving, if you're going to do this with time to spare," Citrosine prompted, changing the subject as quickly as she could.

"Thy words hold true. Well, milady, I take my leave;" it said elegantly, pretending to be Pherkue in a deep bow. Its body began to ripple and meld again. A long tail began to grow, and as soon as the head of a mermaid began forming, Dem dove over the side of the cliff.

Citrosine watched Dem hit the water, watching the silhouette of its tail flash in the fading light from the surface, until she could only see the reflection of the sky. After a few moments of waiting patiently, she sat on the edge of the ground, toes dangling over the roiling river. She made sure to keep a firm hold on the roots behind her, lest she should slip.

She waited still, wondering if Dem would ever reach the bottom of the river. She had to nervously remind herself a few times that Dem was in the form of a mermaid, so breathing was not a problem for it—she?—and Citrosine tried not to worry.

A faint light began bubbling up to the surface of the water, and she recognized it as the shimmering episode that signaled Dem's form changes. She wondered what form she would see next.

That question was answered quickly as water exploded upwards. A huge creature that Citrosine had never seen before flew up out of the water, utterly menacing against the red sky. It spiraled upward, and flew in tight circles over the place from which it had just ascended. Thin, jagged wings protruded in arcs around the black, writhing creature. Embers shot out of its every pore, and six strong legs tipped with razor-like claws clambered over each other. A long spiked tail lashed back and forth from the creature's back, and bright yellow eyes glared at Citrosine.

The creature let out a shriek, and dove straight for Citrosine, who was shaking uncontrollably, face white. She could not move, and attempted to draw on her magic, but was too petrified.

A voice called through Citrosine's mind hysterically. *"Milady, run! Hurry into the water and wait for safer consequences! NOW! Jump in; hold on to something and remain still!"* Citrosine couldn't imagine why she heard Dem's thoughts *warning* her as it attacked, but she obeyed it just the same.

Just as the beast reached the ledge, Citrosine plunged down into the black water. The sun was nearly gone, so she could not tell where the beast had gone. She heard a shriek from it behind her, and a shower of rocks and dust came down into the water. She cried out, and attempted to fight the current to reach for something to hold her still. The water immediately around her shook, as if a large being had just stamped into it, and then it promptly stopped moving. *Did I do that?* The Elf swam furiously over to the nearest wall, the water returning to its angry stampede through the canyon.

Citrosine found a large rock that protruded into the river, and wedged her arms into the small groove between it and the rest of the canyon wall. She held on as securely as she could, and quickly came to realize that it was quite painful. Tears were streaming down her face, and she cursed at herself for showing her emotions so strongly. *That's why the water obeyed my wishes just then,* she mused; *I was frightened.*

Then she wondered why Dem would try to scare her like this. Wasn't it supposed to be her protector? Leader would have a fit when he heard about this plot, not to mention Gya's reaction.

But then…why should Dem warn her to dive into the water?

She looked up and saw the beast lunge out of the sky toward a small black form that had begun to pursue it. The fiery beast let out another shriek that reverberated across the canyon, making Citrosine cringe and lean in to the wall, but it was cut off midway when the black shape raced toward it, faster than the other had managed. Citrosine breathed a sigh of relief, and wished the small, weak shape strength and luck.

The creature shrieked again, this time echoing off all the canyon walls, against the huge mountains far, far off in the distance, and drawing out longer than an Elf's lungs ever could manage. The beast screamed louder, louder still, until Citrosine's ears rang so much that she could no longer hear the sound. Finally, it died down to a small cry and was gone.

Citrosine looked up at the place where the beast had been attacked, and was surprised to see it fly in one last slow circle, and crash to the ground, limp.

Dem...? Citrosine wondered if the beast really *had* been Dem. How could it be so evil all of a sudden? She'd seen the sparkling, shimmering form-change of Dem...Citrosine shuddered, her head pounding in a throbbing headache. She felt something warm crawling down her elbow, and strained her eyes to see. She leaned into the wall even tighter, and brought her head up toward her arm to see what she might be feeling. All she could see was a red line spreading down the back of her arm. She smelled the warm, metallic smell of blood, and realized that she must have cut her hands against the rock they were wedged behind.

There was nothing now—not the shrieking of the monster, no Dem. The rushing, muddy water surrounded her, threatening to drag her away and suck her down where Dem had just explored as soon as her grip on the rocky wall gave way. Citrosine was pondering how long she would wait in this spot when two arms came around her front. They grabbed her firmly, making her start. She twisted around to see who it was, and her hands came out of the channel between the rocks they had been wedged in. She panicked as her head went under the cold water, but before she could move again, the arms around her dragged her up into the air.

Apparently, whatever the being was that had taken hold of her could fly, because Citrosine remembered looking down at the water receding below her, and seeing her feet dangling helplessly through the air. She shivered in the cold air racing by her, and then fell unconscious.

NINE

WAMPYRES

Citrosine awoke with a jolt, every muscle in her body aching. She looked around her sharply, and saw that she was once again on Dem's horse form's back. Now, however, the ride was much less smooth, and she could hardly make out any of the scenery.

"*My repentance for that lurch there, milady,*" apologized Dem's familiar voice, "*but at such a breakneck rate, only a few minutes should elapse until the end of this migration draws nigh.*"

Citrosine inched up into a more erect sitting position. Her head throbbed, and she reached for Dem's neck to steady herself as the dizziness spread throughout her head, eyes, arms, and hands. Her hands were wrapped in black cloths, which were soaked and dripping with cool water.

"*Dem...what... What happened?*" she asked groggily. Dem snorted.

"*My curiosity befell my better senses, down in the river. I am a fool. There was a large hole, or burrow of some kind, and that*

171

creature that sabotaged milady was sleeping inside. She didn't like merfolk, as I discovered too lately."

"But…" Citrosine rubbed her temples. *"I thought that beast was you!"*

"Why dost thou believe I should turn against you? Even if I did, what hell would Leader have in store for me?"

"I…oh, I'm sorry." Citrosine tried to remember what had stopped the beast from killing her. *"What was the black creature that killed that monster, then?"*

"Thou sittest on the creature's back," was Dem's reply.

"What form did you take?"

"My favorite," he said simply. Then it sent Citrosine a strand of its memory. She saw again the fiery beast leap from the water, but now she saw the little black figure in more detail. It was a wispy kind of creature, with no clear boundaries of form. Four slender fangs dripping with river water protruded from its mouth. Its eyes were large and blood-red.

She saw it come up behind the huge monster and sink its fangs into the space beneath the creature's chin. She heard the same long shriek of anguish that she'd heard from her hiding place in the water, saw the beast pale, saw its eyes roll back, and saw it fall to the ground. The Wampyre floated down to the side of the beast, continued its drink, and then wiped its mouth calmly. Next, it floated down over the side of the cliff, and down to Citrosine. It wrapped its arms around her gently, and attempted to pull her up. She leapt in fright, and plunged underwater. Then, as she fainted, Dem scooped her up, brought her back to shore, and bound her cut hands. It placed her on its back, took the form of a horse once more, and ran off.

"Is this sufficient explanation?" Dem asked cautiously, fearful that Citrosine might be troubled. Instead, she laughed.

"Yes, Dem. I understand. Thank you for saving my life, by the way."

*"Thy life is more precious than curiosity—please absolve me…
and wouldst thou mind not to recount this tale to your Leader?"*

An hour or so later, Dem began to slow. Citrosine sensed a change in the air. It tasted different, salty and wilder, somehow. When Dem finally stopped moving, Citrosine saw all the other Changelings and their Elven passengers milling about in a large sandy area. She knew the ocean to be straight ahead, as the half-moon was large and orange, and illuminated the reflections of itself that were thrown across the waves.

Dem crouched, and allowed Citrosine to slide off its back, then reached around and tugged the saddlebags off itself.

"My sincerest apologies again, milady," Dem said courteously, *"but this Changeling thanks its companion for a glorious escapade, despite its own foolishness."*

"Goodbye, Dem, and farewell. I may see you on the ship, but…'bye, 'til then."

Citrosine dragged the saddlebags across the sand for a few steps, and was then aware of the weight being lifted from her hands. She turned, and saw Pherkue picking them up and slinging them across his back.

"I hope you had a safe journey?" His eyes stared into Citrosine's, and she was aware that this was the real Pherkue, not Dem's impression, as she could feel her heart fluttering, her stomach churning unpleasantly.

"I…er…it was…" she stumbled for words, and Pherkue caught sight of her hands, still wrapped in cloth.

"Ay, dear, what has happened?" He dropped all the bags he'd been carrying, excessively dramatic—*"dear"?*—as Citrosine would realize upon later examination, and he rushed to her side. He gently unwrapped her hands, and they both were shocked to see that they were red and scratched, stained with blood. Pherkue looked up at Citrosine's face questioningly.

"It was—er—just an accident," she said breathlessly, trying her hardest to avoid the feelings Pherkue sent through her.

"I'm sure," he said smoothly, stroking her hands tenderly, holding them close to his lips. Citrosine's fingers tingled with his touch. His skin and his breath were both cold. "May I help?" he asked.

"Pardon me?"

"May I use a spell on your hands, to help heal them?"

"Er...all right," she stuttered. A red puff of magic dust floated over her hands, and, when it cleared, her hands were clean and healed, though they still felt raw. She looked at him graciously, not able to find words. He patted her hands gently, sending what felt like an icy shock throughout her body.

"You seem lost. Looking for someone?" he asked suddenly, bringing Citrosine back to reality. She floundered for words. She was looking for...well, she had been looking for *someone*...

"Er..." She shifted, trying to focus on something other than Pherkue's dazzling smile that was like shooting stars in the darkness. His ruby eyes continued to search hers, shining and waiting for her.

Had she not been looking for him all this time? Dem had shown her Pherkue to please her—was it a sign? Of course she had wanted to tell him she was glad to see that he'd arrived safely, to embrace him.

For a brief moment, Tyre came to her mind, and the electric kisses they'd shared. Citrosine's eyes snapped from Pherkue's gaze, and she regretted the series of thoughts the Elf's charms had just given her.

"Tyre. I haven't seen Tyre, as of yet, or my father, for that matter. Do you know where either might be?"

Pherkue's expression hardened. His eyes had gone shades darker, smoldering in the night. "I think," he began, his voice still soft and alluring, despite his obvious irritation, "I think I saw Gya with your sister over near the water. They had a small fire burning." He gestured towards the surf. "Tyre would seem to be absent...you could search for his father..."

"Thank you," Citrosine said, becoming more and more agitated with herself more than Pherkue.

Pherkue nodded curtly as she dismissed him. He gave her a quick kiss on the cheek, and drifted off; leaving her with a rush of emotion that again filled her with regrets and a want to see Tyre.

Citrosine's eyes watered in humiliation. She would have to tell Tyre about how strong Pherkue's charm was becoming. He would have a good solution, Citrosine knew.

"Lissa, Citrosine, what took you so long!" Gya greeted her as Citrosine made her way over to the small fire that her father and sister were warming themselves next to.

"Dem, my Changeling, got a little sidetracked," she said simply. Gya looked at her in alarm.

"Did he put you in danger? Did he hurt you?"

"No, no, nothing like that. We just stopped to look at Jygul's Grin." She sighed. "I, um, cut my hands on some sharp rocks, but both of us are all right." Her father shook his head lightly when she held up her hands, which Pherkue had conveniently healed.

"Ah, yes. Isn't the Grin marvelous, *lissa?*"

"Quite," she said, not wishing to speak very much. Tie ran up and gave her a hug. She smiled up at her sister, and Citrosine couldn't help but smile back.

"Dada," Citrosine began again, "have you seen Tyre anywhere?" She missed his voice, his tender words...it wasn't like him to disappear like this...was it?

Gya smiled crookedly, sensing Citrosine's intentions to visit her love. "No, *lissa,* I have not seen him or his father for quite a time now. Would you like to have a look around for him? I understand that you should want—"

"No, I think I'd rather rest for a while. Maybe it will be easier to find him when it grows lighter." With that, Citrosine curled up wearily on a blanket next to the fire and closed her eyes.

As dawn began to break, golden light rose from behind all the Elves and Changelings on the sand, swimming through the breaking waves, and tickling the horizon with the slightest fingers and touches of sparkling sunlight.

Leader picked his way through some of the milling Elves, and found a raised dune to stand atop. He amplified his voice and called out for attention.

"It seems that all or most of us are accounted for," he began, once everyone had been silenced. "I have received no reports of foul play of the Changelings, and everyone that met at Haerthor's square yesterday has arrived. Thank you for following my rules thus far. We will have a fortuitous journey across the sea if we can follow them just a while longer." He paused, looking out across everyone. *Thank Ghersah that the King is already safe, or I'd be graying around the edges by now,* he thought.

Citrosine looked once more for Tyre, squinting, and looking out as far as she could see through the unmoving Elf crowd. She thought she saw him and his father, but there was a large congregation of Fall Elves in that direction, so she couldn't be sure.

Leader continued. "This new island is barren, save for what the King and his court have established. For the first few years of settlement, all of us will have to remain close, to plant our trees, native flowers, and raise dwellings and governments for ourselves. Remember that the Elves will not, hopefully, be the only populace of the place, as this is to be the new settlement of the Enchanted World. We will not let Men drive us out again. This place will only be home to immortals, and will be greatly protected.

"This island was given the name of *Ilthen.* This stands for a new life, a new home, new beginnings, and, most crucial, a new togetherness. We, as Elves, must unite into a single fellowship. We cannot fray apart and let Men overtake us! We have lived here in tranquility for ages. This new age of discovery for them will not exterminate us from our own world. *Remember this.*

"Now, on this vessel, on our way to Ilthen, rooms have been provided for each family, though they may not be excessively large. If *any kinds of quarrels between tribes ensue,* I will *personally* see to the abating of the conflicts." He paused, casting a steely look around him. Citrosine shuddered at the way his scar and the rising sun contrasted, giving the man deep gash-like shadows over his eyes.

Citrosine, her father, and her sister were jostled into the line up to the dock that led up to the monstrous boat that would ferry them to Ilthen. Tie sat atop Gya's shoulders, and Citrosine followed close behind, dragging along a few of their packs. Most of the Changelings, the antsy ones, that is, had become birds and avoided the line entirely by flying above all the nervous Elves. The more ethical of them took the shapes of Elves or other things and waited in line with the true Elves for their own rooms.

The ship they would all be boarding had been constructed of magic only, so as not to fell trees for wood and leave evidence of the Elven escape. It was a solid blue color, with shimmering patterns running through it every few moments. The ship was long, with a series of corridors in the lower levels that would provide sleeping areas for all the Elves and Changelings from the Big Lands that had chosen to come on this venture. The boat had a deck large enough to fit half the population, with large rails that would prevent inadvertent falls.

The four masts that rose up bore sails with the symbol of the Elves emblazoned in the center, a tree with half a sun peering out from behind one side of the trunk, and half a moon at a lower position at the other side of it.

Citrosine could recall every detail of this from her travel in time, in the vision of herself. She was wary, for her vision had taken her just ahead of this point, when she would learn what she had lost the night before.

By the time the Nakisses reached the dock, the sun had risen up a quarter of the way through the sky. Citrosine took one last look behind her before she stepped up onto the deck of the vessel. She saw the forests and deserts that had once been the homes of countless Enchanted beings. Now, they looked so still, as if the life had been sucked away from them. The green of the trees had dimmed into a sort of gray-brown, and there was no sound from anywhere within the forest, other than that of the non-magical creatures, those that had been too ignorant to bear the sense to evacuate with those of the Enchanted World.

Citrosine sighed heavily, accepting the fate of this flight from all they had ever known. Sparkling, shimmering fibers erupted from her sigh, and flittered back into the wind that was blowing from the sea. She hoped that no one had noticed, and prayed that those few fibers had not caused an inadvertent spell or charm. Who knew what havoc could be wreaked among mortals by just one charm out of their understanding...

The three took a place by the railing on the deck, and waited patiently for everyone to board. The deck was now crowded by Elves wanting to see the launch of their quest firsthand, and watch the land receding behind them, saying goodbye as they raced across the swelling sea.

Pherkue, Egan, and a brief procession of Shadow Elves drifted up from the dock, and as Pherkue passed Citrosine, he flashed her a dazzling smile, causing her body to involuntarily tremble. She nodded back, dazed, and the Dark Elves passed, already descending to their rooms. The younger ones accompanying Egan and Pherkue gripped the railings tightly, seeming to be dizzy with the brilliance of the sun and the rocking of the ship. Perhaps they would be less sick when they finally landed in Ilthen.

Leader was the last of all to board, and as he did, he raised his arms, and the dock vanished behind every one of his steps. The ramp slid up into the deck of the ship, and the anchor lifted itself. With a great creak, the vessel set off of the beach, out to Ilthen, the new land.

Citrosine and Tie waved enthusiastically back to the land in which they had grown up, and wished it well. Citrosine saw the flicker of happiness in her sister's eyes go out after one such remark, and extreme sadness came into her little sister's face. Citrosine assumed that she missed Leenka, who would not be joining them any longer. The sisters hugged each other tightly, Tie's face buried in Citrosine's hair.

Soon after the journey began, Citrosine and Gyardaute learned that Tie was sensitive to the rising and falling of the ocean waves, resulting in a stained tunic for Gya. He took his younger daughter down to find their room, and Citrosine took a place by the rear of the ship. She shivered aside the rail, remembering that this was the very position she took in the vision she had seen by the pond. It, whatever It was, was coming soon.

She watched as the land behind them faded into nothingness, and they traveled further across the ocean.

The land behind them looked out sadly, wishing that the Enchanted Beings would stay. It knew that only malevolence could come out of such a migration, and closed its eyes in resignation as all the others, the Dragons, Nymphs, Faeries, and the rest gathered themselves, readying to join the Elves in this new colonization.

A sigh rang out through the clouds, nothing more than a breath of weeping, caressing air, echoing across the ocean, into the sky, and into the depths of the immortals' thoughts.

The Big Lands would not be graced by mysticism or magical grace for ages to come.

Presently, there was a noise behind Citrosine. She turned swiftly, and saw a man approaching her from around the main cabin between the last two masts. His skin was dark, and he walked haltingly. She couldn't yet make out who he was.

She waited for him to come closer, silently hoping it was Tyre, but soon recognized him as Tyre's father. Her heart leaped. If he was here, then surely Tyre must be!

"Mr. Kendah, sir!"

As the man grew closer, Citrosine could see that his eyes were red and watery, as if he'd just had a crying fit. There were shadows under his eyes, and he walked unsteadily. Was he intoxicated?

Or hysterical?

"Sir," she called out, "are you all right, sir?" Kendah was obviously in earshot, but he did not reply. He ambled ever closer, and Citrosine saw a bunch of paper clutched tightly in his hand. In his other was Tyre's walking cane. The man's eyes grew angrier, and Citrosine tried her hardest not to show fear.

"Citrosine Nakiss?" he asked in a low growl, as if a demon had lodged itself in his throat. He dropped the cane with a loud clatter, not seeming to notice as it fell between them, and stopped walking when he was a step away from the Elf-girl.

"Yes, sir?" Citrosine whispered.

The man's brow lowered to meet with his eyelids, becoming a wall of smoke above his fiery eyes.

Before Citrosine could think another word, the man's hand shot out and slapped against her cheek, making her head snap around to one side. She crumpled to her knees, holding her face in her hands.

"He could have saved himself," Kendah hissed. "We could have protected him."

She looked up in alarm at him, preparing to use her magic, but he was already on his way back from where he'd come. Blood was running out from the inside of her cheek and gums. She swallowed it, her heart thundering through her body. Needless to say, she was totally disgraced, and had no idea what was going on.

She saw Kendah condense the papers he grasped into a rumpled ball and throw the ball over his shoulder. It hit Citrosine's forearm, then bounced across the deck to come to rest beside Tyre's cane.

She crawled over to the cane, eyes blurring, and reluctantly began to straighten out the papers in terror. What had happened to Tyre? Was it her fault, as Kendah made it seem? Citrosine investigated, a gathering sense of dread weighing down her insides.

Dearest Citrosine, Father, Leader, Pherkue;

Many things have just come into play that none of us could have imagined, except, of course, for the latter pair in the four above named. You will understand when, in a future conversation, you hear these words: "Grins se lya Ilthen Wampyre nessa se mikra".

Citrosine paused before reading further. She tried to translate what she knew about the archaic language. *Do not... something—do not do something...Ilthen...in Ilthen, about Ilthen?* She took a breath and tried to focus. *Our Wampyres will...eat? Hurt...no...punish. Our Wampyres will punish... you...* Okay. She'd done it. Now she reasoned it out in horror. *Do not go to Ilthen or our Wampyres will punish you for it.* Wampyres? Whose? Why?

I have recently seen a vision in which my dearest friend—my true love, I feel, to use archaic mortal terminology—Citrosine Nakiss, collapses, poisoned, onto a beach in this new land of

Ilthen. She had been attacked by a Coulf demon in a war of races between Elves. This happens in little time over fifty years. More recently, I witnessed my own near-death. I hesitate to write this, wishing with all my might that it is not possible, that such a thing has never, and will never, be seen in the Enchanted World. Alas, my visions have never been proved untrue, as of yet. Citrosine, I offer words of caution to you for the rest of your days, and wish that I can be seen wrong, at least this once.

The Shadow Elves turn on the other tribes in the very near future. I have seen this. Trust me or not, my visions have always been true. Down to the last detail, unless misinterpreted, which has only happened once out of the thousands of visions I have had. This time I tell you what I have seen, and you may interpret how you wish.

Of my own attack, soon in the future: Leader and Pherkue have had contact and a discussion of some great Wampyre leading a coven that is to be unleashed if Ilthen is settled. Any motives for the moment escape me. I believe this leading Wampyre to be none other than Pherkue's uncle; Egan, the Dark Elf. My suspicions sprout from hearing Pherkue mention his name in urgency to Leader through my passing of the chambers—I was not eavesdropping, only attempting to find my way through the Council chambers; as you must know, I am blind, and thus get lost frequently—only inside buildings, I admit. I suppose this is hardly evidence, but Egan's disposition, his position as the leader of the Shadows, his shady past, dealing with such strong, dark powers…it fits, excusing my bluntness.

Citrosine smirked, remembering how Tyre had excused himself countless times upon their first meeting. The smirk was replaced with a moan of terror as she continued reading.

I am to be attacked this night, presently, the night preceding our migration away from the Big Lands, if I do not help to slaughter Citrosine, daughter of the Stone Tribe Magic Council

Member Gyardaute Nakiss. *This is meant to be seen as a threat to Leader, for to avenge Egan's tribe of being banished ages ago, and for what other possible purpose is unclear.*

The Wampyres have chosen Citrosine, since she is the oldest child of the highest Council member under a Leader, in the direct bloodline of the great Ghersah, and...they already have failed in taking her mother; therefore she can be connected easier to the Council and used as leverage against it. Next in line would be Mychaell, son of Council Member Roebert Laminyé. Third would be myself.

I am very close to Citrosine, so the Wampyres have chosen to attack me, in order to more safely cause her death. By sending me, as a Wampyre, to kill her, she would fall into their trap and accept me without knowing what I will have become. They attempted already to sire Leenka straight off, but she was far too powerful to succumb...I am unsure, but it is my belief that Leenka could have ascended directly back to Ghersah.

I will be attacked in the way of the Wampyres, and made into one myself. They will poison my blood and make me their slave. I will have no choice but to do what they command. This is another threat to the Council. Should someone as loyal to the tribe as I succumb, I could undo all the hope and kinship that is the Stone Tribe Magic Council. I shudder now, in the warm comfort of my room, in spite of the reassuring scribbling sounds of the charcoal pencil that takes my dictations.

I am supposed to be made into one of darkness myself, so that I will follow the orders of the superior, Egan (as I believe; again, it is still imprecise and this is my clearest guess), and help eventually to track and take down every Council Member of Haerthor. How many other pawns said leader desires to create in order to carry out this plot, I am not certain, but it is to be a master coven. In this way the Shadow Elves and all others who join their ranks will be able to prevail eventually over all Elves and take back what they have been forbidden. Again; I am unsure as to motives. Pardon my speculation, but the clearest want of the Shadow Elves I see is retribution for the ageless hatred towards them.

I have few choices. They will sire me as a dark one after I refuse to simply come over to their side to kill Citrosine, since I have an advantage to their cause in that I am greatly attached to her. My bribe is that they will restore my vision if I comply freely, therefore causing there to be no need to sire me and get their hands dirty. This way, Egan (or as aforementioned a different aggressor), would have less risk of being immediately blamed. Never would I do this, you must understand. *I have accepted my state of life for what it is, and would not even be tempted by this offer. To change from such a life I have become accustomed to would not only be unnatural and difficult, but painful…it is hard to adjust, and becoming blind was enough to keep my mind busy for centuries already. Blindness heightened my strength, my powers, and my love of life; it is now who I am. They should not think me so vain; neither should they think that I would ever be able to slaughter anyone I love so dearly and endlessly. They are fools.*

I will not stand to let myself become poisoned by Wampyre venom. To lose my free will to senseless killing and bloodlust has no appeal, no purpose, and no benefit for anyone who still retains a sense of good. At the cost of losing not only myself, but my father and Citrosine, and any who are close to me, I cannot give in. They would be killed without my conscious ability to protect them, which is the worst thing that could ever happen in my life. To reach the day when I rose up over my own father and caused him harm…to reach the day when I have no life in me enough to protect my Citrosine…would kill me. Tortures me…at the very thought. On that day I would tear myself into pieces…

Citrosine could almost feel Tyre's silent sobs as she had the night he held her.

Now I come to the one solution that I have been able to formulate. Hours that felt like millennia have been spent contemplating this problem, and I have known that this was my only option all along, but couldn't admit it to myself.

Because I am afraid.

I have made up my mind. It cannot be persuaded otherwise, and will not, for it is not possible, as in a few short minutes it will have been carried out.

Citrosine could barely make out the last page, through her incessantly tearing eyes and the jagged, crammed script. She could imagine Tyre's voice growing quieter, faster in the dim light of his rooms. The bewitched coal stick would have a difficult time following his terrified thoughts so quickly. Citrosine gulped for air and continued reading.

Rather than carry out a dead life of evil, and help whomever *it might be that leads these vile, fetid creatures, I pronounce the following.*

Tyre Kendah shall soon be no more. If I stay in my current state, I will soon become irreversibly tainted and programmed. I will have no way of fighting this, foretelling of the future or none. I will, in a few minutes' time, have rid myself and the world of the risk of my own becoming of a missionary for the undead. There is no other way to protect myself or the world of my inevitable loss of control than by protecting the world from myself, by way of ridding myself from the world.

The only way that the Wampyres would be foiled would be if they were greeted by a corpse—no use to them at all, unless they should revive their outlawed ways of reanimating the dead. But for this letter, this…suicide letter…I write in warning and earnestness to you; you, at least, shall know the truth.

To the last,
Tyresias Kendah

—Pop!—

The pencil had obviously written down its interpretation of something being opened, perhaps a corked bottle. *No,* Citrosine pleaded, *not poison!* She had lost all physical feeling, and she sobbed uncontrollably. *My Tyre, please, tell me this is not true! Tell me you have escaped!* She struggled to read. *At the end of this letter, he must have been able to reach another solution!* She shook her head violently, trying to pull herself together. Standing over the edge of the rail of the deck for a moment, she breathed in the salty air and spray, trying to fight against the icy blades in her lower abdomen. Citrosine wished for the first time in her life that the Elvish language had some kind of interjections or swears one could hurl out when no logical thought would suffice.

A thick weight had settled in her throat, and she let out a final choked sob before she could mechanically make herself sit and read again. These were to be Tyre's final words, stripped of all reasoning and logic, the pathos of which would reveal the inner emotional struggle he felt in his last moments.

Leader, Pherkue, Egan; I wish all the superiors of our country the greatest of all cautions, and I wish whoever leads this plot damned to remain in the deep abyss with the cursed Jygul of the darkness and shadows. If someone could simply heed my warning and begin necessary preparations!

Father, I am exceedingly sorry to leave you alone, but you must understand that this is for the best of all of us. I make this choice for Citrosine, for Gyardaute, for Leader, for you, for all Elves. I wish not to be used as an instrument of evil, and I pray that you warn Leader or anyone in great power to be wary. Know that this is my only choice. Thank you for all you have done for me. I am truly sorry…I can give you nothing more.

Citrosine, I…I love you more than anything, and you must know that you will be safe, so long as you stay away from Pherkue and Egan, or whomever it is that I may be creating a scapegoat for. Thank you for all that you've shown to me about love, and I wish to tell you that you have more power than any Elf I've ever met. Use it wisely. Do not fear the coming of my vision, of the beach in Ilthen...your...possible place of death. It may not come about at all, which is what I hope beyond hope for you. I wish with all that is left of my heart that this oracle can be altered.

For now, this is the best I can do to protect you. I would not be able to live with myself if I was the one to...who...who had killed you. Even if I were a dark one, what I had left of my own self would die.

Citrosine, remember that the future is always volatile and wavering. The future...I am sorry, unbearably sorry for the future that will never be. I sincerely apologize for that which is impossible as of tonight. I would be with you forever. Know that. I would live eons with you and our little home and our little Dariya... Dariya...hope...in perfect, perfect bliss. Forever. Forever and forever and forever!

But tonight the only choices are to taint that forever in darkness and agony, or to erase the forever that I wish I could have given you, in order for you to have any future at all. The worst thing that could ever happen to me would be to live while you are no more. At least this way I know that you will be safe. I give you all that I can ever give you, and that is my own life on this miserable night...

I love you, Citrosine. My Citrosine! Know that my heart shall fly to you this night...it is already yours; irrevocably, absolutely, without end.

Hello? Tyresias Kendah? Are you at home? May I come in... just for a short moment?

This was obviously a new voice, for the pencil had changed its font—these few words were in a flowing, spidery cursive, echoing a polite yet wicked voice...and Tyre's round, passionate script took over again.

My time is short now…they come. The poison is drunk and there is no turning back now! For I can feel death now, and I understand that it is all I can do for my…final service to the Elven race. I can hear the wickedness in his thoughts—my prophecy is coming true! I wish everyone…in Ilthen well. May magic unite us all…against these times of darkness that lie ahead…The last of my love goes out…Citrosine!

Hello? Open this door now! Hello! Tyresias!

—Crash!—

What is this? No! NO! *Fool of a boy.*

Citrosine clutched the letter to her heart, and gasped and swallowed at the rest of her tears, in hopes that she would not flood the world in black magic.

TEN

TIME IS ALWAYS RIGHT

Citrosine stood there, at the rear of the boat, for longer than she cared to remember. She no longer saw the ocean or the few Changelings in various forms swimming along behind the vessel, but instead nothingness. She withdrew into her mind, seeing Tyre, alone in his room, whispering his discoveries to a charmed pencil that recorded even his last gasping word, as he went into unavoidably suicidal reasoning. The other voice—Egan, or whatever Wampyre had barged in to take Tyre away—pierced Citrosine's mind; she wished upon the owner of that voice a long and painful stay with Jygul at the end of life.

She kept her face stony, although it took an enormous effort.

Trying to think, she turned around and saw a small, hovering cloud, just lower than the rest in the brightening sky. It was definitely of magic, but this didn't surprise Citrosine. She was too deep in shock from the letter to be frightened by what she knew to be her own spirit, looking at this very moment in time; Citrosine crying, with Tyre's father's finger marks across her cheek. The bit of magic that she'd spared to see herself in the future just over a day ago had proven her overwhelming emptiness to come true. It had been pointless, for the sadness and emptiness had come along with a forceful, deathly shock regardless of her and just as his next-to-last vision undoubtedly would.

What she had felt as she slept a night ago—that had been Tyre's death. He had cried out her name as he was dying, and she was so attached to him and his powers were so strongly focused on her that she had felt it, even heard it.

Tyre had seen a Shadow plot, with Pherkue eventually delivering a message from Egan about a Wampyre coven to destroy the Elves. She shuddered. She could see, sickened, how Pherkue could relay messages unobtrusively to and from his uncle, as he had at the meeting before. He had spoken pleadingly, genuinely, on behalf of the "way of life" of his tribe… probably coached by Egan for dark purposes beforehand, and charmed to seem totally innocent and sincere.

Could Egan really be a Wampyre? Was it he who had burst in upon Tyre, with the intention to replace his blood with evil? She remembered how frightening he looked, how severely he had looked at everyone, how they had been seated away from everyone, both at the meeting, and on the beach, possibly restraining the want to lash out and drink the blood of those around him…Could Pherkue be sending his uncle's messages so that Egan would not have to fight the instincts of a bloodsucker? How much chaos there was in this time of supposed fresh starts.

She sat again, slumping against the rail and gingerly touching Tyre's walking cane. She slid it into her lap, running her hands against the handle. The cane itself was smooth wood, with a few quartz inlays. The handle was carved in the shape of a coiled snake, with a small tongue protruding from the head at the top; the snake's way of deciphering where it was going, and if it was going in a safe direction. Citrosine remembered how her father had once told her that a snake's tongue was like its eyes; they were able to tell where a rat was by "tasting" the air; feeling the vibrations in the air to determine the position of the things around it. This cane had been Tyre's eyes.

Her finger ran over a small indent on the underside of the snake's midsection. She tilted the cane so she could see the tiny ridges. There was a small carving there: *TK.* Tyresias Kendah. She smiled wistfully. Up a little higher, on the next of the snake's coils, was another: *CN.* Citrosine's eyes involuntarily allowed tears to squeeze their way out into open air. *Citrosine Nakiss.*

He carved my initials into the most essential object of his life, she whimpered.

Citrosine, I love you more than anything, and you must know that you will be safe... Know that my heart shall fly to you this night...it is already yours, irrevocably, absolutely, without end. His cries had, indeed, reached her on the night of his death... her own name had been his dying cry... If only she had been able to talk to him, perhaps think of another way...or at least see him again before—but that was stupid to wish now. She found herself imagining what could no longer be. She thought back to Tyre's unattainable prediction, of a future...

Of Dariya.

Dariya now will never exist! That beautiful little girl—his baby—our baby...she is dead, too. Citrosine could see her as if she were standing at her side right now. The shining curls, wide smile, and euphoric eyes...Dariya, in which had been hope. The hope had been for Dariya to have a mother and exist. Now she did not have her father, still probably would lose the one meant to be her mother, and could not exist. Dariya—Hope—was lost.

Within many long moments, and between sobs, Citrosine realized what she had seen in Tyre's eyes when she had last seen him—his poor, distant eyes had been uneasy, somehow. He'd been trying to mask his inner thoughts. It wasn't worry, or fear, she saw now…It had just been *knowing*. Tyre had known that he would lose her. Perhaps he did not know yet that he would be attacked and converted into a Dark One, maybe that was in a later vision, but he knew that that last time they were together was when he had to tell her that he loved her, before he couldn't ever say it.

He had only spoken of Citrosine's death, and not his own, because he only cared that she were alive. True, it could have been that he did not yet know that he would die, but he had known somewhere deep inside that he would have died without her, anyway. That was how much he'd loved her. It had been, on that last night, most important to him that she have only as much knowledge as would not hurt her. This way she could protect herself and not worry about the rest—when she would die, that he would die for her if he could, that his own life was also under a countdown of days. Trying to protect her, he had kept the most difficult secret of his all-too-short life…all for her.

A sudden noise startled the Elf. She looked up, deftly wiping her eyes. Pherkue was strolling along the side of the deck, looking intently off the side, at the Changeling-fish and mermaids. He didn't see her, Citrosine knew, strange timing as this was.

"Pherkue," she called out resentfully.

He looked up sharply, but then his eyes softened.

"Citrosine, hello," he crooned. He walked over to her with slightly more purpose. He stopped when he saw Tyre's cane. His eyes clouded, and he looked at Citrosine with an expression of alarm over his face.

"What…what happened?" he asked gently, seeing Citrosine's moistened eyes, her crushed expression. His own eyes were open wide, the blood-red irises brighter than ever.

"Did...*Citrosine?* What happened, love?" he repeated, his words articulated delicately. Was he sincerely worried?

Citrosine closed her eyes and took a deep breath. She held out Tyre's letter to Pherkue.

"I think...you should read this, sir." Her hands were shaking. Now was the first time that she didn't feel the charm of attraction pulling her towards the Elf. Right now, she was disgusted by him, and by his uncle Egan, whom Tyre's evidence wholly accused. After all, he *was* the Dark Elves' leader, and he *had* been extremely hostile towards Leader throughout this whole exodus.

"What is it, Citrosine?" Pherkue asked; hesitancy and wariness layered in his voice. Citrosine took a deep breath, and replied.

"That...is...a suicide letter."

Pherkue read the letter in a rush, almost dropping it several times. Had he let it blow away in the wind, Citrosine would have wholeheartedly jumped overboard to retrieve it. When he was done, he had paled significantly. His face was whiter than that of a corpse. Citrosine studied his face intently, watching for some sign of weakness, of sway, that could persuade her that Pherkue was, indeed, in on this plot.

"His last words..." Pherkue murmured. He forced a weak smile drooping at the edges. "I...I didn't know that...he... never mind." He darkened, unable to continue the thought. "You ought to show this to Leader," he whispered, in such a low, smoldering voice that Citrosine had to ask him to repeat himself. "Leader would love to see this," the Elf muttered. "He could have probably been well-off to have a conversation with Tyresias...get some counsel on how to persecute my uncle, and my tribe," Pherkue's eyes grew sharper, colder.

"I didn't mean to accuse—though his words never lied to me before..." Citrosine argued in a resigned, flat tone. She felt her heart skip a beat. Was she afraid, or was the charm coming back?

"Of course not,"

"I only thought about how it was addressed to you, as well as to Leader and me, and Tyre's father," Citrosine said. Her voice sounded pleading and childish to her own ears. She bit her tongue.

"Yes…" Pherkue walked past her, to the rail, eyes revealing no emotion, and looked off at the clouds. Citrosine suddenly had an idea. She shyly, gently reached out into Pherkue's mind…what could be hiding there?

At first, she saw a blur of red and purple light. Then that cleared, and became a small room, made of dark stone. She saw Egan leaning over a pale, spread-eagled figure, looking down upon it closely…perhaps ready to feed? He moved his hands around, probably talking to someone else in the room, or the figure itself, which from this angle appeared a corpse. That vision began to blur, and then there was Tyre, sitting on the ledge in the courtyard in Haerthor, with the feigned-sleeping Citrosine cuddled contentedly in his arms.

Pherkue turned around to face her, and, panicked, she withdrew from his mind. His eyes were glassy, and he looked at her with an almost timid expression.

"He really loved you, didn't he?" Pherkue asked faintly, catching Citrosine off-guard. She didn't feel that an answer was needed for that question. Her stomach was doing somersaults. She could feel the attraction charm growing, and she was conscious of herself losing resistance. She thought of Tyre, her eyes blurring and heart quaking violently.

Pherkue placed Tyre's letter back into Citrosine's hand, pausing against her skin much more than was necessary. Citrosine was aware of his cool fingertips brushing the back of her hand softly. She looked into his eyes, and was surprised to see them looking wet.

A wave of unprecedented sympathy swelled through her heart towards him, and she couldn't even place why she felt it. Pherkue had barely known Tyre at all, and Tyre hadn't actually gone to Leader and told him to persecute the Dark Elves…but he looked so sad, so forlorn…He was accused, stressed by the thought of a dying tribe, and probably had felt very strongly for Citrosine, competing with Tyre's unmatchable love…and thus Citrosine's common sense evaded her momentarily in a moment of utter loss and weakness. She felt some kind of understanding in Pherkue, perhaps a common bond of the fear of catastrophe in such massive changes in this age.

Pherkue accepted this opportunity to put his arm around the Elf-girl's waist, and he held her gently against himself. He felt Egan's presence slowly creeping into his mind, and raised an impenetrable barrier around his thoughts. This was no time for intrusions: here a single hesitation could ruin everything. He kissed Citrosine's lips, cheeks, jaw, throat…feeling the warmth of her still-flushed and crying face, her rushing pulse, and smelling her woodland scent. Would that Citrosine didn't have to be in such a vulnerable, miserable state when this was possible…Would that she felt so strongly about the Shadow Elf that she would have initiated this…Pherkue held her more tightly, kissed her with more desperation, not knowing how long he had until she would shatter into sorrow.

Citrosine was hardly aware that she was being kissed by a Dark Elf as it happened. She closed her eyes, and all she saw in her mind's eye was Tyre. His scarred eyes, clouded by thin films of blindness, somehow meeting hers tenderly; his hands embracing her, warming and completing her strained heart…

As soon as Pherkue had gone back to the room he shared with his uncle, Citrosine was roughly brought back her good judgment. She crumpled to her knees, and, wiping her mouth with her sleeves in fury, pleaded silently, *Ghersah, how could I have betrayed myself this way! Help me open my eyes when next this might occur. Purify me! Wash away the taste of icy shadows!*

Tyre, I couldn't see him; a Dark Elf! Curse his charms and all those things I have not been able to fight! Please…Tyre, please, forgive me. I saw only you; he fooled my sorrow-filled eyes! She spat anything that might be left of Pherkue in her into the sea.

Tyresias's cane and letter in hand, the distraught Elf ran down to the room she shared with her father and sister. Through narrow passageways, down a spiral staircase, through more corridors, and all the way into the room, she wept.

"Tyre is dead! Dada! He—is—*gone!*" She wildly shrieked, tearing at her face. "I was going to tell him so much—he was going to be my future—he was going to protect me!" She inhaled shallowly, wheezing. "Dada! What do I do now!"

Gya took hold of her firmly, holding her in his sturdy arms. "Speak more slowly!" he commanded. "Tell me what happened. I cannot understand you when you are so excited! Come now, breathe a little. You never lose your head like this, *lissa.*"

Citrosine panted, hyperventilating. She was like a chased animal, with a desperate fire in her eyes and insane tears of fury and pain. The story spilled out of her like sparks.

"*Lissa,* Citrosine, I am so sorry," Gya exclaimed when his daughter had explained her encounter with Tyre's father, up through reading the letter. The red marks that his fingers had made had become bruised, and it hurt to open her mouth. Citrosine allowed Gya a long moment to interpret the letter. He said nothing, waiting for Citrosine to calm down.

"And then Pherkue came, Dada. He…you saw his name in the letter, and his relation to Egan…I was so mad at him right then, but he was there, and," Citrosine sniffed and became bashful.

"And what, *lissa*? What happened then? What did he do to you?" Gya was quiet, but he could have been shrieking for all the wideness of his eyes.

"He took advantage of me…he…he has this charm of attraction over him already…and I was…Dada, he kissed me!

196

And more than just a kiss—it was as if he was my Tyre himself! Like *he* was rather my—my *soulmate*!" She twisted her fingers through her hair, tangling it into a mess to match her state of mind. Her heart was in so much pain, but what was there to do now?

Gya hugged her, cooing and shushing her sobs.

"Citra, Citra, I am sorry," he whispered into her hair, rubbing her back firmly, "but I am glad that he did no more than that! He did not harm you physically?"

Citrosine gurgled a mucous-filled reply.

"That is a blessing. Shh…you're all right now."

Palgirtie had listened with a sick interest to Citrosine's account, and now sat in decorum. "Gone, just as fast as Mother," she murmured, just loud enough for Gya to hear. He looked at his daughter sharply, wondering silently what had brought about this turn towards the cynical in her recent behavior.

Citrosine, her head newly pounding with the day's drama, was instantly dismayed by the size of the room that the three would have to sleep in and while away the hours. Upon opening the door, a small bed was found to the left wall, and a small wardrobe nailed to the wall next to this. The other side of the room was occupied by a small grate that could be used for cooking, and a large basin that could hold water for washing or bathing. All words spoken in the room were instantly swallowed by the rough walls, evoking a distinct feeling of severe claustrophobia. Citrosine didn't understand how her sister could stand this more than the smell of the salt and the open sky above on the deck.

"Girls," Gya claimed their attention again, changing the subject just to keep Tie from hurting her already fragile sister, recognizing the fact that Citrosine would not be listening right now, "I believe I told you that we'd be changing tribes as soon as we arrived, did I not?" Tie nodded. "Well, Leader has announced how this is to be done. He will meet with any who wish to be changed out of their current tribes, and he himself will conduct the spells needed to go about the transfer.

"Our Marks of the Stone Tribe will have to be removed— it should not be painful—and then we are to be initiated to the Realm of the Sea." Seeing Tie's displeased face, he pressed on. "We will be staying in an above-ground city for a small time, however, as the Realm of the Sea has not been completed. Everyone will have a temporary dwelling there, until the tribes' lands are split and things are grown and built up." Tie nodded reluctantly, and Citrosine managed a small nod, although she'd not been paying much attention. Iron hot tears charred her cheeks still, and she feared that her eyes would fall out with all the escaping tears.

Gya looked at both his daughters stonily.

"Are you sure that you are all right with this change, my daughters? We could probably manage to live aboveground if…"

"Yes," Citrosine spoke first. Tie sat up straight and stared at her sister, who continued. "We have to. There are too many things going on, the Dark Ones and all…it's just too dangerous."

"I'm glad to hear that," Gya admitted, surprised, "but… are you sure it's only that reason that's keeping you—"

"Father," Citrosine confessed honestly, "Can we stop discussing this? It is awful to speak of such things now. I need to rest. This day—there has been too much to understand right now." As she spoke, she charmed herself into rest that might help her aching head heal. Gya urged her into her blankets on the floor to rest for a short while, and he and Tie made their way out of the room, to a larger room where Elves could congregate with the other families in the hall.

Citrosine fell asleep quickly, due to her charm; however, it was a fitful, unsatisfying time, full of dreams made of memories.

Two hours later, Tie and Gya crept into their cabin for sleep. Gya was out cold in a matter of minutes due to the stress of all these changes—his wife had vanished, his home was gone forever, and his daughters were growing up too quickly, not to mention the emergence of Wampyres and Elf traitors. It was truly a shame about Tyre. He had been such a good Elf, such a strong part of the Council, so much in love with Gya's daughter.

Tie sat in a corner facing the wall. She had too much to think about, too much of her mother's death to piece together. If only she could have another clue, something that could help her remember the details of that night…a jog to the head, perhaps….She stood silently, and placed a smooth, tan palm on her father's forehead, closing her eyes.

She felt his thoughts from the day he had left his wife for Haerthor…*Interesting storms—almost as if the forces of the earth are willing us to leave…Leenka…home before it catches them vulnerable in the forest…demons, Wampyres, trying to hinder the Council for years…strange, storm from the south, where the Shadow…*Nothing helpful at all, Tie thought. She stood over Citrosine. Her sister had been quieter than she for a long time, more sensitive with her thoughts, so there was great risk in this. Her mind would be receptive and protected. She did not touch Citrosine in her sleep, just tried to draw from her anything of interest from that day—Citrosine's own birthday, that wasn't fair—Tie sulked and felt a newfound resentment for her sister grow.

A dream…transforming into evil…skin ripping away and no longer suffocating…tearing away from former life…something new, careless…powerful—the power—such evil…

Tie felt her stomach twitch…that was what had happened to Leenka. She'd been sired into being a Dark One. Whatever Citrosine had dreamed…did she have something to do with this? Was it a prophecy? Had she *known?* The little Elf's eyes clouded with fear and rage. She would not let this go.

The hours passed on the ship were tedious and uneventful, even for Citrosine, who managed to avoid any other chance meetings with Pherkue. She didn't know what her reaction would be if she saw him again, but she did know that she wouldn't be drawn into that feeling of longing for him again. Why had she gotten Jygul's Blessing if not to protect herself?

Tie fell deeper and deeper into the plot she was concocting, and rarely spoke anymore. Gya noticed this, and tried to introduce her to some other Elves of her age, but Tie only sulked and ignored them. Both of the Nakiss girls spent large portions of their time in solitude, Citrosine pacing the deck, and Tie lying on the bed in their room, scheming. Hours passed, and they drew steadily further from their home, and closer to the mystery and rebuilding that would occur in their new isle of residence.

Eleven

MOURNINGS AND NIGHTS

A few hours later, Leader was making rounds through the cabins, knocking on doors and talking to everyone. He announced to each to gather his things and make way to the deck, as they would reach land in the next few hours. He found Gya and Tie in their room.

"Hello, Gya," he said warmly.

"Hello, sir," Gya replied. Tie raised a hand in greeting but said nothing.

"I would advise you both to order your things. We will reach Ilthen before too long. I have asked everyone thus far to meet on deck in an hour, so that everyone can be counted." Leader's face shone with perspiration, as he'd been traveling swiftly about the ship all day, and there were many Elves that he still had to reach.

"Thank you, sir—but I wonder, how is it that such a small island can have been created so far away?" Gya maintained patience without revealing his skepticism on this whole journey. It had taken much longer than anyone had let on.

Leader smirked. "We have taken a longer route to reach a short distance. For you see, we needed to scout the island before our vessel unloaded such throngs of families, and... due to some misunderstandings on our own part among the Leaders as to which tribes were sending scouts, we were told to circle a little and stall until they were entirely sure that the island was suitable. My apologies, Gya." Leader smiled sympathetically. "We did not want to alarm anyone."

Gya laughed out loud. "Thank you, Leader; I will make sure that my family is ready to depart soon, then." Gya bowed to his superior, casting a brief look over to Tie. She rose, and nodded almost imperceptibly, then collapsed on the mattress and went back to staring at the ceiling. Leader bowed back to the two, and made his exit. As he came to the next cabin, he considered the Nakiss family, giving silent counsel to Gya.

"That Palgirtie...she used to be so enthusiastic about everything. I should know; I did legally register her into the Council records, did I not? She was always running circles around her mother. Now...she's so full of worry! I wonder if her mother's death had a portion to play in such a transformation...She is stronger than that. I wouldn't think that she should withdraw into herself so much. It is probably not so healthy."

"Thank you, my friend. I shall think on this."

Citrosine, restrained if not calmed by her rest, was at the very front of the boat, eyes closed, salt air twisting through her hair and face. Dem was in the form of a swift silver serpent-demon, slithering and twisting back and forth before her. It slipped tendrils of presence into her mind several times, just to make sure that she was feeling stable. She'd had too many emotional extremes recently, and was having a difficult time restraining the black magic within. Every time that she would think about her current situation, she could feel the icy stirrings rising up beneath her skin, and her sight would grow flushed with rage.

"*Citrosine; you must return below. Leader was here in the cabin a few moments ago, letting us all know to pack up our things, as we will be landing soon.*" Gya's voice was quick and excited. Citrosine opened her eyes reluctantly.

"*Yes, Dada; I shall join you,*" she said, eyes hunting for land ahead. At first, all she could see were blurs from having her eyes closed. After she adjusted to the light, she could easily make out the barren edge of the island they would soon have to call home. It was only a few miles away.

"*Citrosine,*" Gya continued, "*Can you see Ilthen from up there?*"

"*Yes, sir, I can, with no trouble.*"

"*What are your impressions of it?*"

Citrosine hesitated. Her impressions were that it was desolate, unprotected, and disgusting.

"*It looks…like it will definitely be able to fit everyone upon it,*" she murmured, choosing her words carefully. Gya said his goodbye, and Citrosine reluctantly leaned over the front rail.

"*Dem,*" she called.

"*Thy voice mourns some loss unbeknownst to my own imaginings. What has happened?*" Dem jerked its head back to look at the Elf-girl for a split-second, leaping into a back-flip above the water.

Citrosine sighed, leaning her elbow on the rail, and cupping her cheek in her hand.

"*Dem…the past few hours have not been well to me, you know that,*" she moaned.

"*We have not spoken since last night. What would have informed me…?*"

"I could feel you prying into my head, you beast!" Citrosine shouted into the surf ahead of the ship. It felt good to let her anger out, if just in small, measured increments. She rolled her eyes, and Dem felt a wave of exhaustion pass through the young Elf. Dem blinked slowly, and told her how sorry it was.

"Doesn't matter," was her reply, and then: *"You ought to start telling some of the others of your kind that we will be landing soon. I need to go with my father, and all the Elves will be meeting on deck again presently."*

"I shall comply exactly," Dem said despairingly, not wanting to irk the girl any further.

As Citrosine strode across the deck, several Elven families were already congregating with their belongings near the bow, gawking at the inhospitable hunk of land with which they were expected to make due.

She marched down the narrow stairs, taking deep breaths, and trying to clear her countenance for Gya. This was done easily except for the presence of Pherkue strolling up the stairs in the opposite direction, coming right into her path.

"Oh!" he exclaimed upon noticing her. "Citrosine; I haven't had the time's luck to meet you since this morning." He bowed his head, stopping right in front of her, so she could go no further. "I trust that you have been well?" His deep, red eyes scanned her face for some hint of...what was it...perhaps attraction?

Citrosine looked at him as if he'd murdered a Faerie.

"I have not been very well at all, thank you," she said calmly, though her eyes were sharp and icy. Pherkue looked at her in disbelief. Citrosine felt a renewed strength of magic, as if he were strengthening the attraction over himself.

"Sir, it is not wise to attempt such a thing," she growled.

"Pardon me, my fair one?" Pherkue took on an amused skeptical expression. He cupped his hand over Citrosine's elbow, simply for the sake of touching her.

"I believe you very well know of what I speak!" Citrosine said, still retaining composure. She relaxed the arm that the Dark Elf grasped, and sent a charge of invisible dark power through it. The burst immediately struck the boy's palm, and he withdrew in alarm. Holding his hand to his neck, his brow furrowed.

"I...what...is this about my earlier boldness?" He floundered for words, and Citrosine wondered if he was this sincerely ignorant. She looked at his bewildered face, and saw a look of deliberation and hurt.

"You didn't know about the charm?" she asked quietly.

Pherkue seemed to suddenly understand. A weight came over him, and then he cocked his head to the side. "Citrosine...I know of no charm." Citrosine looked him over. *Is this just a sham, this whole 'I have absolutely no earthly conception of what came over me' bit?* He could easily be pulling off this little scene as a performance of sorts.

"You had a bewitchment of the nature of a Siren's, or something along those lines, over you. That, I am sorry to say, is the only reason I could have been found... embracing you." Citrosine bit her lip, and Pherkue seemed lost in thought. "Actually, I could say that it was quite more than 'embracing', but the name for that is in the way that you see it."

"Pardon," Pherkue murmured, still thinking to himself.

"I am sorry if I offend you by rejecting your...whatever it is you are attempting to offer me, but I will have none of it. Because of your connection with the Wampyre crisis and how closely you are tied in with your uncle and in my suspicions and—*Tyre's*—" the name caused her a searing pain in her lower abdomen, "I will not have you."

"Pardon," Pherkue repeated, obviously only barely listening to her. His lips were moving quickly, and his eyes had blackened. He could not be still, always his hands or legs twitching and readying for motion.

"So...I am finished chastising now. Forgive me; I was angry with you, for I thought that it all was a sham. If you did truly feel the way you seemed to feel for me, and I gave you some false acceptance of your...love...? I am sorry." Citrosine studied Pherkue's face again, the marble skin of his lips and cheeks giving her no information.

"I am sorry to be so offensive," she began, wondering if she'd just humiliated him, but she saw him change before her eyes. He straightened, lightened, and the brightness of his crimson eyes returned. Citrosine began to realize exactly how close he was to her; he was substantially taller, but stood a step lower on the staircase, so their faces were even. She leaned backwards discreetly.

"No, no: it was my offense," he offered. His voice was again so focused, so genteel. This caught Citrosine totally off-guard. She wondered if Pherkue had perhaps not given up on... whatever it was that he wanted. Involuntarily considering this thought, she decided that she had to leave him now.

"May I proceed down the stair, sir?" Citrosine murmured gently. Pherkue looked into her eyes, placed a tentative hand on her shoulder, and flattened himself as much as was possible against the wall. The Stone Elf passed, allowing Pherkue's hand to slide off her shoulder freely, and finally coming to rest at his side. Citrosine was forced to brush against him as she passed, but she knew that he was trying to be polite, and this was simply the smallest he could make his tall, muscular body. They said nothing more, and she left.

Pherkue watched her descend the staircase and make a graceful exit. Promptly his features snapped back into the distress he had not wanted to show her just before. He closed his eyes, slid down against the wall, and sat on the stair for a few moments. His hands ran through his hair angrily and his mouth uttered incomprehensible words and thoughts that would never have felt the breath of the sea air if the Elf had been in the vicinity of anyone that might have overheard.

When he stood again, he began swiftly descending, reversing the course that he had formerly been upon. He kept his fingers around the railing tightly, all that kept him from beginning into a fit of panic and leaping down to the floor at the end of the stairs.

It was not supposed to happen this way. However now she knows! She must know...she felt my kiss, she was so wary just presently...All I can hope is that all of my methods do not fail so shamelessly!

His thoughts clouded, and he proceeded on his way to seek Egan.

Gathered up on the deck of the ship again, all the Elves and Changelings were cramped and uncomfortable. Each person was in possession of at least one sack of belongings, and almost all of them were squirming and straining for a view of the island ahead. Citrosine felt as if she would be sick. She sent a flow of dark magic into her hands to make them stop shaking, along with one through her inner ears, as the noise around her was deafening; so many Elves, so many questions, so many worries.

"All Elves who have questions about tribe changes please remain on board," Leader was shouting above the din of scampering Elves and Changelings. "Changelings may proceed to their designated leader; please do not ask me where to find it, as it escapes me what form it may be in. All Elves should proceed to *Lothor*, the new city, where the royal family shall hold a court and determine dwellings shortly." Leader's voice was becoming rough and tired from overuse in the last few days. He was to be the organizer of this voyage, and then other Leaders were slated to take over in other matters, so he would be able to rest and resume his role among the Stone Elves.

Gya, Tie, and Citrosine were huddled right at the rail, avoiding contact with other Elves for fear of being distracted from Leader's instructions. They were waiting for everyone to alight, so that they could be changed to Sea Elves and have some peace.

Citrosine removed her outer cloak, as the atmosphere of this new place seemed to be rolling over everyone in waves of humidity. It was hard to breathe. She quickly adjusted her double-swords as she saw Pherkue approaching. She braced herself for any kind of greeting from him, but all he did was nod, courtesy and tranquility coloring his eyes. He passed by swiftly, and without occurrence. This made Citrosine wary, for such a brief change from one's pursuer in such matters was not ever so simple.

"Dada," Tie said nearby in a thin voice, "there are no trees here. Why can I not hear any birds or creatures, other than the Changelings, and those of our own kind?" Citrosine noticed that her little sister's voice had grown calmer and more thoughtful. She wasn't sure when it had happened, but it struck her in full effect now.

Gya chanced a faint trace of a smile. "No other creatures have set out from the Big Lands yet. They will arrive shortly, I am sure. All the trees that will be here are to be planted by all of our kinds together. All of the remaining races will help. We have a large compartment in the underside of this ship that contains nothing but trees, grass, and flowers. See how the ground here is soft and gray? This is the soil that our ancestors enchanted to receive anything that we cultivate."

Therefore we must not cultivate evil, grudges, or discord, Citrosine reasoned.

As the last stragglers were climbing down the ramp of the ship, Leader called the remaining Elves together. There were only a few families left, and the majority of these were in company of Elf-children Tie's age or younger. Citrosine assumed that they wanted to be assured some extra protection just as much as the Nakiss family did.

"Friends," Leader murmured, saving his voice, as this was a much smaller company, "all of you wish to be transferred into new tribes?" Seeing the nods from each family, he frowned in grief. *"Well,"* he continued, *"I can only work with one per moment, so let me have…how about you?"* He pointed. *"The Zjoh family, is it?"* A tall man and his wife, who was being followed with a bombardment of questions from the six children trailing behind, presumably of the Sea Tribe by appearance, stepped forward, and followed Leader towards the rear of the ship, where they could have a bit of privacy.

Gya tried to explain to his daughters what was to happen. "Leader will have our Marks of the Stone removed, though it should not hurt. Then, he'll have to give us the Marks of the Sea, and we'll be free to hurry back with the rest to listen to what King Hendius has to say."

"Is it really that easy to change tribes?" Tie asked morbidly. Gya did not answer.

Leader came back with the Elf family, who had obviously been changed to the Mountain Tribe, as they possessed the swirling designs twirling around the outsides of their eyes, either dashed markings or s-shaped curls. They disembarked the ship quickly, and headed off to where Lothor was in the distance.

Leader looked around him, and picked out a tall man standing out in the back. Citrosine followed his gaze, and recognized the man instantly. Even as Leader called out his name, Citrosine shrank back against the rail, and clutched the cane that she'd held close for hours on end. The man was Tyresias Kendah's father.

Kendah spotted Citrosine on his way forward, and made no sign of identification. He joined Leader, and asked if he could please join the Cavern Tribe. Leader gave his consent, and they went to the rear of the ship again. Citrosine looked over a few heads and squinted in that direction, realizing that she could easily see the two men. Tyre's father was removing his surcoat and tunic, and Citrosine saw that his present Mark consisted of a pair of curved double lines on each of his shoulder blades.

Leader placed a hand on each of these, and with a buzz of magic, they were gone. Now Leader held his hands before the man's face, and there was another transfer of magic. When he turned around, Citrosine saw the three crescents that were the sign of the Cavern Elves, one on each cheekbone and one on the brow. These made the somber man look more aged and alone. Citrosine winced. As the newly initiated Cavern Elf marched past and off the ship, he met Citrosine's eye with an unforgiving, icy look.

"Gya, the Nakiss family, please come with me," Leader was saying as Citrosine watched Kendah step onto the ground, look about him, and proceed toward the gray blur that was their newest city.

The three followed Leader, and, if anyone had been paying attention to Tie, one would have noticed her gritted teeth and repeatedly clenching fists in contrast to her darting, pleading eyes.

"What tribe are you three to be initiated into?" Leader inquired, flashing them a genial smile.

"The Sea Tribe, if possible—temporarily, of course," Gya supposed.

"A shame, that," Leader frowned, "we will all surely miss you in the Council. But, if it is to be; it is to be." Gya nodded solemnly.

"Know that all of us on the Council miss Leenka dearly. She was beautiful, and the best asset to our tribe I have ever known. Not to mention how close of friends she was with all of us. I am truly sorry for you, Gya." Leenka put a hand on Gya's shoulder, and Gya thanked him softly for the thought.

"Now," Leader continued, *"may I see your Stone Marks? This should only take a moment."*

The three rolled up their sleeves, revealing the Marks of the Stone. Leader came to Gya first, and placed a hand on his Mark. A secret word was passed among them, and they both laughed coarsely. A flash of bright light, then his Mark was no more. Leader did the same to the girls, as Tie seethed.

He cupped his hands and held them horizontally at eye level. There was a small sparkling cloud that emitted from his palms, which then turned to water. The water lifted up into an airborne river that spiraled around in a swirling shape. Palgirtie tensed.

Grins jreah nya—Remember never to forget! Her mind screamed, *This must not happen! I must stay in wait…*

Unfortunately, she was too late, and the water was already forming tight spirals around each of her and her family members' little fingers. When the water stopped circling, it hardened, and formed the silver rings that marked the Sea Elves.

A tear wriggled its way from her eye and made its way down the soft, pink desert that was her cheek. As it made its morbid leap from her face, she imagined it as her heart, spiraling and rolling down towards earth, and finally falling into a puddle on the deck.

"Well," Leader said pleasantly, "that should do you well. You may ensue to Lothor now, to receive your dwelling assignments until the Realm of the Sea is completed." He looked at Tie, who had now erased all the evidence of her tear's suicide leap. "Dear Palgirtie, do you know what the word *Lothor* actually means?" Tie looked at him bitterly.

"It means," she glared, "'second beginning'." She clenched her teeth, so as not to say anything foul to her elder. *"But,"* she added, with darkness and hate layered through her voice, *"I am increasingly inclined to think that it means more along the lines of a place where we will all make stupid mistakes. Death will happen here, and we will wonder why we have decided on the things we have."*

Leader blanched, and gave Gya a significant look. Gya had not heard his daughter's threat, and the expression on

Leader's face gave him the advice to talk to the girl as soon as was possible.

Lothor was nearly finished, and yet it was not even close to large enough. The castle was spectacular, unlike any that an Elf kingdom had seen, and Citrosine thought that it fit King Hendius's disposition well; the man was a revolutionary.

The castle's circumference was perfectly rounded and seemed as if it was a mile in diameter. The structure rose up in a massive cylinder of white stone, tapering out just slightly at the very summit, where it was inlaid with gold, and resembled a crown. Alcoves cut into the face, where beveled windows of stained glass rested, arranged in spiraling rows, down to the gate, which was heavily curtained, guarded, and chained. Comparatively to the older structures in Haerthor, this was not as ornate, but more entertaining. This castle resembled a king standing pleasantly to watch over his realm, rather than a conceited, over-decorated sprawl that Hendius had hardly spent any time in, perhaps for this very reason.

A mass of Elves was gathered in a stone courtyard to the rear of the tower, where the king and his family were seated on a large platform. The Nakiss family huddled amongst the throng, and presently, King Hendius rose to speak. Everyone applauded, and he waved his hands for silence. The man looked like an eagle, with flowing dark hair and beard, light, alert eyes, and muscles that seemed to snake and squirm through his body whenever he moved. His mouth was a thin line against his tan face, and his eyes were deep and hooded.

"Welcome all," he said, in a magnificent voice that held the weathering of many battles and ventures. *"I trust that everyone made a safe journey from the Big Lands, as everyone seems to be getting here well. All the Leaders have informed me that their respective groups of tribes have arrived. The only misfortunes I have yet been informed of were those that occurred before the journey was ever begun for certain individuals, for various reasons.*

When a cloud has been born, some rain must fall from it for it to be at correct capacity, though the other water within grieves to see it go. Will everyone join me in giving up a moment of reflection for the following Elves who have been taken from us, for reasons I will explain?" The king paused, letting his bright eyes pass over the silent crowd.

"I regret to be the bearer of these tidings...one of our royal children has passed. Gyrenette, twin sister to Tenthius; my beloved baby daughter, has been called victim to the Red Death, as well as Cavern Elf Kirna Malceste—a strong warrior matron loyal to our armies for many years. The disease has been apprehended by our more skillful healers, but two still fell as we studied remedies.

"A number of Dark Elves have been taken from us, as their magics have failed from the various intermarriages and inbreeding that has occurred within their own extended families. These..."

Citrosine had stopped listening for the moment, as she had caught sight of Pherkue and Egan. They were standing arms' length apart, facing each other, and it was obvious that they were holding a private conversation. Citrosine attempted to break in.

"Egan, I cannot help myself any longer. We must get out of this area...I am too much for her. And you only encourage me. Is it not bad enough that our own families are dying, without the help of your...your thirst? This is not the way. We must collect and come up with something else..."

"My nephew, you have given up so readily? And you blame your inadequacy for planning upon me? You must be mad! I am only doing what I need to do."

"That doesn't matter! But you must understand...it is neither sensible nor possible anymore. I am losing..."

Citrosine was about to reach a conclusion on the ambiguity that was being discussed when King Hendius's voice, leading a train of disturbing thoughts she already knew, barreled into her ears like poisoned arrows, leading all understandings away into the sky; feathers blown away by an icy breeze. King Hendius had not yet finished his elegy.

"Tyresias Kendah. He is the most recent Elf I know of to be dead. He was a blind Elf, a large part of the Stone Tribe Magic Council, and a devoted mage and prophet. Tyresias's life, distressingly, was taken not by sickness or evil means, but by his own volition and a vial of poison. Kalka may see Tyresias's redemption by his contributions to the Stone Tribe and spare him from the punishment that suicide deems.

"I ask humbly for a moment of quiet, as we mourn for all those leaves that have withered and fallen from this tree of beginnings and life."

There was a long, long silence, in which Citrosine cried again, and then King Hendius continued to give instruction to the rest of the body about what would occur during this period of transition.

Citrosine, Palgirtie, and Gya were assigned to a temporary dwelling in Lothor, in one of a series of small tents that had been prepared by the builders who'd journeyed with the royal family. It was very cramped, with a patch of land around it in which they cooked and washed.

For at least a fortnight, every Elf in Ilthen—for everyone had camped around the central Elven city of Lothor—worked patiently planting trees, shrubs, flowers, and buildings in various places. The island was larger than anyone had remembered, and so each tribe was given certain types of plants to place. The Stone Tribe, for example, planted the trees with small trunks and leaves that fell off in the winter, and the flowers which attracted bees and beetles, while the Mountain Tribe planted the evergreens, and small shrubs that would create homes and thickets for woodland creatures.

The work was hard, and Citrosine kept herself planting every day only by imagining Tyre's company, encouraging her and threatening of what might happen if she ever gave in to the strain in her back, neck, and shoulders. *You mustn't let yourself give up,* she imagined him saying, *or whatever will protect you from the Wampyre's attacks? You heard what Pherkue and Egan discussed, did you not, love? They spoke of thirst, of plans... You must stay alert and strong, else they could strike upon you or others at any time.*

So Citrosine bent over, scooped earth from its resting place, and tenderly pressed a seed or sapling into the soil.

Towns and dwellings were created easily, based on what needs the different tribes had. A special assembly of builders created the Realm of the Sea, which was to be the home of both merfolk and Sea Elves.

Races other than Elves arrived every day or so, in varying numbers. Demons and Dark creatures came in the nights, so very few were even aware of their arrival, but in the daylight hours, their presence was obvious, by the small rings of destruction that they left when creating homes for themselves, or even simply gathering food for the remainder of their journey.

The small folk created their own dwellings in and around the one massive, magical tree that had been found already growing on the island. The Dwarves, Faeries, Pixies, and others interwove their dwellings among the massive plant. This tree had already grown enormously, and the branches were invisible in the dense clouds that piled atop each other in the luminous sky. So many of the Enchanted World's races agreed that this was the most majestic growth they had ever witnessed, with its dark, aged bark, and sparkling orange sap seeping from various breaks in wood.

This tree could have quite possibly been Kalka, the Redeemer of the Afterlife, where Ghersah perched in the highest branches of the tree. Perhaps, in another dimension, another plane that was imperceptible to all the living immortals, all the souls of the redeemed and approved lives sat here, looking down upon them all. The city established around and inside carefully arranged knots inside of the massive tree was named Treewall. All the small creatures that flitted about lived in fear and admiration of the massive tree, explained not by their ancestors' tales of this promised land of Ilthen, but only in legend and spiritual tale…

The only other bit of the island that had already been established before the Elves' arrival, apart from a range of mountains and an area of surrounding foothills, was what the immortals called the Ruin. Upon the top of a hill that ran down steeply to the sea on one side and was surrounded by a valley on the other was what looked to be the remainder of some ancient building. One could make out a large entryway off to one side that was a perfect circle, sunken partway into the ground, and also a stone slab on one side of the entryway, facing the sea. None of the races knew its origin, and all could only guess that their fabled ancestors left it here upon creating the island. However, even with this reassuring idea floating about the area, no one dared to give it further exploration or investigation. In fact, everyone let it be, alone atop that distant, secluded hill toward one of the northernmost corners of the island. There it acquired a sacred air, even keeping demons from building anything within sight of it. Citrosine wondered if she'd explore it someday, but it occurred to her that perhaps it would be better left in mystery and isolation.

Nymphs came in small numbers, and it was decided that they would have one city to themselves, built in a protected wood, and called Niklouh, just beyond the mountains. A few wizards and sorcerers came, but there were so few that it was uncertain where they might have gone to settle. A few priestesses and sorceresses appeared, as well, but they, too, seemed to disappear shortly after arrival.

Most spectacular of all was the arrival of all the magical flying creatures. Dragons by the tens, the last of the Changelings, griffins, sphinxes, demons, dark beings, and all the different enchanted birds, serpents, flying centaurs and reptilian flying creatures that one could imagine came in daily, all flying in strands and clouds over the sea, and arriving to their destined places of living. Citrosine agreed with her father: it was beautiful. Almost no one could remember the last time he had seen any of these beings, so it was a wonderful, nostalgic feeling for many, albeit a life-changing novelty for the rest.

All beings helped as much as they could in the development of Ilthen, and soon, even a variety of non-magical animals had arrived. Magic flourished in its various forms, and everything had an aura of beauty and magic flowing through it.

Twelve

Where the Sun is a Memory

A year passed. The planters charmed their trees and grasses to reach maturity faster, and everything got off to a good start. Otherwise, things had been at a standstill. No creatures infringed any others, or made any harm to one another.

But it was time for other things to begin again, like Councils, towns, family lives. Camping Elves drained from Lothor as new colonies were defined. Soon, it was time for the Sea Elves to see their new dwellings. All of those ones who had been living in Lothor joined a procession to the sea. The Nakiss family once again packed their things, and said goodbye to the friends of the Stone Tribe that they had met. King Hendius said farewell to them at the gate, and the Elven flag at the top of the cylindrical wall around the city waved its own goodbye. The green banner boasted an Elven crest, with a white embroidery design of Kalka. The tree was beset by gold stars, winking out a grand wish of hope.

The procession of Elves made its way past the mountains, called the Dragonback Range, for it looked like the spines and wings of the back of a gigantic Dragon. All reached the shore in a short matter of time, where a large, swirling hole was cut into the water.

Tie looked at the excitement on everyone's faces, and ran back to where the grass was superceded by sand. She knelt, her limbs shaking and clammy. Gya and Citrosine tried coaxing her to stand, but the girl was nauseated. She lay on the ground, feeling as if she would be sick. She gagged, but could not vomit, although she felt as if that would have helped her be rid of the sick feeling tracking through her stomach.

"Tie, are you all right?" Gya stroked her back as she shuddered and gasped for breath. Palgirtie tucked her knees into her chest, feeling as if the world was going to collapse under her shoulders. Her fingers tingled; lungs squeezed and constricted. She couldn't explain it to herself, but images of her mother's capture flashed through her mind and she imagined how beautiful the world was back at home and she missed the old cottage and she couldn't leave the beautiful sky and everything was just...*wrong.*

"Are you fellows coming along?" A young Elf-man called out to them. "We're about to descend!"

Gya took Tie under one arm, Citrosine took her other, and they helped her stagger into the globe of air that was waiting to take all the Sea Elves down into their new city.

Once inside, Tie slumped to the ground, shaking and sweating. She twisted to look up at the receding surface. The sun was a wavering ball of hope, morphed by the movement and depth of the water, growing fainter and further away. She took a deep breath of fresh surface air, and the air bubble sealed itself from the water. *Remember never to forget...*Tie shuddered uncontrollably, wishing that her mother was there to sing the lullaby that always had soothed her sorrows, infused with a magic charm of healing.

Citrosine and Gya were quite excited to see the Realm of the Sea, as they had heard so many people spreading rumors of its greatness. A friend in Lothor, one of the leaders in the tree-planting efforts, had mentioned that it was to be enclosed in a large glass sphere, and another copy of it, an almost exact replica, was to be created alongside for the mer-kingdom. The Elves around them whispered to each other heatedly, asking others if anyone knew anything more about the city. They had received dwelling number assignments a few days ago and now fantasized about what the rooms would look like, what kind of jobs they could have, and other such things.

"Dada," Tie groaned faintly from her crumpled position on the floor of the globe. Gya knelt next to her, stroking her hair. Tie had grown to look much like her mother, if not in hair or eye color then most decidedly in the shape of the face, and Gya felt a pang of sadness every time he looked at her. It wasn't completely the fault of the resemblance, but he always wondered about the darkness in his daughter's eyes, and the paleness in her cheeks, the quietness in the energy which she seemed to have spent so much on planting trees and flowers in the last decade. She had always returned home exhausted from the days of planting and sowing, but she never complained.

"Dada, I cannot stay under the sea," she said faintly. Gya tried to smile.

"*Lissa*, I don't wish for it either, not for the rest of our lives," he admitted. "I like studying the magics that all the different races use, and the non-magical creatures fascinate me, but they are gone forever, for they stayed in the Big Lands."

"Then…why must we hide down here? Why can we not show our faces to the sun?" She shot a fleeting look up at the miniscule ball that receded steadily.

"Tie, we have spoken of this before."

"But, father—"

"*Palgirtie.* We are not hiding; we are being protected for the time being. I want us to be guaranteed to be safe from any tensions that the Dark Elves may plan—you know that they—" he shot a look towards Citrosine and broke off his thought, "and if any Men arrive in Ilthen, they cannot find us here. We will wait until everything is settled up on the rest of the land, and then, I will join the Stone Tribe Magic Council again."

"Father, I still do not understand! Why have we spent so long above the water if it is not safe there? If the Men did not come then, how do you know that they will? The Dark Elves would not wait until everyone was prepared with strong fortifications and armies to attack, or whatever they might do! Tell me why you are afraid of the way we have lived for the last centuries!" Tie's eyes blazed with irritation, hurt, and anger. The Elves directly around her family looked to Gya sympathetically, and withdrew a small bit. Gya looked at his child stonily.

"Tie, do you not remember what happened to your mother? What did you say happened to her—she was made a Wampyre? That happened while the royal family was moving down here to wait for Lothor to be finished. Some dark force was trying to exterminate members of the Councils across the Big Lands, in preparation for something that they were planning here. I am sure that it was linked with the Dark Elves.

"They were busied with their own transitions recently, as were we. Now that the majority of that which was to be planted is set in the ground, they will attempt to carry on with that preparation. I have notified all the other members of my Council, and they are all taking extreme measures to protect their families. I have nothing left to protect you two with, and I have decided that this…this migration, is the best defense we have." He stopped, seeing Tie's surprise. She hadn't known completely why her mother had been killed. She had seen, vividly, her mother being transformed into a Wampyre, and now she knew why, after so many endless days and hours had gone by. However, the ideas that she'd harbored ever since then still held true, and this new information only strengthened the motivation to carry out her plans here, under the sea. She did not trust the

Council any longer. Gya folded his younger daughter into a tight hug, which Tie did not return, her arms limply swinging by her sides.

"This was a choice made a long time ago. Your mother and I used to discuss this action at great length, and very seriously. I don't want anything to happen to either of my two favorite girls, and there is too much that could go wrong in the first few years aboveground—you need not be afraid, lissa. I can see the same fire in your eyes as your mother's when she thought of hiding herself from the sky, which is where she came from. Perhaps you have some Air Elf traits in you. Just stay strong, lissa."

Just a short distance away, Citrosine was unaware to all that had happened between her father and sister. She was transfixed with the ocean life outside the slow-moving globe. She watched the brightly colored fish and serpents flitting about in non-patterns through the coral and seaweed that grew in tufts on the ocean floor.

The city was directly ahead, and it was breathtaking. There were two large citadels, one blue-green and littered with stairways, enclosed in large bubbles and glass spheres that caught the sparkling light from above the water. The other citadel was covered in thick layers of coral and barnacles, with open doorways and passages to the water. She saw hundreds of mer-people skittering around; many colors of tails flickering in the wavering light. This city was going to make a beautiful memory in Citrosine's mind, and best of all, they didn't have to plant anything else in the hot, humid air. Nor were there any risks of running into any Dark Elves.

When the globe full of air reached the city, it breached the bubble that enclosed the opening gate slowly, and just like the hole that had opened in the surface of the water. The Elves filed out of the globe slowly and in awe as the globe became a nonentity in the air of the citadel.

They were greeted by the guards at the main gate, and the appointed Sea Elder, who was to oversee the functions and people of the city.

"Welcome, all," she hummed warmly. The Elder was tall and lean, with a long, pale face. She had long, silvery hair, and wore a surcoat with small fish embroidered across it. Her eyes were hazel-brown, and shone with kindness. *"The Enclosed City has been waiting for you. King Hendius informed you of your assigned dwellings, did he not?"* Someone muttered an affirmative answer up near the front. *"Good,"* she answered, *"then less trouble on my part. I am the Sea Elder, and will govern the Enclosed City until further notice. If you need me, you may come to ask me any question whenever you want. I live in the turret at the apex of the citadel. By the way, you may call me Nerine. If that is too hard for anyone, I will also answer to Rina, or Leader. Makes me feel less old."* Citrosine realized that she'd never learned the Stone Tribe Leader's name. She shifted uncomfortably and tried to pay attention as Leader—Rina—continued.

"You must be tired. I have magicked sendings who will see you to your rooms. When you are there, you will find the clothes that our tribe wears; for any who have recently joined the Sea Tribe, that is a long silver tunic and leggings of black. Any clothes you own may be worn, but silver is the preferred color, so that the mermaids and mermen know who we are. The merfolk harbor grudges against some of our people, and we wouldn't want you to get mixed up in a misunderstanding." Nerine snapped her fingers, and a long row of hovering, silver teardrop-shaped forms appeared. Each made its way toward a family of Elves.

"Dinner will be served at sundown. Your sendings will lead you to the dining hall. I would be elated to see all of you there, but you may cook your own dinners in your rooms any time you wish. Have a good afternoon." With that, Nerine turned and swiftly made her way up a flight of stairs.

The sending that presented itself to the Nakisses slowly made its way towards a flight of stairs in the rear of the entrance hall. The three looked around in awe as they walked. Small globes of shimmering blue-green light flickered in their sockets in the walls, and the dancing light reflected off the glass floors and surfaces. The ceilings were all high and vaulted, though some formed perfect spheres with the rest of the walls and floors.

As they followed their sending, they became acquainted with the other Elves whose sendings were leading them in the same direction. One family was made up of two men, two women, and three children of varying ages. The youngest was an infant, and the oldest looked to be older than Citrosine; old enough to have a sword forged to signify his coming of age. She knew this because he showed it off and told her that it was so. Called Paetyr, he was tall and likeable, and talked to Citrosine most of the way. He made very light of everything, and Citrosine made friends quickly with him. Then his dwelling was reached, and they said their goodbyes.

Another person that joined them was an old, hunched Elf-woman who spoke very little to anyone. She introduced herself as Dydae, and had a strange aura, in Citrosine's mind. She seemed as if she could never keep the boundaries of herself in the right place; it was like she couldn't choose how much space to take, and so she just wavered in between a flexible boundary. Tie took an immediate liking to her, the two finding some strong connection, though Citrosine was a bit intimidated by the woman.

Their final company consisted of a pair of Elves, one male, one female bearing child. They walked very close together, fingers interlocked, and each carrying a bag. There was an abundance of love in their eyes, and Gya was left feeling empty inside upon the vision of them walking together.

That's what Tyre and I could have become, Citrosine thought next to her father. Gya seemed to have felt her sadness, empathizing, and he put his arm around her waist.

The Enclosed City was filled with meandering hallways and staircases. Tie looked around in resignation, thinking that this would be a wonderful place to disappear from the world. She always was made to shiver when their party passed through an empty hallway where there were no lamps as of yet. Cool tremors swam up through her spine, and silent voices whispered to her.

The Elf couple parted the company to descend a staircase bordered by solid glass walls that looked out over large shelves in the ocean's floor, and where fish and turtles looked in with surprise. After only a few more turns, the sendings of the remaining four stopped.

"Well," creaked Dydae in her low, shaky voice, "It looks as if we will be close neighbors, doesn't it?" She looked at Tie, and they shared a last glance. *"Tie, child—say something to make your sister laugh. You both seem so sullen. I will not live next to you unless I can hear your laughter every once in a while. Even if you are harbor conflicts…please, just laughter?"*

"Apparently we shall be quite close, indeed," Gya answered the old woman's last spoken words. Dydae looked over at him pleasantly. Gya double-checked the sheet of paper Leader had given him, with their dwelling number written in charcoal pencil. *The Nakiss Family—Dwelling 621, Enclosed City. Good luck, friend. My regards.* He looked up at the door that they were waiting in front of. The door was white, with a blue handle, and a blue symbol of the Sea Tribe. The gold number at the top read *621*. It was indeed correct.

"Nerine did well in creating our sendings." He looked over to Dydae and nodded, then opened the door. Tie and Citrosine followed him in, and were amazed by how comforting the first room was. The carpet was white and soft, and three large sets of green pillows and sheets on hand-carved wooden swings were set on stands to the side of a large living room. Every wall was made of the same glass as the rest of the city seemed to be. A separate room came off to the left, with a fireplace and a large pot where water could be placed for cooking, washing, or bathing. The final room, to the right, was a smaller one, with a wooden desk and chair, and several wardrobes for storage. The greenish lamps were hung every few yards high on the walls.

The sending quickly dissipated, and Gya prompted his daughters to unpack their things.

"Citrosine, I think you were blushing when that older boy was talking to you," Tie teased, putting some of her clothes in a drawer of the wardrobe. She remembered Dydae's last suggestion, and tried to get herself to lighten. Now was not yet the time to withdraw. "He was flirting with you, and you were flirting back."

"I wasn't at all," Citrosine shot back, annoyed. "He was very...well...he seemed quite *dense* to me." She giggled, and placed her pair of swords next to the desk. *Not like Tyre...* "Anyway, at least I avoided the witch next door." She stole a look at her sister, and quickly changed the color of the tunic Tie was folding to a frightening bright yellow.

"Ay!" Tie almost dropped it. "Citra, you tricky one! Change it back—I can't have a yellow tunic!" She laughed, trying to remember the last time she'd been so cheerful. She silently thanked Dydae for the advice. "She isn't a witch, you know," Tie continued their play-argument, "she's just old, and...a bit mysterious."

Citrosine nodded. "I agree on the old and mysterious bit," she muttered, and pointed a finger towards her sister's tunic. It quickly went through a succession of color changes; from yellow to blue, blue to white, white to pink, and finally, pink to silver. Tie rolled her eyes. "Thank you," she drawled sarcastically.

"I don't remember the last time you called me Citra," Citrosine mused, lying on her back in her new hammock.

"*Citra, the profound and macabre,*" Tie joked, recalling a song that Gya had once relayed from a study of the Dwarves.

This was where the nickname had found its beginning, because the name sounded familiar with Citrosine.

"*She sing-ed like oceans and ne'er knew love,*" Citrosine joined in.

"*Ain' if Ghersah kun-nocked, she'd give 'er a swing, ne'er to breath-ie in song!*" The sisters broke the tune in a fit of raucous laughter, uncomprehending of the words' full meaning, but having fun with the far-from-proper language.

Gya walked in to the giggling of the two, shook his head, and smiled. "*Se lissa, nya methia,* calm down, or I'll keep you here for dinner. We can't have you so hysterical in front of all our new neighbors." He gave each of them a hug.

"Dada, I like it here," Citrosine hummed, so that Tie couldn't hear. She knew it would upset her.

"I do, as well, *lissa.*" Then, he added, in a louder tone, "Both of you ought to change your clothes. We are to wear our silver tunics whenever we are out and around the city. Did you find them in your sizes? Good. I think that Nerine did well in preparing for all of us." He walked out to find his tunic, and the girls put theirs on. They were more form-fitting than any of their old clothes, and Citrosine felt a little uncomfortable, revealing more of her body to these people whom she'd never met. Her leggings were tighter, like stockings, and didn't begin until her knee, showing off her lower leg, and the tunic was cut closer to her body, with shorter sleeves, a wider neck, and pronounced curves. Citrosine wondered how mermaid-like she might look.

"If we need to wear these all the time, then what are we to do with our old clothes?" Citrosine asked.

"I think we wear these same tunics forever, even when we decide to go swimming, until they are infested with mold and holes. Then, we wear anything else we have that is silver, and when that all wears out, we paint ourselves with whatever silver paints we can find! Silver everything!" Tie said this in such a declaratory manner that they were both laughing hard enough to be set rolling on the floor. Tie was forcing herself to laugh while trying to discern if Citrosine believed her happiness.

After an hour or so, the sending that Nerine had created appeared again, ready to escort the three to dinner. They followed it obediently, meeting Dydae in the hallway.

"Hello," came Nerine's voice. *"I hope that everyone pays attention to where their sendings lead them, because they will last only for another day. Then, you will need to know where things are on your own."*

The three, plus Dydae, followed, passing the same corridors and passageways that they had before. Things were vaguely familiar.

All of the families they had made the acquaintance of before soon joined them, and all the sendings merged into one, which they followed as a congregation.

Citrosine was immediately awestruck by the dining hall. The shining glass bubble that held the water out continued in a sphere from above to the edges of the floor, and the green, filtered light from above cast ghostly shadows over the long tables upon which food was piled high. There were so few Elves here…The Elf-girl spent much of dinner looking outside, into the sea. At one point, a brown, crusty turtle brushed up directly in front of her, knocking some coral off the structure outside. The coral drifted downward, and the turtle whisked past again. The coral was gone in seconds, crunched up between its jaws.

"Was that not the most gluttonous time you've ever had? It was glorious!" Tie was trying to come out of the sullen mood she'd been feeling all evening, despite Citrosine's tunic color-changing tricks that were an attempt at levity. She waved her arms about and staggered clumsily, as if intoxicated, like grown folks sometimes could be if they drank mass quantities of raspberry wine—very, very rare indeed among Elves, since it took so much to achieve such an effect, but entertaining nonetheless.

"I hope that every meal is as huge, so that we can all just eat forever and never have to think again! Wouldn't that be the loveliest? I think it's just…brilliant to be this overfed, eh?"

Dydae, Citrosine, and Gya, as well as the other neighbors they'd met before, all laughed and played along. Paetyr, Citrosine's friend, stepped forward, next to the girl.

"Aye, I f'il as if I's jus' aeten a gr'wn Drag'n," he drawled in a mocking, coarse accent. He rubbed his belly, and let out a belch. Again, everyone laughed. "An' with'o't ana pause in b'twe'en buytes!" he added. Citrosine laughed at him. *If* that's *being flirtatious,* she thought, recalling Tie's jibes, *then Pherkue must have wanted to ravage me!*

The meal had been quite large, with no limit of platters and courses, it seemed. Their party was all in good spirits, although quite tired and full of warm food. Tie plastered on a forged grin to hide her emptiness. She couldn't imagine how they'd all be able to stand this replica of a living place. The air felt stale and humid, and there was no way possible to see the sun or the moon, unless one or the other should fall into the sea.

Citrosine laughed along with the rest, although she felt it necessary to fall a short way behind them. She looked intently down all the empty passageways that were passed, feeling cold and shivery upon doing so. She noticed quickly that her sister did the same, although she seemed almost eager to leap away from their companions and run down the nearest one. Citrosine was afraid of these passages, wondering why no one was set to live down them, and why there weren't any of the lamps, throwing the swirling, dancing tendrils of light around. She found these lanterns fascinating. They had flames inside, like candles, but nothing was really burning, for it was just a source of magical light inside a glass sphere. They had turquoise-green auras and thus inside the city mirrored the light playing off the surface of the water far above.

When everyone had reached their dwellings and the Nakiss family prepared for their first sleep in this new atmosphere, Tie quickly became secluded and aloof. She lay in the hammock that was to serve as her bed, and listened to Gya and Citrosine as they drifted away into sleep. Tie noticed that Gya was asleep in minutes, while Citrosine didn't seem to be comfortable in the hammock, and was sporadically shifting for hours.

"Child, are you still at wake?" came Dydae's voice.

"...Yes; is there something that you need?" Tie wondered if her father would hear if she just tiptoed outside, into the corridor...

"Would you meet me in my room? It has been long since I have had one as delicate as you to talk with. I mean no harm, my dear. I'm just so glad to have met you, and I feel myself being pulled into a time of need..."

"Give me a moment, and I shall be there shortly," Tie replied. What was there to do, other than try to sort through everything alone?

She listened into Gya's mind, for any sign of consciousness. She saw her mother, younger, swirling and dancing in the old clearing, by a golden pond sparkling with the evening's sunlight. Yes, her father was definitely deep in senselessness.

Then, Citrosine...frightened thoughts skittered around. There was a letter that floated by in a blurry cloud; a huge, fiery monster next, writhing through the air and setting the delicate paper ablaze, and then Tie was met with a firm but not fully protected, private barrier. She wondered if her sister was really as strong as her outer shell made her seem. Anyway, she was deep in the semi-comfort of sleeping rest, which was all that Tie needed to know. She was safe to creep through their rooms and into the hallway, where the eerie, greenish lamps flickered, watching like sentinels.

Dydae was sitting in a huddled heap of blankets and clothing before a low wooden table. Tie went to her side swiftly, sensing that the old woman was very perturbed.

"Dear child," she creaked, "please, sit down. Thank you for joining me here—I have not been feeling myself in this new place..." She waved a hand towards a rough-hewn chair, an exact replica of one which took a place in the Nakiss residence.

"I think I understand," Tie said meekly, remembering how she'd broken down on the way to the city.

"Do you?" The old woman cast an appraising eye on her guest then nodded deliberately. "Yes, I can see it in you." She stroked the young Elf's hair gently, like a grandmother might. "Your face shows so much age, and yet, you are so small..."

"We lost my mother to enemies of the Council that my father worked for, back where the sun blessed the trees and grass. My father thought more of my sister than us, on her birthday...I can't stand them both, sometimes..." she stopped, not believing that she could open up to someone this way.

"Yes?" Dydae seemed to feel her hesitation, and looked at her somewhat warmly.

"I'm sorry...I haven't had anyone to talk to in years...my family..."

"I have none, in the same way. I was cast out for going against their beliefs, and they are all dead now, before I could gather up courage and explain why I crossed them. It has been only me, existing on the company of the creatures around me, forced into living as a hermit. Thank you, again, for choosing to talk to me here..." Dydae rubbed at her eyes, nostalgically sighing.

"If I may..." Tie began gently, not wanting to offend her friend, "what exactly was it that you did, to make your family so angry? My family was the opposite, being too absorbed in their own happiness that they forgot our safety, and now they won't listen…How did you cross them?" Tie's mind ticked and moved like a set of gears.

"Well, I was raised to Wood Elves. We were made to be one with the earth, but not so much as to reject our own kind. We used nature to our advantages, while not damaging nor disowning our own heritages." Tie was a bit confused, but she said nothing, waiting for the woman to finish recalling her experiences. "Getting to the point, dear me; I trained with a Cavern Elf to become a Shape Shifter, as I was not happy in my own skin alone. My family saw this as an insult to our ancestors, Wood Elves, and all others before us that had lived in their own ways contentedly. They discarded me, believing strongly that I had set my life's goal to gain revenge on the world for creating me as an Elf." She sighed again, and Tie gaped.

"A Shape Shifter," she repeated, unable to voice any other words for the mystification in her head. Dydae nodded. Tie floundered for a moment, trying to untangle her words from one another. "Eh…You mean…you can change into whatever you wish? What is your favorite form? What did you try first? Could you teach me? How long did it take you?"

"Ay, child, stop!" The old Elf laughed, the sound like the branches of a tree in the winter, creaking and wavering. "You bombard me so, how can I answer anything?" Tie sat up straight, mouth closed obediently. She felt lightheaded, and realized the possibility that everything she had hereto been planning her life around could change.

Dydae continued. "It took years for me to learn to shift my form into whatever I wanted, but only a short while for the most basic shapes." She thought a moment, gathering her blankets up around her bony, prominent shoulders. "I suppose I could teach you…" she calculated, "but you would have to live with the consequences."

Tie shivered, and hugged her legs to her chest. "Consequences?" The word was like a secret, slipping out of her lips so carefully, ominously.

"Look closely at me, my child. Can you not see that my form is so stretched and worn? I have pulled into so many forms that I can hardly regain my own! You think like the creature you become, with the same instincts, and sometimes it is so difficult to remember who you really are that...your new form changes you."

"How would it change you?"

"Imagine taking the shape of a fish, dear. What are a fish's main goals in life?" Dydae looked at Tie as if she were her own child, being asked if she had done all her chores.

"Well, I think they would be concerned with avoiding being eaten by other fish...finding food...finding a mate, and staying safe...?"

"Correct. If you took the shape of a fish, and stayed that way for quite some time, how would that change your outlook on Elven life?"

"One would only worry about himself, safety, security...and creating little baby fish!" She smiled, and Dydae laughed.

"Yes, that is exactly right. That is how it could change you." She grew quieter. "Tie, I see that you have an ability to think very deeply. I feel secrets in you. I think that you would be well-suited to attempt this...this shifting, but I fear for how it would affect the rest of your mind."

"You don't believe that I can regain my senses, keep focused on my own life?" Tie frowned. She looked icily at Dydae, and was surprised to see her shake her head.

"No, no, by all means, no, dear! Instead, you would be too deep in your own life that you wouldn't focus on the sane thoughts of whatever creature you become!" Tie lightened a little, and Dydae laughed softly, like a wind sighing through the stale atmosphere of the room.

"Will you teach me, then? Or…would I be too much a burden…?" She looked down at her toes, sighing; thinking.

Dydae reached out to her shoulder. "Dear child…" she paused, cupping Tie's cheeks in her frail, leathery hands, "I would be honored, but I fear for what your father might say."

"We shouldn't tell him…then it won't be a difficult situation," the Elf-girl answered mischievously. Dydae sighed.

"Very well…it is a fair price to pay in return for your company and…well, understanding." She smiled, revealing a row of scraggly, stained teeth. "We can begin right now, if you wish!"

Thirteen

Monotony, Melodrama

Citrosine awoke as soon as the first dull rays descended from the surface of the sea, illuminating their quarters in macabre tones; faint shadows lacing every surface, like wraiths waiting for victims to float by unawares. She was covered in a sheen of cold worry, though she couldn't even vaguely remember why. *Dreams can have that way of escaping one in the morning, after they have been experienced, placed into the recesses of the subconsciousness...*Citrosine stretched, yawned, and gingerly slid off of her new bed, attempting not to lose balance and cause the whole structure to flip upside-down. *The ground is so much more reliable,* she reasoned, twisting the soreness out of her back. *One need not worry of falling over the side.*

As she fished through her wardrobe for an appropriate silver tunic, Citrosine cast a quick glance over to her sleeping sister, who had fallen into slumber on her front, arm hanging off the side of the hammock, mouth open against her blankets. Citrosine smirked at her, recalling how happy she'd seemed the day before, despite her resentment of this place.

Tie snorted in her sleep, probably in the middle of some kind of colorful dream. Stifling a giggle, Citrosine pulled off her nightclothes.

Moments later, she remembered why she had awoken in such alarm.

She had dreamed of Tyre. And Wampyres.

Hastily, she scrawled a note to her father: *I need to ask our Leader a question about Wampyres. Had a nightmare. I'll have returned before breakfast. –Citra.* This she threw onto the front table, scurrying out the door. She'd kept Tyre's warning close to her at all times—in the purse she often carried slung over her shoulder—so it was easy to immediately make her way to find Nerine. *"I live in the tower at the apex of the citadel,"* she'd said. Citrosine began climbing stairs.

She walked passage after passage of darkness, and she couldn't help but feel that she was being stalked. Directly above the dining room—she knew it was above because she could see it below her through the glass floor—she arrived at a large, spiraling metal staircase. Ascending, she grew exhausted after so many footfalls. The action of lifting her knees became wearisome, and she whipped her head around every few steps, almost certain that she could hear someone climbing up behind her.

At the top of the stairwell, only a few more corners to turn until she reached the topmost turret, she turned around rapidly.

Tap, tap, scuffle—tap! She heard three hasty footfalls, and a shuffling noise, suggesting someone coming to an alarmed halt. Citrosine's hands began to sweat, and she took a moment to make sure that her breaths were inaudible. Creeping dexterously back down the staircase, she kept her eyes pointed downwards, through the wrought-iron steps. There was no movement for many minutes, as the Elf took one step at a time, gently, gently…

The surrounding bubble that protected the city from the ocean rippled as a snaking, melding form took off through it at top speed. Someone had been standing there, watching her. What it had been, Citrosine had no idea…nor did she wish to dwell on that idea for long.

"Daughter, please call me Rina—it's much more comfortable. I don't know what you called your previous Leader, but do call me by my name." Leader Nerine was calm and inviting when Citrosine arrived in her chambers, breathless and bewildered.

The room was dark, yet warm. A tiny spell-cast fire lit the room from a candle much too large for the flame, which just barely illuminated shelves upon shelves of books and papers, a few overstuffed armchairs, and the various tables with interesting art and glass pieces displayed. Who knew where she had gotten those—they certainly weren't familiar kinds of things to see in a Stone Tribe home.

"Thank you…Rina," Citrosine said, bowing her head a little. She was unused to calling an elder by name, but she had more important matters to consider, so she shouldn't linger on detail quite so heavily.

"Why have you requested my presence?" Rina asked genially. Seeing Citrosine panting and squirming excessively, her smile hardened.

"It's…I told my former Leader of this already, quite a time ago, but moving into this new place…I'd forgotten in all the confusion…I didn't know if you had any information… new information…?" She paused, to gather Tyre's letter into her hands. "I was given this letter from—er—an especially, incredibly close friend, and…I suppose that you could just read it…" She reluctantly slipped the letter into Rina's thin hands and looked down at the plush, intricately designed rug. Her hands grasped the edges of her tunic and twisted them, fingers wishing to hold anything and not remain empty of their most important possession.

Rina's eyes scanned the paper with a sluggishness Citrosine wouldn't have fathomed, her brow growing more concerned with every jump to a new line. Momentarily, she looked up into her visitor's face.

"Wampyres?" She looked skeptical. "You want me to believe that the Dark Tribe has been siring Wampyres…and is going to unleash them upon us to gain revenge and power because of ancient grudges?"

Citrosine nodded feebly. It made perfect sense to her, but…

"And why ever would they want to destroy the very tribes that have helped them settle into their new homes?" She looked at Citrosine as if addressing an immature child, no longer smiling encouragingly.

The inferior paused, anger growing inside her chest. "Having spoken to some of their tribe personally, including those indicated in the letter, I have heard that they are upset with how little land they've been given. They are being forced to diminish, intermarrying because they've been either spread out so much…or…er…" she faltered under Rina's withering expression.

"This sounds like child's nonsense to me," the Leader said carelessly. She thrust the letter back at Citrosine and started walking around the room as if she was drifting in a current. Citrosine scrambled for the letter, which threatened to catch the air patterns Rina stirred. "Nothing but a martyring story written by a child is this. Young Elves often have more melodrama about them than those who consider logical reasoning. You shouldn't worry yourself with such tales, my daughter. The Dark Tribe wouldn't have to narrow themselves so much by going after Council Members—they would have said something to myself or another Leader. It isn't as if they've sent out spies, to follow us around our citadels and know our every Member's exact schedule, now, is it?"

Citrosine stared at her openmouthed. She wanted to scream, *But I saw one of them following me up here to see you!*

"Leader—Rina—*sorry.* I know it sounds childish, but you have to believe me when I tell you now; I am not the kind of Elf to lie in this manner!" Citrosine clutched the letter tenderly to her breast.

"I am sorry, dear," Rina crooned, keeping her voice steady, and not at all angry, "but how am I supposed to keep my time straight? If I had so many juveniles like you coming up to me with this kind of *urgent message,* how would I ever get around to my other duties? What makes your pleas so definite? How do I know you aren't being theatrical?" Her eyes were sincere, and the two Elves stared each other down.

"You should believe that this page," Citrosine waved the paper in front of Rina's nose, "isn't a yarn because it was actually written by the Elf I wished to spend the rest of my life with, and right now, he is *dead*, having poisoned himself to elude capture from an impending *attack*." Citrosine's voice rose into a piercing hysteria, finishing octaves above the tone she'd begun with. She took a step forward, and placed her fingertips against Rina's temples, sending her memories.

Rina saw all at once Citrosine encounter Tyre's father; the acceptance of the letter and his demeaning slap, along with the conversation between Egan and Pherkue she'd overheard in Lothor, and the black form beneath her on the staircase just moments ago.

The Leader's eyes softened, but she still couldn't be sure that Citrosine was being truthful, so she sent the Elf-girl out of her tower, with a quiet apology, and a promise to "look into the problem".

"Please," Citrosine whispered, "just be wary, and please keep in contact with all of us if you hear more. Would you at least do this much for me? Rina?"

Rina smiled sympathetically, gave Citrosine a silent hug, and dismissed her.

Citrosine dejectedly scuffed her way back to where she and her family lived now, collapsing onto the soft, cushioning rug underneath the hammock to rest and reflect.

Days passed slowly, dragging on without end. Citrosine heard nothing from Rina, though she was fortunate, she admitted to herself, that she hadn't heard any terrifying news. Often, she thought she still heard footsteps behind her, and the darkened passageways she passed daily still made her shiver with an unreasonable—and unwaveringly chilling—feeling of being watched.

Tie spent more and more time fraternizing with their neighbor, Dydae, who was to Citrosine an ever-ominous presence, never seeming harmful, but never completely sincere, either. Sometimes Dydae would ask favors of Citrosine that seemed not to make sense, like going down an empty hallway where a supposed "acquaintance" lived, to ask for a parcel, where there weren't any doors to be found, much less dwellings. Another such instance, she was asked to search the thick, stringy carpet for a tiny, tiny pinhead that Dydae "seemed to have let slip". She didn't even understand how a pinhead could have been lost...or realized to be missing.

While Tie was gone, Citrosine and her father kept light conversations and mindless tasks going on for hours. Sometimes Citrosine would seek out Paetyr, and the two would take walks around the city, talking about all kinds of things. They spoke of gossip they had heard from neighbors, what kind of person they would like to marry—Paetyr had sworn off of females for a while because of a recent string of girls leaving him for being too silly. They even talked about their ideas on death.

Most days Citrosine had to help her father with chores, until she felt likely to explode with monotony. One such moment, while mending clothes and blankets worn from the journey across the sea, Citrosine broke out laughing for no reason apparent to her father. She felt that keeping such silence, doing such useless, silly mending was doing nothing to improve anyone's outlook on life, and simply cackled with hilarity at the sheer pointlessness of it all.

"Citrosine, *lissa*," Gya said, amused but not understanding, "what has come over your mind?" He could do nothing but chuckle to himself, watching Citrosine's hands shake and eyes tear with laughter.

"Pardon my impertinence, father," she gasped between outbursts, "but is there something that we could do that actually will help one of us—either of us—in life? I can't understand how days' worth of unpacking and mending will do us any," she laughed again, almost unable to finish, "*any* good once we leave for Lothor again!"

Gya chuckled again, fully understanding his daughter's pleas. He couldn't see how Leenka had managed it all; keeping their dwelling tidy and repaired, watching out for her family, as well as remaining an utterly stunningly powerful magic-wielder.

"Of course, *lissa*," he replied, folding the nearly-frayed blanket he had contemplated trying to repair.

"What can we do?" Citrosine asked earnestly, throwing down a shawl with a hole through the center. She watched Gya consider for a moment, casting a look around the room, until his tight blue eyes fell upon his desk.

"I could teach you the Common Tongue, or some Old Elvish," he suggested. "I had meant to do that before, but now we are stable…" Citrosine forced a smile. She hadn't spent much time with her father since Leenka had been murdered, so any chance was to be jumped upon—even if it meant struggling through dull lessons in a language she would never need to learn.

"It's a much simpler language than Elvish," Gya said later, as they began the day's washing. He meant to teach her the language that mostly everyone, mortal and immortal, learned to speak so as to create a tie for communication between them. He taught as they went about their daily business, so that he could point out terms she would be able to use.

"How is it so much easier?" Citrosine said, groaning as she threw her sister's undergarments into the washtub. The smell of lye pervaded the room, and it reminded her of how Rina's chambers had smelled. It was as if the Leader needed to soak everything she owned in cleanliness. Even her personality, without enough tolerance for such unclean things as melodramatics.

"There are fewer words, and they are all separated a bit more, so that it is easier to put them into their own, smaller sentences."

"Less words? How can that be?" Citrosine thought that every word she'd heard meant at least something—something that one could interpret into a different language…if that was how Common Tongue worked.

"Well…" Gya thought for a moment, soaking up to his elbows in washing. He scrubbed at a tunic, splashing a little water onto the carpet and looking bashful. "Their words are not connected to feelings as ours, since there is no magic involved in speaking them. All right, then—an example. What does the term *'firennyre peant'* mean to you, in Old Elvish?"

"Er…it refers to a stirring of feelings of love, but in speaking the words it kind of summons those feelings themselves. So the words of Common Tongue do not have any magic in them, they are simply used to communicate ideas." Citrosine stirred some leggings through the murky water in the tub. She blushed, feeling the most dim-witted that she had for quite a while.

Gya smirked at her, reminding Citrosine of a small boy. "Exactly." He splashed his daughter's hands playfully. "In the

Common Tongue, there is a distinct word for everything, usually meaning the exact same thing. Also, you should know that there are many words that simply cannot be translated. They are not words that one would speak in daily dialogue, and can only be understood in our language. Words and such that have no meaning except for us..." He stopped, looking a little embarrassed. "Sorry, *lissa*, if I bore you."

"No, no," Citrosine lied, shaking her head, "anything's better than the silence."

They continued that way all day, until Tie came back into the dwelling, looking exhausted. She had circles under her eyes, and she seemed...*grayer*. Her hair had lost its shine and bounce, hanging limply at her shoulders in flat tangles. Even the silver-colored fabric of her tunic seemed less bright and exuberant. Citrosine felt the urge to flick the shirt to another color, brighter and more lifelike, but she felt that Tie would not need that teasing, tired as she seemed.

"Are you feeling all right, Palgirtie?" Gya asked worriedly. "You look as if Dydae has treated you less than well."

"No," Tie objected defensively, making Citrosine start. "No," she repeated, calmer, "I just hadn't slept well last night, and Dydae helped me take my mind off my...dreams." Her tired, encircled eyes slunk to Citrosine's warily, and then darted away again. She went, without another sound, into their bedroom, where the sounds of her undressing and falling into the hammock drifted, muffled, through the walls.

What is happening to my daughter? Gya thought later that night. He was again plagued by dreams of his late wife, as he'd been for ages now. *I'm glad that she has Dydae, at least, as a female influence. I cannot seem to fulfill her needs—I don't even know what those needs might be! Women intimidate me—I cannot begin to imagine what Tie thinks when she comes home nights...or who she will get advice from when she comes of age...*

Gya, Citrosine, and Tie settled into repetitive routine. Every sunup, Tie would be gone, and the remaining bits of the family would look for entertainment; neighbors in other hallways to talk with, pieces of the Common Tongue or the older form of Elvish to learn and teach. Citrosine learned the new languages without complaint, although the Common Tongue was grayer and flatter than the glass separating the Elves from the fish and undersea world. Comparatively, Old Elvish intrigued her to a strong degree. In every phrase of the archaic language, there was power. This was where the incantations for spells came from…by simply saying the words, the magic would come stronger…Citrosine had asked her father about this a few times, but he couldn't explain it any better than she.

"It is what we were left with when those of the Old World fled to the Big Lands…the words *are* power. I cannot understand why…it may have something to do with…" he faltered. *"The… deity…may have blessed us with them. It is a shame that we have strayed from them and become tainted…"* Gya let this thought faintly, only faintly, wisp through Citrosine's mind, as it was unforgivable to ever speak of the deity, the creator of all that was enchanted, before the beginning of time.

This deity was already known in the mind of every born enchanted creature, so that it would never have to be spoken of. It was said among scholars that speaking of the deity, even through thought, would attract Ghersah and Jygul, protectors of the good and bad realms of the Afterlife, and would sentence a being to lose a chance at reaching either…stuck between worlds…for what reason no one knew, as the knowledge had been lost. Perhaps it was not true, but no one wanted to risk being lost in purgatory for eternity.

The two sisters matured in dissimilar ways. Citrosine learned to keep herself looking in a different state of feeling than her thoughts would admit, seeming always happy and content, while Tie began growing more thoughtful, quieter, more controlled in her words and actions than her former energetic self. Gya watched them with proud eyes despite their growing solemnity, thinking of how their mother would have been proud to see them become charming Elf-women.

"Wake up, my daughters!" Gya called cheerily to Citrosine and Tie on a morning a number of days later. The few escaping beams of light from above had yet to diffuse through the water above, and Tie had yet to have awoken and tiptoed out to Dydae's dwelling. "I have quite a surprise for you. You must get up, wash yourselves, and wear your finest. There is a special gift waiting." He prodded the somnolent girls until they submitted to climb out of their hammocks.

As soon as Gya left the room, Tie dropped down onto the lushly carpeted floor, dozing. Citrosine giggled whilst stifling a yawn, and nudged her sister with a toe. Tie groaned, rolling over and stretching out her joints one by one.

"Wear our finest? I thought we were only to wear that ghastly silver." Tie twisted her legs across her body until her back let out a loud grinding noise, and then stood with a dizzy yawn.

"There's nothing even to do here that would be exciting enough to require formal dresses," Citrosine agreed as she pawed through their wardrobe. She threw a few tunics over her shoulder at Tie to clear out a little space. "Hmm," she said, finding little that would suit either of them. "Well, we could always charm on some gowns," was her suggestion. Tie groaned.

"Let me look," she whined, pushing past her sister. "Here— we could wear these." She opened a small drawer underneath where Citrosine had been searching, carefully removing four folded gowns, one not sewn together completely. She laid them out on the floor, and Citrosine attempted to recall where they came from. Two of the silk gowns were the color of the sky, with white beads woven into thin lace; long, flowing sleeves trailing down towards skirts with strips of fabric that, Citrosine imagined, would whirl like rain in the wind when twirled in a dance.

Another of the dresses was not so elegant, but still quite dazzling in a simple style. It was just a pale, delicate, green gown with sleeves that would surely hide the hands of whoever wore it, and a skirt long enough to conceal the feet. This one was still missing a seam along one side of the bodice, but that could easily be finished with a little magic. Delicate, mature patterns of leaves laced around the edges of the fabric, achieving an air of elegance.

The last dress was the one that Citrosine ached to wear. The bodice and inner layer of the skirt were a rich crimson silk, and the whole garment was swathed in silver lace and gossamer. It looked to be too long for Tie, so Citrosine felt a small thrill move through her blood. With a deep neck, long, elegant skirt, and no sleeves, it was miraculous.

Half a moment later, Citrosine imagined what it must look like for her to suddenly want to wear something dark and richly colored. She imagined that her secret Blessing was to blame, but she couldn't help adoring the gown.

"Why have I never seen these garments before?" She appraised Tie intently, searching for an explanation. Tie shuffled her feet, picking up one of the blue fabrics.

"Can I wear this one?" she asked softly, holding it up to her body. It only reached below her knees, and she frowned. The other, identical dress was slightly longer, but still not quite the appropriate length. She sighed, tossing it aside and holding the green gown to her shoulders. Seeing that it looked to be her size, she started towards the door to go bathe.

"Tie," Citrosine persisted, "where did these gowns come from?" She met her sister's eyes and took hold of her elbow. Tie sighed again, turning her eyes downward.

"Mother was making them for the Feast of Ghersah one year, for us to wear. That one," she waved in the direction of the plum-colored dress, "that was for...I don't remember her name...a Council member's daughter that didn't have any gowns. She never received it," she turned her eyes up momentarily, flicking them down again after seeing that Citrosine was still gazing at her face-on, "for she passed on in her sleep—she'd had little of her health, anyway. Her father was a mortal. We two would have worn the two blue gowns and matched, if we hadn't grown so much out of them. This green dress...this was to be Mama's, but it was never finished, for she spent more time on others than herself, as was...always her way."

Citrosine lowered her eyes slowly, knowing how upset Tie was whenever they revisited memories of Leenka. Remembering how their mother always had something to be mending or decorating, she wondered how she'd never noticed the beautiful silks and laces. Citrosine let her hand flit through the air imperceptibly, and the loose thread on the one side of Tie's green dress twined around and around until it was completely sewn.

Gya's voice called something unintelligible from across a few rooms distant.

"Ought to be getting ready," Tie reminded. Citrosine nodded, releasing Tie's arm and washing her face in the basin next to the wardrobe.

Gya wore an embroidered tunic that he usually saved for the excessively important Council meetings, when the king was present, and a cloak that Citrosine had never seen. He was flitting about, making sure that his daughters were ready for their surprise gift.

"Well, now, *lissa*," he asked Tie as they finally left the dwelling, "do you have any ideas of your present? Come, make a guess!" He was smiling widely, looking so comical that neither Citrosine nor her sister could think straight enough to venture a guess.

They wandered up and down hallways, through a few tunnels and staircases, and across a large floor of glass that revealed a large crack in the sea floor, where sharks, morays, and anemones abounded. Citrosine recalled this as being where the couple expecting their child had retreated. Finally, Gya ushered the girls through a final, darkened corridor with only one small, polished door set into the damp wall. Before they could enter, Gya held them against his sides.

"Any concluding speculations?" He smiled again, this time a little more subdued. His daughters shook their heads, winded from all the walking in their hazardously long skirts and pointed shoes.

"Oh, fine, I suppose you wish me to reveal the truth, then?" He took on a weary, teasing tone.

"Yes, Dada," Tie and Citrosine pleaded in unison, giggling together for the first time in ages. They shared a smile, Tie's just allowing the corners of her lips to rise. Gya grinned back, his lightly shimmering aura that had seemed to be so faint in the past few months growing strong and bright.

"I love you girls, but I think I should start thinking of you as young Elf-women. This surprise for you is nothing but a coming of age ceremony, where swords will be forged for you both, and," he beamed proudly, "you may even receive a Faerie's Blessing!" Tie squealed in delight while Citrosine gasped in surprise. Tie hugged her sister tightly, fighting a twitch in her stomach; they had dreamed of this ceremony together since they were small.

In a sudden, worrying moment, Citrosine was filled to the brim of her existence with cold fear. If there were to be Faeries in this room, past this well-polished, expertly crafted door, wouldn't they immediately realize the Jygul's Blessing already on her arm? Would they see this, refuse to bestow her with a normal white magic Blessing, and reveal to her father what dark power was in her blood now? If this was all so, would she be removed from the family forever for shunning his warnings against black magic? This could turn out to be the worst moment her life, couldn't it?

FOURTEEN

FURTHER REMOVED, RECEDING STEADILY

Citrosine's hands were near shaking when the three Elves entered the next room, a small stone chamber that was lit only by a large fire that stood in one corner in a bed of timbers, and the illuminated silhouettes of three Faeries. They wore pleasant expressions, and greeted the Nakiss family with warmth, but their eyes held the tempting, teasing, daring quality that their entire race shared.

Gya took his daughters to two shabby stools against one wall. He held them close, whispering softly into their faces, just barely causing the delicately curled hair around their faces to sway.

"*Se lissa nya methaie,* dearest loves, you must not look into the eyes of these Faeries, promise me! I understand that you have been brought up understanding their dangers, but I just wish to protect you against being taken to the Land of a Thousand Years." He held up a palm, there was a sparkle of

250

light, and the disillusionment charm had been cast. Now, the Faeries would look to be aged, withered, and unpleasant, to dissuade any real eye contact.

"Citrosine," called one of the Faeries, a tall female with wings like a yellow butterfly's, beckoning a finger, "your father has confided that you are the elder sister. Am I correct?" Citrosine and Gya both affirmed. The Faerie smiled politely. "Then you will partake in your ceremony first. Please stand next to the fire, here, then…? Good. Now," she ended mysteriously, "let us begin."

One of the other Faeries, a squat male, probably older than the other, stepped around the fire, to the side opposite Citrosine, and took her hands, making a two-person circle around the flames.

"Please, your name—as full as you know it," he asked. Citrosine closed her eyes.

"Citrosine Leenka Nakiss Rhemaenh Iorae…Manisse Beltha…Ohg Haerthor Nehtli, of the Sea Tribe of Mid-World Elves." She looked at her father for reassurance, glad that he'd told her all of the old stories about her ancestors. Gya nodded, smiling proudly.

"The number of moon-sequence terms that you have lived through—years you have been alive, please," the Faerie said next, leaning closer to her and daring her to look at his face.

"I have lived through three hundred ninety and seven full years."

"Has your magic appeared of its own accord, or haven't you been able to use any yet?"

Citrosine gulped. She tried not to look at her father, and she gave the Faerie her answer. "My magic has appeared," she said quietly, while also talking to him privately. *"It has appeared, indeed, and I have already have had bestowed upon me Jygul's Blessing. This is something that no one else in this room can hear—is that imprudent, or can you oblige me?"*

251

"It is obvious to all three of my kind here, as we can tell what magic you have already. I only asked for you to say it aloud because it is tradition. Yes, you have Jygul's Faerie Blessing, and it is stronger than you may know. Fear not." Citrosine let out a breath of relief, feeling herself lighten almost immediately.

"Have you an idea of what you wish to make of your future life?"

"Er...not absolutely, but I think I wish to fight for the Elves...however...I might study magics, or a combination of those two, as my parents." She hadn't given that much thought before. "In any case, I'd like to utilize magic as much as possible, because it fascinates me so!" The Faerie almost smiled at her, which was almost reassuring.

"Now, a Destiny-Finding, so as to be more suited to match your life with your magic. Close your eyes, please, Citrosine." The Faerie shared a quick glance with Gya, whispering to Tie and he. *"I need utter silence from the two of you, please; else your essence will interfere with Citrosine's. Thank you."*

Citrosine's hands were already resting atop his. She lidded her eyes, trying to think only of the fire before her. She began to feel the rising temperature in the Faerie's hands, and imagined that her fingers were being licked by the flames. She ignored the raw feeling of her skin, growing hotter and hotter with his touch. The flames were blessing her with their attentions, glimpsing into her future, and what was to be of her afterlife. They were using the sacred Faerie magic to outfit her magic for later occurrences; her bones felt as if they would bend and melt, dripping into the ashes and drying out—her skin was almost burning—the boiling blood inside her would soon erupt out of her veins—and then it was over, her hands stinging and twitching, but cooling now.

She met the Faerie's gaze—not looking into his eyes—and he nodded. They dropped hands.

"You are well suited to receive a normal, white-magic-strengthening Blessing, and a pair of light swords. With the ever-changing and adaptive nature of both your personality and future, this will suit you best, if you wish to accept our gifts." Citrosine expressed her thanks, and the male Faerie led her away from the fire, where the other two began pouring metal around in molds. Before the ceremony proceeded, the Faerie gave Citrosine a fleeting, despairing glance, making the Elf deeply disconcerted. Was it sympathy? Of all the Faeries she had ever seen, none had shown such compassionate emotions like this. What had this one seen in her future? A flash in her memory repeated Tyre's dream—Citrosine's own body swept across sands and cast still. Perhaps she would die there, then. The Faerie was really only giving her a little bit more with which to stall her death, but not prevent it. She shivered imperceptibly, and the Faerie quickly returned to his duty.

"Hold out your hand, please, for your Blessing." Obligingly, Citrosine held her arm out, and the white Blessing was bestowed, much like the few she and her father had seen so long ago, back in the woods in the Big Lands. She felt no pain whatsoever, but still cringed when she felt the new magic battling for supremacy in her blood against the dark power.

"Citrosine, listen to me carefully," the Faerie said, escorting her back to Gya and Tie, *"you must find a quiet, solitary place tonight and for the morn. The powers inside you are conflicting. Ultimately, the black magic will prevail, for its power is always more prevalent, but it will be very difficult to suppress either whilst they conflict and overload your body. Unless you wish to make your secret known, spend the night by yourself, and allow superfluous powers to emit themselves from you."*

Citrosine imagined pouring raspberry wine into a cup of water and watching them stir furiously around in each other until either the one clouded over the other or the cup spilled over.

"Don't worry;" continued the Faerie, *"when I say that the black powers will win, that doesn't mean that you will not have good in you, just make sure you are always in control of yourself.*

Do you understand? I plead and lament for your future, as it is nothing like that I have seen. Have strength, young one." The Faerie was now at the back of the room, where the others had waited during Citrosine's Destiny-Finding.

"Ay—and by the way…if my eyes tempted you to our sacred realm, I apologize greatly. In all honesty, I reconcile."

Eh? This was not something that a Faerie would say. Typically, they seemed so resentful…Citrosine closed her eyes in an imperceptible gesture of acknowledgement, her stomach dancing raucously. Her blood twitched, and she could feel the stirring and fluttering of the magics within.

"Palgirtie," the first Faerie, with the yellow aura, called to Tie, who was by this time fidgety with anticipation, "it is now your turn to partake in the ceremony of coming of age. Come stand by the fire, just there. Well done. Let us begin." Citrosine tried to pay attention to her sister's part of the ceremony, but she soon found it dull, and took to watching the swords being swished and worked upon in the back corner of the room—*her* swords, which would be handcrafted to fit what the Faeries had seen in her future.

The third Faerie, who had not yet spoken, took the place of the first. This last female was small, sinewy, and sported a pale orange aura. She smiled teasingly at Tie, who had her eyes fixed on the Faerie's lips, rather than eyes.

With a defeated, groaning sort of tone, the Faerie began asking Tie about herself.

"What is your name—full name…?"

"Palgirtie Mekkih Nakiss Rhemaenh Iorae Manisse Beltha Ohg Haerthor Nehtli, of the Stone Tribe…of Mid-World Elves." She sighed, showing again her resentment towards the sea; she had not realized that she had misspoken.

"Sea Tribe."

"What was that?"

"Are you not an Elf of the Sea Tribe?" The Faerie's eyes clouded irritably.

"Oops..." Tie's face darkened to mirror her superior's. She shuffled her feet, and clenched her fists and teeth.

"Number of moon-sequence terms?"

"Three hundred ten and two years, one more in a few sequences..."

"What are your ideas of your future—do you know?" The Faerie was staring at Tie's eyes, daring her to look up and meet them.

"I want to fight—be a warrior," Palgirtie said without hesitation, her eyes blazing as she avoided the Faerie's gaze. Gya shifted uncomfortably in his seat alongside Citrosine. Such decision! Citrosine cast a glance in his direction and he shook his head to signify that he was not going to share his feelings, smoothing out his face to hide any expressions. With a sigh, Citrosine resisted her curiosity to peek into her father's thoughts.

"Has your magic appeared of its own accord, or aren't you endowed as of yet?" The Faerie continued, Citrosine attempting not to appear apathetic. Her toes were beginning to prickle with lack of use.

"I cannot control my magic yet—it has not emerged." Tie followed the sparkling temptress nearer the fire, and took her hands, just as her sister had done. Citrosine saw that Tie was very sensitive to the heat of the Destiny-Finding, and she felt pity for her. Tie's face grew aggrieved, and her hands shook madly. After a few moments, when it seemed as if she was about to shriek, they dropped hands, and Citrosine let out the breaths that she had been keeping. Seeing others in pain was a terrible thing to see—it made one almost feel the pain oneself.

The Faerie took a moment to consider, and Tie watched her intently. When she cleared her throat, Citrosine could almost see Tie shouting for joy; she would finally get her magic to emerge fully. They shared a quick smile, as Tie's eyes flicked across the room, and the orange Faerie spoke.

"Palgirtie, you seem well-enough suited to receive a double-bladed long sword; you shall not be attaining a Blessing."

Citrosine's stomach slumped; Tie's heart plummeted.

Gya held his daughters' hands as they walked noiselessly back to their dwelling, Citrosine hugging her scabbards tightly across her chest, Tie with her long sword strapped across her back. Every few minutes, Gya would attempt to say something like, "It is so wonderful that both of you had swords forged for you," or, "Magic isn't really all that we Elves have to be confident of—it's also quite crucial for us to understand the physical bits of life," but lively conversations appeared out of the question. Tie kept her eyes lowered, and Citrosine looked over at her cautiously every so often. She was worried about her sister, and she knew not whether Tie could make light of this denial.

As soon as Citrosine was completely positive that her family was asleep, she tiptoed out of their chambers. Tie was sprawled out on her hammock again, face buried in pillows, tears wetting her cheeks and hair. Hating how miserable she looked, Citrosine pecked a small kiss on Tie's cheek and then wandered through the hallways to find a place that was deserted, where she could spend the night.

Unless you wish to make your secret known, spend the night by yourself, and allow superfluous powers to emit themselves from you. The words rang in her ears ominously, and the Elf hummed softly to herself to fight away the fright chilling her bones.

She'd left a note for her father, for courtesy's sake: *Dada, I couldn't sleep, so I will be walking around the citadel for a while. Perhaps I will talk to Paetyr. I will be back by morning; please be well, and have no worries about me. –Citra.* She had added in the bit about Paetyr to seem more convincing, since the two were such good friends. Also, Gya seemed to approve of him—he was a good, strong, patriotic kind of Elf.

Dreading this night, she scoured the nearby corridors until she located one of the empty, ghastly few that usually made her heart feel small and endangered, but now welcomed her into solitude.

She lay down a blanket on the stone floor, and threw her pillow in the middle, curling up around it like a sleeping Dragon with a stomachache. All evening she'd felt flutters and chills flitting through her blood, making her dizzy, feverish, and nervous. What kind of *emissions of power* was the Faerie speaking of that afternoon?

Citrosine tried to close her eyes and relax; however, the magic started overflowing through her body almost before she lay down. The hallway seemed struck by endless streaks of lighting, reversing the colors and appearance of everything she saw. One moment, the air was black and thick, the walls white and transparent; the next, wind whipped across her face and made her eyes tear. Sendings and translucent beings were magicked, and pranced around her in chaos. This was all coming from her? Impossible! What powers would poison this innocent place this night?

Jygul's Blessing had strengthened her blood with black magic, deeply powerful when used in the proper manner. Now, with the white powers attempting to seep into her veins like water into earth, the dark powers were showing their superiority by violently attacking the invading power.

Citrosine clutched her hands to her eyes, which felt as if they were to burst out with the storm of irrationality.

The magic was fighting its way into and out of the Elf, and she felt as if her body was trying to compress into a grain of sand, at the same time as it tried to expand to fill all the sea—this was acutely unpleasant. She closed her eyes, willing her mind not to connect with the pain. Her hands were balled up tight, as if to wring her being out of her skin, and unearthly sounds whispered, shouted, sung their wishes through her head. Her eyes rolled, her hands clenched at the blanket, the ground, her own skin, pulling and scraping against whatever possible, to deny her mouth the pleasure and release of shrieking her throat from her neck.

She couldn't scream, else what would the other nearby Elves think? If they hadn't already awoken, they would hear a scream and immediately alert Rina. She was in enough of a crossing with *her* already. Blood trickled down Citrosine's chin as she bit back her tongue.

Magic flew everywhere, not making sense, and creating occurrences that the Elf never would have wished for. At one point she could swear that she'd turned inside out, with her muscles and bones on the outside, where her skin should be. Before she could make sense of it, however, the sensation had reversed itself. She felt her muscles twitching and straining against the pulling and ebbing of the powers within, as if in a seizure. Her mouth finally opened, and she let loose a single plea.

"Ghersah and Jygul, help me! Tyresias; someone!"

And it stopped.

There was absolute stillness.

FIFTEEN

NEXT TO NO ONE

Time passed normally for years after that incident. Stability returned to Citrosine's blood, black power taking hold of most of her magic store, with enough lightness to sustain her intelligence and sense. Indeed, time behaved well, staying constant and honest as the Nakiss girls matured.

Tie was absent from most of the family activities, save for meals. She slept heavily every night, was absent from bed in the morning, and returned, profoundly exhausted, each day, in predictable habit.

Rina informed everyone about the progress being made in settlements above the ocean, notifying all with caution when it was realized that Men had somehow colonized a portion of the island without their knowing. The immortals had moved far enough away from the shore to be safe, and thus had not kept watch to realize that a mortal city had been built. King Hendius assigned a guardian to protect the Enchanted Realm, lovingly referred to as Lythai Woods. Brou, the new city of Men, became a forbidden territory to the immortals, who had become so tired of running from such clumsily threatening creatures.

Rina reported the immortals' strategy of keeping the Men at a safe distance.

"The Wood Elves have come up with a clever excuse for the Men to stay away. They sent a messenger who had been doing some research on the Men, so he was able to dress and behave like a mortal man himself. He pleaded to the leader of the city that a 'reserve' be set up. This would be an area that Men were not allowed to enter, for fear of disturbing a natural ecosystem that was vulnerable to their influence." Everyone laughed. "So they are protecting us just as well as we are now."

Time went on with little talk of the world of the surface, until one night when Rina called a city-wide assembly in the Dining Hall.

"I have news from the Woods that saddens me greatly to share," Rina began. She looked very sad, indeed, with bruises and rings under her eyes. Her eyes scanned everyone's quickly, almost frantically.

Citrosine's heart sank, as she prayed that the news she was about to hear had nothing to do with the letter that she had received what seemed like a lifetime ago.

"Leaders above have informed me of a growing conflict within our own race. It wasn't said to amount to much, years ago, but now this difficulty has...has spiraled out of control." Rina clasped her hands together, fingers squeezing fingers. "The Shadow Elves claim to be surrounded by opposition: they feel as if they have been cheated by the rest of us." She breathed loudly. "Dark Ones—Wampyres—have been openly released upon the Stone and Wood Magic Councils."

On the bench beside Citrosine, Gya paled, and she understood exactly what he was thinking. *If we had not joined the Sea Tribe, Dada would either be dead or...*

Rina continued. "Ten have been found dead, and it seems…a war is imminent." Almost every mouth in the hall opened with a gasp or a comment for its neighbor. Rina held up her hands for silence.

"The Stone and Wood Tribes are preparing for a great war, and the Shadow Elves are readying with their Wampyres and demons that are possessed with their poisonous magic. Few other tribes have volunteered to assist, for safety's sake, and I believe it is time for us to organize ourselves, before our land is forever ruined." Rina's suggestions were again met with whispers and mutters, but she was unrelenting. Citrosine's eyes clouded with images of Egan's dark scowl, with Pherkue's pleas for equal opportunity and land.

These issues had not been addressed, and now it was the moment for revenge, in their eyes…Egan was to transform many Wampyres, as hinted in Tyre's letter. She remembered clearly the words Tyre had used, and fitted her logic into the empty spaces. He would attack the highest members of Elven society first, as intimidation. Now they would recoil and gather all their power together…perhaps break out in war proper.

"For the sake of light, goodness, and justice, it is our duty. Those who wish to enlist for service in this effort will please oblige me by signing in this book at any time. I will leave it at the head table here." Rina bowed her head and dismissed the assembly.

"Citrosine, *no,*" Gya was pleading that evening, after his elder daughter had suggested that she volunteer to help the Stone and Wood Elves. "I couldn't stand to have you hurt up there. Do you not remember the *purpose* for our retreating under the water?" His voice rose, and Citrosine feared he would wake a neighbor.

"Yes, Dada, I remember, but I have swords, strong magic, and a reason to fight for our tribe. It isn't—"

"*Lissa,* hear me." Gya took her hands, kneeling before her. "I couldn't stand to lose you. This is hardly an ordeal you would be allowed to walk away from. They have Wampyres, of all things! Do you understand me?" He looked up into her eyes. She saw the sorrow in his eyes, and balked in her argument. "I love you, darling; I…need you to be safe. Our family would be crushed forever again if we lost you! I can't—*your mother is already dead.* I …we would be so much the more devastated! *Lissa,* Citrosine," his words faded, and he embraced Citrosine desperately enough that his muscles shook with the force.

"Dada, Dada—" she gasped. Her father loosened his grip just enough to pull back and look into her eyes. "I feel that I have grown old enough to defend our race. I am a part of this world as much as you are. Listening to all the stories…it isn't enough…I don't want to feel useless…I have to *do something.*" Citrosine struggled for the right words, not feeling like she'd expressed her feeling in the right way. "It would be avenging Tyre, and Mother…I think…I think that they would want me to…to do this."

Gya was silent for a long moment. Citrosine felt herself starting to cry, and used her powers to halt her tears until after she'd won her argument. Finally, her father's features softened, his arms tightened around Citrosine's shoulders. Breathing into her hair, he saw Leenka, smiling sadly, affirming his blurred thoughts.

"*Lissa, lissa…*" Citrosine felt her shoulder and hair dampened by Gya's love, his sorrow. "I know you will fight resplendently…like your mother would have wished…"

The rest of the day was spent in a gentler quiet than they'd had for a while. Tie had always sulked and spoke little, making the others feel uneasy, but now, the silence was almost comforting. Gya saw each of them with new eyes since they had officially come of age.

At dinner in the Hall, Gya ate between his daughters, observing them without trying to seem as if he was obsessively watching. He noticed that Citrosine looked out of the bubbling windows for most of the meal, following the all the curious fish and sea life with an open mind. She chewed thoughtfully, seeming content to sit where she was and enjoy what she saw, tasted, and felt.

Tie ate little, poking at the food pushed to one side on her plate. Gya was saddened to see that her eyes didn't move once from her plate, as if she was trying to concentrate on clearing her thoughts, and that involved giving up on normal functions.

When they were all satiated to their liking, Tie departed with Dydae, and Citrosine and Gya wandered up to the head table, where Elves were signing their names for enlistment. They met Paetyr along the way, and stopped to say hello.

"Nakisses," the young man greeted, bowing elegantly. He smirked crookedly, breaking the illusion of being a nobleman.

"Good afternoon, Paetyr," Gya replied. Citrosine smiled politely, too absorbed in her thoughts to contribute. After an awkward pause, Gya continued, "Have you just signed up for the, ah, defense effort?"

"Yes, sir; Mum didn't want me to, but you should see the list thus far." A corner of his mouth came down into half a frown. "Next to no one has volunteered—not that there are really that many in this tribe that could fight...sir."

"I understand you completely," said Gya, his eyes tightening in pain. "Well, we should be on our way. We're to both enlist, and then I suppose we must make our plans for departure." He held out a hand. "It was well to speak with you," he said, as Paetyr shook his hand.

Citrosine gave her friend a light hug as Paetyr departed. "Goodbye," she said, following her father to go sign up for war.

Paetyr stood there dumbly for a moment, watching Citrosine with a sad, yet somehow awed, smile. He proceeded on his way, thinking of the right words to give to his Mum.

The Nakiss family had reached the end of their required time in the Realm of the Sea. Rina called everyone together in the Dining Hall again within the next fortnight, and announced that all of the Elves who would be soon to fight should be packing, and that they would leave very soon; the Shadow Elves had attacked a small band of Wood Elves.

Dwellings had been constructed aboveground for everyone that hadn't intended on staying submerged forever, and they could leave at the same time as the warriors. Few would remain below, most going to return to former tribes and ways of life.

"Tie, I recommend packing your things up," Citrosine called, arriving from the assembly, "as it would probably aid us in leaving earlier." Citrosine herself was already stuffing things into bags. She was elated that her father could return to being on the Stone Tribe Magic Council, but couldn't help the fleeting, dreadful thought of living without him after this battle, should things go awry...

Gya confirmed Citrosine's suggestion from another room, and came into the girls' room, to see what progress had been made. Tie was sitting sullenly, crosslegged, on a suitcase that appeared empty, judging by how the sides gave in under her weight.

"*Lissa,* you should be gathering your clothes," he sighed while leaning against the doorframe. Tie didn't look at him, and made no move to pack.

"Palgirtie," her father grew impatient.

"No," she murmured.

"What have you said to me, Palgirtie?"

"*No.*" Tie repeated herself, arguing into the floor. "You will not make me move again. I will not go anywhere!" Citrosine dropped a tunic into her bag and turned towards them in silence.

"We have a permanent dwelling in Lothor; we can be in the Stone Tribe again, with the wind and the sun, trees, birds..." Gya couldn't muster an angry word. This was the first that he'd heard Tie's voice, apart from "Yes, sir" or "No, sir," in a longer time than he liked to recall.

"*I...am...staying...right...here.*" Tie threw out the words like sharpened stones, like poison darts. She met her father's eyes full-on, and tensed like a predator preparing to spring. Citrosine watched her father's face and her sister's, staying quiet in her corner of the room.

Gya's countenance collapsed. "Would a neighbor care to house you?"

"I will stay with Dydae. She's my friend; she would understand."

"Would you go talk to her, then, *lissa*?" The Elf man was no longer able to fight her. Tie had been so insistent on staying above the ground that it hardly made sense for her to wish to remain away from it.

"Fine," Tie countered, halfway out of the room.

"Dydae," Tie cried, whirling through the old woman's door, "I need your help!" Tears ruptured their way out of the Elf's eyes, and she sat heavily on the floor. Dydae hobbled over to her companion, worry and inquiry radiating from her eyes.

"Sweet girl, my Palgirtie," Dydae crooned. She knelt, joints creaking, and ran her gnarled fingers through Tie's fine hair. "What evil has brought you to this emotion, my dear? How is it that I may help you, child?" Her skin grew warmer, as if she was trying to warm Tie's frozen sorrow.

"They wish me to leave," Tie sobbed, her nose leaking and running horridly. She sniffed and moaned, wiping her nose on her silver sleeve. "I can't go back up there! That's where Mother is…"

"Your mother is gone, my dear. Are you to shun the moving air, the sun, the sky, that you have craved for so long?" Tie looked up into the old Elf's eyes, thinking.

"I…I cannot—she is reflected in everything I see, feel, taste…up on the land. Because my father left us alone… because of Citrosine's magic…"

"You blame her for your sweet mother's being turned into a ghastly beast?" Dydae didn't understand Tie's words. Tie closed her eyes, sighed, and pulled on a string of memory, pushing it toward Dydae.

The storm…hiding in the cellar, darkness; the boulder is forcibly thrown aside…Eerie, grotesque faces with poisonous glares peering in, growled words. "This is the one, the wife, the warrior. The plan was to kill the older child, the powerful one—she appears absent, but this is even better." The demons shoving the young child into a corner, grappling for the Councilman's wife…

Blinding light, rain, thunder, the poor woman's screaming, like a chime, a bell…growing fangs, claws ripping at her own body…her eyes, reflected in every inch of the scarred boulder, her voice in Tie's dreams, explaining why everything had come to pass this way…Remember never to forget.

"Dear, sweet child…"

Sixteen

Understanding...Unlikely

"Warriors, you are here to serve your own interests, your families, dwellings, heritages. Most importantly, remember that you are here to protect the Elven nature of goodness. We must not forget that, like a great river, one bowl of spoiled drink can pervade the whole system of life, and such is the reason we stand here this hour." The Elven King Hendius was pacing up and down a large, armored array of Elves, including Gya and Citrosine, who had been split up, as Citrosine wasn't in the group of elder, experienced warriors who would be along the front lines; she would be more of a sentry.

"Captains, please assemble your troops, and we will make to our posts. Do not fear, my companions. The Elves of Shadow will be taught their place, as well as the demon hounds that snivel alongside. Follow the plans that have been drawn. We will be victorious!" King Hendius shuffled over to his own quarter, leading them to march out to the great field near Treewall.

Citrosine's quarter was headed by none other than Paetyr, who had proven to be a brave and clever fighter, as well as a persuasive, encouraging leader. He unsheathed his sword, and called Citrosine and all of the other sentry fighters into a tight cluster.

"Everyone raise your weapons to mine. If you truly believe that we shall fend off our enemies, wield yours to mine!" His face was glowing with energy and anticipation. Citrosine drew her twin swords, and lifted them above her head, tapping Paetytr's with a clang. They shared a brief, sincere glance. The young Elves nearby all drew their weapons high, and they let out a howl of courage together.

Citrosine's heart was skipping and stumbling as she marched with her comrades. She knew that she was only a foot-sentry, a lookout, of sorts, but still she felt that this was to be the most horrible thing she'd ever done, whether she actually would defend justice in the course of this service or not. The killing, fighting, straining…whether she even partook in it, it would still appear around her at some point.

She had spent the better part of the morning sitting motionless in Lothor, in the new home that she shared with her father. Gya had stood behind her, rubbing her shoulders as she polished her armor and swords.

"You will do well in this fight," he had said proudly.

"As will you, I'm sure."

"Ay…" his voice faltered.

"Dada?" Citrosine turned to face him. His eyes were wet, focused on hers.

"*Lissa,* I grow old…if I do not return…"

"Dada, you will, you will!" *You have to.* "Citrosine, listen to me." Citrosine's scalp prickled. "If I do not return from this ordeal…you must find your sister. I can hardly stand the thought of my family splitting out this way. Both of you must at least reunite…"

Citrosine had taken his hand, and nodded her head, determined to keep her feelings aloof. She had managed to keep her outbursts of magic in check thus far; there was no likely possibility of them taking control of her by their own accord. She and her father went to adorn their battle wear, and Citrosine had taken an hour to sit and think, unmoving. Her fingers had traced Tyre's cane, which sat on her lap. The Dark Ones would be vanquished, and Tyre would be avenged. This was how it had to be…

Now, as the sentries approached the edge of the trees, they could see a black blur across the massive field. The other quarters had arranged themselves as was according to plan; hidden deep in the trees, weapons at the ready, and Paetyr ordered his quarter to thin out, and watch in every direction for their enemies.

Citrosine took a place behind a large oak tree, peering around nervously. She and everyone else knew that these Elves used their dark powers to their advantage, and they could easily appear out of nowhere.

All the pawns in Citrosine and Paetyr's quarter were hidden this way, eyes peering meticulously through the brush. They dared not speak, dared not breathe, for fear of being found. The ranks out on the field would give a cry if they were attacked first, but it was unlikely for such dark, mysterious beings to strike between dawn and midday.

The sun began winking out through the forest behind the younger soldiers, and the night grew still and cool. Stars were visible through the branches, and, her feet tiring from crouching there all day, Citrosine tried to keep her eyes occupied on sighting the enemy, rather than searching the skies for Ghersah's drawings and constellations.

It became dawn, and the sentries grew tired. Still they kept silent, still they waited, still they watched. Paetyr, hidden by a tree not far away from Citrosine, felt a spider web brush his neck and he reached out to sweep it away. He was edgy in the still night, just waiting for anything to save them from this quiet. His fingers were met with the bone-crushing grasp of a smooth, cold hand. He whirled in surprise, eyes inches away from the dark and incriminating one-eyed-gaze of Egan.

"Enemy present!" he screamed. The rest of the soldiers immediately went to action. Dark Elves started revealing themselves from high in the trees, and hidden beneath cleverly concealed thickets. The grating of metal on armor resounded through the trees, and it was apparent that the war had begun.

Egan didn't busy himself with Paetyr, and instead rushed towards King Hendius; Egan a black shadow that seemed to blur and smear through the undergrowth. Paetyr soon found himself confronted with an energetic, lumbering demon.

Citrosine struck at the back of a nearby enemy who was advancing towards the Second Quadrant's captain. The Elf's sword struck hers almost before Citrosine contacted his armor. He faced her in the time it takes for an eye to blink, and her heart nearly froze.

"Ah, Citrosine," Pherkue grunted, lashing out at her but striking only air. "What a pleasure. I have missed you, my love." His eyes were sparkling, taunting Citrosine, but no longer the beautiful crimson coals that they had once been. Now they were maddened in bloodlust, as was his hair and malicious smile. "I once would have felt despair in killing you, but, no matter," he growled. His eyes glowed with a deep, violet glare.

Letting out a spear of black energy, Citrosine grunted. "Your uncle was to kill my best friend," she cursed over the sounds of agony all around them. "Remember when Tyre disappeared? Your uncle was the cause of his suicide." She grunted while straining against the reverberations that passed from his blade to hers in every strike.

"My *uncle*?" He was amused, mocking concern.

"Egan, the very same!" Citrosine sent another jolt of magic his way, but Pherkue clucked his tongue and ducked away. "He burst in upon Tyre's final words and was too late! And you were too enthralled with me to notice. You just enjoyed having me alone and single, free to give myself to you. Charming me, of course."

In one fluid motion, Pherkue had sent the magic back towards her chest. It flew through the air like an arrow, but Citrosine parried with a strong armoring charm.

"Darling, you flatter yourself," Pherkue sniggered forebodingly. "It wasn't you that I wanted."

"No? So why did you throw yourself against me on the ship, I weakened by my own self-pity? You loved me—taking advantage of Tyre's death!" She stabbed at him furiously, missing by inches.

"Guess again," he chided. He was behind her in an instant, the tip of his sword quivering dangerously around her throat. Citrosine squirmed in his grasp, but found that she couldn't break free. She was aware of the Pherkue's lips skimming across her collarbone. They were surprisingly cold, and almost watering—not the same passionate way they had touched her half a century ago. She understood immediately.

"You've been transformed," she whispered.

Pherkue chuckled throatily. "I was transformed while I was, as you say, 'loving' you. Surely you remember the attraction spell? It was a side effect, if you will, of my metamorphosis into this...That encounter years ago, and my apparent pining for your company—was my inability to control my *thirst*, not my passion for *you*." He laughed loudly, making Citrosine indignant. She struggled against him, and her muscles trembled with the exertion, but his undead self had gained an unnatural firmness and immobility.

"Then what made you so much more in control then than now?" His arms held her tightly. His breaths came faster, and

Citrosine was dangerously aware of the terrified drumming of her heart. Surely a Wampyre could hear that...and hunger for all the blood that was rushing around...

"Controlled...?" he whispered, lips to her ear. "Darling, let me paint you a picture...Struggling for survival, rather than struggling to appear normal...taming evils and beasts more foul than your theatrical mind could ever dream... one's priorities become a little, shall we say, reorganized...Not since we established our forces on this island have I ever met any resistance to my instincts, and I have become somewhat spoiled, I admit."

Citrosine shivered as Pherkue gathered the scent of her throat, sending icy chills up and down her body.

"However," he continued, "sometimes a little sport is worth it. The resistance stretches my strength, and makes the taste so much more pleasurable..." Citrosine was sickened, and focused all her energy on the magic within her. Pherkue's lips parted, and he murmured again. "Tyresias was so pitiful, lying on the ground dying, when I came upon him..." Citrosine closed her eyes and fought to ignore his words.

"His hands clutched his heart, and he was giving the last words to his bothersome pencil...so blind, so quick, curse him...Damn him, I was a second late. It was always my duty to get to him, to get to you, to kill your father and those other Council bastards," Pherkue breathed in Citrosine's scent calmly, and she shuddered again with sickness.

"I just never knew that you would be so easy to charm— and now, as I am a Dark One...even your love for the deceased cannot stop me..." The Wampyre's lips touched her neck, withdrew, and came back again, parted, kissing her hungrily. If he were impatient for another second, it would be her blood pouring out, and no longer her fury. She must think of something quickly.

"And his blood...I'm sure you would have gone mad for it, had you been in my situation, but since he was already dead, he tasted so—"

A wave of hot, black, infuriated power charged out of Citrosine's aura, jolting Pherkue away and headfirst into the ground...and she was in control of the fight again. They sparred viciously, until Pherkue took Citrosine by the elbows from behind.

Her arms stretched backwards uncomfortably, and she thought that they would break in another moment, but Pherkue paused. His grasp lessened, and before Citrosine could look behind her, he was in a cluster of trees, kneeling beside a Wood Elf whose arm had just been severed.

Citrosine took advantage of Pherkue's inducement by blood; she turned away to look for fellows in need of assistance and did not see Pherkue gnaw into the soldier's skin, lapping up the precious crimson drippings. She lingered not to watch the soldier collapse, to see Pherkue assaulted and seized by an elder warrior, tied and bound while his legs kicked out, his teeth gnashing against his captors; Citrosine did not see the Wampyre escorted to a powerful Elven mage called Orjeniot.

Citrosine felled an enemy demon as Pherkue was fighting away the most fearsome pain of his life, being reverted from Wampyre to Elf, scarred and burned by Orjeniot, on the outskirts of the battle, as his skin was irreversibly roughened, his eyes drained of the once-awe-inspiring richness.

The young Elf was running behind a thicket to parry an attack while Pherkue was cursed to feel pain in every instant that his name was ever uttered, as punishment for his evilness. He was spelled out in an unbreakable exile to a deserted area of Ilthen, his mind scheming and seething as he thought of a new name for himself, to escape the agony...Farqot, different just enough in pronunciation to allow for some small morsel of relief.

Fires had been lit, ravaging the bodies of anyone unfortunate enough to try and leap them. Citrosine was near when one of these blazes began, and a small, spiky demon leapt across, attempting to chase her. Its scales and flesh were quickly burned, and the Elf girl felt her insides wriggling with disgust. The demon fell to the ground, and Citrosine could smell the blackened, bubbling skin. The scent was more horrible than anything she'd ever smelt, and set her gagging for what seemed like an endless time. The scent pervaded her throat with disgust, and she ran towards the outskirts of the battle, breathing through her mouth.

The Stone and Wood Elves were having a poor time of this fight. The night grew more sinisterly dark, and it seemed that the Shadow Elves were completely surrounding them. Citrosine and Paetyr fought side by side for quite a while, shielding each other from lethal attacks. This could easily be the end.

"Paetyr, *behind you!*" Citrosine shouted in warning as a demon lunged towards the boy. He scrambled out of the way, but still the demon's teeth closed around his calf. Citrosine struck the thing in the head with the butt of her left sword, and it fell, unconscious, to the ground.

Her comrade was wincing with great pain in his eyes, but still he cried out a warning as a huge, purple-pelted demon advanced toward Citrosine. He struck it quickly, making it turn to him and roar furiously before refocusing its attention to Citrosine.

"Let it not touch your body!" he warned. "You'll be poisoned beyond healing!" Citrosine nodded once, let out a knife-like spell, and dodged a swipe from the beast as it focused its attention on her again.

"Run!" Paetyr yelled. The demon, a Coulf, Citrosine remembered, from one of her father's lessons when she was a girl, was quick, and surrounded her with blows. The Elf ducked under a meaty arm and lunged in the direction of the deepest bit of the forest. She sheathed her swords as she ran, pushing branches out of her face.

A look over the shoulder revealed that the demon was following her at a breakneck speed. Citrosine's mind nagged at her: *Demons have never been able to run as swiftly as this!* Still the Coulf followed her, sidewinding through the trees, never once breaking stride. Citrosine wished that she had Dem with her in horse form; it had been so quick that the undergrowth was hardly visible.

"Can anyone help me?" she cried out, hoping that the soldiers behind her could hear.

The beast gained. Citrosine's shoulders and knees started burning with the weight of her armor, and she drew heavy breaths. Looking over her shoulder once more, the Elf lost her footing, stumbling over a thick log in her path. Her head collided with the ground, and her ears rang loudly.

"You always used to run so much faster; what happened, Citrosine?" The demon leaned over her, and seemed to sneer. Citrosine thought she was hallucinating. Demons didn't tease their enemies—she should be dead by now.

"No...you are correct," said the demon, reaching into her mind with a strong grip. *"I am not acting like a demon should, am I?"* It straightened, seeming more Elf-like now. *"Well, that is only natural, under current circumstances..."*

Citrosine leapt to her feet. She pulled out a sword, aiming it close to the beast's eyes. "Reveal yourself!" she shouted, anxiety layering every syllable. Her hands trembled, and she didn't need the use of her intuition to warn her that something here was going to be awfully odd. Who was this demon that it knew her? She had a quick flash to a dream she had had on her birthday a long time ago...

"If you insist, Oh Great Magic Wielder," the demon spoke eloquently, bowing. When it raised its head, Citrosine fell to her knees again in the sheer irony of it all.

"Palgirtie?"

SEVENTEEN

SHAPED BY YEARS OF HAPPINESS

There was Tie, her macabre eyes hardened by her time of solitude; they were underscored heavily with purple, bruise-like shadows from years of staying up nights with Dydae. She wore a foul grin that made Citrosine's eyes swim unpleasantly.

"You..." Citrosine couldn't find any words. Her ears were still ringing from her fall, and her heart tapped a cadence that she felt was impossible for her sister not to hear.

"Surprised? I'm shocked," Tie sneered. "I thought that you might have been smarter than this...Alas, you are more ignorant that I'd remembered, *Citra*."

"When...?" her voice proceeded to moan, as if there was some force squeezing her lungs from the insides. Tie shook her head, tongue clucking. Her form was writhing a bit, as Dydae's had done.

"Every night, Dydae took my shape, and I flew as a shadow to the demon realm. Did you not see me—that day you sneaked out to see Leader Rina? You stared right at me!" Seeing Citrosine's eyes widen further, she continued. "Regardless of your memory, nothing can be done at present…" the girl bristled, "…except for what I've been planning for a century now. At first, I was simply waiting…making sure that Mother was really gone…"

"Mother? Tie…what do you speak of? Are you upset about not receiving a Blessing, as I have? I know that Mother would be proud of you, nonetheless," Citrosine stood now, her swords abandoned on the ground at her feet.

Tie's shape warped, and she was a Coulf again. She lunged for her sister's throat, but Citrosine huddled down out of the way. The demon quickly became Tie the Elf again.

"Guess once more," she teased, tensing. This reminded Citrosine of Pherkue, and she became even more confused.

"Why are you trying to kill me? We are sisters! This is completely wrong. Can you not see what you are thinking?" Citrosine quickly reached for her weapons, if not to fight, then at least to block her sister's claws. "I cannot help the fact that you did not get a Blessing! Let the past be passed." She braced herself as her sister took a step forward, her eyes clouding into fury.

"Stupid Citra! You killed Mother!" Her malevolent voice rose to the skies, resounding through the forest. "You and Father—your magic outings…You left us behind then! You wouldn't protect us from the demons that day—Dada knew that there was a foul storm upon us—the demons attacked her! They had been instructed to kill you, the eldest daughter of Dada, the Council Member. Since you were instead being spoiled, as always, they saw that to take the legendary Leenka would be far more fatal a plan. She is now a Dark One, never to be loved again! In fact, *your tribe* has probably killed her already!" Tie's delicate child's body melded into the poisonous Coulf's once more, and she struck at Citrosine, who dodged in every direction seemingly at once.

"*So you would have rather had me dead than Mother?*" Citrosine taunted, trying to break Tie's will. Tie became frustrated and attacked anew.

"*They wanted you to be happy on your—ugh!—birthday,*" she grunted between blows, "*even if it meant the sacrifice of our family!*" Her claws finally struck Citrosine, but she only hit armor, and Citrosine took a moment to get her breath.

"*You and Father conspired to move us into the sea. This place is so useless; we could still be roaming free through the Big Lands! The Men could not find us if they sent all the armies they had. I hate this place...*" Tie was losing her breath, like her sister, and they took the shortest of pauses. They circled each other warily, and a wind began to pick up. Citrosine knew that her magic was getting out of her control, but her anger was fueling her energy.

"It was to be safer," she tried to say calmly. Tie snarled, and Citrosine's face flushed with irritation. "Can't you understand?"

"*Understand! How can I try to understand either of you hypocritical liars?*" Tie growled again, and ran for Citrosine, who struck at her with all her might. Tie yelped, making Citrosine hesitate and draw back her weapons, fearing she'd hurt her sister too much.

The Coulf took the moment of pause to strike ferociously. Citrosine felt her sister's claws dig through her skin, working their way through a crease in her armor. She cried out in pain as the venomous blades raked through her side, from breast to hip.

Tie laughed. "*How Mother screamed as she changed—I find it amusing...I became this of my own accord, and still, I have felt no pain. Perhaps yours can compensate for this lack...?*" A feral sound came from her throat, and Citrosine knew that she had to get away. Her side was stinging; she could feel the poison deadening her blood, eating away at her skin.

As soon as Citrosine felt this, Tie snarled and jumped at her again, her claws raking through the same path again, deeper. The older sister howled and leapt back, running off-balance and losing her vision. The trees at the corners of her sight darkened and faded away in blotches and blurs. She let out sharp bursts of magic at her feet, willing them to carry her more rapidly.

She magicked a huge orb of light, in the direction of her sister, hoping to temporarily blind her—preventing her the pleasure of following.

Tie's footfalls grew fainter, and she heard a final snatch of monologue. *"Citrosine, the poison will take you. The longest an Elf has ever survived is less than a day with such a wound as yours! You won't escape this! Good riddance to you, my former sister!"* Her voracious laughs and snarls echoed through Citrosine's clouded mind, chilling her bones as she quickened her pace still.

The tunnel vision she was now suffering grew more severe, until she had to slow to a limping shuffle, staring at the ground to avoid undergrowth. The branches and twigs that she trod upon snapped and splintered into the soles of her feet, and as she concentrated on her feet, branches caught in her hair and tore at her face. Her side burned and froze simultaneously, sending nausea through her veins. A limp grew more pronounced as her whole right side went out of her control.

Tie lunged out of the trees ahead of her, and Citrosine did not know what to do. Tie would surely kill her on the spot, she realized now, so Citrosine dropped heavily to the ground and lay, motionless.

"Citra, do you trick me?" The demon paced circles around her fallen sister, hunting for signs of life. She scratched through the same wound again, and Citrosine fainted for a brief time. *"Ah...then I have truly won,"* the beast snarled as she was met with no more resistance. Citrosine felt her right side writhing, and used all her will to keep from moving.

Tie aimed a kick right into the poisoned flesh, making Citrosine lose all thought but for the pain. Then the demon was gone.

Citrosine used magic to help her stand.

Her muscles went from spasm to spasm, and shooting pains laced from limb to brain. She contorted her body in pain, and ran blindly through the woods, branches trying to keep her from proceeding. The wind grew stronger as Citrosine's sight completely stopped functioning. Her feet reached soft sand, and she could hear huge, crashing waves. They grew quieter to Citrosine as she was overtaken with pain.

She screamed again, and in her mind she saw Tyre's premonition. *She was going to die here.* Her side cramped and burned; her mouth screamed a melody of pain, echoed and overtaken by the throbbing ocean. Citrosine's knees gave out, and she felt herself pounded with water; numbing, powerful water, here to sweep her away to the branches of Kalka. She coughed and sputtered as salt poisoned the insides of her mouth, nose, and eyes and made it impossible to breathe. The salt reached into her wounds, burning and stinging, creeping into her blood and muscles that were exposed and throbbing— and she wished she were dead already to spare the pain.

The vision that had just been taken from her returned for one brief instant, and she saw Tyre there, blurred and receding. She reached out to him, fighting her poisoned body writhing of its own accord. *Tyre! Please do not abandon me in this my last moment! If you love me, return and bring me with you!* His robes stirred in the salty air, and he steadily made his way further from Citrosine's painful thrashings, not once even looking back. *Tyre! Do you not care that I am laying here dying, as predicted?*

"TYRE!"

Her strength failed; her magic—both light and dark— stirred once and went completely away. Citrosine fell facedown into the sand, and sand made its way through her lungs. *I am dying,* she thought. *Tyre was completely right about my death… Tyre, I tried…I told you I would hold on, but this is as much as I can muster…the pain!*

Wave after wave rolled over her body, washing her across the sand like a sack of feathers. Thick needles of agonizing hurt sewed themselves through her entire body, and she lost all feeling. Her mind was floating; she knew she only had moments left. There was no possible way that the poison could be evaded, especially when there was so much…

The pain and chaos piercing her broken body slowly dulled, and the water was preparing to whisk her away to a land with no worry, no agony, and no darkness…

Her body sagged, and her last thought ushered out every ounce of awareness from her remains.

You were right; all of you were right…

Book Two

Life through a
Shattered Glass

ONE

CHAIN-MAIL, CODEINE, AND SODA BOTTLES

Colin Baker and his best friend Ant were arguing, as per usual, when their lives changed. It's funny how that can happen sometimes. One either misses the life-changing encounter completely, and it takes one by surprise much later, or one stands up to the experience and embraces it full-on.

"Ant, let's just go to the beach, ok?" Colin rolled his eyes as his younger friend rambled on about how Colin had kept him out too late the other night, which made Ant's mother *so angry* that he'd been grounded for a week straight—and it was all Colin's fault, obviously.

"Fine, whatever, dude." Ant scowled and crossed his arms, as he did whenever he lost an argument.

"Wow! Look at those huge breakers today," Colin yelled over the rising sounds of wind and surf. The dawn was supremely cloudy, with thick gray sheets laid across the whole sky with patches of black, either signaling imminent rain or thunderstorm.

"Yeah, no way am I lugging this thing over there," Ant yelled back, gesturing to the wagon he was dragging behind him, the one they normally used to carry seashells that was now full of empty soda bottles and ice cream bar wrappers they'd just finished off.

"Come on, let's go over without it."

"Man, this thing'll get stolen!" Ant looked at Colin incredulously. With his red hair, long face, and pointless sunglasses he always wore, that had a tendency to slip off his nose, he was hard to be taken seriously. Colin just laughed.

"Fine then, I'll see you after I jump a monster crasher wave! You stay here and guard your little red wagon, you big, bad, eighteen-year-old, you!" He thumbed his nose, and ran off through the sand.

"That kid…sometimes I just…" Ant muttered to himself, taking a seat on the edge of his wagon. He rummaged through it to see if there were any still-full sodas, and was aggrieved to find that there were none. He pouted, like any self-respecting eighteen-year-old man would at that moment.

Colin ambled over to the water, just close enough to get his faded sneakers wet. He leaned down, pawing through the thick layer of shattered shells and gritty sand to see if there were any neat shells that he'd missed earlier this morning. Suddenly he caught a glimpse of something out of the corner of his eye. It looked like a brown figure, laying out on the sand behind him to the right.

Neck craned over his shoulder, he strained to see if there was anything there. All he could manage was a faint brown silhouette. About five yards under the high tide line, the water was on its way back up to snatch the thing back out to sea, or wherever it had come from.

Colin found his feet bringing him closer to the unusual figure. *This is probably just a towel someone left yesterday, or maybe—*

His thought was cut off when he reached the lump. It was a person!

"*Ant!* Get over here! Bring the wagon!" He was answered by some grumbling and arguing, but made no attempt to reply. His attention was focused solely on the collapsed figure in front of him.

The slender body was facedown on the sand, so Colin couldn't tell who it was, or if it was dead. Brown hair spilled out in a tangle into the sand, covering most of the head, and the rest of the body was clothed in black and silver material. Surf, lapping and teasing at the figure's legs, threatened to drag the body away into the angry water.

"What, man? Find a shell you just gotta ha—" Ant came up behind his friend and gasped. The wagon trailed along, leaving large ruts where the wheels had stuck in the thick sand.

"Dude," Ant breathed, "is it…is this a corpse or a live dude, man?" His voice shook, and he poked Colin's shoulder repeatedly. "Oh my God, oh my God…Colin, is it alive?"

"I don't *know*," Colin yelled impatiently. "Ant…help me turn it over? If he wasn't dead before, he's probably choked on sand already." He slid his fingertips under the body's shoulder. Ant hesitated.

"Dude, is this right, man? I think we should, like, call someone!" He grimaced at the body's position on the ground. The legs were crumpled up, and the arms grasped desperately at a wound on the other side of the figure. Ocean water licked at the body's waist now, threatening to pull it out to China.

"There's no time! Just help me, would you!"

"Oh my God…oh my God…" was all Ant could respond.

"*Fine,* call my mom, and *I'll* just do it, so that this dude doesn't *suffocate* on us," Colin growled, as Ant changed his mind and decided to just help his buddy turn the thing over.

Ant's fingers went under the belly of the collapsed, and they gently pulled the—female, they now realized—onto her back. Her face was very pale, and the lips had a pronounced tinge of blue. The girl's shirt...or armor, or whatever it was that she was wearing—it looked like she'd just been to some kind of sci-fi convention—was wet and stained with sand, grass, some kind of purple stuff, and...was that blood? Yeah; lots of blood. Her face was very delicate, and sweat still shone on her nose and temples, so she'd at least been alive a short while ago. It was impossible to tell if she was breathing, as the mail and leather she wore were thick enough to conceal any motion, although her face and limbs were completely limp and cold.

"Well," Ant said, trying to lighten the mood up, "she was pretty hot, if kinda dorky!" He smirked feebly. Colin rolled his eyes again, and threw his cell phone to Ant from his back pocket.

"Call my mom, and tell her to meet us at Jefy, okay? 'Cause the port is easy to reach from the road." He turned his eyes back to the girl, and the task of hoisting her into the wagon. She was surprisingly light, so he lifted her in a fireman's carry, then, after scrambling through the bottles and scattering them all in the sand, he lowered her. Her feet scraped the ground behind the wagon, but she'd not be hurt if they pulled the wagon forward—assuming she was alive and still able to feel pain.

"...Yeah, Colin and I; we found, like, a body on the beach...no, I don't really know for sure...l-looks pretty d-dead to me..." Ant had reached Colin's mother, a doctor partnered with her husband. They were only temporary doctors in the city, but they took over while the others were taking summer vacations. This was of good coincidence today.

Colin waved his hand at Ant frantically to get him to pull the wagon faster. The tiny thing had to be dragged through the sand, which pooled and melded into a high, protective rift just in front of the wheels, making the task even more difficult.

"Um…I guess…yeah, that's probably a good idea…nope… uh, yeah…okay, yeah; Jefy Port okay? We're almost about— *ugh*—there," they pulled the wagon over the curb of the road leading to the port, "…yeah. Okay, see you there. Right…bye." Ant flipped the phone shut, threw it into the wagon, where it bounced around until settling under the unresponsive girl's shoulder. He now used both hands to yank on the handle with Colin, who was looking around frantically for the quickest way to a sidewalk, as they were nearing the southern dock of Jefy Port, the half-closed boat dock for the tiny city of Brou.

"Oh my God, someone better show up soon!" Colin panicked as he looked at the girl. Her whitened skin was like ivory, cold and hard, yet strikingly beautiful. She appeared to be an angel cast down from God's hands, for some reason betrayed and sent away. Why should she have to die?

"This is, like, totally weird!" Ant agreed.

"How often is there anything like this on this island?"

"Much less a *dead* thing like this!"

"Dude, shut up. You're freaking out."

A lone ambulance flashed its lights just around the corner, and some people in white jackets ran up to meet the wagon. Colin and Ant watched in horror as the beautiful girl was lifted up onto a stretcher and shut up in the back of the ambulance. As the sirens started up again and the vehicle took off, they followed, wagon skittering through the cheaply paved roads. There wasn't really a hospital here, so they were headed for Colin's beach house, in which half of the rooms were curtained off for patients.

"Boys, help me get her undressed!" Mrs. Dr. Baker asked of Colin and Ant once the girl had been deposited in a room. "We need to see what happened."

The boys looked at each other, embarrassed. Kathleen gave a huff of impatience as she began removing plates of armor.

"Come on, I know you can do this. You're teenage boys. It's your job!" She winked, forcing a smile.

Colin removed the leather satchel from the girl's waist and began to search for some kind of identification, as he was usually assigned to do for Brou residents who'd had an accident. Ant helped hold the girl's body off of the bed as the doctor removed her multiple tunics and leggings. Colin, finding nothing, turned around just as the patient's underclothes were coming off and blushed, turning away again quickly.

"It doesn't look good," Mr. Dr. Baker said over a cup of coffee, while his wife was in the girl's room again. Colin and Ant were sitting at the dining room table listening, waiting for a good report.

"Well, like, how bad is it?" Ant asked, voice quivering. "Did we drag a corpse all the way up here?"

"It's bad, Ant," Mr. Baker replied with a sigh. Colin's stomach rippled and he squeezed his father's shoulder until his hand shook.

"Is she dead?"

"She was unresponsive when you brought her here, not breathing, stopped heart, so we had to resort to CPR and a defibrillator..."

"Is she *dead*?" Colin shouted.

"She's alive,"

"—which is good," Colin interrupted with much relief.

"—but breathing very, very little, as if it hurts her to do so, which it most likely does," Dr. Baker continued. "She has a punctured lung, three broken ribs, and huge slashes down her side, from breast to pelvis. We had to really work on her lungs, because she almost drowned out there—good thing the tide went down earlier in the day before her lungs totally filled up!

"As if that's not bad enough, her wounds are poisoned, bruised, infected to about black by now, and swelling like nothing I've seen. It would seem to be a poisoning combined with a slashing, but I can't distinguish the elements of the poison. That aside, she's got all kinds of nice little wounds just about everywhere; bruises, cuts, briars in her skin, irritated by the salt and sand of the ocean. This little one's really taken a beating! If we can't cure the poisoning, I think that she will die, if not only from the deadening of her body, then by the sheer pain. Her body will literally shut itself down." He frowned wearily and slurped up the rest of his double-shot-espresso coffee. Ant kicked at the floor dejectedly, but Colin was suddenly struck with a theory.

"What about my *Foreign Infections and Poisons* textbook?" Colin was a first year pre-med student back in Arizona. "It's got some great pictures, so I bet you could figure out how to cure her!"

"That thing creeps me out," Ant murmured bitterly, remembering when Colin had showed him some particularly gross, pustule-ridden photos.

"Why, *that* would sure be helpful right now," Dr. Baker growled, wishing that this kind of information could have been presented earlier, when the patient had had more time they could work with.

"Be right back," Colin said eagerly, bounding to his room. When he'd retrieved his book, it was regarded with a quick glance, followed by a smile of approval to Colin. Dr. Baker exited the room in a flurry to join his wife.

Colin nodded proudly, and the phone rang. Ant's mother had heard about the incident on the beach, but wasn't thrilled to hear that her son was planning on staying and waiting the thing out. Of course, she had a few more words to use to make her opinion known. Colin hung up the phone quickly, which was still sizzling with heated motherly warnings, and looked at Ant like a hurt puppy.

"No offense, man, but your mom has got some *anger!* You're supposed to go home now, apparently." Colin smirked. "I'll let you know how this all turns out, after you get back from your *family reunion.* Have fun, sweetie. I'll miss you!"

Ant's ears reddened to match his hair. "Oh, shut up. I'll see you…er…back at home, I guess. We're back in two weeks—"

"—and we're home in one and a half. Yep. See you back in the States. Bye, dude."

"Bye, man. Tell the girl I said to get well soon…if she's actually, like, alive, eventually. She's really pretty; it would be a shame. Didn't even look like she had anyone with her. Say 'hi' to Becky for me next time you see her. Bye, dude." Ant gathered up his wagon and left. His mother had a summer house just across the street from the Bakers', and his permanent home was back in Arizona, right next door to Colin's.

"Yes!" Colin heard this from the girl's room, where doctors Mrs. and Mr. Baker had been working for the last four hours, while Colin had been trying to see if he could burn a hole through the wall with laser vision. There had been no progress in either case for a long time.

Now Colin swiftly leapt from where his butt had molded into the leather chair and ran to the room that had been transformed into an ICU.

"Colin," his father said excitedly, "your book had just the right cure! We identified the poison, see—right here, it matched all of this information right there—and it said exactly what to dose it with. It's very rare, and I had no idea that this poison was even still around! Thanks, kid! Just don't withhold information anymore!" He gave his son a bear hug, after he'd shed all of his stained scrubs.

"She's still asleep right now, poor thing didn't even need anesthesia—her brain is trying to convince her body that she's dead," Colin's mother broke in, "but *hopefully*," she continued, trying to force a happier tone, "she should wake up and be nice and confused within the week. The poisoning will go away by the end of the day, so we'll keep checking on her."

"What makes you say 'hopefully' she'll wake up?" Colin gulped.

"Well, she has been in pain and unconscious for God knows how long now, and her mind truly thinks it is dead. So...she may be in kind of a coma for a while until she heals a little more. Or...well..."

Their gazes all flew to the girl in the sterilized bed, who had been put into a cotton nightgown and was wrapped up tightly in gauze and cotton swabs.

"Her brain might win. She still could die." Mr. Baker finished, as his wife looked wistfully at the girl with a sudden flash of motherly instinct.

"But you cured her...didn't you?" Colin asked. The pit of his stomach dropped out and all his insides felt cold.

His father wrung his hands. "Yes...but she will only wake up when her body knows that it is alive. If she has lost the will to be alive, then she is as good as dead. It isn't just a conscious decision that she can make. It's up to how strong her body can get, so that it can convince her brain to work normally."

After dinner, they checked in on her again. Mr. Dr. Baker checked her vitals, and the Mrs. inspected her wounds via physical once-over and updated internal imaging. Colin paced.

"Wow! Look at how fast her lung has healed!" Mrs. Baker pointed out the now-closed punctures in her lungs. "That is about two weeks too early for this to have happened."

"That's good, though..." Colin recognized. "How does the wound look?"

She checked. "It's a lot better. Look here, it's already scarring over."

"Great!" Colin said, forcing enthusiasm. He really wanted her to get stronger and wake up. "Are her breathing and heart rate back up yet?" he asked his father.

"No, son. I'm sorry. She is still very weak, and probably very much in pain. It's still too early."

Colin frowned.

"Hey, this is really weird," Colin's father remarked to his son the next day, after another unremarkable check up, attempting to lighten the mood, "but did we ever consider what she had with her?" They all walked over to the small closet in the corner of the room, as the doctors stripped off their gloves and paper gowns. As Colin opened the door to the closet, his father continued.

"She was wearing all that leathery stuff, which you saw, and this," he gestured, "on underneath." Beneath his fingers was a mail coat; tiny interlocking rings that formed protection against swords or arrows. "Knights used to wear this stuff. Along with it were these guys," he said pointing out two swords which had been strapped to her sides. "It's like she was going to a Lord of the Rings convention, or something. I mean, maybe this had something to do with how she got hurt?"

"That's what I was thinking when we first saw her," Colin murmured. The small leather satchel that Colin had hastily examined also had a place in the closet, on a shelf above the clothes. Colin pointed. "I looked in there, too, and couldn't find anything of any help. I don't know…I should have seen… ID maybe? A nametag from a psych ward? I couldn't find anything, but I checked really fast."

His father cocked his head. "What *was* in the bag? Anything?"

"There was an old piece of parchment," Colin said, exaggerating the word *parchment*, "but it had some really strange, made up language written on it, so I couldn't tell what it said." He reached for the little bag, and opened it delicately. Inside, sure enough, was a folded up piece of yellowed parchment. Colin took it, expanding it gingerly, expecting it to crack and tear any second. Black lettering was scratched onto it in hurried, slanting script, but the words were long, grand, and definitely not in English. Some of the letters were not even familiar. Colin noticed a lot of capitalized words that could be names before his father reached for the paper and replaced it in the bag.

They all stood there for a moment, reflecting, when a faint bell sounded.

"The ambulance picked up somebody," Colin's mother muttered, and the two of them scurried from the room, grabbing at fresh gloves and the like on the way.

"Colin, watch for this little girl to wake up over the next few days, will you? I don't want her to freak out on us...Be her guardian angel." his father's voice faded as he retreated downstairs, where someone else was in need of medical attention. Colin rolled his eyes. *Great. Now, if she still dies, it's all my fault.*

TWO

KALKA WITHIN REACH

Once again, Citrosine was drifting through the void of unconsciousness. She'd never imagined how strange it would be to die. Her body was floating through nothingness, separated from her mind along the journey to death. Her disconnected, omniscient mind saw flashes of memory, just little tidbits that she would have told to her children, had she ever grown old enough to have any.

Tyre, shuddering and wincing as he foretold this event, right here, dying on the beach of somewhere foreign…Palgirtie smiling and glowering at the same time, slicing her poisonous skin through her own sister's gut, accusing her of their mother's death…Gya, crying on the inside as Leenka was pronounced gone…Citrosine's own arm being pierced by darkness, Jygul's Blessing that had turned out to be more curse and punishment than gift, all the accidents she'd caused…the stopping of time when she didn't mean it to occur…and finally…

Pherkue…tempting her, kissing her, teasing her…blaming her, punishing her…not being able to go against his fate…

becoming one of the Darkness…making Tyre poison himself… turning against the Elves…tasting her…

She was not thinking in conscious streams or sentences, only in memory and feeling. It was this way for what seemed like as long as her life previously had been…centuries and centuries and centuries. She saw what she had experienced, what she had felt, what she had wished; from her first memories of a birthday to her last memories of fighting her sister. Everything was soft-lit and dull, as if she was seeing reflections and warped lighting from the bottom of a million-mile-deep ocean.

Tie laughing as Gya shared with them the Dwarf song about Citra…happiness, camaraderie, secrets and hiding places, games and contests…childish fights over dresses…regret…best friends… plans and wishes, togetherness…

Suddenly, she began to feel things more sharply. Stinging shards of emotion began to slice into what she could now recognize as her body, preparing her to reach all that was redemption and judgment. These were the stronger memories that would define her afterlife.

Pherkue, Tie, Dydae…hatred-fury-pain, desolation…Tyre… leaving her body as she died…torture…passion…want, Dariya, love, passion-love-want, TyresiasDariya, passion-want-love-regr etneedDariyaTyreTyreDariyaTyrePAINPAINPAIN!

Immediately she knew that something had changed. She could feel her body; every limb, every nerve. All of it was pain. Citrosine could feel the gruesome fire that came with every sip of breath, the suffering labor her heart felt with every thump. She could not move for what felt like another three centuries, and yet she longed to writhe, shriek, wail, for surely she could release some of this torture! In death there was supposed to be peace or even rest, but not such pain as this!

She was conscious of vomiting, and the floating darkness that held her provided a hand to turn her head slantways so that she would not choke. Keeping her from choking and dying? And added to her pain was now a trembling cold nausea within her every muscle.

Please, let me die after all! I can go no further.

The lessons she'd learned when she was small flashed through her head; those about how Ghersah had awoken from death in a torture chamber…subjected to all of the pain in her life being relived, made to feel each sigh, each stab, and every near-fatal blow all in one massive ball of searing pain, so that she hung on the edge of life, that thread of miserable pain and desolation in which one can only weep and keen for death and quietus.

Have I not been touched by Kalka's slender, cradling fingers after all? I knew; my body was gone…and now I am to be as Ghersah was—reprieved of death by most evil of torturers…I can't fight this—what is happening? Is it not possible for me to simply die, get this pain over and finished…what…? I can see light! I can feel my scars…oh, glorious foul magic, am I to continue or to finally reach my end! I am DEAD—WHY IS THERE SUCH EVIL PAIN UPON ME! PLEASE KILL ME NOW!

She moaned in pain. Tie raked her claws through Citrosine's torso repeatedly at the same time as Pherkue strained her emotions, at the same time as Tyre showed her her death, at the same time as Tyre died, at the same time as Dariya died, at the same time as the conflicting magics warred within her blood, at the same time as the salt water filled her lungs, at the same time as Citrosine died—and she fainted.

When Citrosine could feel her body again in what her mind perceived as a few centuries later, she opened her eyes and let them adjust to the darkness. The first thing she was aware of was a bed underneath her. The coarsely woven blankets scratched her skin, and she felt all of her bruises being scraped and itched.

The roof above her was strange…it was white, but very rough-looking, not of a material she recognized. The walls were decorated with a few small mirrors hanging up in frames, and the room was painted a light shade of green. A matching curtain bordered one side of her, blocking her view of the other half of the room.

There was a tube that ended inside her nose, breathing cold air into her, making her insides itch. She promptly ripped that out, and the tube hissed at her as she cast it aside to the floor. *Could be poisoned air*, she reasoned, and coughed a little, just in case. The effort of coughing was too much for her injured lung and slow heartbeats, and she grew extremely lightheaded. Her surroundings grew dark again as she lost feeling and fainted.

She awoke a short time later, quite alarmed, when she began to acknowledge a strange, muffled noise, like a high-pitched squeaking; but it echoed her very heartbeat! Her pulse quickened, not understanding, and the shrill noises sped up to match. She saw a gray, lumpy...*thing*...with a lit, greenish-glowing square. The square was a moving picture of some sort, for it depicted green mountains that rose and fell with each screech. A thin wire sprouted from the side of the device, coming to its end in a small white patch stuck to her upper chest, not quite underneath the tight bandages she now was aware of around her waist. Many more patches like this adhered to her skin, in all different sizes. Most, however, were more skin-toned and covering stinging wounds.

Something was very strange here. Magic power seemed to flow by itself, into this device and others close to it, as they hummed and buzzed by themselves, and she saw no other beings but herself in this area, although...she sensed no magic whatsoever. In fact, the level of magic was so low that she heard the thin buzzing of magic coming from herself more than anything else, and her head began throbbing severely in response to such disorientation. *Where am I?*

Nearby, the sound of a yawn came muffled through the curtain, and she started. So there *was* another creature close, though she knew not if it was friend or foe. She decided to keep quiet. The thing was probably listening to her heart, monitored by the thing with the green mountains running across it.

Citrosine gently pushed herself up to a sitting position, regretting it in an instant. Her head swam, and everything went darker. She felt dizzy, and collapsed onto her back again, attempting to stay conscious this time. Everything slowly regained lightness and the spinning sensation began to fade, her side burning and stretching out. Her heart was slowing again, back to normal. She reached down at the itchy white patch, and stuck her fingernail underneath a corner. *One, two, three…*She yanked the patch off all at once, and grimaced at the explosion it left in her skin, so close to her wound and pulling on the deadened flesh.

The device monitoring her heart started letting out longer squeaks now, until the green mountains turned into a flat red line, and there was a single note held out loudly, making the Elf's headache increase. She heard a voice behind the curtain.

"Huh?"

The green sheet was ripped aside, and a boy that looked to be about her equal in age stumbled through sleepily. He didn't give her a glance, but ran over and pressed a button on the lumpy thing. The high note was suspended, and faded to silence. The boy turned to her frantically, and a look of surprise and relief came over his face. His eyes fell on the white patch in her hand, and he laughed and shook his head.

"Too itchy for you, huh? That's the first time anyone's ever tricked that LCD screen that way." Turning away again, the boy pulled a wire out of the wall that connected to the machine. The lit square went dark and the humming of the monster, the LCD, the boy had called it, went silent.

"Well, we can't just be pulling wires out of ourselves, now," he said playfully, trying to scold, but laughing too much in relief to accomplish the desired effect.

Why isn't he speaking Elvish? Citrosine wondered. She was internally elated that her father had taught her of the Common Tongue, for now she could figure out why she wasn't dead, like she was supposed to be.

"I—I'm sorry," she managed. The boy frowned in concentration. Citrosine slouched and tucked her hair behind her ears. Her fingers noticed that it was dry and salty. *How long was I laying there in the water?* she wondered.

"That's all right," the boy answered, gaping blatantly. "I'm just glad that you finally woke up! We didn't think…"

"Yes?" She was trying to be polite, but her headache was starting to get her irritated with things, along with not understanding her current state of living.

"Um…nothing," he answered shyly, "I was just…uh… supposed to, like, make sure you woke up and everything. Eventually."

This isn't an Elf! Citrosine grasped. *He's just a young Man! Why…how did I get here? Where am I? Why am I not poisoned? Well, thinking about all this won't help me find out.* She rubbed her temples.

"Does your head hurt?" the boy queried, "'Cause I could get you some medicine for it." He looked at her earnestly.

"Medicine? All right, I suppose…" Citrosine was confused. Yes, Men used medicinal remedies, since most possessed no magic abilities whatsoever.

"Okay. I'll be right back—just a sec," he assured, before hustling out of the room. Citrosine saw that the door he used exited into a hallway with many more rooms. There was a window across the corridor, where a beach was visible. Gulls flew over the water in loose formations, and she wondered if that was where she'd fallen, certain that she was headed for death.

Colin jogged down the stairs to the bookshelf-sized master medicine cabinet. Beach Girl had a headache, so he would get her some aspirin. He stifled a snicker as he located the bottle and filled a glass with water. The way she had looked when he unplugged the heart monitor! She seemed so confused now, as if she had never seen any of these things before in her life. Even when he had opened the door to come down here; the skepticism on her face was so dominant.

Taking the stairs two at a time, Colin did his best to stay quiet. It was, after all, not even past sunrise yet, and there was another patient he knew of, along with his parents, that needed to rest. The client ringing the bell yesterday had been a guy who'd gotten slammed against a pier surfing in the stormy waves yesterday and broken his arm. Seemed so mundane after the poisoning/drowning/beating/dying of Beach Girl.

The girl was moaning in pain when he returned, so he quickly moved toward her. He handed her the glass of water and the two oblong ibuprofens that he'd fetched for her. "Go ahead and swallow those babies with a few good swigs," he prompted, sitting on the foot end of her bed.

She looked at him with cynicism again, then took a drink of water, threw both the pills into her throat and drank again. Her eyes widened, and she coughed, but no harm done. She grabbed at her chest as she coughed and fell back to the bed. *Mental note: Hey, stupid! She has a punctured lung!*

"Good," he said, taking the glass back and placing it on the swinging, adjustable tray alongside the bed.

Citrosine looked at him in horror as she felt her pain blurring...she was drowsy—what had this beast given her? Would she regret this? The Elf couldn't think anymore, as she was asleep. Never being administered such a kind of medicine, her body reacted to it immediately and tenfold compared to a normal mortal.

Colin smirked as Beach Girl was asleep in seconds. Shaking his head, he backed out of the room.

Wow, is she weird. It's like she actually is from some fantasy story. I gotta call Ant. He drew out his cell phone and called his best friend, not caring that it was two in the morning in Arizona right now.

A few hours later, Beach Girl was inspecting the bandages over Tie's slashes when Colin came back in the room.

"You took a pretty hard beating there," he said, "from whatever you managed to get yourself into." He meant to sound teasing, and the way the girl smiled distantly proved his tone to be correct. "So," he began awkwardly, "what's your name?"

"I am Citrosine Nakiss," she said softly, "and you are…?"

"Colin Baker, son of Mr. and Mrs. Dr. Baker, who fixed you up so that you could be sitting here talking to me." He smiled, and Citrosine looked at him blankly in reply. "Sitter-seen, huh? I've never heard that name before."

"Er, it's *Citro*sine. How about calling me 'Citra' instead?"

"Citra?"

"All right." She struggled for a topic of conversation but found none. "I've never…heard the name 'Colin' before." There was a pause. "Your parents healed me? But I was sure that I had died…Did they use medicine like that you fetched for me?" Her eyes fell to the bandage around herself.

"Some," Colin answered, shutting the door so that the other patients wouldn't be awoken, "but mostly they were just trying to clean up that big chunk you got out of your side there—it was poisoned, some of your ribs were broken, and your lung was punctured. There were some other cuts and bruises, which I'm sure you can feel."

"I thought I was certain to die—I could feel my life slipping away. I…there was nothing, I was dead—and I could almost touch…" *Kalka,* she finished silently.

Suddenly, she thought of Tyre. He had shown her that death on the beach. And yet she had not died. *Tyre's premonition was not wrong…* the Elf realized. *It was just that he misinterpreted. He didn't see me die, he just saw me almost reach death…* She exhaled heavily, the pain of losing Tyre fresh all over again.

"Well, my friend Ant and I found you on the beach," Colin continued heedlessly, "and it looked like you were done for. Then my mom showed up and brought you here…they had to use all kinds of machines and crap to get you to start breathing again, including the respirator that was hooked up in your nose, which I see you got rid of…and we found an antidote for whatever you were poisoned with." Colin cursed under his breath for making her relive this experience.

She shifted. "But it felt like so long, and you speak so unaffectedly…"

"Oh, er…Well…I mean, honestly, we thought you were going to die, and it has been a good week now…" Colin explained softly.

"My father will be so worried! He hasn't seen me for that long…"

They sat in silence.

Colin made small talk. "So…like I said, my friend Ant and I were on the beach,"

"Your friend 'Ant'?"

Colin laughed. "Yes. His real name is Anthony, but I like Ant better. It's kind of a nickname for him, since we were little."

"Ah. I see. There is a name behind the animal title." She joined in laughing with the boy, then winced and grasped at her waist.

"That's not pleasant," she whimpered.

"Oh, I'm sorry," Colin said, hands reaching out in attempt to find something to help with.

"No—not your doing," she fragmented, being in too much pain to elaborate a sentence. She laid down on her back again. "Citra is also a kind of 'nickname', I suppose," she related as the pain receded. "There is an old song, very irreverent, that talks about some kind of temptress 'Citra', and it was close to my name, so they used to joke that the song was about me."

Colin was curious of her dialect now. She sounded faintly British, or maybe Irish. He wondered also about the pointed ears that he just began to recognize—was she a leprechaun, or something?—as well as her Middle-Earth-style clothing, then rolled his eyes at himself for making fun of a patient. However, she must have gone through a lot of work to perfect her Elf-y costume.

Citrosine didn't know how to respond when Colin asked where she was from. She wasn't supposed to tell Men about the enchantment on Ilthen, but this boy seemed different. He was friendly, treated her like an exact equal; whether that was right or not was yet to be seen.

She'd spotted a brightly colored world map on a display stand outside the room when Colin went out to get the medicine for her earlier, and she asked him for it now.

"Round world map? Oh, the globe…yeah, sure." He walked out of the room and retrieved it, sitting on the end of her bed again.

"Thank you. Come sit aside me so I can show you without splitting my side open again," she said, giving him a mock pout. He complied. "Now, can you show me where we are right now, please?"

Colin pointed to the spot off the coast of the shape that Citrosine recognized as the Big Lands. His fingertip rested on the exact spot where Ilthen—and Brou—should be.

"We are in Brou," Colin confirmed, as if speaking to a child.

"Yes, of course," Citrosine said lightly. "I live in the woods outside of where we are right now." She stopped herself from saying more.

"But…" Colin seemed confused. "But that's only forest. That's the Brou Tropical Wildlife Reserve. Nobody's allowed in there!"

Citrosine nodded thoughtfully, as if she'd heard this argument many times. "Well, my people live in the Reserve, kind of as stewards of the…" she struggled for the word Rina had used years ago, "ecosystem." Citrosine saw the bewildered glance Colin gave her and stopped.

"So what's with all the armor? The pointed ears? The accent? The scroll of parchment in your bag?" Colin countered quickly. He reconsidered his hostility briefly. "We had to inspect your things when we treated you, so that's the only reason that I ask…"

Citrosine was lost for a moment. She looked at Colin silently, measuring him. Gently, imperceptibly, she reached into his mind. There was nothing there to even hint that he was treacherous or menacing…he had never told a malicious lie, he rarely broke his word on things. *Can I tell him?* She felt true goodness in this boy, such as she'd felt in very few people before…her mother, Tyre, her father, King Hendius…but he was a mortal! He wasn't supposed to know! *I mustn't,* she affirmed, *I just mustn't! It isn't natural!*

"Colin, I am tired. I…I don't wish to talk about this anymore." She forced a yawn, and curled up under her blanket."

The boy reluctantly accepted her avoidance of the conversation and left her to think. "That's okay. I guess I could tell my parents you're up."

Citrosine struggled for a few hours as the sounds of other Men moving about the house began to grow louder. After all that the immortals had gone through, it could destroy everything that they had just established, everything that they had just escaped, if she spoke of Elves to Colin.

But he was so concerned about her health. After all, he had turned out to be no torturer, and was quite sympathetic to her dislike of being in this place…which, if this was his and his parents' job—healing others with these set procedures—he must have had to bend a few rules to let her disconnect herself from the "machines", as he'd called them.

I should at least let him know the truth. I think that he is a friend. What would Tyre say? *Tyre would be blunt. 'Are you trustworthy? This is important. I can answer your questions, but you must be willing to keep some secrets, for my sake.' Tyre…is this wise?* He would say, *Just be wise, dearest. Just be clever and wise.*

Colin entered a while later with a glass of water for Citrosine. "I bring a peace offering," he offered, handing her the glass, which she accepted gratefully. The cool water helped ease her headache, which had receded to background pain compared to the rest, although it still hurt. She took a few slow, deep breaths, which felt a lot better now than they had when she woke up.

"Ah, I wonder…" she said softly, "if I can answer your questions from this morning…?" She hesitated, deciding how best to approach this situation.

"I'm listening," Colin prompted.

"Can I trust you?" Citrosine asked.

"Is there something that needs trusting, Citra?" He looked skeptical.

"It is of utmost importance that I know that you can keep these words secret. Should you speak them to your parents, or others, then my existence could be threatened."

Colin stared at her.

"Our kind live in secret, so I am not supposed to speak of this to you…and you mustn't tell." Citrosine saw the transformation from bewildered to interested, and gave Colin a moment to respond.

"Your *kind?* What *kind* would that be, exactly?" He grasped the edge of his chair, as if radically new information, which he expected, would make him too heavy and he'd fall through the floor.

Tell him, Tyre would suggest. *It will be hard, but he can be trusted. Just ask him directly one more time.*

"Do I have your honor? Can I trust you?" Citrosine pressed once more.

Colin's eyes refocused on hers more intently, and he leaned towards her. "Whatever you are about to tell me, I swear that I'll keep it quiet. Now what the hell are you talking about?"

Citrosine took this as confirmation. She smiled. "I am a part of the Elven race."

Colin didn't react for a moment, and then smirked.

"You have got to be kidding me. What do you think I am, four years old?"

Citrosine looked at him for a moment. She tried another approach. "Have you never heard the legends of magic? Of creatures which used to do amazing things? Dragons?"

Colin frowned. "Well, yeah, but they're just stories. Like... fairytales, movies, bedtime stories. I'm eighteen. I'm past all of that." He gaped at her and tried to imagine what kind of family she'd grown up in if she thought that all this fantasy stuff was real.

"Would you listen if I told you they were true? Or...well, I don't know exactly what you've heard..."

"No, I probably wouldn't," Colin persisted. "Do you...you think that you can actually do magic, then?" He cleared his throat and tried to force his outrageous grin away.

"Yes."

He laughed. "Really? But it doesn't exist!"

"It does, at least for us," Citrosine murmured seriously, keeping track of his reactions. If worst came to worst, she could just erase his memory, yes?

"We...um...they, at least, they...my culture says that God was the only one with that kind of power..." Citrosine looked confused now. "Creator of Heaven and Earth? He made everything, and had a son that was the Savior of humankind, who died, then came back and went to Heaven...you have no idea, do you?"

Citrosine's eyes widened as she slowly comprehended. "We have something comparable to this...but it is forbidden to speak of."

"Forbidden? Like how?"

"Like 'forbidden'. I can tell you nothing." The Elf hesitated, trying to remember if she had broken any rules in these statements. If one mentioned anything about the deity to a *mortal*, Jygul and Ghersah would immediately collect one's soul to use as a plaything in the Dark Realm of the Afterlife. The tales told that the goddesses were much less lenient with talk of the deity than with other moral codes. The deity was a force that united all the world's living, nonliving, thought, and spoken things, and was in danger of being disproved. For the creatures that it created were always on the verge of knowledge and discovery, so if they were to ever try to dissect the deity's power and workings, they might try to come up with some grand explanation of why the deity did not, in fact exist. Should one, for example, think, 'This song is so beautiful, and the deity cannot have the talent it takes to have any part of producing these notes; therefore the deity must not be all-powerful or omnipotent!', then the deity's very existence, which existed only through the belief of its creations in it, would be threatened. It was, in short, a thing to be believed in and not challenged.

"Go on; you were saying?" Citrosine prompted, to distract Colin's questions.

"Well...I'm not supposed to believe in magic, because... um...God is the only being that can make things, destroy things...there's rules." He ended weakly. "Maybe it works out for me, too, that I not tell anyone else about this. No one would believe us, anyway."

Citrosine nodded in understanding. They both breathed in relief. His parents were very conservative and revolved around religion, while Citrosine's whole realm could unwind if anyone in Colin's world held this information in ill will.

"There are rules in our magic, likewise." Her eyes went a little harder.

"You have rules in making things appear, disappear, change, or come back to life? No way!" Colin was amazed, but still a little skeptical. Citrosine giggled, sensing that he was making fun of her persistence in the subject.

"Well, for one, I can't just make things disappear out of thin air. They have to go somewhere! And as for making things appear from nowhere, they're not of very good quality, and we have to get rid of them within a short time, in most cases." She held up a hand. "Would you care for a demonstration?" She smiled, knowing fully that Colin had never seen magic, and that this could be a fun thing to do.

Colin nodded weakly, and Citrosine giggled again. He wanted to see her interpretation of the real deal, as if the pointy Elf-ears and battle armor didn't explain that enough. If she could actually pull off this stuff, then maybe she would win back some of his respect. Otherwise he could just send her back to whatever cult or convention she belonged to.

She waved her raised hand, smirking. All show, this was. She closed her eyes, breathed sharply, and all was dark. The only thing Colin could see was a small blue ball of light hovering close to Citrosine's hand.

And then there was a Dragon sitting across the room from them. Colin, who had never seen a real one before, shrieked and flung himself against the wall. Citrosine slowly diminished it in size, until the Dragon could flit about the room to land on Colin's arm, letting out a breath of smoke, and then vanishing. Colin went back to Citrosine, unable to think of a thing to say.

She laughed, and the flickering blue-green ball she held faded away, letting the electric lights took over again.

"Okay, okay; I believe you," Colin said in a resigned tone layered with conflicting sarcasm and amazement. Citrosine giggled again, forgetting for just an instant that she had lost a mother, a best friend, and been attacked by her transformed sister.

"So..." Colin started, after the humor had died down a bit, "how did you end up here? I mean, if your side of the island is so magical and awesome, why'd you come to the boring, non-magical, humanoid Brou?" He smirked, and then frowned, seeing Citrosine's reaction.

The Elf slouched and traced the bandages on her side. She bit her lip, and Colin watched as her eyes went back in time, hardening and saddening at the same time.

"I'm sorry—I didn't mean to make you feel bad about it..." *See, why did I have to go and say that to her? She's just recovering!*

"No, it isn't your fault, it is done," she murmured. "You have a right to know why you're keeping me alive..." She looked up, and said levelly, "I was *supposed* to die on the beach."

Colin didn't know what to say, but his cheeks flamed in reply. "Supposed to...as in it was, like, ordained?"

"A prophecy of my late friend...well, more than just a friend..."

"Ooh, how much more?" Colin interrupted immaturely. Humor was his thing; anything to get away from sad moods. Citrosine wasn't bothered. The sidetrack gave her more time to plan her words.

"I loved him. He loved me. We wanted to spend the rest of our lives together, have children, live together, be married..."

"Awesome. So this dude's a boyfriend."

"You could say that…though I'm not entirely sure what that entails in your culture. Boyfriend? Is that what you'd call him? Someone in that relationship?"

"Yeah, although most of us don't know that we want to spend our lives together. We just like kissing each other, so we get girlfriends or boyfriends." Colin sent a silent apology to his girlfriend Becky, who he very much liked kissing, but there was at least a little more to the relationship than *that*…although they'd been together more than most teenage relationships, so they were kind of a freak of nature.

Citrosine blushed just hearing the mention of kissing—not something often spoken of in normal conversation.

"Then I suppose he was my boyfriend. He foresaw our life together. We would have a lovely home, and a child… Dariya…" She broke off, unable to control herself. She began sobbing, and asked Colin to excuse her emotion for long minutes.

Colin let her sob in silence, his eyes making circles around the room, focusing on the machines, the walls, the white, plastic-and-paper-covered bed; anything but the Elf. Citrosine's tears burned her throat, and as she heaved breaths, her wound began to ache more and more sharply, the muscles below contracting and twitching, irritating the dying skin above. She winced. *Dariya and Tyre…dead…I must face this someday. But they are both so precious! Would that I were dead, too, in whatever place they are.*

"I can give you some time, uh, alone. Citra?" Colin hedged.

Citrosine shook her head and motioned for him to stay.

"In any case," Citrosine said as she began to control herself, "…he prophesied my death here…There was a war… our tribes—the different groups that use different kinds of magic—one of those tribes disagreed about the amount of space they were given. They use black magic, and are associated with darkness and evil. They were, well, diminishing, having to mate at young ages, like animals, for survival. None of the others trusted them, so they weren't granted many freedoms..." she paused. There was a noise in the hallway, but Colin waved her on. It was just his parents downstairs.

"Well, this tribe...the Shadow Elves, had staged a revolt against all the rest of us...they had Dark Ones—Wampyres. Are you familiar with these creatures? They are evil...they drink blood to live, and breed more of their kind," her voice lowered, and she hesitated. Colin nodded. He had dressed as a vampire for Halloween last year, for a party that one of Ant's friends had thrown.

"Wampyres," she continued, "started the attack on us. Our tribe declared war on the other, to defend the rest of our realm, and it turned into a huge mess with a few tribes against the other few. My father and I...er...fought against the Shadow Tribe's side. They were almost defeated—no, were about to bring us to our end, set their negotiations—when their Wampyres appeared again, along with demons..." she lifted the side of her nightgown carefully so that the bandages were fully visible, along with the blood caked to them. "One demon ended up being...she was...it—" she couldn't finish, and her cheeks reddened. She caressed the vein of magic on her forearm absently and made her face blank.

"It's okay..." Colin floundered, "you don't have to—"

"The demon," she continued, inside Colin's thoughts, scaring him fully, *"was my sister, who had shape-shifted. She chased me down, attacked me, and accused me of killing our mother, in which I had no part whatsoever. Such an unreasonable Elf, always, but this! The demon she'd become was poisonous, and dug into me so many times...it should have taken me few more minutes, to die...and it would have been only seconds, I believe—it was difficult to distinguish time while 'dying'—if you and...Ant hadn't found me. Or perhaps I was already dead and you revived me, I don't know.*

"*I'd had to run from the wood, where I had tricked her, and along the water to here. I didn't really know where I was, just delirious. I...I suppose I just thought I should die...that was what the vision had warned me. Everything matched. The waves, the storm, the way I had to drag myself on any further.*

"*And all the time while I suppose you were healing me, I believed I was dying. I lost all my senses, but for a little bit of memory...which continued during what I thought was my... journey to Death. And then the pain began to return, and I felt all of it even more sharply, in crisper detail and more agony and torture. As if I was being burned alive and I could not even open my eyes.*" She couldn't think of anything further, so she grew silent. Colin stared. He knew that it sounded impossible, but he really thought he believed her.

"Well...Citrosine, thank goodness for low tide..." he didn't even hear himself say this until Citrosine spoke.

"Thank you. I would never have had a chance of living if I hadn't found my way ...er...*lost* my way to this place," She forced a small grin.

"Colin?" A voice floated in from the hallway.

"That's my dad," Colin said softly. Then, to the door: "Yeah?"

"Is our friend awake yet?" He was very curious. Colin assumed that he could hear snatches of conversation from the hallway.

"Yeah," Colin said disdainfully. "Would you like to meet Our Friend?" His eyes met Citrosine's, and he moved his finger around in circles next to his head and crossed his eyes. Citrosine smiled faintly as the door opened.

The bear of a man, Mr. Dr. Baker, opened the door jovially, beaming at Citrosine like she was a newborn baby that he had just helped to deliver. That was how Colin's mother had met him. She had had a husband before, but when she got pregnant—zing! He left—and Colin's father delivered her baby (Colin's older sister, who was in grad school), making an instant connection and falling in love with Colin's mother, causing them to go on some dates, grow closer, eventually get married, etc, etc. Happily ever after.

"Well, hello," Baker said, a little quieter than he'd been before. "How are we this morning?"

"Make up a story about me that he'll understand, please," Citrosine whispered to Colin as she said, "I am well, thank you. It is good to speak with you, now that I think that I am actually alive." She smiled sweetly, and Colin knew she would blend fine into Brou.

"Of course; I'm so glad you're up!" Dr. Baker boomed. "I hadn't imagined I would see your beautiful eyes for quite some time. We were pretty worried about you." Citrosine blushed. "How did you ever manage to get such a slash like that?" He meant it to be funny, and Colin thought that Citrosine would understand that, but she lowered her eyes to the wound and said nothing.

"Dad, *Citra,* here, is from London," he said, thinking quickly, trying to explain everything at once, "and is doing a project on olden cultures. She was given permission to do a little research project in the Reserve, and she said that she tripped and fell in the water by the pier on the morning when we found her; you should have seen all the breakers out there! I thought it might've had something to do with the storm." Citrosine nodded faintly. "She tripped down at the cove by the port—with all those rocks with the barnacles on them—and got sliced on some kind of er...I don't know, a rare fish, like a lionfish or something! Pretty crazy, I think." He sneaked a look at Citrosine, who was nodding slightly, eyes still lowered.

"Wow! That's one of the more exciting ones, isn't it? Hey, just last week there was a patient who only came here because he was dehydrated! Now that's just boring, right? Not to harp on people's health nowadays, but..." Dr. Baker laughed, and loped off to check on Surfboard Kid down the hallway.

Citrosine looked up at Colin through her lashes. *"Thank you. I would not have known what he would accept as truth. That was a riveting story, quite interesting. I found it more unbelievable, somehow, than what was truth, but I suppose I can't complain, if it pleases him."*

"It wasn't quite as complicated as the true thing, that's for sure. I just needed something to explain all of your battle gear," he admitted, nodding towards the closet where Citrosine's swords and the like hung.

"Yes; I was starting to wonder where my things were—" Citrosine suddenly blushed, then tried to cover her face. She collapsed into the pillows, which muffled her soft laughter. Her hands clutched at her bandages as she gasped for air, still giggling.

Colin looked at her intently, not knowing what was going through her mind. *Um? What's her deal? Is she, like, going insane?* "Citrosine? Uh—what did I say that's so funny? Anything?"

This only made her laugh more. She shuffled out of the pillows, face red, smile plastered onto her face. Her breaths came quickly, and she clawed at her side, somewhere between agony and hysteria.

"I'm sorry," she panted, trying to cover her remaining laughter. "If there's one thing I cannot mask, it is most definitely happiness and embarrassments."

"So, what's so funny?" Colin was laughing himself.

"You didn't—you weren't there helping me be undressed, were you? Did all of you undress me whilst I was..." She giggled, covering her mouth with a hand.

Colin's face turned a deep shade of red. "I—I didn't mean—it's just—like—um—Strictly business, of course... y'know, we had to see your wounds!"

"Yes, then, I presume?" Citrosine asked, laughing harder than she ever had. *"It's just that Elf culture is so much stricter than yours...! I don't believe that our Healers would even do*

such a thing...I feel as if I have been so violated!" However, she continued to laugh.

"Well...yes. Sorry—we were trying to figure out how you were poisoned, and put you into that little smock-thing—I didn't—oh, gosh!"

Citrosine was in silent laughter, grasping her side tightly, slipping a charm of healing into it. "We aren't even allowed to talk about kissing!" She gasped, "and already you have spoken of it, and your girlfriend, and undressing me!"

"Dude, we talk about everything here," he winked suggestively. "Everything."

"Please—do not;" Citrosine could no longer make sentences.

"You have a wonderful body, by the w—" Colin said sheepishly. He couldn't finish, so they laughed for a few more moments. When they could no longer smile so widely, Colin regained composure.

"We just put all your stuff in the closet...You had a little purse-bag-thing in there, too, right? Sorry—we had to go through everything, just to see if you had any identification or drugs or anything...we didn't take any of your stuff, just, like, looked at it a little bit."

"That's okay...er...what all did you see in there?" She looked a little suspicious, and Colin gulped.

"All I really found was, uh, there was a piece of paper, like a note or something...it looked really old...did you know about that?"

"Yes," she said quickly, her voice immediately hard. "Did you...read it?"

"No—it's in Elvish, I guess, otherwise it's really bad handwriting," he tried to joke, wondering if he should have just left well enough alone.

"Yes, of course..." she trailed off, staring into space. Colin decided not to push his luck with too many questions.

"Hmm. Well, all of this talking has made me very hungry. Wouldn't you agree?" He smiled, and Citrosine drudged herself out of whatever quandary she'd been in.

"Absolutely; I think a good snack should be in order, eh?" She winked.

"Hell yeah!" Citrosine winced at the cursing in his words, even if it didn't make sense in her language. "Do you think you can walk down the stairs, or would you like me to bring you something? You could eat on this tray thingy here or..." he eyed her bandage, and remembered all the cuts and scrapes she had. "You know what? I think I'll just make you something. Is that okay?"

"Er...yes. That is a brilliant thought. Thank you so much, Colin."

"No prob," he replied, halfway out of the room.

When Citrosine awoke the next morning, almost all her pain was gone, if she remained sitting still. This was good. As soon as the first little shards of light trickled into the room, she sat up delicately, pushing the scratchy sheets away. She swung her naked feet to the cold floor, and groaned as the scratch Tie had inflicted stretched out with her spine.

She padded over to the tiny closet that her clothes were stored inside. The door opened with a startling screech, and Citrosine looked quickly behind her. No one seemed to have heard, so she reached for her shoulder bag.

Taking a deep, preparatory breath, she pulled out Tyre's letter, and went back to curl up amongst the pillows encased in paper. She raked a hand through her hair, prolonging the wait before she read the letter, which she knew she would end up doing. She braided her hair. She unbraided her hair. She picked up the letter, replaced it on the bed. Took it up, unfolded it...

Many things have just come into play that none of us could have imagined...dearest friend, Citrosine Nakiss, collapses, poisoned...Rather than carry out a dead life of evil, Tyre Kendah shall soon be no more...

...refolded it again. She took in gulps of refreshing air and reminded herself that she should not revisit these feelings. Her life was still going on; she was in a new chapter. Tyre was gone, but she had a whole life to continue. She set the letter back down, and tucked her hair behind her ears. She began braiding a section of it.

Citrosine irritably abandoned her hair, and resumed her reading.

To the last, Citrosine—I love you more than anything. Know that my heart shall fly to you this night...it is already yours, irrevocably, absolutely, without end...May magic unite us all against these times of darkness...

I had not remembered the power of this letter. He was so strong, in his darkest moment...too young, too old in spirit, as all of us have become. Would that we could feel humor instead of pain like the mortals, she wished. Citrosine looked up as a soft knock came at the door, eyes dripping just like they had the first time she read this.

"*Nehtle vye,*" she suggested, accidentally saying "enter" in Elvish. Colin's face peeked in, befuddled, hoping that *nehtle vye* didn't mean "go away" or "I'm naked" or something.

"Are we decent?" he pronounced, mocking an English accent. Citrosine sniffled, chuckling. He wasn't very good at that; his voice was too energetic and hurried to pronounce each letter with precision and delicacy, as the accent that was distantly reminiscent of Citrosine's own demanded.

"Of course, sir, apart from the half-sized nightclothes, I am perfectly decent!"

319

"Sorry about that," he laughed. "We underestimated your lovely womanliness." Citrosine blushed, and Colin snorted. He squeezed through the door, holding a tray of breakfast in his arms. "Pancakes, bacon, scrambled eggs, and some French toast," he announced, noticing her glance toward the warm food. "I didn't know what you wanted, so I just picked some stuff out. We can share, if you're not that hungry."

"Actually," Citrosine said bashfully, "I have no idea of what any of this food is."

Colin laughed, placing the tray in front of her and sitting on the corner of her bed. "So..." he said slowly, "Who wrote the letter there?" He nodded towards Tyre's letter.

Citrosine hesitated. She didn't know if she could retell what had happened to her first love. Seeing Colin's friendly face, however, she gave in, but not after a heavy, reflective sigh.

"It's a bit ironic," she began distantly, thinking back, "that the first Elf I loved was also the first Elf to ever die in my name..." Colin looked at her in horror.

"Explain," he encouraged cautiously after an awkward pause.

"The, er, what did you call him? Boy-friend? His name was Tyresias...and he was warning me about the Wampyre that I think I told you about...?" Colin nodded reassuringly. "The creature was going to sire him to get him to destroy me, so that my father would be weak. My father was a member of an important council, and they needed to threaten him into giving the Dark Elves more land, or rights, or whatever it was that they wanted."

"When you say it was gonna 'sire' him...?"

"Poison him with its venom, in order to make him one of them..."

"Yeah, yeah. I just didn't know there was a word for that. Okay."

"The letter was dictated by Tyre himself—he was blind, so he'd enchanted the utensils—while he warned me of all this. I was to inform my elders, and Tyre was to protect me, and himself, by..." she stopped, leaving Colin with his eyes open wide and waiting for an ending. Citrosine's mind was spinning, and she knew that if she didn't relax and disregard her story soon, she would lose control of her emotions again.

Colin moved closer to her, as if that action was going to keep her from crying, or whatever he presumed her to be ready to do. She smiled halfheartedly.

"He wanted to keep me safe, and didn't want to lose control of himself and become one of them when the Dark One ambushed him, so he poisoned himself. The letter reads exactly what he said aloud in his room that night, when he was ready to drink the poison, up to his dying words...He didn't finish his thought...and the Wampyre bursting in on him is recorded..." Citrosine was actually amazed at how she managed to keep herself in check by leaving words out. She wasn't as crushed as the first time she'd read it, but she was, nonetheless, crying, throat stinging.

"That's so sad," Colin muttered. "I can't think of, like, *anything* I've heard that's more depressing than that."

Citrosine nodded, folding up the letter and putting it on the swiveling tray where her breakfast was waiting.

"I think I recognize that name from somewhere... Tyresias?" Colin's eyes wandered the room. He quickly snapped his fingers, eyes lighting up in recognition. "That was the name of this blind, like, oracle in a really old Greek story! That's pretty cool, that it was the same kind of person, huh? They were both blind prophets!"

Citrosine did not answer, pretending to be too distracted on her food. She pensively stabbed an egg with her fork and moved it around on the plate for a moment.

"So, what, this dude, like, proposed?" Colin looked at Citrosine's slender hands that were currently poking through her breakfast.

"What?" Citrosine snorted. "Sometimes I have the hardest time attempting to understand your dialect." Colin smirked. "Are you from somewhere outside of Brou altogether? I've heard Men speak, but it's been a long time, and they were different…"

"Um…well, we're actually from the USA—er—the Big Lands? Right next to the Grand Canyon—"

"A big crack in the ground in the middle of the desert?" Citrosine wondered.

He smiled.

"Jygul's Grin," the Elf added. "That's what we call it. I had…some adventures there, a long time ago…I almost drowned."

"Drowned? The water is way, *way* down at the bottom— you can't mean that you fell—right?" Colin stared her down.

"Back then," she informed him, "it was still full of water."

"So," Citrosine continued in another direction, "what am I eating here, exactly?" Her fork was poised in the center of a pile of yellow, writhing lumps. Next to them on the plate was a small piece of bread that had been roasted and smothered with what looked like butter, but the Elf couldn't be sure. Another plate on the tray was the resting place of some oversized *paliz*, or sun cakes, but they were drowned in thick brown sauce.

Colin laughed at her expression of wonder and skepticism. "That," he said, pointing to each one in turn, "is a pile of scrambled eggs. That's toast—not too weird, I hope—and then pancakes, with bacon hidden underneath somewhere, maybe…"

Citrosine was still baffled, but she ate without objection, wiping her eyes periodically.

Throughout the afternoon, Citrosine took alternating dozes and periods of lying on her back, staring at the ceiling and thinking about what seemed like a past life now. Sometimes she tried out small spells and charms, just to be sure that her powers still worked.

Colin visited several times, apologizing for not being able to talk for long each time. He was, apparently, very involved in helping his parents take care of the injured Men in the house. Citrosine figured that it had to be irritatingly tedious to heal all of these mortals, seeing how no magic could be used.

She began to feel as if Colin was like a brother. If only Tie had ever been this understanding. She could tell him so many things about herself that she'd never realized alone, and every time she began to feel self-conscious, talking about her own life so much, he asked her another question with renewed eagerness and honest innocence. He was so honest, asking her whatever he could think of and not continuing if she wasn't comfortable answering. The Elf's aura shimmered brightly when they spoke together, and her mind lightened as she focused not on her past worries, but on laughing and learning, growing stronger every hour.

THREE

CITRA, FROM LONDON

"How long have you been, like, a warrior-Elf-ess, or whatever?" Colin asked near noon the next day, when his parents had run out of errands to send him on. His day had been flat and monotonous, whenever he wasn't around the girl that had changed his life so abruptly.

Citrosine giggled, holding her laughs in slightly, and ever so gently grasping at her side. "I have been taught in the ways of swordplay since I was very little; my mother was a prestigious warrior, and my father has been a kind of guardian for as long as I know."

"Is it, like, a requirement of your race to have to fight off evil all the time?"

"It isn't as if we have always been plagued by war, but we need protectors to fend off the more evil creatures that creep among the woods and such in that manner..." Her brow furrowed, and Colin wondered if that was an unpleasant memory. *Hmm...*he thought, *I think I should stop asking her questions eventually. She's probably getting really pissed at me for* *making her think about all that bad stuff...*But he had so many things he wanted to know about her! Here was a girl who had lived for centuries—really! Actually through centuries!—and experienced so much more than Colin was ever allowed to believe existed. How could he just let her disappear back into her own secret world again? He had to get the most out of this, to know, at least within himself, that it all was actually happening.

"I know this sounds jerk-y, but I have to ask," he began. "Why did you decide in the first place that you would fight your own race? I mean, couldn't you be, like, a medicine-woman, or...I don't know...some kind of Council-ish person, like you said your Dad was? Is there really that much point in 'dying with honor' or whatever?"

"Colin...I don't know..." her eyes looked out of focus, trying to remember. They wandered the room without really seeing it for a few minutes, then their eyes met. Citrosine's dark eyes were troubled, and almost frightened. Colin tried not to break his gaze away, but she stared through his so intensely that he looked over at the wall for a second or two, and then turned back.

"I think it has to do with our Afterlife. Supposedly...your death is more honored if you've defended your Tribe, or race... but if you put it that way, fighting against our own kind, the Elven War of Races...it doesn't seem to make sense..." She twisted around in her wool blankets.

"What's the Afterlife have to do with it—like, you spend it with the other warriors in an eternal hunt kind of thing?" Colin was inwardly glad to have read so many fantasy novels, so that he could at least have some root from which to guess about what Citrosine couldn't tell him.

"I don't know...maybe I wanted to be higher on the Tree of Redemption by protecting what I knew...but it sounds so selfish, now that I say it aloud...I don't even recall that I met anyone I would've been forced to spend my death with...just my cohort Paetyr," she whispered this last bit, and Colin noted that her hand was pressing against her side so hard that her fingertips were turning white.

"Maybe you should try being something else," he reasoned gently, "so that you could see—er—Tyresias?" He nodded to himself. "Then you could see Tyresias again, even if you aren't honored for fighting, or whatever. Maybe your mom would be there, too...You'd be happy, even if you weren't glorified so much." He forced an almost-smile, making Citrosine nod distantly.

"Do you think," he continued, a cold lead weight dropping into his stomach, "that mortal people—like my family and I—have the same Afterlife as you and the...immortals?" His parents would probably have excommunicated him, or given him some dreadful punishment, for doubting God at that moment, but he wondered if all beings alike met in the same kind of place after death...then it seemed kind of silly to be so closed-minded that one's God was the only one, and everyone else was wrong, because their god couldn't exist. But were they all the same god? Was it possible, if magic really did exist? Now that he knew magic was real, what kinds of other things could there be that he had been disbelieving all his life? Was all that he had before known a lie?

Citrosine looked at him softly, most likely hearing his doubts in his thoughts. She sat up slightly, wincing, and placed her hand on Colin's wrist. Her touch was cool and silky-smooth, sending an almost instant reassurance through Colin's body.

"I don't know," she whispered again, "but I do understand that I can't find out if I remain a warrior." She paused, stroking his hand—not lovingly, but comfortingly, warming up the weight in his insides and making it lighter and less of a burden. Was that a spell he felt?

"Colin Baker, you have encouraged me to forfeit this practice...and I thank you. Maybe—though let us hope it does not come soon—our deaths will be better off without so much violence..."

"I think you'd be great at doing something else magic-related," Colin assured her as she paused to think. The Elf took a moment to herself in silence, as Colin watched her almost angelic face, with its inhuman aura of shimmering lights and magic.

"Could you help me stand, sir?" she murmured, nearly humming. Colin most eloquently replied, "Huh?" and then realized what she wanted. He took her hands as she gingerly rotated her legs off the bed and onto the cool floor. Her back straightened slowly, and Colin saw for the first time that he was a substantial three or four inches taller than the centuries-old, powerful-as-all-get-out being.

Citrosine drew a sharp breath, her hands instantly flitting to her waist. Colin put his hands on her shoulders to steady her, and, after a few heaving breaths of pain, in which the boy felt more helpless than ever, watching his parents' patient suffer, Citrosine was stable.

Colin took a moment to see Citrosine's body for the first time, really *see* it, and noticed that the Elf had no self-consciousness about how much of her legs were showing, how rumpled the hospital gown was, or even how the bandages all over her body stood out against her pale skin. He envied the perfectly shaped Elven form before him, wondering what Citrosine's Tyre had looked like, if someone like *this* fell in love with him. Would that he could be as hot as an Elf for his girlfriend Becky...she'd melt for him!

Citrosine raised her hands to her heart, and Colin cocked his head.

"As you stand there, my witness, and as my name is Citrosine Leenka Nakiss, daughter of Gyardaute, I make this oath now—never to use magic nor physical strength, nor any of my powers whatsoever, to harm another being of my conscious will unless the situation is too totally dire for me to resist.

"I am finished with making my life a short and reckless one, and all of my being resolves to keep my life a peaceful part of the Enchanted World for as long as I am able. I do not believe that my fighting was even strong enough to help this world of good and evil divided. May Kalka and Ghersah understand my deliberation, and know that I will devote my life to magic; I shall find better ways to help my realm.

"Ghersah se rathka lya ayasnt; iore se nae hretu; Kalka solaie le lissa!" This was truly in Old Elvish. Citrosine smiled as the words came out of her mouth—she knew what they meant, of course, but they had been given to her through some kind of connection with Ghersah that moment. Ghersah above had given her the understanding of those words so that she could use them right then.

Colin was openmouthed, and he prayed silently that no one else in the building had heard Citrosine just then, for fear of them both being locked up in the nearest asylum. Citrosine met his eyes, and gently took his fingers in hers, touching them to her forearm.

Almost immediately, the room was filled with black, dark purple, and indigo colored smoke, swirling out from and dissolving back into Citrosine's body again. Her eyes were closed, and her hair and gown whipped and waved in a breeze that seemed both to emanate from and blow directly into her body in swells.

Six seconds later, the room was back to normal, and Citrosine was lounging on the edge of her temporary bed, smiling coyly. Colin's hands shook, and his heart felt as if it was about to take off running, straight through his chest and into the Elf's slender palms.

"What the hell was that?" Colin breathed.

"That, my friend, was an Elven Destiny Oath. Irrevocably and irrepressibly powerful, unable to be broken, and stronger than any kind of combat spell an Elf can wield."

"That wasn't…wasn't hard magic for you…was it?"

Citrosine sniggered. "Not at all."

Footsteps creaked across the hall, and Colin recognized the gait of his mother, who would undoubtedly be entering the room to check on Citrosine in a moment. Colin noted that the LCD where Citrosine's heartbeat should be displayed and monitored was still blank.

"Let's just tape this patch onto you again, shall we? My mom's kind of a freak." He gave her the gray tape from the top of the machine, punching the POWER button. Nothing happened, and Colin panicked for a brief moment, hoping that he hadn't broken the stupid thing. He realized that the monitor wasn't plugged in, and fixed the mistake in a matter of nanoseconds.

Citrosine didn't respond, but within seconds, her calm, relaxed heartbeat was echoing in short beeps across the room.

The door opened, and Colin smiled innocently at his mother. Dr. Baker smiled warmly back, looking extremely pleased that Citrosine was sitting up and conscious.

"Good morning," she sang, coming over to check on some of the machines about the room. "Colin, your dad said that this young lady"—Citrosine sniffed silently, thinking, *Young? I am older than you and all of your ancestors, thank you—six hundred years earns me "young lady"?*—"had quite an interesting story!" She smiled again, her eyes crinkling merrily around the corners. Colin rolled his eyes.

"Yep," was his only reply.

"Well," his mother shot back, growing impatient with her son's persistent apathy, "what was it exactly that happened?" She looked Citrosine in the eye, plastering on an "I really want to be your friend so tell me your life story" smile.

Colin thought quickly, trying to recall the story he'd told his father, so that Citrosine wouldn't get confused and say something to reveal herself.

"Mom, this is *Citra*," he began, sneaking a wink at Citrosine, "and she's here on vacation from the UK—London, right?" He looked over at the perplexed Elf, who nodded reassuringly, as if she'd lost her voice, and Colin was her interpreter.

"Yes, Citra's from London. She was walking over by the pier, climbing around on the rocks over there—then this high tide storm came in, and she slipped off of a ledge—she managed to get attacked by some lionfish or something pretty badly."

"Oh, that's absolutely *ter*rible!" Dr. Baker exclaimed. She gave a sympathetic, motherly look towards the slight girl in bandages. "Haven't your parents or family come to check on you yet? Won't they be *wor*ried, sweetie?"

Citrosine flashed back a look that made Colin's mother want to bite her tongue. She whispered, "I came to the country with only myself. My family…it was so horrible! Such an accident—Mother attacked in an alley…brothers ran off… Father…!" she buried her face in her blankets, apologizing wetly as she did. Colin looked at his mom in scorn, rolling his eyes, as if to say, *You shouldn't have asked, shouldn't have gotten involved.*

"I'm so sorry, Citra, dear," she muttered, blushing to a deep plum color, "I didn't mean to bring it up—I'll just excuse myself; so sorry—stupid of me…" she was still making amends as she scurried out of the room, shutting the door loudly behind her.

Citrosine's eyes peeked out from behind her hands, and she grinned widely at Colin, who couldn't help but laugh his head off.

"That was, like, so, *so*, awesomely cool!" He nodded eagerly, making Citrosine laugh at how much he looked like Tie—the *old* Tie, before time and darkness had changed her.

"But you actually have a place to go back to, right? Dad's house or something?" Colin wanted to make sure that he had the real story straight.

Citrosine checked herself, letting her words pronounce themselves one by one. "To the last of my knowledge, I have my father's home in the main city."

"I am growing weary of this room. Could we go outside, perhaps? My head throbs terribly with the oppression of this non-magical realm."

"Uh...would the beach be okay?"

"Perfect...but I think it would be helpful to don something that doesn't reveal my body—or at least so much of it—to the world."

Colin snorted. So she was a little embarrassed about her body. That was a shame. "Let me get you some clothes. Be right back."

The boy hustled himself out of the room, leaving Citrosine alone, feeling as if stuffed with fur or cotton. Her head hurt, and she could still feel herself vibrating with magic, alone and lost in such a mortal place. When Colin returned minutes later, he held a pile of bright clothes in one arm. Throwing them down on the cold floor, he grinned.

"Take your pick," he chortled, as Citrosine picked herself off the bed to sit amongst the clothes. "These were donated especially for people like you who don't have enough clothes while they are patients."

"Are these normal clothes of Men? They are so much different than the Men I encountered back in the Big Lands," she asked, wanting only to blend in if they were to walk the mortals' streets. Colin winked at her, making the Elf smile.

"No; these are the normal clothes of *wom*en, *Citra*." Citrosine laughed loudly, making her wound contract in a quite uncomfortable manner. She pawed through the piles of fabric, finding an odd yellow tunic that she liked, with a primitive smiling face on the front, and a blue skirt made from all different kinds of fabrics of similar shades. It was the longest skirt she saw among the other clothing, but still only just reached her thighs—not acceptable in Elven society.

Citrosine changed quickly, the clothes fitting a bit tightly around her, and met Colin downstairs in his kitchen.

She was astounded by all the shiny surfaces and strange lights in the room, but didn't ask what they meant, her head too full of humming and ringing to add more information to it.

"Are you sure that I do not look silly in these clothes?" She shook out her hair a little, tugging on the bottom of her skirt to lower it an inch or so.

"Beautiful," Colin remarked. He tried to reassure Citrosine that she looked normal, but she hardly agreed, muttering about how "Men would stare" at her, but Colin seemed to quite enjoy ogling her. If not making her any less uncomfortable, it made her feel prettier. Colin took her arm in his, after scrawling a little note to his parents that the two of them were "going to the pier for some air" and to "look for Citra's wallet", but assured them that they wouldn't "get too close to the water" or the poisonous lurking organisms.

"Shall we?"

"Let us make for the beach."

Colin led Citrosine down a few sidewalks and around a few parking lots, which Citrosine lingered in, amused.

"What are these things? They are so…there aren't even words in this language that are quite right!" She pointed to a dented blue Volvo station wagon in the sandy parking lot that they were passing through.

"Those are cars," Colin explained. "Um…You get inside them, press a few buttons, turn a key, and you can go places, like, really fast."

"But they *aren't* fueled by magic? How does it work?" Her eyes were wide, making Colin shake his head. *What a deprived childhood this one's had.*

"They burn gas inside there," he gestured towards the gas flap, "and that makes the wheels turn when you push down on the pedal..." Seeing Citrosine peering at her reflection through the windows, he gave up. "Come on, the beach's right here."

The salty, humid air cleared Citrosine's head easily. The wind whipped through their hair, and muted the sound of the concentrated magic in Citrosine's ears, almost as if there was another presence of magic here. She closed her eyes, breathing in the sweet peace of the ocean. Today it was so peaceful... nothing like the day of her "death", when it was so gray and stormy.

Colin was mesmerized by the look of ecstasy on Citrosine's face. She was almost glowing, shimmering in the warm sun, so pale, delicate and out of place...and yet...perfectly at ease with the world, and so naturally versatile. He found himself staring, apologizing in his mind to his girlfriend back in the States.

Citrosine opened her eyes, and Colin quickly turned his gaze to the sea. The gray-green waves shushed lazily toward their outstretched toes, carrying with them hints of mysterious other lands. It was miraculous to think that this same water had once been somewhere thousands of miles away, that once it may have been flying down as rain...

"What's the hardest part?" Colin heard himself ask faintly. He hadn't even known that he was thinking this until the words crept from his mouth, as would a spider tiptoeing out into the sunlight. He wondered if she'd even heard.

"The hardest part of what, sir?" Citrosine angled her head towards the mortal boy, not needing to squint in the sun, as her unnatural pupils naturally adjusted.

"...Um," he started dumbly, "Being all magical and immortal, I guess." He bit his lip, trying to think of what he was talking about.

Citrosine seemed to understand, for she stretched out on the sand, and took a breath.

"It isn't really complete immortality," she explained evasively.

"Yeah, I figured that when I found you dead on the beach. But how does that work?" *Stop looking at how much her skin glows!*

"Hmm, how to explain this? Most of us could live for as long as time would permit, but there are certain limits."

"Limits, like, if your head got chopped off, then you couldn't just stick it back on and live?"

"Correct. Magic can tire one, however, or that is as I have heard." She chose her words carefully, thinking back to the lessons Gya had given her in this language. It was necessary to make sure that she could find the right words to express the correct ideas she meant to convey. "If magic sprouts recklessly from us, too powerfully or too much at a time…or if we have been judged by—er—the protector of the Afterlife, as being unworthy, we could be plucked from the world and thrown into the Underworld. Typically you live forever if you remain a virtuous and honorable figure." She hesitated, about to say something, then continued on. "Anyway…the hardest part to magic? I cannot think…"

"Come on, anything. If you could, like, change one thing—just be like, 'Poof; I want it to be this way!'—what would you do?" Colin's dialect made the corners of Citrosine's mouth threaten to lift, but she kept thinking seriously about his question.

"I would make life and death easier to understand," she said simply. Her fingers touched each other, letting out small black sparks and making Colin's heart speed up.

"Easier to understand? What—"

"Being immortals, death is something less intimidating to speak of. But there is so much that we cannot know! Where do our souls go? Are they split up, like Kalka is supposed to make them? What does the next plane look like, *feel* like? Sometimes you must wonder…Being so close, almost losing reach of my life…I didn't have to die yet, but is it not strange?" She left the words hanging awkwardly in the air, and a chill coiled around and up Colin's spine. *Will I be older and grayer before she ever is married? Will I…die…before she even thinks about bearing children?*

"My apologies," the Elf said more lightly, putting a hand on Colin's arm for a fleeting moment of tingling warmth. "I should not speak of such abstracts on such a glorious day!"

The boy did not pay attention to this, still fighting the cold, metal weight in his stomach. "I need to know something…" Colin's hands grew sweaty and his stomach roiled—the same symptoms he'd felt when he had asked Becky, his girlfriend, out for the first time. The wind blew firmly, almost—but not quite—erasing the cold weight formed by thinking about death. Death was a taboo, here in Mortal Land. You just didn't talk about it with people in casual conversation. "I think that if you can answer this, maybe I can finally accept the fact that you…that you are…immortal…"

"Eh?"

"You keep hinting that you've been around for a really long time. Your immortals moved to Brou—"

"Not Brou; Ilthen—Lythai Woods," Citrosine interjected.

"Right, okay. You moved there, like, before any of us built anything, but I can't remember back that far. All my life, we've had this beach house…so you've been around since before I was born…You moved before even the 'Big Lands' were fully colonized. That makes you older than the establishment of my home country…and…"

Citrosine stretched a tendril of awareness into his mind, wondering what the persuasion behind his questions would be. She felt nothing from him but sheer curiosity, perhaps blended with a little bit of fright and anxiety.

"Citrosine, how old are you?" Colin braced himself, feeling ever the skeptic.

The Elf shifted her position and gathered her hair up on her head, away from her face. A flash of memory threaded behind her eyes, and she sighed, answering in a passive voice.

"Five hundred, seventy and two years."

"Holy crap!" he couldn't help himself, and he ruined the peculiarity of the moment by making them both laugh with the sheer disbelief in his voice.

FOUR

A GLIMPSE OF MORTALITY

Citrosine was, by now, feeling almost no pain in her side when she raised her arms, but her head felt as if it were stuffed with wood; heavy, dull, and aching. Colin talked to her every day, asking questions about Lythai, and answering Citrosine's own wonderings of the world of Men.

Lives had been ruined to create this realm, Citrosine knew. She could feel the absence of trees, animals, free air, and of course magic, in her bones and blood, and agreed with her body in deciding that it was just about the time to remove herself from this place in which she didn't belong.

On the thirteenth morning of her stay in Brou, the Elf picked up her armor from the closet, strapping everything to her body again; leaving her armor unlaced just slightly, so as not to rub against her side. She gathered all of her belongings, not turning around when she heard the door to her room open.

"Are you going home?" Colin's voice sounded frighteningly ominous in the still, cool air. The words echoed against the linoleum, and still Citrosine did not turn. "Citra?" He watched from over her shoulder as she adjusted her sheathed swords tight to her waist, which was still beautifully delineated, despite the lines of her more bulky armor. "Is it time for you to leave?"

"Yes."

Colin was crestfallen. Yes, he realized that she had to go home sometime, obviously, but she had become like a mysterious knot that he had felt obliged to untie. Did he love her? Well, Becky was still his girlfriend, and he'd only fleetingly imagined kissing Citra...once or twice...but it was just that she was so freaking *otherworldly*. The Elf was so like an angel, one who had fallen from the sky and become so vulnerable—she was such a strange part of Colin's life that it had felt like she would be more permanent.

The "British" girl wasn't expected to heal so quickly, Doctors Baker and Baker would admit later. The poison she'd suffered was harsh and had a very slow half-life—it would scientifically have been predicted to heal fully in another few months.

"Do you need me to carry anything for you?" Colin offered hopefully. "I could bring something along for you, if anything's too heavy. Do you need any more aspirin for your head? It'd make you feel better, I bet." He was stalling, and it was pathetic, but he felt like it wasn't time to let her go yet.

"No."

The boy grew frustrated. Citrosine raked her fingertips through her silky brown hair, tying it up with a thick black ribbon. Her hair had never been much less than perfect this whole time and Colin knew that she hadn't needed to use any shampoo whatsoever past that first time she'd washed all the salt off of her a few days ago.

"Are you sure that you're feeling okay? I mean, you can stay a few days longer, if you need more medicine. I'm sure

Mom and Dad wouldn't mind—it's what we're here for, you know. Does your side still hurt?"

"No."

Citrosine finally turned around, a pained yet angelically beautiful expression coloring her features. She placed her hands firmly on his shoulders. Colin saw her dark eyes flick to the door for a split second, icily, and then soften and warm like dark, bittersweet chocolate.

"Stop trying to make me stay," she whispered, her soft, pink lips barely moving. "You're forcing me to wish to." Her voice wavered, and Colin saw her trying to steel herself.

"Can't you—just for, like, one more day?" He wished irrationally that he'd taken a picture of the Elf so that he could show Becky when he got back home to Arizona.

"No," Citrosine mourned. *"I cannot; for the sake of my magic, and that of my tribe. I fled before I could search for my father...I don't know what is left of my family, or my race."*

"But..." Colin racked his mind for some other argument. Finding sufficient words, he lowered his voice to the same whispering volume as Citrosine's. "I won't have anything to remember you by. If you stayed, I could take a picture... remember what I told you about cameras? Just so that I could remember you by it—you don't have to freaking leave! Just one—"

Citrosine touched a smooth fingertip to his lips. She used her opposite hand to pull the ribbon from her hair. With the cascading halo of hair falling around her face, she tied the black ribbon that had been a part of one of her mother's dresses to Colin's wrist. *This has linked me to my mother's memory for as long as I have possessed it; I wish of it to link mine to this wonderfully innocent boy's that long and doubled...* She smiled gently.

"I must leave now," she whispered almost inaudibly. "In the beginning, I wasn't even allowed to come into contact with mortals. Now I have told you everything about myself." She closed her eyes and took the last breath of non-magic-filled air that she would enjoy.

Without warning, Colin wrapped his arms around her shoulders, hugging her tightly. The armor she wore dug into his skin, but he ignored it. Citrosine was overwhelmed, and let out a soft, bewildered cry, her throat tightening. She dug her fingers into the fabric of Colin's shirt, and whispered an imperceptible blessing of thanks to him. He had, after all, helped to save what remained of her life.

"I'll miss you," Colin breathed. Citrosine nodded, agreeing on her own part.

"Thank you," she said, "for talking with me, for curing me, for reassuring me. I know now that my life has been a mess, but...I believe that you have shown me how to mend it. With innocence."

Citrosine pulled herself away from Colin, and the two silently walked to the beach, Colin following her to prolong the farewell.

The surf was gentle that morning, hardly breaking to the shore at all. They stood in the quiet for a moment more, and Citrosine took a long, slow breath.

"*Sahme—phennea.*" This was sung gently into the boy's mind, and, although he didn't understand it, it felt beautiful in his thoughts.

"What does that mean?" he asked now, still attempting to stall Citrosine's disappearance. The Elf shook her head in reply.

"*Untranslatable.*" The words meant nothing in his language. She knew no way to explain them, but that the phrase was a kind of a thank you, a well-wishing, and a goodbye. There were powers in those words, of the ancient Elven heritage all Elves could access in the deep recesses of their blood. She feared briefly that she'd done something to make the boy less mortal, but then reconsidered, and hoped that these words could carry him through a graceful life.

She grasped his hand delicately, kissing his palm like the breath of a ghost. "Goodbye and farewell. May life be good to you."

Citra walked swiftly away in the direction of the forest—Lythai, she had called it. Her footprints were close to imperceptible on the wet sand, and the clinking of her armor was swallowed rapidly by the moist wind.

It took until she was a tiny dot receding into the "Brou Wildlife Reserve" for Colin to accept that she would be out of his life as swiftly as she'd entered it. He looked down at the ribbon tied around his wrist, totally unsurprised to see it pulsing faintly with the same aura that had surrounded the Elf's body. He nodded his head, as if to finalize the week's events, and convince himself that he hadn't been dreaming the amazing-yet-real magic that had occurred.

Citrosine's words, "Sahme" and "Phennea", rang in his ears, and as Colin closed his eyes many nights afterward, he would hear them sung through the voices of angels, yelled by happy children, chanted by Death, and whispered by the earth. He would later go on to become a brain surgeon at the Phoenix City Hospital for the rest of his record-breaking hundred and twenty-three years of living. He would marry Rebecca Morris, and, in honor of just one week of his life, albeit a miraculous one, he would modify the last two Elvish words he ever heard to form the names of their two children, Sam and Penny. He would never tell anyone of this experience, but it would ultimately change his life, leading him subtly in the direction of grace, goodness, and happiness.

Colin turned, walking along the shore in the opposite direction. His eyes scanned the beach, looking for interesting shells, or otherwise...

Citrosine walked through the great field of Lythai, seeing a plume of smoke where the dead carcasses from the battle had most likely been honorably burned, as was the custom. She breathed through her mouth, instinctively. The smell of burning flesh…she wouldn't let any of it get into her lungs this time. She trudged across the field, over the hills in the center, where she could see the Dragonback Mountain Range, rising up like so many ravenous teeth trying to nibble at the clouds.

She could see the giant tree that protected Treewall; called Kalka in the stories. In the next plane—the dimension after death that exists in the living world, but is only seen by the dead—the tree stood in the same place, but was taller than the sky, reached past the moon, and all souls scurried among the branches, Ghersah sitting as a powerful mother, matriarch, at the tree's crown. Once more, Citrosine wondered what branches she and the souls of her close friends would be confined to.

*I will not think about death yet; there is still much to find out about the war…*Citrosine scolded herself as she felt a cold fear swelling in her stomach. *If I get home, and Dada isn't…* She shook her head. *No! I shall not find myself thinking about this! I am* not *thinking these thoughts…*

Citrosine reached Lothor by midday, greeted by crowds of Elves rushing around, most likely preparing for the restoration of peace. She noticed Paetyr, limping lightly down a path. She called his name.

"Eh? Ay, Citra! You are well, then! We thought that surely…" He smiled widely, hobbling toward her more quickly. "No harm done, then, you?" He grabbed her in a tight hug, making her groan and pull away.

"Actually quite the opposite, much harm done, but I am healing, I hope."

"Ah, damn me, I am sorry, Citra." She could see the sobriety that she rarely saw in this Elf presently enter his eyes.

"No matter. I shall tell you of everything soon. It makes for a great story." Citrosine tried to bring herself to smile sympathetically, but she was apprehensive enough that she only really wanted to dash home. "I've been lost—truly thought I was dead for a while," Citrosine said in explanation to her absence of thirteen days, "so I have had no opportunity to ask what happened at the end of the fight..."

Paetyr smirked, looking like a child overeager for dessert. "Well," he said, rubbing his hands together, "after the demons were all slain—that's after you disappeared, I think—the Shadow Tribe had us all surrounded, our whole quarter, and the Third Quadrant—our soldiers who were to back the rest up when we grew weary—appeared out of *nowhere*. I think that they'd made a wrong turn through the forest—ended up in Niklouh, the Nymph City—and they turned up just in time to ring outside of us, so it was a circle-within-a-circle-within-a-circle sort of chaos! The Shadows got all up in a dither, and had to fight fore and rear.

"We beat them down, until they finally had to surrender. That one-eyed fellow saw that there were only about ten of his left, so he was shouting 'We concede! We plead for truce!'" Paetyr laughed boisterously. "King Hendius and Prince Tenthius—that prince lad's only a small sprout yet—ran up to them to negotiate the terms."

"What are the terms? And what of the Dark Ones?" Citrosine interrupted him, wishing to know what had come to pass, but too weary for Paetyr's jibes and colorful stories.

"The Dark Elves are in exile. Their lands were nearly completely seized, and the demons that remained were forced to a huge hole in the sandy, desert-like area in the west. We aren't to *touch* their lands, and they aren't to disrupt ours. Anyway, I'm just glad that they can't attack again. They don't have any kind of leader, just those few Dark Elves—the few that were spawned into Dark Ones have been reversed back to Elves—and the demons are too stupid, in general, to fight back."

Citrosine nodded absently. "Thank you very much. I would stay and discuss this more, but I must return home, for I have not seen enough comfort of my home in the last moon."

"Very well—but, Citrosine," Paetyr caught her by the arm as she started to turn towards the path that would circle around to her dwelling. "Did you hear about our hierarchy? The whole ruling system is to be changed."

"What do you mean? I thought that King Hendius was doing a wonderful job at governing us."

"True, he is, ye'h, but all the races—except for the exiled ones, obviously—have had a council just yesterday. They want all of the remaining races to be united among each other, so that we don't have any more wars."

"Then what is to be done?" Citrosine gave Paetyr a skeptical look, growing impatient with his enthusiastic remarks.

"The Leaders have no power anymore, and King Hendius is to be a kind of second for a newly positioned Nymph leader; the *Seer*. He's really a wise man—can see into the future, do destiny-findings, and all those Faerie things...doesn't have all the political power, but can delegate it among..."

"That is truly wonderful. I wish him the best of luck, seeing how we do need some unity in Ilthen...But, Paetyr, I really do need to go home now." Citrosine pulled her arm from his grip, and took her leave.

"'Bye then," Paetyr called, blowing her a knightly kiss. Citrosine rolled her eyes back, and jogged to her dwelling, armor and swords weighing her down and clanging together. She reached dwelling number 241, with its empty little patch of dirt in the front. Even though she had not spent much time here yet, she was greeted with warm memories of the short stay in which it had kept her.

The Elf closed her eyes, steeling herself for who she might—or, she gulped, might not—find inside.

Palgirtie entered the Sea Realm's main atrium, feeling numb. She felt like her mother had been avenged, but she couldn't believe that Citrosine, her older sister, was really dead. In her mind, she thought that she would have felt something, a memory, a twinge of magic; *something*—if Citrosine's life had slipped away. That was what she had heard happened to siblings; if one was hurt, the other would feel it.

If this was accurate, why did she feel so proud of herself when she'd struck Citrosine, hearing her cry out as her side was slashed? What was the electricity that had surged through her skin when she'd kicked at her sister's dead flesh, seeing her own claw marks echoed in black poison? Would Tie be punished after her life was finished for this? She knew, somewhere in the back of her mind, that it was wrong...

But she felt no guilt whatsoever.

When she opened the door to the rooms that she and Dydae inhabited, she was greeted by a small, scaly creature that was an exact replica of a miniature Dragon, with pearly gray scales, gold whiskers, and a snakelike tail.

"Dydae?" Tie knelt next to the creature, stroking the space between her white, leathery wings.

"Yes, my child. It would appear that I am at the age of forfeiting my Shape-Shifting powers." The voice came into Tie's head gently, like Dydae's wrinkled hands would sometimes comb through her hair on a dismal day.

"You mean...you can only have them for a certain length of time?" Tie panicked. She had so looked forward to living out her life able to try new forms, to alter her appearance and become one with all the creatures of the earth. Would she, too, have to give up these powers eventually?

Dydae laughed, the noise sounding more like a snarl. Smoke curled from her nostrils. *"Yes. One can only practice this magic until one's form cannot stand the stress anymore. My body is frail, my aura is stretched...and now I am one being until I die. At least I was able to choose..."* The tiny Dragon curled herself around Tie's legs, like a feline might.

"Why…how?" Tie paused, rephrasing her question. "If I take too many shapes in a short time, will I have to give my powers up more quickly?"

"I wouldn't worry about all of that. Your form is still young, stretchable. You aren't as weary and stuck as I."

"Dydae…surely you aren't…you're not confined to this forever, are you? Oh, I'm so sorry…"

"Don't be! It has been long since my muscles have been so lithe, since my energy has been so built up. Mind you, I will have to leave you in the nights, to hunt…and I can't hug you anymore, child…" She chuckled through her thoughts, unsuccessfully masking a note of disdain.

"Oh, that is perfectly all right. I can still wrap my arms around your neck! I have only one question." Tie hopped up onto her bed, and Dydae fluttered up beside her, landing gently on her side to avoid tearing the hammock. "Will you grow to the size of a normal Dragon? I don't think that you would fit in this room at that size…"

"This form of mine isn't truly a Dragon's, dear daughter. I am a hybrid of a Grouhrl demon and a Dragon. So, no, I will not grow larger. I may start developing a pair or two of fangs, though…" The two of them laughed and talked together until the sun was no longer visible, and the green lamps illuminated their dwelling.

Tie curled up in her hammock, with Dydae snuggled under her arm. They had become the best of friends, even though they were separated by years of life experience and wisdom.

"Good night, Dydae."

"Sleep well, dear child; sleep very well."

Citrosine opened the front door as slowly as was possible. She called through the doorway that was gradually widening: "Father?" She kept her eyes closed a moment, straining her ears for his voice. She heard nothing but the squealing of the door pivoting open, the Elves rushing around behind her, the wind passing through the trees above.

I will see you some other time, then. These words came unbidden into her mind, making the girl shudder. The hairs on her arms stood up underneath the mail she wore. She was rooted to the spot for a moment then, as she said the words to herself.

"I will see you some other time, then...who said that to me...Colin?" The words made her shiver again as she said them, and then as she realized the source of the phrase, she felt as if her stomach had been wrenched out of her body.

The last words Tyre ever spoke to me...He didn't know it at the time, but what he spoke was a lie. What did I last hear of Dada? 'Good luck, lissa'? I should hope right now that I have luck *enough to see him again!*

A forceful peal of thunder struck close above Citrosine, and she knew that she had to control herself. Her worry had created a storm! A deep breath made its careful way into, and out of, her lungs, and after she steeled herself, Citrosine walked into her house.

"Father? Are you here?" Her words sounded as empty and alone as Colin's had just hours ago. Citrosine found a small oil lamp in the front room and lit it up with a flick of her fingers. The soft glow of the fire illuminated the room warmly, although shadows flickered and skirted about behind chairs, tables, blankets...

"Dada?"

There was no answer. The storm outside grew harsher, and the sounds of other Elves rushing inside were ignored by Citrosine's hopeful ears. Her vision blurred, and she put her hands over her temples, attempting to calm her magic. This was the second time in years that it had betrayed her this way, the first being the storm of desperation created at the beach.

"Dada!"

FIVE

WHAT IS LIFE BUT A JOURNEY?

Citrosine was alone.

She breathed as quietly as she could, tiny gasps that nonetheless hurt her still-recovering lung, and yet it was the only sound she heard. *In...out...in...out...*Who would guess that such slow air could shriek so cacophonously?

She was alone.

Gya had told her to speak with her sister, to reunite if the concept of father and daughter was no longer possible for the Nakiss line. She would send a letter to her sister first, warning her that she was actually alive, no thanks to family, and she would write of the news...*Dada has been killed in the war,* she would write. *We have to be able to speak to one another, so that our family isn't completely destroyed. That was his last request to me.* She must go to the Realm of the Sea eventually, plead forgiveness and explain her side of things, and Nakiss would again be the name of a close family. Or at least she could hope. That was all that she had left.

Citrosine was alone.

The bereaved Elf girl lay on the blankets in her room, stroking Tyre's cane once more. *I have no one but the one who placed me in your vision; my treasonous sister,* she said to what she imagined as Tyre's soul.

You must be strong, she imagined his soul would speak back. *Your sister will understand in time, will she not?*

Citrosine rested her cheek on the polished snake's head, the handle of the cane, with the initials etched into its coils. TK and CN.

*Love has been so difficult for me, Tyre. Everyone I have loved, even just with proper friendliness, even if not of my own accord, has been separated from me in some way or another…*She listened as the rain outside—the rain that she in her misery had conjured—lightened, slowed, and stopped.

What would Tyre reply to this?

Should that stop you from trying? he might say. *Write to Palgirtie, tell her you love her, and tell her of Gya. If she has a heart, she should at least permit your presence once more—she must see you, as you are family, excusing my bluntness, barging into others' families this way.*

That is all right, Tyre. I would always have thought of you as my husband and therefore my family.

And I would feel the same. So send Tie the letter you thought of moments ago. Why not try? At least it will shake her overconfidence in herself.

Yes. Always the perseverant one, Tyre was—even when all hope seemed lost, he would continue to fight for light and goodness.

Dragging herself off the floor, Citrosine located her father's desk behind the front door in the dim light. A yellowed, untidy stack of parchment was already atop the desk, threatening to fall to the dirt floor with a wink of the eye's notice. Citrosine snatched the first page of the pile, and then pawed around on the shelves for a charcoal stick. Finding a decently sharpened one, she moved to the table where the lamp sat, so that she could actually watch her hand form the correct letters.

Dear Tie, she wrote.

The paper which she was using seemed kind of worn, and she moved the lamp closer to herself. Citrosine drew a sharp breath, cursing herself. This paper already had the beginnings of a note—but here, what was this? Her name was within the first line, written so faintly…almost as if the writer had been unsure of whether it would be read. She leaned closer.

Dearest Citra,

I write this in the hopes that you are returning home soon. It has been days since the battle ended, and yet I still wish.

That aside, if you are reading this, I am in Niklouh. I have an appointment with the Seer there, for my magic studies. He is said to have almost as much power as the Faeries, and what seems strange is that he presides over them!

I will be returning in a day or so, depending on when I have the chance to begin walking home. The moon will be gone and black when I expect to arrive—that's easier to measure, I suppose, for you have not been home and I have no way of recording the date; the war jumbled everyone's minds a little.

If you are home right now, then I thank Ghersah heartily for keeping you safe, guiding you from the peak of Kalka! I have missed you, and worried of you with all my mind for these past days. You must understand; it is so difficult to write these notes every time I step out, only to crumple them into balls and feed them to the hearth when I return.

Please return safely and with happiness in your heart. I dream in hopes that you are well and light of worry. Perhaps we can study the Nymphs' magic together to strengthen ourselves?

Citrosine, you are all that is left here of my family—know that I love you and am prouder than Ghersah as she looks down upon the souls on Kalka's limbs.

I wish you the best, my dear, sweet lissa—for you are my nearest, dear, sweet love now;
Dada

Citrosine laughed through her tears and stepped outside to look at the sky. She saw nothing but stars straight ahead of her so she turned her head all the way up and back. There was the moon—a tiny sliver of a smile, or a wink, laughing with her. That winking lunar eye would lead her father home into her joy in just a night or so. Hopefully it would also smile down at Colin in Brou, help him understand how things needed to be in their own places…and also wink up in trust to all the lives that had been recently lost.

A single cloud flitted across the moon for just a moment, illuminated to a translucent silver sheet as the Elf watched. The ground and trees around her home were lit with the faintest, most beautiful of silhouettes and shadows, making the renewed, energized dark magic within her blood warm her cheeks in the most pleasant way possible, love welling up like it had not done for too long. She gave a cry of satisfaction up to the sky, just as the moon was unveiled into nakedness, showering the slumbering world with the promise of remembrance.

Sahme, Phennea

Returning inside, Citrosine gathered Tyresias's cane and letter,
along with the dress that Citrosine had worn to her coming of
age ceremony, the tunic and skirt that Colin had allowed her
to keep, and a tall white candle. She opened the door to a room
in the dwelling that would have been Tie's or her mother's, and
stepped in for the first time. A tiny window peeked out into the
woods behind the city of second beginnings on the far wall.

She carefully laid out the dress, tunic, and skirt on the
ground, as if they were being worn by invisible sleeping forms.
She placed Tyre's letter atop the clothes carefully. Drawing her
small dagger from her belt, she took up Tyre's cane and began
carving as precisely and carefully as she could. In one coil was
already carved *TK*, the next *CN*. In the smallest lettering she
could manage, she carved *Dariya* into the next coil down.
Caressing the cane once more, she brushed her lips against the
handle and placed it alongside the dress.

She knelt, lighting the candle she'd brought not with magic
but instead a taste of fire from her father's oil lamp touched

to the virgin wick. Natural fire would eventually burn out, the candle would collapse into a pool of wax and not be able to burn anymore, and this room would grow dark and dusty, perhaps forgotten and locked. The clothes would be eaten by invading moths, growing darkened and stained with damp, bleached and stiffened by light entering from the high, narrow window. The cane would rot away, as dead wood eventually will with damp and still air.

"Thank you, Colin, for showing me the way to what I wish of myself, though I knew you little," she whispered into the room that was now to be like a tomb; quiet and sacred to the memories of those she would not see for a long time, if ever.

"Thank you, Mother, for protecting us for as long as you could from all the evil in the world, and for teaching us of the innocence which we have all been deprived of, but must at least try to remember. I will remember this, and remind myself not to let it be completely lost." She stood and crept to the doorway, not wanting to disturb the precious quiet. Before her feet left the room, she turned around.

"Thank you, Tyre, more than you know. You gave your life for goodness, love, and loyalty. You opened my eyes to so many things, even if it was only your memory and my own fantasy these last years. I love you so much; you have taught me what love truly is. I wish for Dariya to accompany you until I arrive and may hold you again someday. Perhaps I can still find as good a future with someone else as I could have with you, but I owe all the knowledge of such a powerful, perfect feeling to you. Thank you again, and goodbye."

Citrosine closed the door.

About the Author

Andrea McKerlie is entering the freshman class at Meredith College. She plans on double-majoring in English and Flute Performance. Andrea began her first novel, Until We Meet Again, when she was eleven. She enjoys playing flute, watching House, canoeing, writing on random scraps of paper, and watching movies. She was her high school's head drum major for three years.

LaVergne, TN USA
21 August 2009
155466LV00001B/2/P